The Longhunter

The Longhunter

An American Tale

British Colonies, 1777

E.P. Lewis

Copyright © 2022 by E.P. Lewis.

Library of Congress Control Number:		2022906107
ISBN:	Hardcover	978-1-6698-1857-1
	Softcover	978-1-6698-1856-4
	eBook	978-1-6698-1855-7

All rights reserved. No part of this book may be reproduced or transmitted in any form or by any means, electronic or mechanical, including photocopying, recording, or by any information storage and retrieval system, without permission in writing from the copyright owner.

This is a work of fiction. Names, characters, places and incidents either are the product of the author's imagination or are used fictitiously, and any resemblance to any actual persons, living or dead, events, or locales is entirely coincidental.

Any people depicted in stock imagery provided by Getty Images are models, and such images are being used for illustrative purposes only.
Certain stock imagery © Getty Images.

Print information available on the last page.

Rev. date: 04/13/2022

To order additional copies of this book, contact:
Xlibris
844-714-8691
www.Xlibris.com
Orders@Xlibris.com
840629

Contents

1777, East of the Cumberland Gap 1
Elspeth 7
MacEwan Cabin 9
Mr. Boone 11
Shadow Bear 15
Home Again 17
A Contest 23
A Spring Journey 30
Bears 35
The Cherokee 40
Little Cornstalk 49
The Shawnee 58
Manhattan Island 74
Home 77
MacEwan Station 79
The Trail Home 86
The Road East 96
Little Cornstalk 98
The Road to Philadelphia 103
Broken Tree 104
Stevenson 108
Philadelphia 113
Eleventh Virginia 119
Alden 128
Colonel Morgan 133
The Murphy Clan 139
The Weatherly House 148
The Shawnee Trail 153
Philadelphia 158

Little Cornstalk	165
New York, South of Saratoga	171
West of Saratoga	173
The Weatherly House	177
Olaf Stevenson	193
Saratoga	205
Offices of Lord Jeremy Skelton, Manhattan Island	214
Murphy-Borough	216
Outside Philadelphia	220
A Field of Wounded	231
Seamus and the Blacksmith Witch	243
Rescue	250
Broken Tree	264
Alden	270
Little Cornstalk	278
The Delaware Crossing	281
Little Cornstalk	288
Headquarters of Maj. John Clark	291
Philadelphia	297
Two Virginia Cousins	302
New York Harbor, 1778	306
The Ohio	312
Headquarters of Major Clark	318
HMS Victory	324
Tenskwatawa	329
New York	332
West of Philadelphia	335
Murphy Settlement	339
The Victory	343
The Letter	356
Manhattan Island	361
The Shawnee Village	363
Woolwich to London	370
Western Boundary of New York Colony	376
London-Greenwich	380

Number 10 Downing Street 382
Cell Number Six, Royal Barracks, Greenwich 386
Lenape 388
The MacEwan Homestead 392
Chambers of Lord Jeremy Skelton, New York 396
The MacEwan Homestead 398
Number 10 Downing Street, London 400
Cell Number Six, Royal Barracks, Greenwich 402
Number 10 Downing Street 405
The Royal Barracks 408
Number 10 Downing Street 409
Murphy-Borough 410
One Mile South 416
Manhattan 419
Number 10 Downing Street 421
Cell Number Six, Royal Barracks, Greenwich 423
The Cherokee Way 427
Royal Barracks, Greenwich 431
Quaker Settlement 434
France 437
Murphy-Borough 442
Philadelphia 449
Tenskwatawa 456
Murphy-Borough 459
West 462
Murphy-Borough 465
The LongHunter 471
Farewell 474
Alden 476

1777, East of the Cumberland Gap

IT WAS A simple arrangement of cabins located in the territory south of the Ohio River. Surrounded by slash pine, its stockade stood just under five feet. The entire property line encompassed an area of ten acres and a bit.

Inside the settlement were two cabins, a barn, a smokehouse, three outlying sheds, a deep water well, and a large privy outfitted for three. The entire place ran alongside a narrow creek with modest palisades. This time of year, the water ran quick and shallow.

The lands lay just east of the Cumberland Gap, which had only been explored by Daniel Boone some four years earlier. The Tennessee and Kentucky borders ran east to west of the creek and just three miles north.

The cabins and barn were made up of rough-hewn pine similar in fashion to the stockade-timber-stacked crossway Swedish-style. Each member was notched for a stable interlocking of the mating corners. The seams in the layered timber were packed with red clay and canebrake to keep wind and weather out. The low, slanted roofs were sealed in similar fashion. Split pine board covered the floor of the main cabin, laid over hard-packed earth mixed with red clay. Dry straw lay scattered about, mingling with the dirt and dust created by several busy feet. Each cabin was well aired and neatly arranged.

The main structure was long with a low-set roof. Constructed with frontier settler hands, it was dry and healthy, able to sleep eight. This was the MacEwan trading homestead. A popular way station that straddled the westward trail, the MacEwan family place was worked and operated by Elspeth and Ian MacEwan along with their six offspring.

On this cool spring morning, a wisp of woodsmoke drifted skyward from the large stone fireplace enclosed within the main cabin. Dying embers continued to warm the inner space of the central room. It was early, daybreak only minutes away.

In the early darkness, a tall young man quietly closed the door behind him as he stole outside the big cabin. The leather hinges swung silently closed as he sniffed the morning air eagerly. He carefully tiptoed his way about the water bucket just outside the door. Chickens wandered aimlessly around the enclosed compound, clucking softly. The birds were paying little attention to the young man as they methodically pecked the damp ground for insects and seed corn scattered throughout the grass.

Gingerly treading his way through the standing livestock, he crossed the open space to the compound outer gate quickly. He slid the heavy gate pole back and pushed through enough for him to squeeze out.

He wore only a thin white linen nightshirt. It was the same nightshirt he wore every evening to his bed. His mother, making certain it was clean, washed it whenever needed.

He hurried along, knowing his mother would be up soon along with a gaggle of his hungry siblings. He made his way toward the creek as quickly as his bare feet allowed. He could hear the water rushing gently southwest as he approached the little stream.

The musket he carried was loaded, ready to fire. It was a common British Brown Bess, a gift from his father, which he now nestled in the crook of his left arm in cradle fashion. He only hoped his little trick would work and that he would be able to bring home fresh meat to his mother.

The young man crouched low as he advanced to the water's edge. He spied the tree he had used for his trap, a tall oak with a good stout branch that could bend some but not break. On it, he had tied two fat catfish with a thin rope taken from his father's work kit. He knew his mother would chastise him for that, but he didn't care. She would have disagreed about the trap as well, settling on the two fish without the use of the rope. She was practical in that way. What did she always say—"a bird in the hand"?

He was close now. Quietly bringing the musket up to ready position, he settled in. His shoulder was tucked in comfortably against the stock as he pressed his cheek lightly along the polished wood.

His nightshirt briefly tangled underfoot. He carefully pulled it out. Except for the running creek and a few morning birds, it was stone quiet. He leaned forward and took into view three, not two, raccoons as he had expected. His father told him there would most likely be two.

Hanging just above the raccoons were the bony remains of two catfish swaying gently under the bending branch. They hung a little less than two feet off the ground.

The young man studied the animals for several seconds. If he moved to the left, he might have a better angle. If his position was good, he could hit two of the raccoons with a single shot. The third racoon had wandered off a few feet from the others.

He shuffled sideways, slow and silent, pulling the Bess back so as not to catch any branches from the thick brush that concealed him. Bringing the musket back up, he had a sharp view of his prey and a good sight line for striking the two animals sitting along the water's edge.

The raccoons were busy cleaning themselves after their meal, bobbing down and back and vigorously scrubbing their paws. Their ducking motion played in unison every few seconds. He waited for the perfect shot.

Across the creek, the quiver of a low branch among the canebrake caught the young man's attention, distracting him momentarily. Staring across the running water, the raccoons sat upright in a locked pose, their paws clasped together as if in prayer. It was the perfect shot for the young hunter.

Suddenly, a branch visibly shook on the far side of the creek, alarming the raccoons. They quickly separated, backing away from the water's edge. Losing his target, the young man aimed at the closer of the two. But he did not fire. He was as curious as the raccoons about this unexpected intrusion on the opposite bank.

Sitting as still as a tree, the young hunter pondered his next move. Staring hard at the opposite bank of thick brush and low trees, he saw nothing, and his eyesight was excellent. He could spy a gray squirrel perched in a tree at two hundred yards off. His father had often complimented him on this ability. He had the sight of a good longhunter.

At first, it was just a glimpse of a thing; but as it moved behind the dense brush, a dark feather and then a lighter one came to be seen, and the young man became excited. A turkey, he wondered. If he brought home a fat turkey, his mother would be very pleased. Roasted turkey meat was her favorite dish. The two raccoons stood frozen in concentration, staring across the slow running water. Then they ran. They scampered away so quickly the third raccoon was equally startled and ran wildly in the direction of the young hunter.

He took aim at the oncoming racoon then quickly pulled his musket left, aiming across the creek. As he stood up, he could see a dark feather clearly jutting out just so from the brush. He fired.

As the echoing roar of the Brown Bess exploded over the creek, the fleeing raccoon slid to a stop, turned sharp left, and ran for its life, dodging the flash and thunderous sound. Across the creek, a figure that was clearly not a turkey stumbled out from behind the brush and canebrake. Clutching his left side with a bloodied hand, the Indian dropped to one knee and fell forward on his right side, moaning.

The young hunter stared in shock at the sight. The Indian moaned again, louder this time. Then it was the young man who turned and ran. He was so shaken by the event that he couldn't recall how he suddenly appeared in front of the cabin doorway, his heart pounding in his throat as he tried to call for his mother. The only sound that came out was a strangled croak. He took a sharp breath.

"Mother!" he hollered as loud as he could. "Mother, I've shot an Indian down at the creek! Mother!"

The cabin door swung open, and a dark-haired woman stepped outside.

"William MacEwan," scolded the woman fiercely, "what're you doing out the cabin this time of morning in nothing but a nightshirt?" She looked down on her son's feet. "And not a shoe on your foot. What is this then?"

William repeated more calmly, "I shot an Indian down at the creek, Mother."

"You what?" she asked, spinning about in a desperate scan of the property boundary. She saw nothing. "Where was this, William?"

"It was by the fishing oak on the far side of the creek. I didn't know it was an Indian, Mother. I thought it was a turkey."

"How many Indians?" she asked, fear in her voice.

"I've only seen the one."

She scanned the horizon carefully again, rotating her head slowly. She knew it was unlikely the Shawnee would raid this far to the southeast, but it was possible. It was also possible that a band of Delaware could have come down the creek to raid white settlements.

She quickly entered the cabin and returned with a loaded flintlock in hand. It was always loaded and at the ready. "Let us go then," she said, gathering her courage and nightclothes about her. Mother and son headed toward the creek.

"Load that musket," she ordered tersely.

William did as he was told, loading the Brown Bess with ball and powder as they hurried down to the creek.

The Indian had not moved from where he fell. Painful moans and grunts came across the running water as mother and son stopped on the opposite bank. Elspeth MacEwan waded across the shallow water in her bare feet, the water running painfully cold over her toes. She ignored it. She approached the wounded Indian carefully. Looking about, she bent down toward the writhing figure and slowly rolled him on his back.

"Why, he's nothing but a boy, William," she announced. "He's no more your age. Why did you shoot him?"

"It was an accident, Mother. I thought he was a turkey. I saw the feathers through the brush, and I thought he was a turkey. By heaven, it was an accident true. I am sorry, Mother. Will he die?"

William's words held genuine grief. Elspeth looked up at her son's stricken face and slowly shook her head. "I don't know, William. We'll have to get him back to the cabin. He's losing some bit of blood for certain. Sling that weapon and help me carry him up."

She deftly tucked the flintlock into her nightdress pocket. Mother and son wrestled the injured Indian to his feet. It was a struggle. At first, the wounded Indian resisted but soon calmed down. As he studied the white woman and young hunter, he began speaking and making painful sounds. Neither William nor his mother understood a word.

The Indian boy continued babbling in his tongue as they carried him up to the cabin. It was clear he was trying to say something as he repeated the same phrase over and over. As they passed inside the cabin door, the Indian jerked once and fainted cold.

"God have mercy!" cried William. "I've killed him!"

"Quit your whining, William, and help me get him onto your bed."

Elspeth

ELSPETH MACEWAN WAS born thirty-four years earlier in the year of our Lord 1743. She still carried a good form and was very handsome to look on. Her hair was soft and colored dark henna, which matched her large brown eyes. She weighed seven stone and had a strong will about her. When she left Wales as a young girl, she did so as an indentured servant. She was almost thirteen years old then.

She sold her service to a wealthy landowner from the new colonies in America. The work was hard, but that was fine with Elspeth. She never shied from hard work. It was in her soul from an early age.

At first, Elspeth labored in the fields, pulling tobacco and what cotton and corn that managed to grow in the hard black earth. It was backbreaking work, but Elspeth didn't care. She knew what she wanted, and she would get it someday. Hard work was nothing compared to her dreams.

After a time, the landowner's wife took some notice of this young Welsh girl. The woman quietly moved Elspeth into the large house, making her a domestic. Elspeth's work ethic and sharp mind soon displayed itself, and it was realized she was not your average house servant.

Elspeth began to teach herself to read and write. She understood and worked numbers as well. This was highly unusual for an indentured soul and especially prized given the circumstances. Good help such as Elspeth was rare in this part of the world. She was considered a treasure by her employers and was soon running the household, much respected and even loved.

To his credit, the landowner held to Elspeth's indentured contract and, after seven years, set her free. When she told them she would be leaving for Philadelphia to find a husband of substance, the lady of the house openly wept. She begged Elspeth to stay and be part of the family, but Elspeth had her own notions. She would find a good, solid man and start a family of her own. She would move west to free land and make a life as she had always dreamed of.

MacEwan Cabin

"WILL HE LIVE, Mother?" queried William, anxiously pacing the wooden floor.

"It looks worse than it is, William. The ball passed through and hit meat on the way but no bone as far as I can tell. His insides seem to be in place as well. I smell no waste in the wound. Get your da's whiskey and start some water to boil."

William hurried off and soon returned with a dark clay jug in hand.

"Bring that soft cloth I have hanging by the door and get the fire up and that water boiling."

Elspeth probed the wound efficiently. She was familiar with all manner of injury—broken bones, bullet holes, animal bites, and knife wounds. She had even fixed up a scalp victim once who had survived the vicious mutilation. She quickly cleaned the wound, taking advantage of the young Indian's unconscious state. She pulled some cobwebs from the bedpost and gently tucked it into the wound, stemming some of the blood flow. The boy moaned as she pressed the clean cloth onto the small hole. Then she wrapped a long scarf about his waist and pulled tight. Her patient let out a sharp cry and then fell silent again.

"Why did you shoot him, William?" asked Elspeth sharply.

"I told you, Mother, it was an accident. I thought he was a turkey hiding in the brush. I swear to it."

"Accident or no, this boy was shot and by your hand. Your father will have your ears for this. I'm sure I don't know what to make of it myself."

William shook his head in sad realization. Indeed, his father would have his ears for this. It had taken three hard years of settling this place. It was a good piece of land with a clear running creek not far off and plenty of timber to build such as needed in the wilderness of western America. When his father heard of the shooting, William was certain his concern would turn to the friendly relations the MacEwans had with the natives.

"Your father will be home come a fortnight and a bit. I expect he'll have something to say about this surely. I don't recognize this Indian, but he looks to be from the Cherokee people. Your father would know for sure."

"Do you think his clan will be missing him, Mother?"

"In time, I'm certain someone will. He must have a mother and father. It could be some days before he's missed though. I really don't know for certain."

"Will he live, Mother?"

"I think so. It's hard to tell with these things. If he gets a blood fever, it could turn bad. I cleaned the wound best I know how, and that's all there is for it. Bullet wounds are hard to predict. He may have caught something in the wound, a piece of cloth or leather, which sometimes happens. That could bring on a blood fever. I just don't know, William. We'll have to wait and see. Now go cut some of that smoked ham up for me, and I'll make a broth. He'll be hungry when he wakes."

Mr. Boone

ELSPETH STOOD AT the open door, observing her children. The older children were busy around the cabins and lodge house, gathering kindling for fire, feeding the chickens small corn, and pulling eggs whenever found. Two Guernsey cows stood stock-still in the field, chewing on new spring grass. They were yet to be milked, one of William's chores.

The six-year-old twins, Brian and Duncan, sat quietly just beyond the cabin doorway, playing in the soft grass and dirt. Elspeth had instructed her second eldest, Mary, to clean up the lodge, wash and hang the bed linen, and make the morning meal.

Mary was two years behind her brother William; still, Elspeth could see a maturity in her daughter that was lacking in her son. This sometimes worried her, but as her husband, Ian, often said, the nature of young men was difficult to gauge. Much had to do with the challenges they faced as they grew into their life.

Each child of the household closely examined the wounded Indian lying in William's bed. David stared at the young Cherokee with great curiosity. Although he was fourteen years old, he had only spied a few Indians in his lifetime. Being this close to one was thrilling. This was clearly a different morning for the MacEwan household. Many questions flew about. Without answering, Elspeth stiffly instructed them all to get to their everyday chores.

It was going warmer to the weather, and most hunters and trappers were still well south and west of the MacEwan place. They had not had an overnight patron for some days, but that was fine as this would give Elspeth the time needed to clean the place properly and make ready for the returning longhunters. She knew her husband would be coming home soon as well. She wanted to have the place done proper for Ian's return.

"Mother!" called William. "There are some men coming up the low eastern trail. It looks to be hunting men with horses—and a dog."

Elspeth stepped out of the cabin and stared off in the direction of the well-worn road. Sure enough, a clutch of rough men adorned in buckskin and fur caps were visible, coming up the trail. A large black dog of mixed breed was leading the group. Elspeth immediately recognized the tallest of the visitors and broke into a friendly smile as she waved her arms over head.

"Hello, the house!" called the tall man of the group. He cradled a long rifle in his left arm as did most of his companions. He waved his free arm in greeting.

William's dog, Stick, rushed to the compound gate, spinning in circles, barking, and wagging its tail furiously.

"Stick, get back here now!" called William. The dog sullenly obeyed.

In time, Elspeth marched up to the east gate and swung it out. "Good day to you, Mr. Boone," she announced with a smile.

Daniel Boone nodded in recognition. "Howdy-do, Missus MacEwan? It is a fine day for a visit."

"I should say it is, Mr. Boone. Come in and be welcome, gentlemen. You can put your animals in the field back of the sleeping lodge. I'll have food set up for you all quick as I can. You'll find the drinking well round back."

Daniel Boone stood some measure over six feet, considerably taller than his companions. These were rough-cut men, bearded and dark eyed. The odor of fresh skins lingered about them. Each wore a cap of raccoon, possum, or squirrel. Vibrant feathers adorned their caps while some wore them tied alongside their braided hair. They dressed in a curious mix of buckskin, feathers, and store-bought colorful fabric.

Every man carried a long rifle tucked neatly in the crook of his arm. A large hunting knife sheathed in fringed leather and colorful beads hung from their belt, tied securely to the leg. They were half savage, half civilized. Men such as these trapped the new land of the west struggling and fighting to carve out a life in the American wilderness. It was travelers such as these who made up most of the visitors to the MacEwan homestead.

"William," called Elspeth, "pull some corn for these gentlemen, please, Three or four dozen ears will do and bring the big ham hanging in the smokehouse."

William dashed off in pursuit of his mother's request.

"That is most kind of you, Missus MacEwan," said Boone, removing his coonskin cap and revealing a dark mass of uncut hair damp with sweat. "I have a fresh turkey here, shot this very morn. It should go well with the ham."

Elspeth smiled, nodded, and stated her business. "It's a half dollar a day for food and lodging. That's my usual price, but if you bring your own meat, I'll reduce it some. Animal feed is separate, of course."

"Agreed, Missus MacEwan," replied Boone. "You always did run a fair house."

Elspeth looked down at her feet and said, "Since you are here, Mr. Boone, I would ask a favor. My son William shot an Indian boy down by the creek. I cleaned the wound, and now he lay inside on William's bedding. He has yet to awake. I would appreciate it if you would see him. He is Cherokee, I think. Maybe you'll know?"

Boone raised an eyebrow and looked askance at the man standing to his right. He was a stout fellow with broad shoulders and a full dark beard. The stranger dragged a muskrat cap from his head. He nodded politely to Elspeth. "Pleasure to meet you, Missus MacEwan," he said in a soft accent.

"This is Mr. Stevenson," announced Boone. "Mr. Stevenson lived with the Cherokee for some years and knows most of the tribes running along the Appalachia, north and south. I believe he'll know what tribe your Indian is from, if I'm not mistaken."

***

Boone looked down on the Indian boy, lying motionless on the thin mat. He peered in closer. "What say you, Mr. Stevenson? He looks to be Cherokee to me with fine moccasins. They look all too fine for a boy his age."

"He's Cherokee all right, Daniel. And I think this one I know. His father is Black Feather, the Cherokee chief. The boy is called Shadow Bear."

"Black Feather, you say?" asked Boone. "What's his kin doing up this way, I wonder?"

"I heard there was a fight between them and the Shawnee west of here. It may well be the boy was scouting."

"Well," announced Boone, "if he is who you say, it's best we get him home before any more mischief occurs."

Elspeth shook her head with concern. "A chief's son, you say, Mr. Stevenson? That is bad fortune."

"Well, he's not too shot from the look of him. Did he say anything?" asked Stevenson.

"I'm sure he did, but I have no idea what," replied Elspeth in her lilting Welsh. "Would you be willing to take him back to his own people, Mr. Boone?"

"We can take him as far as Murphy-Borough and then send word back to Black Feather. I don't know if he's looking for his son just yet, but if he's due back before summer weather, he surely will be."

"I do appreciate that, Mr. Boone. I'll have some food ready for you gentlemen in no time."

"And where is Mr. MacEwan, may I ask? On a long hunt?"

"No," replied Elspeth. "He's gone to Philadelphia for sundries, powder and ball. We haven't been east for supplies in nearly two years. I expect him back in ten days or so."

"I shall wait for him if my companions agree but no more than ten days. Your Cherokee boy should be awake and feeling better by then. It would do no harm."

"Your company is most welcome, Mr. Boone. I'll tend to your meal now, gentlemen, if you will excuse me."

Shadow Bear

THAT EVENING, A feast of boiled corn, smoked ham, bitter greens, and venison stew was served up. The food was seasoned with salt, Jamaican pepper, and what little mace Elspeth could spare.

The visitors queued up in silence as each man was passed an overloaded plate from Elspeth. Soon they began to scatter about in a loose circle, lounging on their packs and skins, softly grunting as they ate with obvious appetite. There was little to no conversation. Before long, Elspeth appeared bearing two loaves of coarse bread and mounds of cut-up roast turkey. This was followed with a cool clay bottle of creek water and a jug of warm rum with maple sugar.

Afterward, the men gathered about a healthy fire. The evening air was cool and pleasant. The jug was passed among the drinking men each in turn. Soon they began telling harrowing tales of wild hunts in fine weather and foul. They told of vicious fights with bloodthirsty Shawnee and Delaware who populated the trails and valley ranges of the northwestern Appalachia.

As the rum jug emptied, both the stories and volume rose in intensity.

Three or four of the hunters pulled out their Dutch clay pipes, stuffing them with kinnikinnick. Mr. Stevenson offered his pipe to William in a polite gesture, but he shook his head no.

The young man had tried kinnikinnick once and found the mix too foul for his consumption. His mother frowned on such behavior. William was much too young for smoking.

"It's no pastime for a gentleman your age, William."

"But I'm not a gentleman, Mother," answered William honestly. "You've told me so many times."

"You will be," replied Elspeth with conviction.

"So, boy," said, Stevenson in his slight Swedish accent, "is that the first Indian you ever shot?"

William blushed heavily at this. "It was an accident, Mr. Stevenson. I did not shoot him deliberately."

Boone laughed aloud at this, spitting into the fire and smiling broadly.

"Well," continued Mr. Stevenson, chuckling, "if ever you do shoot one deliberately, I hope it to be an accurate shot."

Three mornings later, William brought a bowl of corn pudding to Shadow Bear. William was happy to see the young Indian awake and looking about with frank curiosity. William offered the bowl gently while making eating gestures with his free hand. Shadow Bear simply stared at William in silence, making no move to accept the food. Setting the small bowl beside the bed frame on the floor, William went back outside, oddly offended.

Once his chores were complete, William would wander over to where the hunters gathered after their morning meal. Each man was tending his gear and pack carefully. Great care was taken to ensure their powder horns were dry and free of any debris. Every hunter pulled a share of hides from their pack for trade. They wanted tobacco, sugar, salt, and corn—whiskey, if available. "Was there no powder and ball for trade?" several asked.

"I do have some," answered Elspeth. "I will trade what I can, but my husband, Ian, has asked that I trade it out small as we are low ourselves."

William walked back to the main cabin and, to his surprise, found the pudding bowl now empty and set proper on the rough-hewn table. He looked over at Shadow Bear, who made no move from the cot in which he lay.

Ten days passed filled with hard work and clear weather. By this time, it was obvious even to William that Shadow Bear would survive his wound.

Home Again

OUTSIDE THE CABIN, there came a loud hallo and huzzah from Boone and his companions along with the ringing fire of several rifles. William rushed to the door, and as he did so, Shadow Bear suddenly sat bolt upright on the bed frame, startling William. They hesitated at the open doorway as the two young men stared intently at each other. William saw concern and a mix of curiosity in the young Indian's eyes but no hostility as he had expected.

The men were hailing someone coming up the eastern trail. Stick rushed from the cabin, wagging its tail vigorously with joy. William knew instantly his father was coming.

Stepping out into the bright morning sun, both boy and dog raced up to the rail fence. William vaulted over in one throw, and Stick dived under. William could hear his mother calling but paid her no mind. His father was home.

As the column of men and train wagons crested the small rise, William ran headlong into his father. The big Scotsman laughed as he held his eldest boy in a crushing bear hug, spinning round in a tight circle, all the while surrounded by a large blond dog whirling about like a small tornado.

"Hold yourself, William. Let me catch my breath, son," said Ian MacEwan in his thick Scot accent.

He reached down and rubbed Stick's head until the dog calmed a bit. "Good boy, Stick. Did you miss me then?"

"Oh yes, Father. We thought you were coming home week next. I'm so glad you came now. Mr. Boone is here for a visit. He has some Longhunter's with him."

"Is that so? It will be a pleasure to see Mr. Boone again. I have news for him as well."

"Father, I shot an Indian," announced William. It came out of his mouth just like that, surprising himself and his father.

"It was pure accident, but I shot him all the same," finished William, hanging his head as he prodded the earth with a booted toe.

Ian MacEwan stopped short and gave his son a questioning look. "What do you mean you shot an Indian? What Indian?"

"It was down by the creek, Father. I was hunting, and I thought this Indian was a turkey, and I shot him in the canebrake. Mother said she thinks he'll be all right though," he added brightly.

"William," said Ian MacEwan carefully, "how is it you could mistake an Indian for a turkey? You had best have a good explanation, son. Did ye not look before you fired?"

William continued to stare at the earth beneath his feet but said nothing.

"Well then, let us get up to the cabin so I can hear this tale properly."

MacEwan spied Elspeth in the distance wearing a simple pale green linen dress with a white apron overall. He stepped lively, now marching with singular intent.

Ian MacEwan never loved anything in his hard life until he met Elspeth. She was working in a tavern east of the Appalachia when they met. She was a handsome woman and so attracted a good bit of attention from the men passing through. For some strange reason that Ian could not fathom, he found himself returning to the tavern every evening.

Eventually, Elspeth noticed the handsome silent Scotsman sitting in the shadows of the Pillsman Tavern. He would quietly ask Elspeth for a flagon of ale and a cut of rough bread, some roasted venison perhaps. He would smile. Elspeth would smile. This went on for nearly a fortnight until finally, one evening, Ian asked if she lived here with her husband, the tavern owner. Elspeth laughed and said, "No, I do not. I am not married, if it's any business to you, sir."

"I mean no offense, lass. It's just that you are always here. It would seem possible your family would be running this tavern."

"I have no family here, sir. I work the tables and clean up nights. In the morning, I do the accounting for Mr. Pillsman. He pays fair, and I do not mind the work."

"You are an educated woman then," said Ian with surprise. "That is a rare bird in this part of the country."

"I thank you kindly for the compliment, sir, but I am sure you'll find that I am not such a rare bird."

After that, Ian and Elspeth spoke to each other every evening. Ian was fast falling in love with this beautiful girl, and the more they spoke, the more he wanted her.

One evening the tall Scot stood up slowly from his back room table, took Elspeth by the hand, and announced, "Elspeth Thomas, I am a good and honest man. I may not look so from my dress and manner, but I come from a strong Scottish clan. I am well educated, and I am a fine provider. I am in stout health and possess nearly sixty pounds sterling as well as a full pallet of fine furs. I also have a mule and a good saddle horse. I carry two guns, one a Brown Bess, the other a Philadelphia rifle handmade by two *deutsche* brothers. And I am more than a fair hunter. I would hope that you consider these things as I ask for your hand in marriage. You have told me you have no family here in America, so I must ask you directly. How do you answer?"

Elspeth looked at him and slowly shook her head. "Well, Mr. Ian MacEwan, all I can say to that is it's about time. I was soon to give up on you. It so happens that I know you to be a gentleman, and I am sure you come from a fine family. I also know you carry two guns. I know you have a full pallet of fur hides, and I know you have a mule and a saddle horse. You may be aware that I feed that mule and saddle horse every evening and morning as you have paid for. My answer to you then is yes. I will marry you, and we will make a life right here in this country or west."

Ian nodded certainly and let out a rush of air. He did not realize he had been holding his breath. He said, "West, I think. Aye, west it is."

* * *

Ian stepped up to Elspeth and swept her into his arms, raising her off the ground in a hard embrace. He then kissed her mouth with the thirst of a man gone without water for some time.

Boone and his companions stepped up as Elspeth untangled herself from her husband's arms, blushing and smiling.

"Daniel, it is good to see you again, my friend. And you as well, Mr. Stevenson." Ian nodded politely to the remaining hunters, calling those he knew by name, welcoming all to his home.

"I have news from the east, Daniel," continued Ian. "Washington's Continental army has taken Trenton and Princeton. It was a remarkable feat. He defeated the Hessians and captured the lot."

"I have heard much the same," said Boone. "Rejecting taxes is one matter, but fighting the British is something else altogether."

"What will you do now?" asked Ian.

"I stand with the Continental Congress along with my friends and family. The Congress has taken the right course. Independence is the only answer. I will fight alongside them."

Ian nodded in agreement. "I feel the same. Let us go up to the cabin and drink some good Scots whiskey from the British store." He laughed.

Shadow Bear emerged, standing just outside the cabin. Ian looked up. "Who is this then?" he said, nodding toward Shadow Bear.

"This is the young Indian your son William shot," announced Boone. "It was a clean wound. Missus MacEwan did a fine job."

"Has he spoken?"

"Not yet," answered Boone. "Mr. Stevenson, could you speak with this boy? I want him to understand we mean no harm. He can travel with us until we reunite him with his people."

William stared at Shadow Bear in simple wonder. It was the first opportunity he had to study the young Cherokee while fully upright.

Shadow Bear stood straight as a tree as he viewed the white men standing before him. He was nearly as tall as William with long limbs and a narrow face displaying a short hooked nose. His hair was black as pitch, straight, and long. A braid ran down one side of his head, accentuating the narrow face in a peculiar fashion. Portions of his long black hair were tied and bound with small, thin strips of leather and jutting out like the branches of a thorny bush. A colorful band of leather and beads was wrapped about his neck in a high collar. He wore a dark fringed tunic with a deerskin loincloth lapped in a calico fabric. The tunic was adorned with vertical lines of colorful river stones and beads arranged front and back with small fringed strips of hide gathered at the seams.

His bare legs, set slightly apart, displayed a pair of long fringed moccasins covering feet and shins just below the knee. They looked beautiful to William.

Shadow Bear raised his arm, pointing directly at William. He spoke in a guttural singsong fashion, his voice soft and clear.

Daniel Boone turned to his companion. "What does he say, Mr. Stevenson?" asked Boone.

Stevenson spoke, raising his hands in a gentle gesture; he swept one arm across the group of white men and continued.

Shadow Bear replied.

Stevenson said, "I asked him of his people. He is Shadow Bear, son of Black Feather, as I suspected. He has a question. He wants to know why the Longhunter shot him. He is no enemy of the white man, and so his father will be angry that his son was shot for no reason."

"The Longhunter?" queried Ian. "What Longhunter?"

Stevenson simply nodded toward William. "Your son," he answered.

"But William isn't—" began Ian.

"Please tell him, Mr. Stevenson," interrupted William firmly, "that it was by accident. I believed him to be a turkey bird in the brush. I meant no harm to him."

Stevenson relayed the message. Shadow Bear spoke again, this time at length.

Stevenson translated, "He is pleased he was not seen as a man. This was his intention."

At the age of seventeen, William MacEwan was a gangly youth with strong long arms and broad shoulders to match. In casual observance, the boy appeared clumsy and uncoordinated. This was deceptive. Tracking through wooded trails among the tall trees and heavy brush, he traveled near catlike, making little sound as he moved along. He was well built for his age and carried his load at the MacEwan place.

His handsome square face displayed small pink freckles, and his hair, which was his most striking feature, was a rich golden red. Bound in horse tail fashion, it hung to his shoulders.

"Shadow Bear has asked for the return of his weapons," announced Mr. Stevenson quietly.

"He carried no weapons," replied William. "Did he, Mother?"

Elspeth shook her head in answer. "None that I have seen."

Stevenson spoke again to Shadow Bear. He replied.

"He had hidden his weapons by the creek. We best go and collect his things," said Stevenson. "They will be needed for his journey home."

A Contest

TOBACCO, POWDER, AND ball exchanged hands as a flurry of trading took place. Along with salt beef, corn seed, and whiskey, there were barley flour, dried beans, and peas. Bolts of cloth were cut and passed around as a free offering from the MacEwan family. The men quickly tucked the welcome gift into their packs for trading or adornment. Everything carried value in the frontier.

The pelts offered were good quality, properly dried, and combed clean of any animal residue, blood or fat. Beaver, raccoon, and fox were all included along with deer, squirrel, and possum hides.

One man named Alden had collected colorful feathers to trade.

"Now these," said Alden in a clipped English accent, "these are best for trading with the northeastern tribes. I have plenty in my store. Indians treasure such feathers. They bring great power to the savage."

There were deep red northern cardinal feathers along with blue jay, black crow, woodpecker, blue heron, and robin feathers, all carefully gathered in a thin deerskin leather wallet displayed in fine order. Turkey, hawk, eagle, and quail feathers were all present.

As William studied the line of plumage, he was taken with the shimmering iridescence that could magically change hue in the sunlight when tilted this way or that.

Shadow Bear had been wandering among the white hunters, studying each detail of the homestead and the men surrounding him. As the trading came into full swing, the young Indian became caught up in the fascinating array of goods on display.

Ian had brought out steel tomahawks, sturdy long knives, sewing needles, and small mirrors. He piled tall bags of English tea along with four pewter cups with fancy cut images on the sides. Small pouches of salt, nutmeg, and Jamaican pepper were on display. The quantity and variety of items were a delight to the hunters, and so many pelts and furs were soon traded off.

As William studied the line of feathers, he realized that Shadow Bear was standing beside him. William looked at the Cherokee and said, "They are the most beautiful feathers I have ever seen."

Shadow Bear replied softly in his own language, seeming to understand William's words. As if on cue, Mr. Stevenson stepped up beside the two young men. "Feathers have a special meaning to the Cherokee. This one favors the spirit of the forest trees, and this"—he pointed to a hawk feather—"has the power of wisdom."

"Is this true, Mr. Stevenson?" asked William.

"Oh yes, the Indian can be savage, but I have seen white men equally savage. I have also seen nobility, compassion, and love in the Indian. My mother used to say that white men and Indians are cut from the same cloth of God's design, just different patterns and colors. In this way, we are much the same as well as different. I think she was right."

Shadow Bear spoke at length then, and as he did so, he pointed to one of the feathers.

"He would like to trade for this feather," said Stevenson, addressing Alden. "It would be a gift for his father."

Alden leaned forward. "What can the lad trade?"

"He will trade two good beaver pelts in the summer if you will let him have the feather," said Stevenson.

"That is no trade." Alden laughed. "I trade on the barrelhead. If the lad wants the feather, he must have the goods to trade."

"What would you take in trade, sir?" asked William.

"Pelts, good powder, hard silver money, or some of equal value. Yes, I would trade that," answered Alden, nodding.

"Please, would you hold the feather until I return?" asked William.

William returned carrying three pelts in his arms, holding them outward fur side up—a beaver, one raccoon, and a rare northern silver fox fur.

Alden eyed the fox, realizing its value. He said, "I'll take that silver pelt."

Ian MacEwan strolled over. "What have we here, William? Are you trading, son?"

"Yes, Father. I'm trading for this feather. It is a gift that Shadow Bear wants for his father, but he has nothing to trade. I thought it the least I could do after shooting him. It's an apology, Father."

"And a good one, I see," answered Ian, nodding in approval. "This silver fox pelt has some value, son. Are you sure you want to trade that? As I recall, that Canadian trapper gave you this for taking care of his animals the whole of last summer. I would think it holds some value for you as well."

"Oh, it does, Father? But that is what a gift of meaning is about, is it not? If it has value to me, then it will be of value to Shadow Bear."

Alden smiled at the senior MacEwan, and Ian nodded back. "I'll have no advantage taken of my son, Alden. I think more than a single feather in trade would make this right."

Alden smiled and nodded in agreement. "I think several feathers would be a fair trade at that."

"Is this all right with you, son?" asked Ian.

"Oh yes, Father, that would be fine."

"If that is what you wish, then make your trade."

The transaction was quickly made, and William solemnly handed the four beautiful feathers to Shadow Bear.

Shadow Bear passed his hand across his chest and spoke.

Stevenson translated, "He said the Longhunter is generous, and Shadow Bear will not forget this gift. He takes you as a friend, lad."

William smiled broadly as did Ian and Stevenson.

By early afternoon, a revelry of sorts broke out at the MacEwan homestead. Everyone was chattering, eating, and drinking in cheerful company. It was not long before a shooting contest broke out.

William sat munching a long ear of boiled corn neatly coated in coarse salt. Swinging his feet to and fro from his fence rail perch, he watched as Shadow Bear approached and stood nearby. William smiled at the young Cherokee. They had come to understand each other in a way that was peculiar to youth. The barriers of prejudice and hatred were undeveloped in these young men, replaced with simple curiosity. It drew them toward each other. It was a happy feeling.

The sounds of a bone flute and stringed wood fiddle began to fill the air. Song accompanied the music, but to William's ear, the tunes had little in common. It did not seem to matter to anyone present.

Ian MacEwan was unfurling a long heavy package wrapped in muslin and oil-soaked cloth. He carefully withdrew a long rifle. Even from a distance, the rifle caught William's eye. He watched as his father marched toward him, rifle in hand.

"Father," he declared, "you bought a new rifle?"

"Aye, William. Come have a look."

It was beautiful. Long and slender, it had a dark hardwood stock perfectly feathered into the polished steel body of the trigger mechanism. The stock was thinner than his father's rifle. Each side was carrying a silver plate intricately engraved with swirling designs. The stock butt, too, had a polished silver plate attached with two ornate screws. The barrel tip was sheathed in silver with a delicate end site. The ram was good hardwood with a silver tip to help keep powder dry. It was as straight as a Bible verse.

Shadow Bear and some few of the other hunters gathered about. They all agreed it was an extraordinary rifle.

"By the lord," said Boone, eyeing the piece, "this appears to equal my Tick Licker, MacEwan. Is she Philadelphia made?"

"Aye, she was made in Pennsylvania by the hand of two German brothers, same as my rifle. They are the finest rifle makers in the colonies. She shoots an accurate ball," said Ian. "Why not try her and see, William?"

"Me?" declared William, surprised.

"Aye, son, this rifle is for you, a gift from your mother and me. It's time you carried a proper rifle in support of the family. We'll need a good longhunter to provide meat. Let us see what ye can do."

William quickly cleaned and buffed the rifle. He gathered up his powder horn and ball and deftly loaded the piece. He fired a shot at a small dry cone hanging among the pine. The cone shattered, disappearing in a cloud of brown dust.

***

Seven men lined up along the small pasture edge that spread out beside the Indian Creek. A tall oak 160 yards from the line would be the target base. One man approached the tree and hacked three small vertical cuts down the center of the trunk. Into each cut, he wedged a sliver of wood no more than an inch wide, gently tapping them in place. The object of the contest was to hit and split the sliver of wood best in count. It was a difficult target given the late afternoon sun.

"Gentlemen," announced Ian as he and William approached the cluster of men, "I would like to enter my son William in your contest if you allow."

"Who?" asked a drunken marksman. "The turkey shooter?"

This brought a line of laughter from the grizzled hunters.

"What of his wager?" asked another.

"I will wager for William," said Ian flatly. "I say three English pounds in silver coin. And I will wager it all he takes the lot of ye."

This brought a measure of excitement to the men. They gathered up to consider the bet. They argued backward and up, deciding how best to match MacEwan's wager. They finally agreed on a mix of coin, eight fine pelts, and some of their newly acquired tobacco, equal to three pounds and a bit.

Ian MacEwan examined the lot and declared it fair.

"Father," said William nervously, "this is too much. What will Mother say if I lose?"

"Now, William, you don't think I would wager such an amount if I thought you could lose, son. Ready that rifle as I have taught you."

The contestants lined up perpendicular to the target. Each man poured a spoon of dry powder down the long barrel, followed by a small wad of fast-burning fabric. A hand-polished ball was rolled in, finishing with a final pack of the ram.

Each man would fire three shots at three slivers of wood. Hitting the same sliver twice was a miss. All three slivers must be struck in turn from bottom up.

One member of the party, not a contestant, would stand out by the oak and announce the accuracy of each man's shot. He would then replace any slivers of wood as needed.

This task fell to Mr. Boone due to his known sense of honesty. Besides, everyone knew that Boone was the finest shot in the colonies, and so he excluded himself from the competition.

Soon the air filled with black powder smoke and the acrid odor it brought. The near-constant explosions from the rifles alarmed horses and stock alike, driving them outward as far as the stockade fence allowed. The hollers and whoops from the men did not help.

The boisterous racket scattered every chicken within sight as they began roosting and populating the nearby trees. Elspeth, letting out a sharp cry, grabbed her long-handle broom from the cabin in a desperate attempt to drive the birds back to the ground.

Of the seven men who fired, only one hit the mark. The last to shoot was William.

Side wagering began among the men, with William's skill raising the odds. After all, he was a strip of a youngster, built to a man's size but without the experience they had. Had he not proved himself to be a poor shot, striking an Indian rather than a turkey?

"Let us show these gentlemen how a MacEwan shoots," said Ian, resting his hand on William's shoulder. "Remember, son, calm and steady."

William quietly nodded and began swiftly and silently reloading his rifle. Just then, Boone stepped closer to the target by a good margin, prompting Ian to shout, "Halloo! Step back, Mr. Boone! Take care! You are too close to the target, sir!"

Boone replied with equal volume, "Have no concern, MacEwan! I have seen your boy shoot many times! I am perfectly safe!"

William stepped up to the log and took position. Breathing slow, he held his stance. Carefully drawing the rifle up into a firing pose, he tucked the slender stock firmly into his right shoulder. The ornate plate felt cool and certain against his cheek. He could clearly see the three targets and, judging the center of each, took aim. Pulling the trigger, he fired with a small jump of the long barrel.

The bottom wedge of wood exploded, disappearing into splinters. Loud howls, laughter, and shouts followed this shot. The tall golden-haired boy had hit his mark.

The second and third shots fired from William came quickly, each hitting the target in similar fashion. This drew an odd silence from the gathering. Several had lost fair goods on the wager. As they studied the youngster, Shadow Bear leaned in toward William and lightly tugged the sleeve of his blouse. William looked over at Shadow Bear and smiled.

Alden stepped up to Ian. "I wouldn't think it possible, MacEwan. I certainly would not believe such a thing had I not seen it with my own eyes. The boy is truly amazing," finished Alden. He quietly laid his coin pouch before Ian, shaking his head in wonder.

"How far can your boy shoot, MacEwan?" asked Alden.

"William can hit the mark at over 250 yards," answered Ian carefully.

As he walked away, Ian MacEwan eyed Alden suspiciously. There was something about the man that brushed Ian rough. He had this very feeling when they first met. It was as if there was something false about the man, untrue. Ian shrugged off the feeling as he had seen his fair share of scalawags along the Appalachia. Some ran from indentured servitude or the British navy while others were murderers of men and common thieves. It was difficult to know which type Alden was. He had the drawl of a British tar but the manners of a gentleman. He carried well-made goods and a newly manufactured Brown Bess. This he held in the fashion of a British redcoat. He apparently carried money as well. It was an odd mix for certain.

The silence among the hunters was now complete. Those men who had bet against William broke out with a string of profanity while those who bet with William smiled broadly, pounding the young man's back and declaring him to have no equal in the company of all.

Ian MacEwan, smiling broadly, carried an irresistible pride with him the whole of that day.

A Spring Journey

BOONE AND HIS companions gathered their packs and animals together, ready for the trip up to Kentucky lands. Despite losing money as some did, everyone agreed that the time spent at the MacEwan place was fine and proper. Warm beds and comfortable food had a way of healing a man. And the company was more than pleasant. These Longhunter's would tell a tale of the golden-headed boy who could shoot the wings off a fly at two-hundred-plus yards.

Shadow Bear and William stood silent as Boone and Ian MacEwan, surrounded by a clutch of men, discussed what to do with the Cherokee boy. It was determined that the best course would be to send Shadow Bear home rather than up to Kentucky with Boone and his troop. William stood just back of the men, his head turned slightly to catch every word.

"I'll not consider it proper for the boy to travel alone. He must return to his family," announced Ian. "The sooner, the better. I canna take him myself just now. It will be a fortnight or more before I can leave with any time to spare. There is too much work to be done here."

William piped up, "I can travel with Shadow Bear, Father. After all, it only seems right that I go. I should be the one to apologize to his mother and father. I will explain what happened and tell them how sorry I am."

Ian looked at his son. As a father, he was proud of William for making such an offer, but he also twisted with concern as William was only seventeen. Other than an occasional trading visit to the homestead from a friendly Indian or two, William had not spent time with such men and could speak no language other than his own.

"No," said Elspeth, who had somehow entered the circle of men and boys unnoticed. "I'll have no son of mine wandering the wood among savage Indians and god knows what. These are just boys, Ian. Can you truly say a trip to the southern edge of nowhere with every possible danger along the way leaves you comfortable?"

She nearly shouted these words at Ian and William in her agitation. It was clear Elspeth was greatly perturbed at the notion of William traveling off alone, more upset than Ian had ever seen her. Still, William was seventeen years of age, and Ian himself had traveled halfway across the world when he was no more than fourteen.

"Come into the cabin," said Ian gently. "Let us talk this over, Elspeth. The Indian boy must go home. I am sure his own clan is as worried as you would be given the circumstance. We must make this right, Elspeth."

"He came here alone. Why not let him leave the same way?" said Elspeth logically. "I took care of his wound. He seems fine now."

"He leans to his left, Mother," said William quickly. "He also turns slightly when rising from a seat. I believe he still has pain, Mother. I could help him."

"Let us talk, Elspeth," said Ian forcefully as he deftly guided her toward the cabin.

William and Shadow Bear stared at each other, understanding in some way that their immediate future was now being discussed by the man and woman walking away from them.

"Elspeth, do you think we can hold William forever? He's a grown man now. David will be taking his chores, and William would naturally come along with me on long hunts, a dangerous thing itself. These are our bairns, and this is our way. You know this yourself. If William is to be a man of his own fortune, then he must go his own way.

"Mary can read and write with a fine hand. She composes her own poems. David is a natural farmer. He cares so for the crops and takes the livestock straight to his heart. Who knows what life will hold for Aelwyd and the twins? It will not be our wish but theirs. You know this, Elspeth. You have spent your entire life gaining those things that are precious to you. Did you think our children would be any different?

"William has the hand and heart of a Longhunter, Elspeth. You know this. I do not intend to stand against his wishes. What he asks is only right and for the right reason. Be proud of our son, Elspeth, and rely on the fact that we have done our best to bring him to this world with a strong back and a sharp mind. We canna ask for more than that."

To emphasize her words, Elspeth knocked the table with her knuckles as she spoke. "The only precious things I have in this world are you, our children, and this home. If you think I could abandon that for even a second, you are very wrong, husband. I know William is capable and strong, but this trip he wants to go on rings with hazard. Can we only wait a while? Maybe the Cherokee boy will be well enough to go home of his own. Can't we do that, Ian?"

"We could, I suppose, but then William would only wish to go when that time comes. No, he wants to make amends for his mistake, and he has a desire for some adventure. Surely you see that?"

"Don't make me do this, Ian."

"I'll not make you, Elspeth. This is something you must decide on your own. But be aware that we canna tie the boy to us and expect him to grow to the man we want him to be."

After several minutes, Ian MacEwan stepped outside, followed by Elspeth, looking concerned but resigned. She shed her wishes but no tears.

"You will go with Shadow Bear, William," said Ian. "You will make your apologies to his father and clan. You must be at your best behavior, son, as you will be acting in some measure as the head of this house. We wish to remain friendly with the Cherokee. I will expect that you can explain what happened to Shadow Bear. Ask the Cherokee people to come to our home in peace and trade. Then return to us."

"Yes, Father," answered William with a broad grin.

"You are to keep an eye while on the trail, William . . ." began Ian.

"And a quiet ear," finished William. Father and son smiled at each other in a way that brought color to William's face along with the feeling of simple joy.

Mr. Stevenson stepped up and looked on Elspeth with a benign expression. This woman had greeted Boone and his companions fearlessly, opening her arms and sharing her hospitality. She had fed these rough men and provided them drinks and a warm place to sleep.

She was a very handsome woman, and it was in Stevenson's nature to assist a lady whenever possible.

"I would be happy to accompany your son and the young Cherokee, Mrs. MacEwan. It would be my pleasure," said Stevenson in his clipped Swedish accent.

Elspeth smiled up at the big man, and indeed, she did feel a measure of relief. A seasoned fellow such as Stevenson would be most welcome. Ian MacEwan offered a hand to Stevenson and thanked him heartily.

"I planned to visit the Cherokee myself, Mrs. MacEwan," announced Alden. "I have hopes of trading with them as I have in the past. I will go along as well if no one objects."

"There now, Elspeth, you see," said Ian MacEwan. "Four souls will make a safe trip surely. Mr. Stevenson speaks the language, and he is a well-known fellow among the Cherokee. I'm sure their journey will be safe."

Elspeth did feel better knowing Stevenson would travel with the boys, but Mr. Alden's inclusion inexplicably concerned her. She did not know this man. He seemed odd.

Whenever she looked at Alden, she found the man glaring at her. It was unsettling. A gnawing grip entered her belly. She knew not why. She did have confidence in William. He was a capable young man educated well as she insisted. She knew him to be an excellent hunter, hardworking and sensible. Still, she could not shake the worry from her apron.

Stevenson explained to Shadow Bear the plans they had made. He was pleased.

The young Indian explained to Stevenson the importance of Shadow Bear telling the tale of his adventures with the white men. If Stevenson and the Longhunter came along, his people would know he spoke true. He would tell his father and the tribal council how he had been shot by a white man and survived. He did not cry out like a woman in his pain. He would proudly tell his father how he traded with the white men and had come home with powerful feathers.

He would sit at the Cherokee fire telling of the white men's food and the peculiar sounds they made on wooden boxes with strings, how the white men sang so badly. And he would tell of his friendship with William MacEwan, the longhunter who could strike a bird in flight with his rifle.

Stevenson smiled at Shadow Bear and agreed that it would indeed be a fine tale to tell his people.

Ian MacEwan emerged from the main cabin carrying a pair of long-legged moccasins that he used when hunting. He handed them to William in silence. Elspeth gave William a coat made of good pelts with a felt cloth lining. She also gave William a small Bible to carry. She nodded at her son, silently indicating she was all right. She smiled, but her eyes betrayed the concern she held for her eldest boy.

William was so excited about the prospect of adventure that he barely noticed his mother. Ian nudged his son gently and gave a quick glance toward Elspeth.

"Mother," declared William, suddenly aware, "I will be fine. Do not worry."

With uncharacteristic emotion, Elspeth grasped her son in her arms and hugged him in a fierce embrace. Then just as abruptly, she turned on Shadow Bear, doing the same. She whispered softly in the Indian's ear. Shadow Bear could not understand a word she spoke but knew the words were kindly meant.

Shadow Bear spoke, and Stevenson translated, "The boy wishes to thank you for saving his life, Mrs. MacEwan. He will ask his ancestors and the Mother Spirit to watch over you."

At this, the small group gathered up and began their long trek south to west.

Bears

THE MANY TRAILS that led east and west were worn and popular among longhunters. Those that ran south were equal in nature. Good hunting ranged every direction. The four travelers from the MacEwan Station walked a single line, with Stevenson leading, followed by Shadow Bear.

William felt that the necessaries he carried—his long rifle, winter coat, and food pack—would wear him down over the trail. Still, he was determined to push along with the rest, uncomplaining. Mr. Stevenson and Shadow Bear barely spoke. For miles on end, they padded their way along the beaten path in total silence.

Alden was not so constrained. He spoke incessantly. At first, William was grateful for the constant chatter as it filled the time nicely. After some days, though, William noticed an irritation in both Stevenson and Shadow Bear with respect to Alden's unceasing dialogue. Before long, William, too, had gone silent as he carefully studied his companions.

Shadow Bear and Stevenson displayed a quiet certainty as they navigated difficult sections of the trail. The Indian and the seasoned Longhunter scanned their surroundings constantly, one pointing, the other responding. No words passed between them.

The weather was fair and bright. An early spring sunshine brought new leaves to the trees. They had yet to fill out completely, which afforded a good clear view ahead. *Keep a sharp eye and quiet ears*, recalled William. His father had been most insistent about this. So he followed suit along with Stevenson and Shadow Bear. Their silence had no apparent effect on Alden.

Rain came on the eighth day. It varied from a sudden rush of hard-driven sheets to a lighter and consistent pattering through the trees. William was near soaked through after a full day of such weather. Shadow Bear and Stevenson tightened the distance between them as the trail became slick among the dead winter leaves and pine needles.

Footing was precarious in some places and deep with mud in others. For once, Alden went silent, struggling to keep pace.

As they continued along, the wide path narrowed to a deep hammock of tall pines. The sun arrived, but in among the pines, it did little to help dry the men out. The chittering of birds and the soft rustle of tall grass disappeared as the trees closed in, muffling the surroundings.

Shadow Bear was leading, with Stevenson trailing close behind. Alden held a place some twenty feet in front of William, who came last. A short crying bleat just right of the trail suddenly broke the morning quiet. Shadow Bear stopped. He folded up on his haunches in a low squat, staring intently into the unbroken line of pines. He held his hand up, which halted Stevenson and then, with slow realization, Alden. All four travelers were looking to their right now toward the direction of the sound. Stevenson looked at Shadow Bear and nodded.

There was a second bawling cry, much closer now. Shadow Bear slipped an arrow from his quiver and silently drew back his bow. Stevenson checked his rifle and quickly blew the pan clean. Drying it with a small cloth from his pocket, he added new powder. Alden began doing the same as a roar suddenly shattered the quiet directly facing the men. William took an involuntary step backward. He quickly brought up his rifle, pulling an oiled cloth from the breech. His powder was dry, ready to fire.

The bear charged out of the trees with an awesome thundering stride, crashing through the smaller pines, heading directly for the line of men. Within seconds, the beast was nearly on them. Shadow Bear fired first, releasing an arrow with swift efficiency and striking the bear on its right side to little effect. The animal pounded onward toward the group and, when close, reared up on his hind legs, letting out an ear-shattering roar of fury.

Stevenson, with no more than ten feet between man and bear, fired his long rifle directly into the bear's throat. The roaring suddenly ceased, but the bear did not. From its forward momentum, it bowled Stevenson over onto his back while taking a violent wide swipe at the man, catching his shoulder.

William took ready aim at the black monster, but as he did so, a flicker of motion to his left brought his head round. Smashing through a line of thin pines down a sloping rise from behind the group, there came a second bear somewhat smaller than the first and driving directly toward William's position. William swung full left and fired point-blank, striking the bear in the right side of its head. This was a female, realized William. They had stumbled on a family.

The smaller animal tumbled down the slope and rolled straight into Stevenson, knocking him down a second time. The larger black bear then came straight at William as if knowing who had killed its mate. William dashed behind a large pine as the bear came on slashing and slicing its claws into the tree, shearing off tiles of bark. William wiggled around the tree and pulled his large hunting knife. As he did so, the bear reached around the tree, catching William's shirt. In desperation, William drove his blade to the hilt into the bear's paw, nailing it to the tree. A gurgling scream arose from the animal as it struggled to free itself.

Alden stood stock-still during the entire brawl. He never moved an inch as if frozen in place. Holding his Brown Bess close, he began stepping back away from the fray. Shadow Bear watched as William dodged the great black around the pine tree, and he fired yet another arrow, hitting the bear squarely in the back.

Pinned to the pine with William's knife, the black bear struggled in grunting frustration, spinning left and then right to free its paw from the tree. It strained in ferocious effort, stamping its great feet and pulling with all its might. As Stevenson struggled to his feet, he pulled his French flintlock, preparing to fire. Shadow Bear dashed over to Alden and ripped the Brown Bess from his grip. Racing toward William and the thrashing bear, he raised the Bess and fired directly into the back of the animal's skull. The bear fell dead, leaning backward with its great paw still nailed to the pine.

There was silence again. The powerful odor of spent powder, bear musk, blood, and rotting leaves filled the air. Save for Alden, the remainder of the group were all panting loudly, leaning over at the waist, taking in great gulps of cool morning air.

After catching his breath and examining the bears to ensure they were truly dead, Shadow Bear marched up to Alden and flung the now empty Bess into his arms, startling the Englishman. He turned back toward William and, with struggling effort, pulled the knife from the tree, releasing the bear's paw.

"Mr. Alden." Stevenson snarled. "You never fired, sir. Is this a moment of fear?"

It was obvious that Stevenson was very angry. He ground his teeth as he spat out these words. William looked up slowly as if in a daze. He was still trying to find his footing as his breath slowly returned to normal. Shadow Bear spoke with equal venom to his words, unmistakable in its delivery.

"He calls you a coward, Alden," translated Stevenson. "How say you, sir?"

"I am no coward, sir," declared Alden angrily. "Everything happened so quickly I was startled. Which of these monsters posed the greatest threat, I ask you? I held my shot in reserve, which I would consider wise under any circumstance, let alone mayhem such as this. Any sensible man would have done the same."

"I think not, Alden," stated Stevenson flatly. "Any sensible man would have placed that Bess up against that bear's head and fired to save young MacEwan here. You held your fire, sir. If Shadow Bear had not the good sense to relieve you of your weapon, it is almost certain the bear would have killed William."

William looked at Alden, not quite comprehending the conflict between the three men. He had no view of Alden's actions, let alone the time to consider them.

"Apologize to Mr. MacEwan, Alden," declared Stevenson as he pointed directly at the man. "That is the very least you could do, sir."

As William was trying to make sense of this sudden argument, he stood up in a weak stance. He began to shake slightly as the realization of what had just happened came over him. He bent slightly and so leaned backward with his hands outstretched, flopping down to a sitting position, possessed with exhaustion. He stared at the great mass of black fur in wonder. Did this really happen?

A bleating cry broke the silence as a small black cub trundled out of the pine brush, heading straight for its dead mother. The men simply stared.

Stevenson walked calmly over to the wailing cub, and placing his French flintlock to the top of the animal's head, he fired.

"Get your knives out, gentlemen. We have two great bears to skin. We must make haste. A fight like this would surely be heard for miles."

He spoke briefly to Shadow Bear, and the young Indian swiftly gathered up William's blade, returning it. He let out a shrill. "Ayee-ah!" And he began the bloody task at hand.

The hides came off quickly as they sliced away the muscle and fat. With Alden's behavior temporarily forgotten, he, too, helped with the work. By the time they finished, a mass of black flies had gathered, buzzing around them, seeking blood and meat.

The hides along with the bear meat were far too heavy to carry, so Shadow Bear quickly cut down pine saplings thick enough to drape the massive skins across. The makeshift travois allowed them to drag the skins and meat along the footpath. Shadow Bear cut the claws from both bears, storing them in a pouch that hung from his belt.

As they approached a small clearing, Stevenson stopped. "We'll make a site here and take some rest." The weariness in his voice told all. He spoke to Shadow Bear, and the young Indian trotted back along the trail they had come up from. Stevenson explained, "He will scout the trail back to make certain no one follows."

They made no fire that evening, eating a cold meal of coarse bread and smoked meat. When Shadow Bear, returned he told Stevenson the trail behind was empty. No one followed.

No one spoke. The heavy odor of bear meat and blood permeated the air along with a cloud of buzzing flies.

"I am happy you are with us, Mr. Stevenson," said William. "I would not care to think of your absence while we fought for our lives. I am most grateful. I do feel humbled though. We destroyed a family as such, even if they were bears."

"Yes, Mr. MacEwan, it is a shame," said Stevenson sadly. "Being forced to shoot a defenseless cub is not my idea of a fine hunt. I had little choice, of course. It would never have survived alone."

The Cherokee

TWO MORE DAYS of trekking through thick stands of southern pine had brought the four men to near collapse. Hauling haunches of meat and bear hides along with their own necessaries had taken its toll on the little group. Alden complained bitterly.

William bore the task in silence. Only the buzzing flies would test his patience. He had never been this tired. He felt certain in his mind that if he laid his head down on the soft pine needles, he might never rise again.

"The tree line is clearing ahead," said Stevenson. "We'll camp the meadow just farther."

The path they traveled ran alongside Indian Creek for miles. The little stream widened farther south and was now thirty or forty feet across bank to bank. The water ran swiftly here deep in places as it flowed east, joining the network of waterways ending in the Atlantic Ocean.

As they passed the tree line, they came on a large grassy field that stood along a lake just beyond. Shadow Bear turned, dropped his burden, and with some lively chatter in Cherokee began to wave his arms about as he turned slowly in a tight circle.

Shadow Bear babbled on excitedly as he waved his arms in the air. Picking up his pack and grabbing hold of the travois, he gestured southeast and began to struggle with renewed energy toward lakeside. The others followed his path.

Stevenson turned to his white companions. "He said he can smell his father's lodge fire. We are close to the Cherokee village. He knows this place," continued Stevenson. "There will be fish in the lake as well as ducks and other fowl. Come along, Mr. MacEwan, or have you given up on your adventure already?"

William eyed Stevenson with a look of affectionate malice. Alden collapsed in a heap, unable to take another step.

"Come, Mr. Alden," said William. "It appears we are close to the end of our journey."

Alden mumbled an inarticulate sound but remained firmly grounded in the tall blond grass.

"Leave him," said Stevenson. "He can trail behind. Let us go lakeside and start a fire. You, young men, drop the hides in a suitable place while I collect firewood."

Settled in close to the water's edge, William and Shadow Bear gratefully stretched their legs after dropping the heavy travois posts. They sat gingerly on the grass, flattening out a small circle. Stevenson came along only steps behind and began to kick out a patch of the grass in preparation for a fire. He dropped his load of wood and went to work. Before long, a comfortable and smokeless flame grew, warming the morning air.

Shadow Bear sat cross-legged, pulling tall reeds from the canebrake and weaving them into an intricate patch like a small basket. He hopped up onto his feet and headed toward the water's edge. Curious, William followed, carrying two wooden canteens ready to be refilled.

Shadow Bear carefully placed the reed basket into the water, squatting down, silently staring at the placid surface. He dusted the water over the basket with a handful of dry grass seeds.

As William watched, Shadow Bear thrust his hands into the shallow water. Gripping the grass basket, he threw it backward over his shoulder up onto the muddy shoreline. A variety of small fish and pollywogs thrashed about in the basket at Shadow Bear's feet. He smiled broadly at William. William returned the grin with pleasure but little understanding.

Shadow Bear quickly gathered up his tiny catch and headed toward the fire. He carefully folded the homemade basket in two, encompassing his catch; he pushed it close to the fire. William watched with frank curiosity.

Mr. Stevenson looked on. He said, "The fire will smoke and dry the little fish. He will eat them when ready. It is a common thing among young Cherokees. For them, these little fish are a treat of sorts."

"Should I taste one, Mr. Stevenson?" asked William cautiously.

"I should say so, William. I have had many over the years, and they are tasty."

Alden suddenly appeared. "You left me," he stated flatly. "I could have become lost. If not for the fire, I might have passed you along the trail."

"You were not lost, Mr. Alden, only alone," said Stevenson. "I believe you fear that as most men do. Out here in this wilderness, it is the men who cherish solitude that survive. Sit now, and we will roast some of this bear meat."

Shadow Bear collected his little fish basket and offered the fare to each man in turn. Alden screwed up his face as the basket was passed to him. He declined with the wave of a hand.

William, determined to make the most of things, picked up two of the small fish, chewed slowly, and then swallowed the remainder. They had a smoky flavor with a mild saltiness. He was surprised that he liked them so.

"They are good, are they not?" asked Stevenson.

"Yes, Mr. Stevenson. They are quite good," agreed William.

"Disgusting," muttered Alden under his breath. He stood up and walked off for some distance.

"I cannot abide these horrible flies," he said as he batted the empty air with flailing hands and arms.

William stared hypnotically at the lake, watching the fine ripples as the traveling wind disturbed the surface. He suddenly jerked his head up, pointing directly across the water.

"There is an Indian there on the opposite side of the lake," he announced excitedly.

All turned in the direction William was looking. Sure enough, a small figure in the distance stood solidly at the water's edge just opposite the group. Shadow Bear stood up and, spying the figure, held his hand up high, fingers spread. He called out in Cherokee. The solitary figure made an identical gesture and swiftly disappeared.

Before long, a gaggle of young Cherokee trailed up alongside the lake and stood quietly in front of Shadow Bear and the strange white men. These were young boys mostly. They did not seem surprised to see Shadow Bear. And to that, there was no welcome or fanfare on his return.

Shadow Bear spoke and, as he did so, waved his arm along the three white men. He indicated William with a steady hand. He spoke at length, repeating the phrase *ganivhida ganohalidohi* (the Longhunter).

The group of young boys stared at William without hostility. They seemed curious only. One slowly approached and reached out to touch the long rifle held firmly in William's hand.

Shadow Bear stepped between the two and restrained the young Indian's hand. He shook his head firmly, barking three sharp words.

"He tells them never to touch the Longhunter's rifle, for it has no equal." Stevenson chuckled.

"Why, it is only a good rifle, Mr. Stevenson. It holds no special power, I assure you. Please tell them so," answered William anxiously.

"They are a simple people, William, steeped in magic and the mysteries of life. They believe in the spirit of all things. Even the wind that blows and rocks that lay about carry a spirit. To the Cherokee, there is life in everything. A charmed rifle would certainly fall to that category."

A line of women, young and old, began arriving. Leading them was a tall girl dressed in a snow-white deerskin blouse bleached from the sun. Covering her from the waist down was a heavy blue flannel skirt. She wore a colorful beaded sash about her waist that carried a good-sized blade in a heavy sheath. Her hair as black as a crow's wing was long and unbound. A delicate white feather was tied in her hair with a thin red leather strip. Her face was young. *She is very beautiful*, thought William.

Her silver-gray eyes, which William found to be most fetching, wandered over the scene as if searching for something. She walked deliberately up to Shadow Bear, silently nodding.

She reached out and held him by both arms in a stiff embrace. She spoke in solemn deep, throated tones, and then they gently touched foreheads.

Shadow Bear stepped back and spoke, puffing out his chest some. As he did so, he gestured to William, then Stevenson, and finally Alden. He spoke at length to the young woman, repeating his phrase "Longhunter." Then he pulled up his short tunic and displayed the wound he had received at the hands of this white man, William MacEwan.

The young maiden suddenly turned on William with obvious fire in her eyes. She stepped up close to the Longhunter and began to shout at him in her native tongue. She reached up with both arms and struck William solidly in the chest, forcing him two steps back. She followed and once again slammed William with both hands.

William stumbled awkwardly backward and looked across at Shadow Bear, seeking some understanding about what was happening. Shadow Bear remained stoic, his face impassive. William looked over at Mr. Stevenson and, to his shock, saw the old hunter smiling. Once more, the young girl hit William; but this time, he did not budge, anticipating the blow. His face flushed, but he held his feet fast to the ground.

As the girl moved, attempting another assault, Shadow Bear suddenly interrupted, moving quickly to intercept her. He spoke calmly to the young girl, who stepped backward and lowered her head.

"What is happening, Mr. Stevenson?" asked William, perplexed. "I am sure I do not understand."

"She is Black Feather's daughter, William, Shadow Bear's sister. She is scolding you for shooting her brother. Her name is Little Cornstalk, and she is quite angry with you."

William's face flushed a brilliant red; he nodded, slowly understanding. Expecting anger from Shadow Bear's father, Black Feather, he understood. This battering, however, came as a surprise. "Please explain, Mr. Stevenson, that it was purely accidental. I had no intention of harming Shadow Bear."

"She knows that, William. Explaining will not temper her anger. You shot her brother, and it could have ended badly regardless of the reason. If you had killed Shadow Bear, she would have happily taken your life."

"And to think I only feared Black Feather," said William, wagging his head in wonder. "I had not considered any other relatives."

"The girl is sixteen or seventeen seasons," said Stevenson. "That would place her about your age, William. She is often called Little Mother. She has scolded nearly everyone in the tribe, much the same as any mother would do with her children. Most of the Cherokee accept her behavior because of her father, although some of the warriors have small tolerance for the girl. I have known her from previous visits and can see that she has changed little over time."

"Gentlemen," said Alden, "can we move on to the village now? I have business to attend."

"In due time, Mr. Alden," said Stevenson. "In due time."

As they approached the village of the Cherokee, William was stunned at the size of the community. It was a very busy place indeed. Activity of every sort was on display. Hides were strung up, stretched over wood frames made of pine, while others worked on the roofs of their huts, piling heavy branches up and weaving them into the wood framing. The cabins themselves were made of woven saplings, plastered with mud, and roofed with poplar bark and heavy branches. Each was large enough to house a family of ten or more. There were a hundred such cabins scattered about the low valley along the lake edge. Woodsmoke lingered through the sunny air and seemed to encompass the entire village. Large bubbling pots stood over wood fires.

As William and the others approached the center of the village, he could see many hands at work. Corn seed was pounded and mortared on large flat stones, making a harsh scraping sound as the Cherokee women bent to their task. Several dogs barked, circling the group as they entered the village. The smell of roasted meat wafted nearby.

Several Cherokee men led a group of horses to an open field in the distance. Cattle wandered about on the outer limits of the village, silently chewing grass. Fields of early corn bordered the entire community on the north side.

In the center of all stood a large ornate cabin adorned with shields and lances. The front entrance was bordered in red paint. A tall Indian maiden ducked out of the enclosure and stood quietly by the opening. Shadow Bear approached her with outstretched arms. They embraced.

"This is Adsila, Black Feather's wife and Shadow Bear's mother," explained Stevenson. "Her name means 'blossom.'"

A remarkably tall and beautifully attired Cherokee male emerged from the lodge. He wore a heavy red and black striped blanket across his left shoulder. Black strands of thick hair hung down from the crown of his head. His forehead was plucked bald near the top of his head. Pale red paint covered his forehead down to the eyebrows. Black tattooed bands of horizontal and vertical lines adorned the center of his throat all the way down to his waist. He stood stock-still as if waiting.

He smiled broadly as Shadow Bear came up to greet him. Father and son grasped each other's arms in serpentine fashion, finishing with an embrace. Adsila chattered in Cherokee and began shooing the young ones away. Black Feather spied Mr. Stevenson and gave a hearty shout. Much to William's surprise, Black Feather spoke English. "You have returned to your Cherokee family, Stevenson. It is good to see my white friend. Come to my lodge. We can smoke and speak."

"I would be honored, Black Feather," replied Stevenson.

The great chief waved his visitors toward his lodge. They all entered. As William passed among the onlookers, some of the young boys reached out to touch his rifle. He did not pull away, allowing several to stroke the beautiful wood and silver-plated stock.

It was midday as they entered the lodge. A small fire glowed in the center of the space, smoke rising lazily through a hole in the center of the roof. Many skins along with cloth blankets and canebrake straw covered the ground. William's eyes slowly adjusted to the shadows surrounding him. He could make out all manner of ordinary household utensils much the same as his own mother's kitchen. There were pots, iron pans, knifes, and stirring spoons. Wicked little hatchets adorned one wall. The smell of damp earth and sodden straw filled his nostrils. It reminded him of home.

Shadow Bear sat next to his father with Stevenson perched on his left. William and Alden sat opposite in a cross-legged pose. Adsila passed a long pipe to Black Feather and quietly slipped outside.

Black Feather spoke briefly to Shadow Bear as he passed a long taper over the fire and with it lit the pipe. Then he said aloud, "I will hear my son."

Shadow Bear told his story, and as he did so, Black Feather nodded quietly without comment. The tall chief raised his dark eyes to William occasionally but displayed no emotion as far as William could tell. Shadow Bear continued and then suddenly stood up, lifting his shirt to display the wound he had received at the hands of the Longhunter. Passing the pipe to Stevenson, Black Feather spoke softly.

"My son has good fortune. His spirit is strong. This is something we have always known. He is young and sometimes foolish. When he wants a thing, he does not always measure the cost. He ranges far from his people and travels alone. This is not good," finished the great chief, shaking his head.

Shadow Bear bowed his head as if understanding and began to speak.

Black Feather held up a hand to interrupt his son. Addressing the three white men, he said, "I am proud of my son. He carries the strength of the Cherokee. But this must be said. His mother suffered in her heart while he was gone from us. We did not know if our enemy, the Shawnee, had captured him and burned him in their fire. We do not know if a white man with a broken mind has taken his life for no reason. The hurt of not knowing these things injures his mother and father. This wounds the Cherokee people. We weep for him when he is away."

William looked at Stevenson as if seeking permission to speak. He said, "The fault of this is mine, Black Feather. If I had not shot Shadow Bear, he would have come home sooner. I am sorry for this. My own father has passed judgment on me, and in doing so, I have come to apologize to you and Shadow Bear's mother."

Black Feather studied William closely. "It is good that you have come to me to say these things. You are a friend to the Cherokee. We will keep this friendship."

Stevenson leaned forward and passed the pipe to William, who took a quick pull, handing it off to Alden. It was not tobacco, but it was likewise not kinnikinnick either. It had an earthy musty flavor, much like softened wood. It was not unpleasant.

Black Feather once again spoke to Shadow Bear, sweeping his arm across the small fire; he then pointed to the lodge entrance. Shadow Bear quickly departed.

William began to feel odd. He was light-headed and suddenly thirsty. He turned toward Stevenson and began to smile for no reason. As Alden passed the pipe back to William, Stevenson said, "I think Mr. MacEwan would rather not smoke just now, Alden. It appears that our young friend has little experience with the Indian pipe." He turned to Black Feather and explained.

The chief smiled knowingly and, with that, said," Bring your young hunter to the lodge we have prepared by the lake, Stevenson. Rest now. You have journeyed long. We will have food together this night and rejoice in the return of my son."

Stevenson rose to leave, but Alden stayed where he sat.

"I wish to speak with the chief, Stevenson," said Alden. "I have business with his people." Black Feathered looked at Alden with a question in his eyes but said nothing.

Little Cornstalk

OUTSIDE, WILLIAM FOUND himself surrounded by a crowd of small children and curious women. The children poked and pulled at William as he was a novelty to the youngest Cherokee. They had never seen a white man with such colorful gold hair. William smiled benignly at them, oddly unperturbed.

Stevenson came out of the lodge and looked about. At a distance, he spied Adsila waving her arms. Gathering William's attention, both men walked steadily toward the lodge where she stood. As they approached, William could see that Shadow Bear and Little Cornstalk were also present.

Adsila was smiling, and so was Little Cornstalk. For the first time, William looked closely at the girl and realized she was quite tall and beautifully handsome. Her face and arms were bronzed by the sun.

Little Cornstalk was a curious mix of high cheeks, round chin, and a petite narrow nose. Long black hair with short cropped bangs framed her face.

Her smile was brilliant with straight, even teeth. It was friendly and warm. She had full black eyebrows above silver-gray eyes. The eyes glowed and seemed to sparkle to William. Her long lashes were winking rhythmically. Full lips with a rosy tinge accompanied the smile. William was taken with the girl.

She wore a single triangular earring of silver in her right ear. Hanging with it was a delicate white bird bone.

She still wore the white buckskin shirt, but this time, it was held close to her body with a wide belt that was fastened in the back with slender leather strips. Her moccasins were light gray and as tall as William's own. Beautiful beads adorned them. The blue flannel skirt was hitched up higher due to the added belt. Her waist was narrow, and her breasts swelled visibly as William approached. She smelled of leather, woodsmoke, and sweet corn.

Bowing her head and extending her left arm, she said simply, "Home." Then she smiled again.

William was so taken with this expression of hospitality that he was stricken to the core. He had an unexplained feeling of happiness. Stopping in front of the young woman, he could not keep himself from looking in her eyes. Little Cornstalk suddenly laughed out loud as if mocking William. His response was to blush bright red. He coughed.

Stevenson said, "Shadow Bear will come for us later. He wishes to hunt with you while you visit."

"Yes, of course, Mr. Stevenson," stumbled William without taking his eyes off the girl. "I look forward to it."

Adsila waved her arm toward the lodge entrance and announced, "Come, please."

Stevenson stepped inside, and William reluctantly followed.

The lodge was large. It had good light in comparison to Black Feather's. This lodge also had a fire in the center of the floor surrounded by several clean furs. Along the walls were four sleeping blankets with a thick layer of soft grass tucked beneath. A long wooden pipe lay among the hides. Stevenson dropped his pack heavily onto a far blanket bed along the wall. He turned and then sat wearily with an audible thump.

"Ah, this is a nice soft bed, William." He laid back and stretched his legs. "I will sleep well this night." Then he scowled. "I do not trust this Alden, William. First, he shows himself to be a coward in our fight with the bears and then demands a private council with Black Feather. I think he came along with us to do some mischief. I do not know what it is, but I will find out." Then he yawned deeply, stretched, and fell to sleep.

William was impatient to speak with Stevenson about Little Cornstalk, but the older hunter was already snoring in his comfort. Their conversation would have to wait.

As the day waned and night came along, Shadow Bear and Little Cornstalk entered the lodge. They looked about the shadows. Stevenson was the first to sit up and take notice. William rolled over groggily and tried to focus on the two visitors. When he realized that Little Cornstalk was present, he shot up from his nest, wagged his head with vigor, and then brushed his hair back with a flourish. He smiled.

"There is a great feast happening, and we are to attend," said Stevenson in a flat voice. He looked about and noticed that Alden had yet to join them in the lodge.

Many large fires burned throughout the village. Whistles and wood flutes played lightly along with a series of gourd rattles. Water drums were pounded with deep, hollow resonance, shaking the night air. There were many people dancing alongside the fires, shuffling and stamping their feet while bobbing to and fro. They shook their rattles and bangles and leaned backward, calling into the night sky.

William began looking for Little Cornstalk in the jumble and mass of Cherokee in constant motion. Stevenson looked about with a large grin on his face. The colorful dancers' lively chatter and thrumming music invigorated the older man, but the whereabouts of Mr. Alden began to concern him.

Shadow Bear led his friends to a ring of heavy logs, which surrounded a great blazing fire. Here, the music and drumming were loudest. Rounding the log boundary, William could see Black Feather seated on a raised platform covered in blankets and hides. Beside him sat Adsila and Little Cornstalk. Nearby, Alden could be seen displaying some of his feathers. He was smiling and nodding as one warrior reached out and grasped a colorful quill.

"Still trading, Mr. Alden?" asked Stevenson from behind the man. Alden turned quickly.

"If it is any business to you, sir, yes, I am still trading."

"And what is it you seek in return, Mr. Alden? Is it hides, pelts, gold? These people have few hides this time of year, and I know of no gold in their possession. I am quite sure you did not come for their corn crop, so what really brings you to this village, Mr. Alden?"

"As I said from the outset, Mr. Stevenson," Alden said stiffly, "I am here to trade and build a good relationship with these kind people. What else could there be?"

"What else indeed, Mr. Alden? That is what I am trying to discover." At that, Stevenson turned his back on the man and walked slowly toward Black Feather's low dais.

William was so delighted that he had found Little Cornstalk; again, he could barely contain himself. He looked at the girl and smiled broadly. She returned his smile in kind. William and Stevenson were seated on the left side of Black Feather, affording a poor view of Little Cornstalk, which frustrated William. Still, he was happy just knowing she was there.

Stevenson began a low conversation with Black Feather. The chief nodded gently in reply. Stevenson went on at length, stopped, cleared his throat, and took a cup of cool water. Black Feather looked unconcerned by what Stevenson said, but his eyes turned toward Alden. Black Feather then spoke to Stevenson softly. Stevenson frowned deeply.

The evening ended far too soon for William as he was never afforded an opportunity to speak with Little Cornstalk. He was disappointed. As he followed Stevenson back to the lodge, he asked idly, "Do you know if Little Cornstalk is married, Mr. Stevenson?"

Stevenson turned on William and replied with his own question. "What interest to you would this be, William? She is a beautiful girl as anyone can see, but she is still Cherokee. Do you fancy this girl, William?"

William blushed red and bent his head, looking down on his moccasins. "I . . . I do like her very much, Mr. Stevenson, but I am unsure what to think. What do you say, sir?" he asked eagerly.

"It is none of my affair who you fall in love with." William suddenly snapped his head up. "But I would venture to say such a union would be most difficult. I suppose you know that the girl is half white."

"What?" blurted William, almost choking on the word. "What did you say, Mr. Stevenson? She is not Cherokee?"

"I said she is half Cherokee, William. She is Shadow Bear's half sister. Her father, as I understand it, was a Spaniard.

"Years ago, Black Feather's clan lived farther east. While away hunting, a raiding party of Florida Spaniards attacked their village. Black Feather's wife, Adsila, was terribly violated by these Spanish and left for dead. When Black Feather returned, he found his wife barely alive. She was brought to the tribal shaman and, by some miracle, survived. Many months later, she gave birth to a black-haired child, a girl. Black Feather was overjoyed to have his wife back but never spoke of the child's origin. He has loved Little Cornstalk as his own and, I imagine, always will."

"How is it you know this, Mr. Stevenson?"

"Adsila herself told me. Over time, we have become good friends."

"What should I do, Mr. Stevenson? I am completely addled, sir. I cannot seem to think properly. My mind is all a twist."

"Well, I for one, William, will be laying my tired head on this sweet bed of blankets, and I will sleep until I can no longer. I advise you to do the same. In the morning, your head will clear, and things will appear better, I am sure. Good night to you."

With that, Stevenson fell face-first and began snoring almost instantly. William looked over at the older man and wagged his head in despair. He carefully checked his rifle hidden among the blankets and gently nestled it back under the grass bed covered in two heavy blankets. He removed his moccasins and coat, folding them neatly at the end of the bed. He removed his cocked hat and lay on his back, staring at the few stars that shone through the gaps in the lodge roof. He slowly faded to sleep.

It was early morning and still black as pitch when William felt a light rustle beside him. He rolled over half awake and came face-to-face with Little Cornstalk. Her white buckskin blouse was untied, exposing her left breast. She wore no skirt. William gasped audibly and jumped to his feet. The heat in his face and body was near overwhelming. He looked down on the girl. She smiled up at him.

"What is this then?" said the deep voice of Stevenson from the dark.

William looked up and stammered desperately, "It is Little Cornstalk, Mr. Stevenson. She is . . . she is lying in my bed, sir. Truly, I know nothing of this."

"She came to your bed, William. She likes you," stated Stevenson flatly, turning back to his blankets.

"Please, please tell her, Mr. Stevenson, I cannot have this. It is most improper. My god, she is half-clothed, sir."

"I understand," said Little Cornstalk. "You do not want me."

"No, miss, no, I do like you. It is just . . . you speak English?" William gasped. He trailed off helplessly. "Please, Mr. Stevenson, help me explain."

"Step outside, William. Since you have spoiled my rest, I may as well assist you. However, I have no idea what to say."

William did as he was asked and quickly left the lodge. He made no more than ten strides when he came on Black Feather himself. William stood stock-still in front of the tall chief and groaned audibly. Black Feather simply stared at the young hunter, his head tilted in mild query.

After a few moments of silence, Little Cornstalk emerged from the lodge fully dressed again. Her father looked on with surprise and then turned back to William. If ever guilt were written on a man's face, it was surely written on William's. Black Feather turned toward his daughter and simply swiveled his head in the direction of the great lodge. Little Cornstalk walked quietly away.

"I see you have taken my daughter to your lodge, Longhunter. Is this why you come to the Cherokee?"

"Oh no, sir, upon my word, I have never touched your daughter. I swear to it."

This was delivered in such earnest that Black Feather was taken aback. Stevenson emerged from the lodge then and walked up to the chief and his young friend.

"I fear you have found William in a poor situation, Black Feather. It is not of his making."

"He declares innocence, Stevenson, but my daughter leaves his lodge before the sun. How is this?"

"It is true, Black Feather. The boy is innocent. It appears Little Cornstalk came to his bed of her own mind. William slept unawares. She cares for him. She cares for him very much. She has told me so."

Upon hearing this, William's face broke out in a brilliant grin, which he displayed to both men in turn. Stevenson could not help laughing aloud. Suddenly, Black Feather joined him. William continued grinning at the laughing hunter and chief, but he did not care. He had never felt so inexplicitly happy in his entire life.

The days that followed passed swiftly for William. In the span of three weeks, he had already gone hunting six times with Shadow Bear and a league of his brother Cherokee. His thoughts of home and family were now brief, if at all. He missed his mother and father, of course, but felt differently about it somehow. In his time away from home, he had changed a bit. Would Elspeth even recognize her son? He now wore feathers in his cocked hat. His tied and braided hair was adorned with thin strips of leather, which carried a row of beads in varying colors. A broad dark leather belt crossed his chest with a large brass buckle in the center. Inside was tucked the knife that had impaled the bear claw. Next to it was a loaded French flintlock that Stevenson had given him. Across his back, he slung his short Brown Bess. His britches were held up with a good leather belt that accommodated a small hatchet, a short thin blade, and an elegant tomahawk with a colorful banded grip—all gifts of the Cherokee.

From each hunt, William brought back meat. This he shared with members of the tribe, making him welcome to the Cherokee and even popular. Wherever he wandered about the village, Little Cornstalk could be found nearby, bringing cool drinks from the lake and small touches of food. His favorite dish was roasted duck livers with a rough corn mush flavored with salt.

It wasn't long before Little Cornstalk took charge of William's kill. She distributed meat to the Cherokee women who depended on the tribe's charity. She was also wise enough to share haunches of meat and good pelts with the Cherokee tribal council including her father, Black Feather. William willingly delegated these tasks to the girl. To him, it all seemed natural.

For the first time in his life, William felt a freedom that was hard to describe. He loved his mother and father, but when measured against the life he was now living, the family homestead seemed distant and confining. He understood that this freedom that he now enjoyed was fleeting at best. His family called to him, but so too did this wonderful new freedom.

His fondness for Little Cornstalk grew each day. The girl often amused William when she scrambled her English innocently, maiming the language. He would correct her while laughing simultaneously. They would each smile on the occasion.

His rifle and belongings along with the lodge were in constant maintenance, and he was concerning himself more and more with providing meat, hides, and firewood to his Cherokee friends and neighbors.

Stevenson would often seek out his young friend, finding him seated among a group of braves, making motions with his arms and hands, demonstrating his long rifle. In the evening, William could be found sitting quietly, smoking a pipe beside a fire, Little Cornstalk ever present. The girl had taken over Stevenson's job of interpreter, and with her help, William slowly began to learn some of the Cherokee language.

Alden was also seen moving about the village. He seemed to be well liked and accepted by the Cherokee. Still, Stevenson would often follow Alden, observing the man at a discreet distance. William had noticed his attention to Alden and, one evening, asked Stevenson about it.

"You seem to take special notice of Mr. Alden's whereabouts, Mr. Stevenson. Is there something you look for, sir?"

"Black Feather has confided to me that Mr. Alden is a British representative of His Majesty's government. Mr. Alden, it appears, is attempting to enlist the Cherokee as allies in the war against the Americans. Black Feather has yet to commit in any fashion, and so Alden seeks to win the hearts of the Cherokee. I fear he may succeed."

"What could Mr. Alden offer the Cherokee but a bundle of pretty bird feathers? There is nothing to fear from this."

"He has already promised Black Feather that the lands taken by the Americans east and north of the Cumberland would be returned to the Cherokee by order of the British government. This would be a great temptation to the chief."

"I do not understand, Mr. Stevenson. Why do we fight the British? I thought we were all one and the same. What is to be gained by this? We will always live here, and they will always live there. What could possibly change by fighting one another?"

"William, I am sure your father and mother have explained why they came to America. They came to be free as did we all. They came to ensure that you as well shall live free.

"In the empire of the British, there is one man who makes the law, the king. It is the king who decides what land can be owned and who can own it. It is the king who can make war. He can enrich the lives of his subjects or destroy them. It is his choice and his alone. The king answers to no man, only God."

"Does a king truly have such power?"

"Yes, he does, William, and the colonists have come together to tell the world that they will not live as a subjugated people under one man's rule.

"Your father and Mr. Boone would rather fight for their freedom as will many men. I fear the British will not stand for such revolt, and so they have brought war to America. If Mr. Alden succeeds in gathering the Cherokee to his purpose, it would go badly for the Americans."

William frowned. He had not considered Mr. Alden a friend but had otherwise not considered the man an enemy. He frowned again. "I will speak with Black Feather myself, if I must. He will hear me."

"I think not, William. The return of Cherokee lands is far too great a promise for Black Feather to ignore."

"What can we do, Mr. Stevenson? Surely, there must be something," asked William.

"We must wait, William, wait and discover what the Cherokee will do."

"I do not care much for waiting, Mr. Stevenson. It is not in my nature."

"Nonsense, William. A good Longhunter must always wait."

The Shawnee

THAT EVENING, A great commotion rippled through the village. Many Cherokee began rushing toward the central lodges. William and Little Cornstalk hurried toward the mass of Cherokee braves, children, and women. Wild shouts and piercing cries rang through the air. Three or four musket shots were fired into the sky as if in celebration.

As they approached the village center, three braves could be seen dragging an Indian by his hair and arms along the ground. The man was badly wounded, possibly dead. Beside them walked another Indian who was variously poked, prodded, and pushed by the crowd of shouting Cherokee.

Dressed differently from the Cherokee, the walking captive wore a red cloth wrapped about his head. It was decorated with a single feather. This man wore no shirt and so was bare skinned from the waist up. A simple breechcloth covered his waist and hips. As they moved past, William could see the man holding his head high, looking neither right nor left. He bore several wounds and was bleeding steadily from them. There was no fear in the man's eyes, only resignation. He knew well he was walking to his death.

The party came to a large fire and stopped. Both Shawnee prisoners were thrown roughly on the ground, and their arms and legs were swiftly tethered to deeply driven stakes. Flat on their backs, spread-eagled, they could only look into the eyes of their enemy and the sky above.

A Cherokee brave named Dragging Canoe straddled the body of the unconscious Shawnee. He pulled out a great knife, grasped a fistful of hair, and yanked the Shawnee's face upward. With a thick gathering of hair held tightly in his fist, he swept his blade across the Indian's forehead, ripping and tearing his scalp from the bone. The knife made a sharp, scraping sound at the finish. Dragging Canoe then stood erect and, holding the bloody Shawnee's scalp up high for all to see, let out a great cry of triumph. He then reached down with his knife and plunged it to the hilt into the man's chest. A soft groaning whisper arose from the Shawnee as he died.

At first, William thought Dragging Canoe might perform the same horrible act on the second Shawnee, but he simply stepped over the tethered man and walked toward his lodge. He began to sing a Cherokee victory song as he moved away.

William and Little Cornstalk looked on as one or two older women of the tribe stepped near the second victim and quickly thrust a small blade into his exposed side. The Shawnee brave made no sound. A young child ran up and punctured his left thigh with a muddied stick. Blood flowed from the wounds. All the while, the mass of Cherokee surrounding the scene shouted encouragement with great yelps, cries, and piercing screams. Then the dogs arrived.

The first bitch to reach the dead Shawnee tore into his arm and pulled furiously, swinging its head left and right in a vicious motion as it attempted to tear off meat. Before long, every dog in the village had arrived. Shouts of jubilation and the growling of several dogs tearing at human flesh could be heard. *It is an insane frenzy of animals and people straight from the gates of hell*, thought William.

As he looked on the sight, he turned to Little Cornstalk and said, "I am leaving. I will not witness this."

The girl looked at William with a curious expression. "The Shawnee are the enemy of my people, William. They must die."

"If they must die, then shoot them and let them be," said William with sudden venom in his tone. "This is the hand of the devil." At that, the Longhunter strode away.

The first shouts of alarm were heard before sunrise. The sound of many feet rushing outside his lodge woke William abruptly. Horses could be heard whinnying in the distance. William and Stevenson stepped outside, gathering their weapons as they did so. Shadow Bear came quickly up beside his two friends and spoke. William was able to catch only a few words but still understood that a large party of Shawnee was outside the village, preparing to attack.

Knowing the Shawnee would come, Black Feather had called a tribal council last night after the capture and death of the two Shawnee scouts. He knew well that the arrival of these scouts meant that greater numbers of Shawnee were surely nearby. He sent messengers to all the surrounding Cherokee villages. The Shawnee were coming and would soon attack. As they followed Shadow Bear to the western edge of the village, Stevenson explained, "The Shawnee and Cherokee were once friendly, William. Then the war with the French came. The Shawnee fought with the French and the Cherokee with the British. The Cherokee and British forces drove the Shawnee northwest as far as the Ohio Country. They have remained bitter enemies ever since. I hear the Shawnee fight with the British now. Perhaps this will convince Black Feather not to side with the English."

Scattered along the north side of the lake and surrounding wood, many Cherokee braves prepared a defense. Arrow quivers, lances, tomahawks, muskets, and knifes were swiftly passed among the defenders in an efficient manner. A single wide trail led to the village from the west, and the Cherokee intended to ambush the oncoming Shawnee as they passed through.

"What shall we do, Mr. Stevenson?" asked William.

"I will follow Shadow Bear," answered Stevenson calmly. "I think it best you return to the village center and ensure that all is ready for the coming fight. Keep an eye, William, as it may take a long shot to slow these devils down."

"Yes, I will do so."

William rushed back to the village and scanned a scene of hectic activity. His eyes searched for Little Cornstalk, but she was not to be seen anywhere among the others. Adsila was directing several women of the tribe. They were laying defenses. Using long poles as levers, they rolled large pine trunks in a single line, nearly crossing the entire village from east to west. This took many hands. To this was added a healthy quantity of brush kindling and pine saplings. The resulting construct bisected the village from lake to cornfield. Several women held brush torches at the ready.

William began shouting out Little Cornstalk's name, desperately seeking any sign of the girl. He finally spied her at the edge of the cornfield. As she ran along, she fired the corn with a long torch. This would delay the Shawnee from making a northern approach into the village. Once burned, the open field would then afford a clear view of the invaders.

Smoke began to envelope Little Cornstalk as she fired the remaining field. William ran toward the girl with the energy of desperation. At the field edge, a hundred or more yards off, two Shawnee could be seen running toward Little Cornstalk from the opposite direction. William took a knee and fired his long rifle at the oncoming pair, hitting the Indian on the right. Up and running again, William headed in the direction of the fire line, looking for Little Cornstalk through the dense white smoke.

The girl suddenly emerged through a wave of crackling fire. She was running for her life. Fifty paces behind and chasing at full stride was the second Shawnee. William swung his Brown Bess around and fired, striking the Indian in the throat. The running brave staggered forward ten paces and collapsed in a heap. Little Cornstalk rushed past William and continued onward toward the village.

Over her shoulder, she cried, "Run, William, run!"

William snatched up his long rifle and followed the girl. The two crossed the remaining distance in short order and made their way to Adsila's side. Adsila had not given the order to light the defense line yet, and so all was held at the ready. William scanned the southern side of the lake and, to his horror, spied a large band of Shawnee attempting to cross. If this maneuver succeeded, William knew that the village would be caught between attacking Shawnee from both the west and southeast. The defensive firebreak Adsila had prepared would be useless.

Musket fire, the terrible sound of clashing weapons, horses, and the cries of battle could be heard from a distance at the western edge of the village. William briefly pondered the fate of his friends as the fight continued unabated.

Directing his attention to Little Cornstalk, William shouted, "Stay here!" He bounded over the line of heavy logs. He headed directly to the lake edge.

On the opposite shore, a line of Shawnee began probing the bottom, searching for a crossing. William knew that, farther east, a shallow sandbar afforded just such a crossing. The distance across the lake was more than three hundred yards, too far for an accurate shot. William would have to wait until the enemy was within range, but what then? He only had the three weapons on hand, and he knew, with the Shawnee in such numbers, he would soon be overwhelmed.

As he turned to assess the fight to his rear, William nearly bumped into Little Cornstalk.

"What are you doing here?" he shouted. "I told you to wait back with the others."

"I fight with you, William," said the girl simply. She smiled and nodded in affirmation.

"You must go back now!" cried William. "It is not safe here. A band of Shawnee are attempting to cross the lake at the shallows. They will soon be behind us, trapping everyone in the village."

Little Cornstalk looked up sharply and peered across the water. Sitting astride a large gray and white pony was a Shawnee warrior wearing a chest plate of Spanish silver. Around his biceps were thick silver bracelets. His hair was bound in the familiar red cloth of the Shawnee, the tails of which hung down below his shoulders. He wore a dark overcoat with a white blouse beneath. Two red bands of red cloth crossed his breast. His upper legs were bare. He wore tall moccasins. He used no saddle, only the animal's bare back beneath him.

He appeared confident and commanding in his motions, directing the probing Shawnee in the water as they ventured farther east toward the shallows. His bearing was regal as William watched with fascination.

"Tenskwatawa," whispered Little Cornstalk.

"You must shoot him, William," said the girl urgently. "Shoot him now."

"It is too great a distance, Little Cornstalk. I cannot hit him from here. I must wait."

"I will tell Father."

"Go then. I will watch and follow them down the lakeshore."

Little Cornstalk quickly disappeared.

William felt deep relief when the girl departed. He was near certain he would die this day and prayed that Little Cornstalk would somehow survive.

The Shawnee moved methodically along the lake bank, reaching out, with their feet searching for solid footing. Lances pierced the deep water, gauging the depth as they went along. William realized it would not be long now before they discovered the place to cross. He checked his rifle, Brown Bess, and flintlock. He reached down and felt the soft leather pouch that held the balls he would fire. He counted them deftly through the pouch and estimated he could fire twelve, possibly fourteen, shots before he ran out. He crouched low so as not to be seen by the advancing Shawnee. He heard a rustling sound from behind. Whirling about, anticipating Little Cornstalk's return, he was surprised to find Alden not ten feet away, crawling toward him on all fours.

"What are you doing?" asked the Englishman sharply.

"I am following the Shawnee on the opposite side of the lake. They seek the shallows. When they find it, they will cross the lake and join the fight, trapping us all."

Alden stuck his head up and, through the brush, looked across the lake. He immediately summed the situation. His face was stricken white with fear. His eyes were bulging out so that William thought they might burst from his head. A rivulet of spittle ran down the man's chin. He was terrified.

"We must flee, MacEwan. Can you swim?"

"What do you say, sir?" asked William, shocked at the notion.

"We must run. This is not our fight. Let the heathens murder one another. What matter is it to us? If you can swim, we can cross the lake farther west in silence and then head south and thus avoid the Shawnee."

"I thought the Cherokee people were to be your ally, Mr. Alden? Do you hold your own life so dear that you would abandon them? Shadow Bear was right, sir, you are a coward."

"Have you lost your reason, William? These savages will roast you over a fire. They have no notion of mercy. They will kill us all."

"Believe this if you will, Mr. Alden. I would rather die on my feet or even roast in a fire before I drowned as a coward in the bottom of a cold lake. I cannot swim a bit, sir, so as you can see, I am here to stay. If you wish to turn and run, then do so. You are no help to me."

William turned his back on the man and continued his vigilance. Alden stuttered some unintelligible sound and began scrambling crablike toward the water's edge. He was soon gone.

By this time, William had positioned himself directly across from the searching Shawnee. The distance across the water from north shore to south had narrowed considerably, but the range for a shot was still too far. Once again, the sound of someone approaching caught William's attention. This time, he was happy to find his friend Stevenson advancing on hands and knees. A long arrow shaft jutted from his left hip, and a bloody patch radiated outward and down along his britches. His face was pale but incredibly held a smile.

"You are wounded, Mr. Stevenson," said William, alarmed. "Are you all right?"

"I believe I will be, William, but I will have to attend to it later. What mischief occurs here?"

William explained as Stevenson observed the state of things across the lake.

"Well, this explains the reason for the Shawnee retreating west of us. We had hoped they had lost their will to continue the fight. I see now that they are holding back to attack from the east and west as one, trapping us between the lake and the fired cornfield. That Indian on the south shore riding the gray is the great Shawnee chief, Tenskwatawa. He planned this attack well, and it is rare to find him in defeat."

"Little Cornstalk tells me I must shoot the man if we are to survive. What say you, Mr. Stevenson?"

"I would doubt that, William. There are at least two hundred Shawnee around us. Many are led by other tribal leaders. They will follow the plan Tenskwatawa has set. They would be foolish to do otherwise."

William nodded as if in agreement, but in truth, he was not sure what he should do. He searched the south lakeshore and noticed that a small number of Shawnee had begun to swim across farther east. At first, there were only a few, but then several could be seen hauling large tree trunks from the wood and throwing them off the bank into the water. They leaped out and grabbed hold of the floating logs, kicking their feet furiously and thus crossing the water safely to the Cherokee side. They began to fan out, heading north and west to encircle the village.

By this time, the Shawnee chieftain had discovered the sandbar crossing the lake. William watched as they began their advance to the other side. Three Shawnee led the way across, followed by a single Indian holding the reins of the gray pony as he carefully guided Tenskwatawa into the water.

"Are you loaded and dry, William?" asked Stevenson in a rush.

William nodded again. He seemed unable to articulate his thoughts; there were simply too many. The distance for a shot was fast closing, just over two hundred fifty yards. William gauged the wind and distance. He rubbed dirt on his rifle barrel tip to cut the glare off the water. Stevenson crawled up to his side.

"Take this rifle as well, William. You must strike the lead Shawnee when they are within range."

William took careful aim at the first Shawnee crossing, but he did not pull the trigger. His mind swept back to Little Cornstalk. *You must shoot Tenskwatawa, William.*

The Longhunter pulled his rifle right and fired. The shot struck the Shawnee holding Tenskwatawa's horse squarely in the center of his chest. Still holding the reins, he fell back, jerking the horse's head violently downward. The horse stuttered backward and, with the soft sand beneath its hoofs, swayed unsteadily.

William then took hold of Stevenson's rifle and fired a second shot, which was followed by the sound of a loud, clanking bang as if two large pots had been struck together. Tenskwatawa rocked backward and rolled off the gray, making a hearty splash in the cold lake.

A great cry echoed over the water as several Shawnee rushed in to help their fallen chief. Every Shawnee within sight suddenly stopped moving. All turned in the direction of the great Tenskwatawa as he floundered in the shallows.

"By god, William, you have stopped them cold. What in heaven's name possessed you to shoot Tenskwatawa and his horse lead?"

"It appeared to be the right choice, Mr. Stevenson. The horse would rattle and perhaps lose its rider. If so, then I could claim two with a single shot, thereby saving a ball, but Tenskwatawa held his mount. And so you see, I had to shoot him as well. Little Cornstalk was most clear on the matter."

As if responding to her name, Little Cornstalk spoke. "They are coming, William."

William turned suddenly and stared in shock. There before him was Little Cornstalk, kneeling and quietly loading his rifle.

"You must go back, Little Cornstalk. Go back now!"

The girl answered simply and calmly, "I fight with you, William. They are coming. We must fight."

William turned to see three Shawnee racing toward his position; he snapped his head back, only to see Little Cornstalk beginning to load Stevenson's weapon. Facing the oncoming Shawnee, William pulled his flintlock with his left hand, checked his powder, and then took hold of his tomahawk with the right. As the leading Shawnee rushed up, William leaped from the brush, swinging the tomahawk in a high arc. The Shawnee attempted to dodge the blow but to no avail. William raked the wicked blade across the left side of the man's head, catching his jaw, ripping open his mouth, leaving a huge gaping wound. The Indian fell at his feet.

The second Shawnee came on as Stevenson's flintlock reached out from the brush and fired, striking the man midchest. The first Shawnee began to rise onto his hands and knees. William ignored him as he carefully aimed his flintlock at the third oncoming Shawnee. Little Cornstalk scrambled up to the wounded Shawnee at William's feet and drove her large blade deep into the man's back. He collapsed dead.

The third Shawnee rushing up on the three defenders threw a small hatchet, narrowly missing the Longhunter. William fired at very close range. The Shawnee warrior tumbled past William, tripped over his dead companion, and crumpled to the earth.

"We should head back to the village center," said Stevenson. "At least we will have a better defense than this brush and thin canebrake."

Little Cornstalk said, "Wait, can you hear?" She stood up fully next to William, pointing northeast past the Shawnee who were heading for them.

"My brothers are coming," she said simply.

A great cry rang through the valley as a horde of Cherokee burst through the distant northern tree line. Scores of Cherokee warriors came out of the wood, screaming and running toward the Shawnee on the north side of the lake. So many Cherokee were coming that William could not count them. The Shawnee, knowing they were very much outnumbered, ran to the lake edge, attempting to escape the onslaught. Those who could jumped straight in and swam for their lives. Others grabbed what floating wood was available and began to paddle back across. They were soon cut down with a rain of arrows and musket balls. The brisk rate of fire struck most of the slow-moving targets in the water.

"By god, William, it is White Owl and his people," said Stevenson with a rush of relief in his voice. "We may live yet."

Those Shawnee who chose to face the oncoming wave of Cherokee were soon slaughtered to a man. William stood in awe of the bloody scene. Scalps were torn from skulls, brains crushed in with heavy blows from hatchet, club, and tomahawk. The Shawnee were literally hacked to pieces.

"Come, William, we must tell Father," said Little Cornstalk.

A Cherokee warrior came running up toward Little Cornstalk and the two white men beside her. Little Cornstalk spoke rapidly to the warrior as she pointed to William and Stevenson. The brave stared hard at both men and then looked down on the fallen Shawnee warrior at William's feet. He let out a great cry and began to hack at the dead man with heavy blows from his hatchet.

William turned to Little Cornstalk. "Go to your father now. He will want to know of this. I will help Mr. Stevenson back as he is badly injured."

Little Cornstalk ran up ahead as William and Stevenson limped back toward the village. It was slow progress as William struggled to support his friend while carrying their weapons. It was a painful trip for Stevenson to be sure. Nevertheless, the old hunter kept up a cheerful monologue that William barely heard for the ringing in his head.

A keening wail echoed through the air as William and Stevenson made their way to the great lodge. A large group of Cherokee could be seen surrounding an open space in front of Black Feather, who stood a head above the others, perched on his dais. He looked down on his people.

Many of the Cherokee women were weeping, rocking, and raising their arms to the sky. Ten prone bodies lay at the foot of Black Feather. A group of squaws broke away from the others and took hold of Stevenson, whisking him inside the lodge.

As William approached the ring of Cherokee, he realized that the loudest cries came from Little Cornstalk. She knelt closely beside one body, bobbing her head in silence and looking into the heavens. As William stepped up to the girl, he realized the dead Cherokee beside her was her brother, Shadow Bear.

At first, William could not comprehend the moment. He began to shake as he feebly inched his way closer to his dead friend. He knelt alongside Little Cornstalk and gently raised Shadow Bear's hand in his own. He looked down on the battered face.

Holding Shadow Bear's slender fingers, William recalled how they had once woven a small reed basket to catch minnows and pollywogs. He was beyond heartbroken.

The Cherokee mourners began to look on William with a mix of curiosity and wonder. Little Cornstalk stopped her chants as she, too, stared at William. She suddenly grasped William's hand, crushing all three into a tangled knot. William looked at the girl and ran a sleeve under his nose, wiping away his tears. They sat quietly for several moments.

William released the hand of his dead friend and stood up. He looked at Shadow Bear for the last time.

Three musket wounds that had taken Shadow Bear's life were clearly visible. William turned and shouldered his way through the silent Cherokee. He walked to the great lodge in a sort of daze, not knowing where he was going or why. He wished he could speak with his father now. This was not possible. He felt as empty as a Sunday whiskey jug. This only increased his misery. He would speak with Stevenson. Just now he needed the calm certainty and wisdom of the older hunter.

As he stepped inside Black Feather's lodge, William could make out the form of Olaf Stevenson. The hunter lay on his right side, leaning up on his elbow. The offending arrow had been removed. The arrowhead was cut from the flesh of his leg and replaced with a large patch of poultice over the wound. As Stevenson sat up slowly, William observed a bottle of whiskey held firmly to the older man's chest. It had been well attended.

"What has happened, William?" asked Stevenson quietly. "You are as white as a linen shirt."

William began to speak but choked on the words. He shook his head violently.

"Shadow Bear has been killed, Mr. Stevenson. He lies not thirty yards from here. I don't know what to do, sir. I am confused and so very tired. Why did my friend die?"

"The answer to your question is the price we pay for living," said Stevenson, shaking his head and taking a long swallow of whiskey. "Adsila herself lies just there." He waved his arm toward the opposite end of the lodge. "She is badly wounded, having taken a fire arrow. Her burns are terrible. I do not think she will survive, but I pray she will."

William simply shook his head and stared down at the earth beneath his feet. He had come to the Cherokee to return Shadow Bear to his people in safety and good faith. Now his friend was dead and possibly Shadow Bear's mother as well. It came to him that he was somehow responsible for all this. Guilt began to whittle away at his thoughts.

"Take this," said Stevenson, offering the bottle to William. "Go and sleep, William. Empty that bottle and thank god you survived the day. Take your weary bones to bed and sleep a peaceful sleep."

The tribe began to prepare the dead for burial. This period could last seven days as the family deprived itself of food and drink in sufferance. It was Black Feather's wish that Shadow Bear be buried the old way, and so large stones were collected for his son's burial tomb. It was understood that no conflict among tribe members be demonstrated during this period of mourning, and words exchanged were spoken in gentle, peaceful tones without anger or heat.

The pursuing Cherokee could be heard firing on the last of the Shawnee as they fled west. The sounds of musket fire and wild shouts soon died away, and the late afternoon gave itself up to cool air and quiet.

William sat outside his lodge, staring into a small fire. Holding on to the whiskey bottle with one hand and his rifle with the other, he leaned back and took a sharp swallow. The harsh liquor burned as it slid down his throat, lighting an equally small fire in his belly. Bands of three and four Cherokee braves wandered past, speaking in hushed tones. Some greeted William, "Longhunter." Others simply stared at the young white man, who had shed tears over a Cherokee warrior.

As the day waned, William longed more and more for that peace Mr. Stevenson spoke of, the peace that only sleep can bring. He was so tired. He took another sip and began to rock back and forth slightly.

Little Cornstalk attended her mother, who was barely clinging to life. Adsila suffered silently until she was told of her son's death. In a halting shout, she cried and began singing Shadow Bears' death song in whispered breaths.

The village was strangely silent as the sun set. There were few fires about the lodges this night as the tribe mourned their dead and wounded.

William's small fire died to glowing embers, yet he still sat motionless, staring at the wisp of smoke. The bottle, near empty now, was cast aside, and William wobbled slowly into his lodge. He dropped his rifle and shrugged the Brown Bess from his shoulder. Unbuckling his belt and chest strap, he dropped all onto the ground without care. He pulled off his shirt and fell solidly onto the blankets, bumping his head in the process. He instantly fell to sleep.

In the darkness of middle night, William opened his eyes. He had a fierce headache and dry mouth, and his stomach was jumping like a butter churn. As he rolled over on his left, he stared directly into the face of Little Cornstalk. She lay quietly beside him, wearing a small smile. William looked at the girl and realized she was completely naked. She reached out for William. He took her in his arms and kissed her mouth. The close and tender sensation was overwhelming and thrilling at the same time.

Little Cornstalk had never been kissed before as this was not done in Cherokee culture. And William had never kissed a girl. As they lingered in this pose, they drew closer together in their embrace.

Leaning back, William slowly ran his hand down along her body from breast to hip and along her thigh and then back again, feeling the dimple of her lower back and up along her spine. His passion rose, everything else forgotten. They clung to each other desperately.

They made love quietly with a slow, gentle motion, seeming to engulf each other in the process. William had never felt such bliss. It was a discovery that filled his heart with the greatest measure of love he had ever known. Through the night, they made love three more times. William felt he had found the notion of heaven on earth or as near to it a man could get. He felt true love for someone.

When William woke in the morning, he was alone. He studied the blankets that he and Little Cornstalk had lain on and smiled to himself. He quickly dressed and stepped outside. The village was fully awake by this time. Cornmeal was being ground, and meat roasted over small flames. He looked about for Little Cornstalk, but she was nowhere in sight. He was hungry. He pulled a strip of dry, salted meat from his pack and marched up toward Black Feather's lodge.

Stevenson was sitting up now and looking better for it. He eyed William curiously as the young man ambled over to Stevenson's side. At the end of the lodge, William spied Little Cornstalk kneeling beside her mother, Adsila. He smiled at the girl. She displayed no notice of William.

"You appear to be in better spirits this morning, William. I take it you drank the last of my whiskey?"

Not really listening to his friend, William turned his gaze from the girl and simply asked, "What did you say, Mr. Stevenson?"

"Never mind, William. It is of little matter. There are more important concerns just now. Did you see Mr. Alden during the fight? I have asked after him, but no one seems to know his whereabouts."

"Oh, yes," said William. "I saw Mr. Alden just before you came along by the lake. He asked that I join him in swimming away across the water to escape the fight. He was frightened for his life, I believe. He did not care a fiddle for the Cherokee or the village, only himself. He ran away, sir."

"Ran away, you say?" said Stevenson.

"He jumped into the lake and swam for his life. If he made it to the south side as intended, he could very well have run directly into the fleeing Shawnee on that side. If so, I would think he is quite dead."

"If only that were certain, I would feel the better for it, William. Two nights ago, I took these papers from among Alden's possessions. They were hidden inside his feather pouch. I assume he realized they had been taken and, in his desire to save his skin, had not the time to discover where they might be. It is a copy of the treaty between the Cherokee and the British. It also carries plans for the British invasion of the southern colonies. Come and see, William."

William sat beside the older hunter as the two men read the documents carefully.

"What does this mean, Mr. Stevenson?" asked William.

"You must bring these papers to your father, William, as quickly as you can. The Continental Congress must know of this. It is vital that they do."

William's thoughts immediately flew to Little Cornstalk. He turned his back on Stevenson and looked to where she sat quietly beside her dying mother.

"What troubles you, William?"

He did not turn to answer but merely said in a hushed tone, "Little Cornstalk."

"You can always return, William. I am sure your family would understand, and the Cherokee would welcome you as a friend always. They speak of nothing but the longhunter and how you wept for their brother Shadow Bear. Your fight with the Shawnee displayed magnificent courage, William. You have the affection of the whole tribe."

William continued to stare at the girl he now fully loved and shrugged, unsure of his reply.

"The world is turning too quickly for me, Mr. Stevenson. I have love in my heart and now great fear."

"Love is a blessing, William, as well as a burden. We live as best we can with what we have. What remains are those things we must do. Loving someone is a responsibility I could never face myself. You are a braver man than I am, William.

"Don't concern yourself about Little Cornstalk. She is stronger than you know. She loves you, and she will understand if you must leave. I promise, no harm will come to the girl. I will not allow it." He smiled broadly at William, whose face was now drawn with uncertainty. "You must leave soon, William."

Manhattan Island

LORD JEREMY SKELTON leaned back heavily in the hardwood chair. The red-dyed leather was cushioning him comfortably as he stared up at the heavy crossbeams overhead. The desk behind which he sat was hewn from American oak; its sturdy legs and solid piece top displayed intricate design and artistry. Skelton had to admit the beauty of the American woodwork was nearly comparable to his own sixteenth-century English desk.

Only a few years ago, Lord Jeremy's uncle Lord George Germain, first viscount Sackville, had been court-martialed and summarily dismissed from the British army. Recently, the viscount regained his reputation with the king. This fortunate turn of events had placed Skelton in his current position, liaison to the home secretary and the king's personal representative in the American colonies.

That ridiculous Dartmouth had left the secretary's office in chaos. British regiments in America were doing better now, but there were still needed supplies in some areas. It had taken Skelton nearly a year to correct his predecessor's fumbling mistakes, but now things were running smoothly.

Skelton's constant argument with line officers was wearing on him. Many of those same officers had little to no experience in war. His uncle Lord Germain would correct this. For too long, the army had taken a modest position in America. After General Howe was forced to vacate Boston and sail his troops to Halifax, the feeling in London was one of despair. Still, the rebels were forced from New York; and once again, Howe was considered the man for the job. *Clinton and Burgoyne are good generals*, thought Skelton. Nevertheless, he knew with certainty that Charles Cornwallis would bring the real fight to the Americans. Then they would know the might of the British Empire.

Lord Skelton was a tall man, just over six feet. He was overweight but in general enjoyed good health. He wore his usual white wig tightly powdered the way he insisted. Too much loose powder was most vexing. Tied neatly in the back with a dark blue ribbon, the wig displayed unmistakable British aristocracy.

He wore no uniform but nevertheless chose a coat of brilliant red with a short stiff collar. His white blouse and ruffled sleeves were arranged in military fashion, and he often wore a blue striped sash across his chest, much the same as an English general officer.

His britches were soft velvet dyed light tan. Bone-white stockings finished his dress, covering his lower legs down to the black leather shoes that carried high polished brass buckles.

He slowly lowered his eyes to the desktop and realized with some annoyance that a silver tray had been set before him. He had not heard the orderly enter. Sitting beside the tray lay a stack of messages and letters neatly arranged in order of importance and tied with a banded ribbon. A sharp knock brought his attention round.

"Come," called Skelton.

The door opened, and Colonel Sims entered. He carefully closed the door behind him and stepped smartly to the secretary's desk. He gave a quick salute. "Sir."

"It is unnecessary to salute, Colonel. I am not commissioned, nor have I ever been." Skelton snarled.

Colonel Sims disliked this pompous civilian. Skelton had insisted that all senior officers report to him, each on a given day and time of the week. *Ridiculous*, thought Sims. The man held no service in the army, and his bloody uncle had been drummed out in disgrace. He had no right demanding such from his officers. Sims and every man in this command thought Skelton an ass. Still, he was the representative to the secretary of the Americas and held sway over every order received from London. Much of the army's supplies, weapons, even command orders came through this man. Sims would have to dance the tune he called for now.

"I was just about to go through today's correspondence, Colonel Sims. Please take a chair, sir. I will call for more tea."

"That is most gracious of you, Your Lordship, but I am afraid I must decline your kind offer. I have a great many things to attend to. Another time perhaps?"

"Ah yes, of course, Colonel, your trip to Philadelphia. Nevertheless, please take a seat. I do have a question. Have you had any success with this gun-smuggling problem?"

"Yes, sir, we have. We have discovered the names of several men involved as well as their source of supply. Our Indian allies have provided us with valuable information."

"Very good, Colonel. Mr. Washington's disorderly retreat will most likely depend on a new supply of men and weapons. The cowards dropped theirs in the field when they ran."

Skelton leaned forward, sipping tea. "And now, Colonel, what is the latest news of my cousin Captain Alden?"

"We have had no contact with the captain, sir. It has been nearly three months. He should have returned weeks ago with the Indian alliance in hand, but we have not heard from him yet."

"He is a very resourceful fellow, my cousin," pondered Skelton aloud. "I expect he will return shortly. We will wait a little longer, I think. We have already secured treaties with most of the savages. If you receive any information concerning Captain Alden, I am to be informed immediately. Is that understood?"

"Of course, sir, the instant I hear."

"Thank you, Colonel. You are dismissed. Please attend to your critical duties as you must."

Sims stood up and, forgetting, gave Skelton a quick salute. Tucking his white-trimmed tricorne under his arm, he turned sharply and left the room.

If Sims did hear anything about that lapdog cousin of Skelton's, he would send his lieutenant to deliver what message there may be. Sims could barely tolerate Skelton's presence. Captain Alden could go to the devil for all he cared.

Home

WILLIAM LOOKED IN on Little Cornstalk through the open lodge entry as she knelt beside her mother. His heart was beating in his chest with so mighty a thump that he felt it could be heard by others. He knew he would have to leave Little Cornstalk for at least a month, possibly longer.

Little Cornstalk attended her mother, bringing cool water, bandages, and small food. Still, William could see, as anyone could, that Adsila was dying. Black Feather came to his wife daily but did not stay long, his face a solemn mask.

As the day passed, William began to pack his things for the journey home. He did this out of sight, feeling guilt about his coming departure and still having no words to explain why he must leave. He considered asking Stevenson to have one of the braves from the village carry the papers to Ian MacEwan, but he knew that would not be right.

He did wish to see his mother and father again. He felt certain that both his parents would understand his feelings, but would Little Cornstalk be welcome in the MacEwan family? He had no idea. Love was expressed every day in his home. Would it be the same with Little Cornstalk?

William gathered his pack into a neat arrangement. He stepped outside the lodge every few minutes, hoping to see Little Cornstalk, but as the sun faded, so did William's hopes of seeing her this night.

He would have to explain. That is what a man will do. He realized now he had no choice but to tell her he was leaving. If he truly loved Little Cornstalk and she loved him in return, then it became a matter of necessity. He gathered his courage and stepped outside.

Little Cornstalk stood quietly in front of the small fire. She held a bundle of firewood in her arms. She smiled at William and casually placed the wood beside the fire. William was happily startled by the appearance of the girl. She always seemed to know when he needed her most. He smiled.

"Do you have all you need for your journey, William?" she asked quietly.

Her English had improved over their last several weeks together. He was not surprised at the question and suspected the girl knew of his mission from the very start. Even so, he felt a wave of relief, grateful she understood. It was this calm, knowing attitude that so endeared her to him.

"I think I have everything," he answered carefully. "I must travel quickly, and so I travel light. Mr. Stevenson has given me a promise to look after you while I am away. Please allow him to do so."

She looked oddly at William, tilting her head with a questioning look. "William looks after me, and I look after William. Stevenson will drink his whiskey and eat too much."

He laughed suddenly and pulled her into a hard embrace. Kissing her mouth, he whispered, "I will miss you so."

They spent their last night together, not leaving the lodge once. William would be on his way at the break of light.

He traveled fast. Keeping just off the main trail into the trees, William paced himself carefully. He stopped only to relieve himself or take a drink from his canteen. Without pausing, he chewed and swallowed the rich brown juice from the dried, jerked meat that Little Cornstalk insisted he carry. Making little sound as he traveled along, he noticed the leavings of the invading Shawnee along the trail.

At night, moonlight illuminated his way, allowing him to make good progress through the dense trees and brush. As he neared the site of the bear fight, he was drawn down into the hammock and stopped. He examined the scene closely. Little was left of the awesome battle with the bears, just stripped bones and small tufts of black fur. William could see that a good many moccasins had trampled the surrounding area. The tracks were days old, but there were many. With an uncomfortable knot growing in his belly, William began to pick up his pace. He began to run.

MacEwan Station

ELSPETH NEEDED NO words from her husband as Ian burst through the door of the cabin. The look on his face was enough. Elspeth quickly scanned the room for her children.

"Out back now!" shouted Ian.

The young German couple who had arrived only the evening prior were just packing up some of their belongings when Ian crashed into the room. The tall blond-haired woman was holding an infant no more than three months. She became instantly frightened with Ian's behavior. The young man looked at Ian and simply said, "Was ist es?"

"Indians," replied Ian as he took hold of his long rifle. Sweeping up his powder horn and shot, he raced to the doorway and latched it shut. He ignored Elspeth, knowing she would do what was necessary and planned.

With the children in tow, Elspeth pulled out the wooden hatch at the rear of the cabin and began pushing David and Aelwyd through the opening. She hoisted the twin boys up and out the portal and wiggled her way outside, turning to help Mary.

Looking through the escape hole, Mary declared, "I'm not leaving, Mother. I am staying with Father."

Elspeth stared at her eldest daughter open mouthed. "You will not! You get out here right now, Mary MacEwan, right now!"

"No, Mother. Father must have someone who can shoot, and I doubt that German boy knows one end of a rifle from the other. Father will need someone to load for him as well. I am staying, Mother."

For the first time in memory, Elspeth was truly frightened. She must get the young ones to the safety of the shelter, but to do so, could she leave her eldest daughter behind?

"Please go, Mother," pleaded Mary. "I can help Father, and if there is any chance, we will have it together."

Elspeth pulled her flintlock pistol from her apron and tried to pass it into to her daughter.

"No, Mother, you will need that for yourself. I have my own, remember?"

Elspeth turned and saw David and Aelwyd making their way up the steep hill, dragging the twins behind them. She turned once more to face Mary.

"I must close this now, Mother. May God be with you. I love you, Mother."

With that, Mary picked up the wooden patch and nudged it back, closing the opening. Elspeth could hear the heavy wedges being pounded in place from inside. She turned and raced up the hill after her children.

The hide itself was unique even by settler standards. It consisted of a great mound of animal scat and manure piled high across the hillside. Near the center of the pile was buried a stiff panel of wood covering a dugout that Ian had made almost from the day they arrived here. The panel was well hidden. Elspeth grabbed a bush branch and began sweeping the trail behind her to cover her tracks and those of her children as she made her way to the hide.

Dropping the branch, she reached down through the black manure to secure the panel edge. It was very heavy. She strained her back pulling the panel upward, with David assisting as best he could. Leaning her hip into the sharp edge of the wood, she had all four children scramble down into the hole. Elspeth sat heavily, holding the panel against her back. As she rolled left, she simply slid down into the dark muddy hole. The panel came down with a loud clap. Manure, mud, and dirt shifted and rained down through the slender gaps, slowly extinguishing the slivers of daylight that seeped through the wood and muck.

The sounds of musket fire mixed with Indian war screams penetrated the heavy layer of manure. Elspeth understood. This was no small-band Indian raid. This was different. As her sight adjusted to near-total blackness, she could just make out the face of her daughter Aelwyd. The girl was silent, staring upward as if seeing the terrible sounds emanating from beyond the heavy layer of manure and dirt. David was looking at his mother. He seemed calm, but the concern on his face was all too real. The twins clung to each other as they listened to the terrible sounds as well. Not one child cried out.

The frantic screams of a woman could be heard just then, and Elspeth knew instinctively that the voice was not that of her daughter Mary. She realized it must be the young German girl with her baby. Elspeth also knew that the tall girl and most likely her babe were being taken or killed.

A loud explosion shook the air above them, knocking down more loose manure, vibrating the air as it echoed up the hillside. Elspeth had never heard cannon fire before, but she knew that this was no musket. *Since when do Indians carry cannon?* she asked herself. *This is no Indian raid*. She knew then that both her husband and daughter would be killed by these people, whoever they were. Tears rolled down her face as she sat back in the wet muck, soiling her dress. She pulled her children close and quietly wept.

It seemed like hours before the sharp cries and musket fire from outside died away. When all seemed calm, the crackling sound of burning timber could be heard. They had fired the cabin and possibly the barn as well. The smell of woodsmoke seeped into the hide, confirming Elspeth's suspicion. More Indian cries followed, but they soon fell away to silence. Sharp calls from several directions approached the hide, but no one stopped to inspect the rotting pile of manure. Elspeth could hear the tramping feet of men as they passed. The sun was falling. It would soon be night. The pop and crackling of burning timber continued.

When Elspeth woke, the sun had yet to rise. It was pitch-black in the small hole, and she could see nothing as she crawled about the space on hands and knees. She gently felt the warm bodies of her children. All were sleeping. She sat back and took note of her pistol firmly settled in her apron pocket. As soon as she felt it was safe to do so, she would push her way outside. She waited in silence.

Light began to seep through the darkness. The heavy smell of burned wood lingered in the tight space. She waited patiently, concentrating on every bit of sound.

The crack of a musket broke the silence, and Elspeth stiffened at the closeness of the shot. She began to hear voices just outside the hide and slowly reached down for her pistol. As the voices came near, she was certain these were the words of English-speaking men.

Who are they? she wondered. *Surely, they are not Indians. Did they come with the raiding party, or had they come to save my family?*

The sharp sound of digging came clearly through the wood panel. Elspeth tried standing up, but the headroom of the tiny hole was too low for that. She spread her feet apart for a solid stance and slipped her hand over the pistol in her apron pocket. The digging continued until one shovel finally struck the wood panel with a firm clunk. Hands began pulling at the panel. Her children had awoken. She hissed. "Stay behind me."

A flood of light struck the small space as the panel was thrown aside. Elspeth stood up fully. Blinking in the sudden light, she looked up to see a tall Indian standing just outside the opening. As Elspeth began to pull her pistol, she heard an English voice.

"Mrs. MacEwan, I am so very happy to see you alive, dear lady. Please come up from that filthy hole. We will not harm you."

Elspeth recognized the voice. It was that strange man, Alden. He stood beside the tall Indian poorly dressed and half-covered in black soot. Caked with mud and charred ash, he pulled a coonskin cap from his head and smiled broadly through a dirty blond beard. A band of similar white men stood about, all staring at Elspeth.

"Mr. Alden, the feather merchant," she said simply.

"At your service, Mrs. MacEwan," replied Alden briskly. He then bowed politely.

"What is it you have done, Mr. Alden?" asked Elspeth as she nodded toward the tall Indian. "You have brought these savages to my home?" Elspeth began to shake with anger. Her realization that there would be no rescue from these men boiled inside her. These badly displayed white men were little more than highwaymen and murderers. Elspeth eyed them closely as they gathered around, smiling. She had seen this look in other men's eyes.

Elspeth noticed that a hatchet hung loosely in the left hand of the tall Indian. Noticing her attention, the Indian responded by placing the hatchet carefully into his belt.

He was very tall and well built for a native. His hair, pulled back in a tight queue, was adorned with several feathers. A long red blanket hung over his shoulder, covering the left half of his body. He wore midhigh moccasins and a colorful loincloth. He carried no musket as the others but held a long staff, which he leaned on heavily. Two long knives and the hatchet protruded from his belt, which was heavy, beaded, and broad. It held hundreds of colorful beads with wide strokes of blue, red, and yellow stones. He took a step forward, and Elspeth responded by taking one back. She gripped her pistol tightly. He held his hand out to Elspeth, offering to assist her. Then he spoke.

"No one will harm you, Mrs. MacEwan."

Elspeth was struck speechless as she investigated the face of this Indian. His English was perfect. She had never seen the like of it. The Indian smiled gently as if to reassure Elspeth he meant no harm. He remained motionless, holding out his hand patiently. Elspeth took a tentative step and gripped the rough hand. He was very strong, lifting Elspeth out of the hole with ease.

"I will say again, Mrs. MacEwan, no one here will harm you or your children. I am Broken Tree of the Shawnee people."

"What has happened here?" asked Elspeth. "Why have you come? Where are my husband and daughter?"

"I am sorry to tell you, Mrs. MacEwan, but your husband and daughter are both dead." Alden pronounced this as if it was a common, everyday comment. These were no common words to Elspeth.

"Dead you say, Mr. Alden?"

"I am afraid so, madam. You see, when the Shawnee arrived, your husband very wrongly assumed they were attacking your homestead. And so your husband fired on the Shawnee, killing two of Tenskwatawa's braves. Naturally, the chief viewed this aggression as a challenge and so attacked in force. Everyone in and around the cabin was killed. Your husband's body is only steps from the cabin door. I'm afraid he did not get very far. I was terribly saddened to see your daughter take her own life. She was determined to prevent the Shawnee from having her, a brave young woman indeed. Her name was Mary as I recall." He hung his head in mock grief. "So sad."

Elspeth drew the pistol from her apron, pointed the weapon directly at Alden's chest, and pulled the trigger without hesitation. The powder did not ignite; it was too wet from her night in the hide. Only the sharp clack of the pistol mechanism could be heard.

Alden flew backward at the sight of the weapon, but he was slow to respond. If the powder had been dry, he would certainly be dead. Broken Tree leaned over and gently retrieved the pistol from Elspeth's hand. He looked back at Alden with curiosity, slowly shaking his head.

Alden's face took on a blood fury of rage. "You will be coming with us now, Mrs. MacEwan!" he shouted. "Gather your children, madam, and follow these men to the wagons!"

"I wish to see my husband, Mr. Alden," replied Elspeth with equal volume.

"We have no time for that, Mrs. MacEwan, and it is Captain Alden, if you please. Gather your children as I have asked and follow these men."

"I will do no such thing until I have seen to my husband and daughter."

"I'm afraid that won't be possible. We must follow the Shawnee immediately. To delay would invite a visit from the rebels. We must move now."

Elspeth helped her children up from the hide and turned abruptly on Alden. She charged the man, knocking him aside with a furious shove. The surrounding men looked on in surprise as Elspeth dashed down the hillside toward the ruins of the cabin.

"Stop her!" cried Alden.

At that, three men quickly took after Elspeth. Broken Tree appeared unconcerned over this event as he quietly examined the four children. Alden angrily stomped his way down the hill after the running group, mumbling under his breath.

Elspeth rounded the stone fireplace, and there lying facedown, horribly disfigured, was her beloved, Ian. She knelt beside his body and wept. The tears so washed across her face that she could no longer see clearly.

He had been scalped, of course, but there were also four arrows protruding from his side and back, the shafts burned to cinder. A large bore shot had passed through his body as well, leaving a hole big enough to look through. His left hand had been amputated, and a series of musket holes ran from his shoulder down his back. From the waist down, he was burned black.

Alden stepped up and shooed his men away. He grasped Elspeth by the arm, pulling her to her feet, but Elspeth resisted.

"Where is Mary?" cried Elspeth through her searing tears.

"She lies in the remains of the cabin. I doubt you will be able to recognize her."

"We must bury them," choked Elspeth as she rocked back and forth in the rhythm of grief.

"We cannot, Mrs. MacEwan. We must follow the Shawnee before they range too far ahead."

"We must bury them!" shouted Elspeth frantically.

"You must think of your children, Mrs. MacEwan. If we linger much longer, these loyalist villains will have their way with you and leave you dead alongside your husband. Without you, your children will be left to the mercy of these men or, worse, the Shawnee. You know what that means."

Elspeth looked up into the hated face. She slowly nodded. Yes, she knew what that meant.

The Trail Home

CLOSE TO THE MacEwan Station, William pushed himself to exhaustion. He had run nonstop for nearly two days. The trail he followed was littered with small cold fires, food leavings, and moccasin prints. They drew him ever closer to his home.

As he came up to Indian Creek, William dropped the small pack he carried and hurried up the embankment. Approaching the tree line that stood as a natural boundary, he swiftly scanned the ground for tracks. The smell of burned timber and rotting flesh came to him like a wave on the breeze.

As William crested the low rise, he saw only devastation. The stockade was torn down and all of the MacEwan cabins burned to the ground. The fencing and cornfield were burned out as well. There were no persons nor animals seen.

William approached cautiously from the south. As he did so, he could see that the destruction of his home was complete. Not a stick of wood survived. Moccasin tracks lay everywhere. The terrible odor of rotting flesh came to him again. In the field lay two horses crumpled into a pile. Meat from the animals had been stripped in a hurried fashion. Stick, the dog, lay dead beside the carcasses, several arrows protruding from his golden fur.

If any of his family survived the attack, they would be hiding in the shelter his father had built. William raced to the hide on the hillock. As he approached, he could see the heavy wood panel carelessly tossed aside. Reaching the edge, he looked down, hoping to find someone who may have survived. The mud floor displayed only footprints, nothing else.

William sat back on his haunches and looked over his burned-out home. It began to rain. He stood up and called out, "Ian MacEwan! MacEwan, is anyone there?" There was only silence.

Walking back toward the remains of the big cabin, William searched the debris for any sign that someone had lived through the assault. He found nothing but a small round iron ball. The rain began to beat down harder. William peered into the trees and cloud-covered sky, pleading with God Almighty that his family lived.

The rain came throughout the night. William sat on the remains of the river stone fireplace that had once given warmth and comfort to his family. Without cover, William remained silent, leaning against the fireplace, rivulets of water streaming down the stones, washing away the ashes at his feet.

At daybreak, the rain let up a bit. William sat there the entire night, soaked through from the unrelenting rain; he felt nothing. He began to shiver from the cold, trying, wishing to be wrong about his family's fate.

The sound of approaching voices caught William up. He searched the trees in the direction of the voices, crouching low behind the standing chimney as he did so. The stamp of hoofs could be heard. William quickly reloaded his rifle with dry powder. He slipped his tomahawk, knife, and flintlock from his belt, placing them close by his side.

He leaned the Brown Bess up against the stone column, reloaded the flintlock, and waited. A fury began building in William. If these men proved to be the group that attacked his home, he was determined to kill as many as possible. If they wished him harm, they would pay dearly.

An Indian afoot came into sight, stopping suddenly at the tree line. He searched the homestead grounds and footpaths that approached. Then the Indian stepped back behind the pines, waving his arm. The only sound was the soft patter of the rain as it struck William's hat. He carefully removed it, placing it over the flintlock.

"Hello, the station!" called a voice from among the trees. "Who is there?"

The voice held a soft Irish accent that William seemed to recognize. The stranger called again.

"Who is there now? Are you a white man? My name is Connor Murphy. I live just the way north. Do I know you?"

Connor Murphy, thought William. *Yes, I know this man. He has come to visit a time or two with my father. They have hunted together.*

"Who is it with you, Mr. Murphy?" called William. "I have seen an Indian in your lead. If you come here falsely, sir, you will pay a price, I assure you."

"Who are you?" called Murphy.

"I am William MacEwan, son of Ian and Elspeth MacEwan. Step out from the trees, sir, so I may see you plainly."

"I will, young MacEwan, but do not shoot me. I am your friend."

A rough-looking man in hunter skins stepped forward of the tree line and presented himself clearly. He dragged a coonskin cap from his head, and William could see that it was indeed his neighbor to the north, Connor Murphy.

"Don't shoot me now, boyo. I have come with me son as well as two Indian friends. You know us, William, so hold your fire."

William stood up and faced the man across the open space. Murphy replaced his cap, and the men advanced carefully as William held his rifle on the approaching group.

It appeared to be five—no, six men. William made out four whites and two Indians. The white men led three horses. They approached slowly. Stopping well short of William, each man nodded in silent greeting.

"Why are you here, Mr. Murphy?" asked William.

"We come back for the guns, William," answered the hunter.

"What guns?" said William. "Where is my family, Mr. Murphy? What has happened here?"

"It was a party of Shawnee, William, them and a group of murdering Tories. There was a great many of them. They came at the place, and . . . well . . . you can see for yourself. I am sorry, boyo, but your family is gone."

"Gone where, Mr. Murphy?" said William, raising his voice. He had the wild look of a cornered badger. "Where are they, sir?"

Murphy simply pointed in the direction of the hide.

"I have looked in the shelter. There is no one there."

Murphy dipped his head, saying softly, "Beyond the shelter, William. That is where we buried them."

William stood in silent shock. He heard the words Murphy had spoken, but his face showed only incomprehension. "What do you mean buried them?"

"They were killed, William, murdered by the Shawnee. The savages massacred everyone here, and then they burned everything—the bodies, the cabins, everything."

"All . . ." William trailed off, again silent. Looking in the direction Mr. Murphy had pointed, he began to walk. His knees were wobbling as he started along. His thoughts were as black as the charred timber he stepped away from. He began a steady cadence now, one step following the next.

All four white men trailed slowly in his wake. They offered no comment as the rain continued to pelt the trees and sodden ground. A series of stone and earthen mounds came into view as they reached the crest of the hill.

The stones covered five grave sites lined neatly along the ridgeline of the hill. Each of the graves had small rough crosses at their head.

William looked down and noticed that four graves were large while the last was suited for a small occupant.

William looked over at Murphy. "Who is it that lay here, Mr. Murphy?"

"That would be your da there on the left. I know it was himself because they did not burn him so much. Beside him is your ma. Next to her is a young woman we could not recognize. We found her under some timber at the back of the cabin. They were burned just so.

"That one I do not know. He was burned badly, and so it was impossible to recognize him as well. The fact is we thought it might be you, William. Then, of course, the last is the little one. Found among the ashes he was. Don't know was he boy or girl. We buried them proper."

William said nothing. He continued to stare at the graves, slowly wagging his head. "Something is wrong," he said simply. "Why did you come back here, Mr. Murphy?"

"As I said, for the rifles," repeated Murphy, bobbing his head for emphasis.

"What rifles?"

"Why, the rifles your father bought in German towns and the like, round Philadelphia. But surely, you know this. We thought we should try another look. The Shawnee may have missed them, you see. I know your da would hide them well if he could. If you've no notion of where they might be, then the knowledge of his hiding place rests here in the ground."

"I know nothing of any rifles, Mr. Murphy," said William, shaking his head.

Murphy bowed his and continued, "William, your da bought rifles for the Continental Congress. He was bringing them west to freedom-minded men. These weapons were paid for, free for the taking as long we pointed them at the British, which we are only too happy to do. Your da was for the Americans. He worked with the army, General Washington, and the like. And so we are." Murphy nodded toward the men about him. "Did you not know this?"

"Where are these guns, Mr. Murphy?"

"That's what I been trying to find out, William. It's the devil who knows, for I do not. If you think on it, maybe you know a place your da would hide such things, maybe?"

"Maybe," repeated William absently as he continued to stare at the graves. "These graves do not seem right to me, Mr. Murphy."

"Well, as I said," muttered Murphy apologetically, "we buried them best we could. It was done proper. These boys and I carried a good number of stones to cover the graves. What is it you find to be amiss, William?"

"Oh, no, Mr. Murphy, the graves are well attended, sir. I thank you for that. What I mean is there should be more. And it would be unlikely my mother would cling to a single child. She would have had hold of all for certain. Did you witness this attack, Mr. Murphy?"

"It was seen by my Indian friends here, Samuel Blue and Gray Wolf. They come from the Catawba tribe, the river people. They tell me your da fought like the devil on judgment day. He killed many Shawnee."

"I would like to speak with your Indian friends, Mr. Murphy. I have questions."

The two Catawba sat beneath a large oak, trying to keep out of the rain. Each man sat squat with a blanket stretched overhead. They studied the tall white man with the bright golden red hair. As William approached, they stood.

"This is Samuel Blue, William," said Murphy as he indicated the taller of the two. "He speaks English well enough. He and Gray Wolf saw the fight."

William turned to Samuel Blue. "You were here when the Shawnee came?"

Samuel Blue pointed to a thick line of trees to the north. "We stay in the shadow, those trees. The Shawnee do not see us. We stay quiet."

"What happened here?" asked William.

"Shawnee come from west across the creek, many Shawnee. Man in cabin fire two guns and kill Shawnee warriors. Then Shawnee come all round. They fire many arrows at cabin. White men with wagons help Shawnee fight."

"White men?" asked William.

"Aye," claimed Murphy. "They say they are loyal to the British, but they're little more than highwaymen. They claim loyalty to king and country. It's loyalty to bad deeds as I see it. They have raided all along the frontier, thieving and killing."

William turned back to Samuel Blue. "What happened?"

Samuel Blue continued, "Three white men bring big gun and shoot the cabin. Man inside comes out to fight. He has hair like you, red fire.

"This man kills four Shawnee with knife and hatchet. Then white men shoot him many times. He falls there." Samuel Blue pointed to the ground where Ian MacEwan had lain sprawled in the dirt.

"A big gun?" asked William, confused.

Connor piped up again, "'Twas Tories that possessed the cannon, William. Tory raiders carry light cannon, a gift from the British."

Samuel Blue continued, "Man, woman come out of cabin, holding hands out to surrender. Woman holds her babe up, but the Shawnee do not care. They kill man, woman, and babe."

"What did this woman look like?" asked William.

"She was fat woman with corn straw hair. I do not understand her words. She shouts strange words, but the Shawnee do not care. They kill her quick."

William looked up at these words and smiled at the Indian. "Corn straw hair, you say, and she was a big woman?"

"Yes, she carry a babe."

William's heart began to pick up pace. He turned on Murphy. "I think my mother may still be alive, Mr. Murphy. As you may know, my mother is slender in stature, and her hair is as black as a crow wing. Another woman must have been here at the time of the attack.

"There are too few graves as well, and I found several footprints in the hide. If everyone at the station were killed, there should be eight graves, not five. My mother and possibly younger brothers and sisters may have survived."

"Aye, the Shawnee often take the young ones," said Murphy. "Women as well. Do you think it so, William?"

"I do, Mr. Murphy. And if that is true, then I must find them. Where would they go?"

Samuel Blue answered, "North and east, they move fast."

William swung his rifle up, cradling it. "Then I must follow."

"Please, William," said Murphy with some urgency, "you must tell me before you leave where you think your father may have hidden the rifles I told you of."

"I do not care about rifles, Mr. Murphy. It is my family I am thinking of. I must go, sir."

"These weapons are too important, William. It is most likely the reason your father was killed."

"How can that be?" asked William.

"The only reason a band of white loyalist scum would track this far west to meet with bloodthirsty Shawnee is for those rifles," said Murphy.

"Hold on now, William." It was Connor Murphy's eldest son, Timothy. "You can't chase after a flock of Shawnee yourself. What would you do when you find them? You'll likely get yourself roasted alive."

"I do not know what I will do or what I can do. I only know that I must do something. Many in these woods knew my father. I will pass neighbors. They will help."

Timothy shook his head. "If the Shawnee have not burned them out, then surely, they have taken to the mountains. You will find no neighbors on the trail of these Indians.

"The wagons will head for Philadelphia. That would be safe ground for the loyalists. As for the Shawnee, they will continue north to their own lands.

"Your problem, William, is which of these parties has your family, the Tories or the Shawnee?"

William looked toward the trail east. Timothy was right. If his mother was taken by the Shawnee, that would be the worst of it. If the white men held his family, there was a chance he could retrieve them. William had to do something. He would follow and catch the raiding parties as quickly as possible to discover what he needed. He turned to Timothy.

"I must follow them. How many days are they ahead?"

"Three and a bit," said Timothy. "They're traveling fast, but this rain will slow them some."

"Then I must go. I thank you for your kindness, Mr. Murphy. I know my father would be grateful."

William gathered up his weapons. "Could I take the loan of a horse, Mr. Murphy? I would be very much obliged."

Murphy shook his head. "No, William, I cannot. These animals are promised to the Continental army. We have been asked to provide what we can to support the Americans. Horses and men are most in need."

"Well then, I am afoot. Thank you again for your kindness." Gathering up his tomahawk and musket, he turned to go.

"Hold up, William," said Timothy. "I have been asked to bring these horses and these men back to our regimental headquarters. I am a rifleman with the Eleventh Virginia. I serve with Col. Daniel Morgan and his company of volunteers. Our camp lay some distance outside Philadelphia. If you can stand the company, we will go with you."

The two young men standing beside Tim nodded in agreement.

"Me brother Dermot and I joined up with Timothy. We can ride two on the black. You and Tim can travel ahead."

William looked at the young man with the thin smile standing before him. As if seeing him for the first time, William asked, "What is your name, sir?"

"Myles Fallon. This is me brother Dermot. We settled north of the Murphys. And we are with you, Mr. MacEwan."

"Then let us depart, gentlemen. There is no time to waste."

William swung up onto the tall speckled sorrel. The blanket was soaking wet. There was no saddle on the animal, just a bridle, bit, and reins.

Connor Murphy held up a hand, halting the group. "Before you leave, William, I must ask you again if you know where your father may have hidden the rifles."

"They might be along the west side of the Indian Creek, Mr. Murphy. It is the only place I can think of."

"Show me," said Connor.

The men followed William in single file as he traversed the MacEwan land at a slow trot. The small cornfield had been burned to cinder, and as the men stepped over it, clods of black soot clung to their feet as delicate ashes wafted into the air with each stride. No one spoke.

As he passed over the blackened field, William recalled the happy days he had spent planting corn with his mother and father by his side. Surveying the field now, William felt only dread, anger, and grief.

They approached the creek where it turned southeast. As he looked down from the high bank, William pointed across the water to the opposite side.

"Do you see the large oak leaning down and covering the opposite bank with roots?"

"Aye," said Murphy, squinting.

"My father often hid things there, whiskey mostly, but I have seen him bring powder and shot there as well. He claimed it to be well hidden and far enough from the cabins so as not to attract the attention of Indians or thieves. If the rifles were not discovered by the Shawnee, then they may be there."

Connor Murphy turned to the two Catawba. "Come," he said as he raced to the creek bank. Here, it was low enough to jump to the water's edge. The three men crossed the shallow creek and approached the old oak. Samuel Blue began pulling branches and brush from the heavy roots and soon uncovered Ian MacEwan's hidden hollow.

Being small in stature, Connor Murphy bent low and scooted inside. He came out holding a long rifle in one hand and a bottle of whiskey in the other. "We found them, William!" shouted Murphy across the water.

"Other things as well," he said, shaking the bottle he held up high.

"Then I am on my way, Mr. Murphy!" called William. "I thank you again, sir!"

Then William wheeled his horse about and raced toward the eastern trail.

Tim Murphy looked over at the Fallon brothers. Wagging his head, he climbed his horse and took after William.

The Road East

THE RAIN STOPPED.
They trailed the Shawnee and wagons by days. Taking to the main road, they traveled quickly over the muddy track. Moving faster than the wagons, William and his companions continued at a good pace. The loyalist wagons stayed mostly with the rough, crude road. The Shawnee tracked farther west. William decided it would be best to come up on the slower moving wagons and so pushed on steadily, following the deep-wheeled ruts. They rode until dark, stopping only to rest and water the mounts.

"How far ahead would you take them, Timothy?"

"We've gained more than half a day, William. At least the rain has stopped, and the road to Philadelphia turns hard east up ahead. It's good road there. We should be able to make up some distance."

The two men pulled the worn blankets from their horses and laid them out on drying ground. They debated a fire but, in the end, decided not. They would sleep only a couple of hours and then continue on before dawn.

William sat down cross-legged on his blanket. He asked Timothy, "Do you think we can catch them?"

"Hard to tell, William. Given the distance we have left, it could be a close thing."

William absently reached down to the pouch hanging from his belt and pulled out a handful of soft corn. He tossed the kernels in his mouth and chewed silently.

"That's a fine pouch, William," said Timothy. "The beadwork looks Indian. Was it your ma who did that?"

William looked down on the ornate pouch made of fine, soft leather, fringed edges, and colorful stones. Little Cornstalk made it for him using the hide from a whitetail he had brought to her one morning. William suddenly jumped to his feet. He looked straight south into the trees as if he could see the beautiful Cherokee girl standing among the pines.

"What is it, William?" asked Timothy, alarmed at the unexpected turn.

"Little Cornstalk," said William, not turning his gaze from the trees.

"What?" asked Timothy, confused.

"Her name is Little Cornstalk," answered William quietly. "She is a Cherokee girl, the daughter of Chief Black Feather. We met when I stayed with her tribe for some weeks. She made the pouch for me."

He fondled the pouch gently. "She is the most beautiful girl I have ever seen. I think I love her."

Timothy pulled his cap from his head and began scratching his scalp with vigor. "You love a Cherokee girl?"

"She's half Spanish, or so I was told. She was the reason I stayed with the Cherokee for so long. If I had not, I would have been at home with my parents when the Shawnee came. I am at fault for not being there when they needed me most."

"William, if you had been at your home, I would be speaking to your grave and not your ears right now. You cannot blame yourself for such things. God has ways that are difficult to understand, William. But in your case, I see it clear.

"You are alive to rescue your mother and whoever else of your family survived. Yes, I think God made a wise choice in this. You must think on this and believe what I say is true. You know full well your father would believe the same."

William paid small attention to Timothy as he spoke. His mind lay elsewhere. Consumed with thoughts of his family, he felt a shame not thinking of Little Cornstalk until now. He wondered if he would ever see her again. Guilt now pulled at the young longhunter from two directions.

Before daylight, William was up, gathering his gear. He poked Timothy with a moccasin toe. "We must hurry now, Tim. I mean to catch those wagons before they get to Philadelphia."

Timothy opened one eye, looking out to a dark morning sky. "I am with you, William," he croaked. "I need to only get the wrinkle out of my legs."

"Hurry then, Tim."

Little Cornstalk

LITTLE CORNSTALK BUSIED herself all morning, preparing her visit with Stevenson. The girl was determined to gather some knowledge of William and his whereabouts, and she knew the best source would be the older hunter.

Why did William leave? If it was to visit his white family at the top of the north trail, then he should have returned by now. The thought that William may never return was too painful to consider. Was he really coming back, or did he leave with no thought of Little Cornstalk? The girl could not bear the notion.

She had come once again to the duck woman's lodge, visiting nearly every morning. Since Adsila had passed, Little Cornstalk seemed to find a comfort in the old woman's company.

This morning, she came to trade a bag of dried corn and a good knife for two of the duck woman's fat birds. It had taken hours for her to collect the corn; the knife had belonged to her mother. Picking through the charred remains of the burned cornfield, she plucked out the undamaged kernels one by one. It took most of the morning and produced only a small bag of the now precious grain.

The duck woman had demanded more, but Little Cornstalk had only what she carried. The girl haggled with the old squaw and in the end made the trade along with a promise to return next morning with more corn. The old woman swiftly denuded the birds, her hands flying in and out, with feathers sailing in every direction. She carefully cleaned the birds, retaining the prized livers as Little Cornstalk instructed.

"Will you give these livers to the hunter Stevenson?"

"Yes," replied the girl.

"You should eat them yourself."

Little Cornstalk looked strangely at the old woman, who nodded firmly.

"Is Stevenson your man?"

"What?" said Little Cornstalk, shocked at the notion. She laughed suddenly at the thought.

"No, he is not," she said emphatically.

"That is good," said the old woman, wagging her head. "He is a fat white man and will not be able to provide for you the way a young brave can. White men beat their wives every day, it is said. If not Stevenson, then who?"

Little Cornstalk did not answer the duck woman, instead, she looked down at her mother's moccasins and smiled. Turning away from the old woman, she carried her ducks off, gripping them by the neck. Little Cornstalk had to admit that the birds were fine for roasting, and so she set about doing so.

She was careful not to burn the tender meat as she slowly turned each bird on a low spit over a smokeless fire. She sprinkled precious salt and herbs on the sizzling skin of the roasting fowl. As the fire grew, rivulets of fat dribbled down, sending up bursts of flame, turning the pale skin a golden brown. She pierced each liver with a fine, sharp stick and held them under the dripping fat. Then she placed them on flat stones close to the embers, cooking the dark brown flesh until firm to the touch.

The bottle of whiskey she had taken from her father's store was carefully hidden in her lodge. She knew the whiskey would do more to loosen Stevenson's tongue than the duck, but she also knew the older hunter loved roasted duck. She had taken great care with Stevenson's wound, and largely due to this, his injury healed nicely. She had visited Stevenson several times even as her mother lay dying. Now that Adsila was gone, Little Cornstalk had only one thought, William. Where was William? When will he return?

Stevenson sat down heavily on his blankets and began to scratch the scarring arrow wound. The hole had closed neatly, but the remaining itch was terribly vexing. Still, the pain was mostly gone, and he was able to walk without too much difficulty.

He had not seen Black Feather for some days now and was beginning to wonder what had become of the chief. He wished to have words with the great Cherokee. He would do his best to persuade the chief not to join with the British against the Americans, even though he knew in his heart that Black Feather would never agree. Still, he had to try.

Daily life in the Cherokee village was returning to normal. Every hand in the tribe was now busy with the tasks of life. Little Cornstalk had come almost every day, bearing corn mush cakes and roasted meat. After Adsila passed, it seemed to Stevenson that the girl was walking about dazed. Stevenson recognized that Little Cornstalk was suffering, but he could think of no way in which to relieve her grief. Shadow Bear and her mother, Adsila, were both dead now and William far away. The girl no longer smiled when she came to visit. She seemed busy with her daily chores, but she rarely spoke, and when she did, it was simply yes or no, nothing more.

Stevenson had hopes of hearing from William by this time. His concern for the young man was growing. The papers he had retrieved from Alden's pack were too important to ignore. They carried an alliance between the Cherokee and British but also nascent plans for the British invasion of the American south.

It would begin in the Carolinas, from there heading south to Georgia, splitting the colonies in two. British soldiers from Florida would then head north, joining up with those in Georgia and the Carolinas. Even Stevenson could see the value of such a plan, and in this realization, he knew that the Continental Congress and Washington's army must be made aware of the danger. He knew full well that Ian MacEwan would have the wherewithal to get those papers to the Congress and Continental army, but would he be in time to make a difference?

Little Cornstalk came to Stevenson's lodge laden with duck, whiskey, and crispy livers. When she entered, she delivered a broad smile to Stevenson for the first time in weeks. The old hunter studied the girl with a close eye. As Little Cornstalk laid out the food, she chattered on about her morning with the duck woman. The secondhand conversation meant nothing to Stevenson, but he was curious about Little Cornstalk's behavior. She placed a small cloth across Stevenson's outstretched leg and then brought out the clay whiskey jug.

"What is all this now?" asked Stevenson cautiously. He sensed immediately what Little Cornstalk was after. "This is a fine meal and even better whiskey, Little Cornstalk. It must have cost some. What is it you want?"

Little Cornstalk stood up and, being as she was, asked frankly, "Where is William?"

Stevenson knew this was what the food and drink were about—William. Still, he was surprised at the abrupt question and wasn't certain how to reply.

"William has gone to see his mother and father. You know this. Why ask a question you already know the answer? He will be back soon," finished the hunter with a wave of his hand.

Little Cornstalk fired back, "When, Stevenson? When will he be back soon? It has been many days since he left. William should be here now. I worry for him, Stevenson. You must tell me what is happening with William and why."

Stevenson was taken aback at the ferocity of Little Cornstalk's inquiry. The girl was leaning forward over Stevenson close enough for him to smell the lingering woodsmoke about her clothing. Stevenson looked at the girl and felt a stir of pity. He wondered how much he should tell. He had no wish to frighten the girl, but how to reassure her?

"William's father may have asked that he stay a while longer with his family. There could be many reasons why he has not returned yet."

"What many reasons?"

"Well, I don't really know, but I'm sure William is fine, and he will return soon." Stevenson took a long swig from the bottle and winced. Little Cornstalk was making him uneasy.

"You are not telling me true things, Stevenson. Why did William leave? You have told me he wants to see his family. Why? Why did he leave so quick, and why has he not returned? You must tell me now."

"All right, girl, I will tell you," answered Stevenson, exasperated.

Little Cornstalk sat back, expectantly looking at Stevenson, who wore a blank face. Placing her hands in her lap, she waited for the hunter to speak.

"I gave William some important papers to carry to his father," said Stevenson. "His father must take these papers to his friends. Once that is done, William will come back." Leaning back, Stevenson took another long drink from the whiskey jug.

Little Cornstalk sat quietly, peering at Stevenson. She considered the hunter's reply in silence. She looked up. "How long?"

"I do not know," he answered in a tired voice. "It may take many weeks, many days for William's father to return, and in the meantime, William must stay with his mother and family. Please, Little Cornstalk, you must believe that William will return safely. In two days, I plan to travel the north trail and come on William's home on my way. I will find out what delays William, and I will send him straight back to you. I promise."

"You leave in two days?" she asked excitedly.

"Yes. I have business of my own to deal with, and if I had not been shot with this Shawnee arrow, I would have left weeks ago."

"It is good you have been shot with this arrow because now I am going with you."

"What is it you say?" said the hunter, stunned.

The Road to Philadelphia

"THEY ARE NO more than a day ahead, William," said Timothy. "We should come up on them before nightfall tomorrow. If your family is safe with the wagons, then we'll have them. If the Shawnee has your family, then it may be possible to seek the aid of Colonel Morgan as I said."

"Can the wagons enter Philadelphia freely then?" asked William.

"Aye. There are many ways into the city. These brigands know how to travel, and they have safe haven within the city. The British army and loyalists hold Philadelphia in a tight grip now. Colonel Morgan knows this. General Howe and his army have not moved outside the city, and so the colonel waits."

"I will not wait," said William.

"I know that, William. Still, right now, we must stop and allow these animals to rest. It took a good deal of trade and hard work to gather these horses for Colonel Morgan. We have driven them hard, and I've no wish to lose or injure them."

William was anxious to continue, but he knew that Timothy was right. Not only were the animals weary but they all were as well. They dismounted and began walking the horses toward a small open field.

Broken Tree

ELSPETH WAS TIRED, so very tired. She looked over her children and despaired. It pained her terribly to see them in such a way. They were filthy with mud and wet from the intermittent rain. Just now she struggled with the twins, one on each side of her. They were fussing in abject misery. The fleas from the animal hides had worked their way over to the children, and it was a constant effort on Elspeth's part to pick the bugs off, pinching them dead and discarding them over the side of the wagon.

Although the rain had finally stopped, she and the children were wet through to the skin. She had tried covering them with a few of the drier hides, but the water still found its way, making the journey as miserable as it was frightening, not to mention the fleas.

These low-bound men constantly tormented her children, shouting at them to stop crying or speaking. It was an impossible task given their exhaustion and hunger. The worst of these men would ride up and stare at Elspeth for long moments. He would come alongside and begin poking and pulling on her thin dress, sneering or smiling all the while, whispering how he would take her.

Elspeth and the children rode in the forward wagon that carried several bundles of skins, both traded and stolen. There were small barrels of powder and ball along with many guns tied in a tight bundle. There was a small water bucket, but it had no water now and hadn't seen any since the rain ceased. The children were getting thirsty.

She was angry at these cruel and ignorant men for not understanding how frightening this all was to her children. David and Aelwyd were calm for the most part. The twins were another matter. Constraining them was near impossible. Although she knew the children would be hungry by this time, she dared not ask these violent men for anything. It would only invite another session of torment.

The ride had been rough as well. The road they traveled on now was better than before, but it was still a jarring experience and long. Elspeth began to wonder where they were going. Mr. Alden seemed settled on some destination but gave no clue about where that might be. They had been traveling east for more than three weeks now, or so it seemed. It suddenly struck Elspeth that she did not know what day it was. That had never happened to her before, even when she sailed to America, locked in a ship's hold for eight weeks.

A large brown hand suddenly slapped over the sideboard of the wagon, making Elspeth jump. A second hand followed the first, pulling back along with the wagon. The head of Broken Tree appeared. The tall Indian began stumping alongside the wagon, waving up and down like a boat on the sea. He looked over the occupants as he tossed his staff into the wagon and then held out a large bag of soft corn to Elspeth. She took it gingerly.

"I thank you, sir," said Elspeth, grasping the swaying bag with a quick nod.

"For the little ones," said the Indian.

Broken Tree had come to the wagon every day. Each time, he brought food for the children and Elspeth, water too. On several occasions, he helped the children relieve themselves, hoisting them up and out of the wagon with his strong long arms. He would guide them to a bush or tree and wait patiently as they finished. Returning to the wagon, he would lift them again, gently depositing them back among the animal skins.

"Why do you help us so? I do not understand," said Elspeth.

She had watched Broken Tree closely whenever he came to the wagon. The big Indian was kind and helpful, but she did not trust him.

"I have told you, Mrs. MacEwan, you are the mother of the longhunter. It is simple, really. I do not understand why you do not."

"You are speaking of my son again, and I have told you many times his name is William MacEwan."

"Yes, William MacEwan," piped up David. He smiled at Broken Tree as he said this. David had become fond of the crippled Indian.

"The longhunter is a powerful enemy, Mrs. MacEwan. If not for his Spanish armor, Chief Tenskwatawa would have been killed by your son. I have seen this with my own eyes. He killed several Shawnee warriors as well. He is a powerful enemy, and the Shawnee are the greater for it. You see, Mrs. MacEwan, the Shawnee measure their greatness through the power of their enemies. The stronger the enemy, the more powerful we Shawnee become. This is well known to everyone."

"This cannot be my son you speak of. My son is only a boy. Yes, he has red hair and carries a rifle, but so do many men. My husband . . ." Elspeth stopped herself, shaking her head slightly. She looked over at her children. Except for David, they had all fallen asleep from sheer exhaustion.

Seeing tears well up in Elspeth's eyes, Broken Tree said, "Your husband was a brave warrior, Mrs. MacEwan. Many tales will be told of him in our Shawnee lodges. He died bravely. You must be proud to be the wife of such a warrior and mother to another."

Elspeth had no answer to this. She simply hung her head and closed her eyes.

"Good morning, Mrs. MacEwan."

Elspeth looked up to see Alden trotting alongside the wagon on a dappled horse.

"We have almost reached our destination. I think perhaps another day of travel. We expect to be in Philadelphia before twilight tomorrow. When our British escorts arrive, I want you and your children under these skins. Is that clear? It is important that you are not seen as we enter the city."

"Why, Mr. Alden? What possible difference would that make?"

"Spies, Mrs. MacEwan. The rebels have spies everywhere. I do not want your son knowing exactly where you are. That could spoil my plans, you see."

"What are you saying, Mr. Alden? How is my son involved in this?"

"Oh, Mrs. MacEwan, surely, you know that your son and probably Stevenson as well are following us. I would expect nothing less. Yes, they are following. Unless Stevenson was killed, then it would be your

William alone. It doesn't really matter. I expect our business to conclude in short order."

"What business would that be, Mr. Alden?"

"In due time, Mrs. MacEwan, in due time."

Elspeth looked over at Broken Tree, who was following the conversation closely, but the Indian held mute as he concentrated on Alden's words.

"What could William have to do with any of this?"

"Just so, Mrs. MacEwan, just so," answered Alden as he turned his horse away from the wagon.

A feeling of panic began to rise in Elspeth as she considered what Alden said. If William was following, then he was in danger. She looked out along the wide serpentine road heading west, wishing with all her might that William was far, far away and safe.

Broken Tree heard Alden's words. He considered the idea that William MacEwan, the golden-haired longhunter, might be trailing them now. He, too, stared out at the receding road and wished just as fervently as Elspeth that the deadly longhunter was indeed many miles away.

Stevenson

"WILL YOU SLOW down?" Stevenson was moving quite well considering his recent wound, but it still held him back some. Little Cornstalk was at least fifty yards ahead of him, and he was beginning to lose sight of the girl.

"The old duck woman was right," replied Little Cornstalk over her shoulder. "You are a fat old white man."

Stevenson wagged his head in resignation. He quickened his step, but it did little to shorten the gap between himself and the determined girl. They had been speaking Cherokee for the most part, but Little Cornstalk asked that Stevenson speak English so she would know the words of William. It was turning into a mix of English and Cherokee that Stevenson was beginning to lose track. He wasn't sure what he was saying any longer.

They had been traveling now for several days, and after some time, the realization came to Stevenson that they were somehow on the same trail of the Shawnee who had attacked the Cherokee village. The Shawnee had certainly passed through here some days ago. The remnants of small fires, trampled prints, and food littered both sides of the trail.

Stevenson had assumed the Shawnee would be traveling much farther west along the Appalachian Ridge straight to their own lands. As Stevenson and the girl moved closer to the MacEwan homestead, it became clear what direction the Shawnee were taking. This did not bode well for the occupants of the MacEwan settlement. Stevenson became more and more concerned the closer they came to their destination.

Complicating matters was Little Cornstalk. She had insisted they stop at the hammock where the bear fight had taken place. Stevenson told the girl there was little to observe, but she made him promise, and so they stopped for some time at the lonely copse of pine and small oak. She peppered Stevenson with questions.

"Where did William stand? Is this the tree he trapped the bear with his knife? Where was Shadow Bear when the bears came? I was told there were three bears. Is that true?" There were many more questions. Stevenson answered all to the best of his recollection.

He patiently waited for the girl to finish as this was now a sacred place to Little Cornstalk. She placed small tokens alongside the scattered bones—a colorful river stone here and a small robin feather there. As she moved about the area, she chanted a Cherokee song. Singing to the Mother Spirit, she slowly stamped her feet among the decaying debris. When she finished, she smiled at Stevenson and explained that now her brother, Shadow Bear, and the bears who lost their lives in this place would be together with the Mother Spirit. This seemed to make Little Cornstalk very happy.

Stevenson stood in silence as he observed the girl make final preparations. Just then, Little Cornstalk jerked upright and said, "Ooh." Then she bent at the waist and threw up her morning meal.

Stevenson looked at the girl. "Are you all right?" He rubbed his stomach and pointed at Little Cornstalk's belly.

"I am very much good, Stevenson," she replied in English with a great smile on her face.

"Well, I am happy to hear it. Now if you would, please stop wasting good food. That is the third time you have ejected your meal since we left the village. Are you sure you are well?"

Little Cornstalk answered with a question. "What is 'eejectated'?"

Stevenson looked at the girl and said simply, "Wasting food."

"I will stop 'eejectated.'"

"Good. Now let us continue."

Stevenson did not say it aloud, but he was truly concerned for the MacEwan home. If the Shawnee did attack, they would surely find a fight in Ian MacEwan, but would he be able to hold off such a large number? He was hopeful that the station would have several longhunters in residence as it often did. The Shawnee had already met defeat at the hands of the Cherokee, and it seemed unlikely they would wish to lose any more of their braves fighting a pack of wild longhunters.

As the sun retreated to the west, Stevenson pulled up short, stamped his long rifle heavily on the ground, and shouted, "Stop!" He was done for this day. The hip was paining, and he was thirsty as well as hungry. Little Cornstalk stopped and retraced her steps back to the older hunter.

"You are tired now, Stevenson?"

"Tired and hungry," he said.

"But there is good moonlight now. The rain is gone from the sky. We see much better," she pleaded.

"I am not taking another step. We will make a cold camp here. We are less than a day from William's home, and as you see, many Shawnee are just ahead of us. They may have already attacked William's home."

"If the Shawnee attack William's lodge, he will kill them. Is that not so? He will shoot Tenskwatawa, and the Shawnee will run away as before," she said, nodding for emphasis.

"We will see when we get there," replied Stevenson cautiously.

They passed the evening exchanging new words in English, with Little Cornstalk showing no desire to halt her education. Stevenson was fond of the girl, but he was becoming weary of these constant explanations that sometimes confused him. As much as he enjoyed her company, he was more than willing to return Little Cornstalk to William just so he could get some rest.

The morning came bright and soft. Little Cornstalk naturally took the lead as they moved farther up the trail. When Stevenson found the Indian Creek, he called to Little Cornstalk to hold her place.

Standing beside the small creek not far from William's fishing oak, Stevenson spoke in hushed tones.

"You stay here by the creek while I go up."

"No," she said.

"This is no time for discussion," whispered Stevenson angrily.

"What is 'dish-kus-shone'?" asked Little Cornstalk, slowly pronouncing the word.

"No more talk," said Stevenson flatly. The look on his face did nothing to dissuade the girl.

"I do not like this word."

"It's far better than getting raped and killed by a Shawnee brave."

"I know *kill*. What is *raped*?"

"Good lord," said Stevenson, exasperated. "Just stay here as I told you. Do not move away from this place unless you see someone, then hide."

"I can hide good," she said, smiling. She was becoming more excited about seeing William again and could barely contain herself.

"Fine, now just do what I say."

With that, Stevenson checked his powder and began walking slowly up the ridge toward the MacEwan place.

The first thing he saw was the studded remains of the fireplace. His heart jumped as he slowly circled the boundaries. Not a cabin stood. Everything had been burned to the ground. The field he traversed was burned to ash. He came across the rotting carcass of the dog Stick. Two arrows jutted from the small body. The lingering odor of charred wood was nearly gone now, but the smell of death still clung to the air. He cautiously approached the place where the main cabin had been. The only thing left standing was the fireplace. It was eerily quiet.

He thought about his last visit here with his friend Daniel Boone. The place had been full of life and sound. The cornfield was half grown, with mooing cows and nickering horses wandering about. Children were squealing in delight as they chased wandering chickens about the cabins, laughing just for the delight of it.

His worst fears were now realized. The Shawnee had attacked. They must have driven everyone from the station, or they killed them all and burned everything to the ground. He walked across the rubble that was left of the barn and privy. Holding his rifle at ready, he was prepared to fire. There was no one to be seen.

Olaf Stevenson had been ten years old when his family farm was attacked by a band of Delaware. His mother and father had been killed and badly used by the Indians. His brother Bjorn and little sister Elsa were taken. If not for his daily chore of collecting water from the small river that ran near the Stevenson farm, he, too, would now be dead or a Delaware slave.

The force of this unhappy memory slammed him like a shot. His anger was rising higher with every step he took across the blackened earth. He scanned the property from where he stood, searching for a possible hide, which Ian MacEwan was sure to have.

"Where is William?"

The words came from behind. He spun about, swinging his rifle round, nearly smacking Little Cornstalk with the barrel.

"Good god in heaven, girl! I could have shot you. What the devil are you doing sneaking up on me like that? I told you to stay by the creek."

"Where is William?" she repeated.

Philadelphia

THE CHILDREN WERE hungry. Broken Tree brought water and food to Elspeth and the children, but it was a small portion. Elspeth felt a weakness in her bones, not just weariness but real exhaustion. The constant harassment and jostling of the wagon had taken its toll. Her grief was always near. She would wake from a fitful sleep, only to realize that Ian was gone and everything that had happened was only too real. She held fast her tears for the sake of the children, but still, a hard sob would choke her occasionally, and then she would shake her head to steady herself.

The calamity that came to her family was brought into stark clarity the farther they ranged from their home. Reality settled in her mind. She began considering the future and how best to deal with it. Elspeth could be single minded when it came to this.

She knew now that Alden was bringing them to Philadelphia. She had no idea why. Certainly, the Shawnee should have taken the children and most likely herself as well. This seemed to her to be a mystery. And why did Broken Tree stay with them rather than travel with the Shawnee? Another mystery.

As she tried to make sense of this, the crippled Indian rode up beside the wagon on a small black and white Appaloosa. He leaned over his horse and dropped a water canteen and a small bag of soft corn into Elspeth's hands.

"I thank you for your kindness, Broken Tree. It is appreciated."

"You are most welcome, Mrs. MacEwan."

Elspeth shook her head in wonder. If she closed her eyes, she could swear she was listening to an educated Englishman. "I am amazed you speak our language so well. I would suppose a white man has taught you this?"

"Yes, of course," he said cheerfully. "He was a Jesuit priest, an educated man. His name was Fr. William Faraley. He taught me many things—reading, writing, mathematics."

Broken Tree paused and stared off to the horizon as if recalling his lessons. He continued, "He was a good man and very pious. I have read the Bible and even Shakespeare."

"Where is your priest now, Broken Tree?"

"He is dead," he replied simply. "My father killed him with his tomahawk and then took his scalp. It hangs on my brother's lodge pole now."

Elspeth winced at this casual description. "I am sorry to hear that. Why did your father kill him?"

"I was taken to the priest because of my injury. Father Faraley told my father he could cure my leg and I would walk like a man again. Alas, that was not to be.

"My father came for me one day, and the good priest told him that my injury was a gift. Because of this, I was close to God now, and it would be a sin for me to go back to my Indian ways. Then my father killed him. He took his life and his scalp. He did this to remind me that I am Shawnee."

Elspeth leaned back slowly, looking down at her hands cupped in her lap. "That is a sad tale, Broken Tree."

"When my mother spoke with me," continued the Indian, "and heard my words, she asked me something I have never forgotten. 'My son,' she said, 'you stand one foot in the white man's world and one foot in the Shawnee.' Can you tell me which of these is the broken foot?"

Elspeth had no answer to this. She carefully considered Broken Tree's words and decided this Indian was more dangerous than he appeared.

"I take it you have abandoned your teachings then?"

"On the contrary, Mrs. MacEwan, I have a better understanding of the world for it, far better than my Shawnee brethren. Father Faraley was correct, I was given a gift."

He looked at Elspeth impassively and then inclined his head toward the children with a nod. "I am leaving you now, Mrs. MacEwan. I go to join my brothers. They are heading north to fight alongside the British."

Elspeth felt a moment of regret hearing this, but the emotion faded rapidly. She was wary of this tall broken Indian and inexplicably grateful for his kindness. She wondered again how all this might end.

"Will we see you again, Broken Tree?"

"That is unlikely, Mrs. MacEwan, but you never know. I have traveled far, and I see many people."

The wagons came to a halt just then, and Elspeth turned toward the driver. "What is it?" she asked. She received no reply.

Alden rode up to the wagon and nodded curtly to Broken Tree. Then turning to Elspeth, he said, "The British are preparing to enter the city in force. We will wait here for the regulars who will escort us in. When we move ahead, I expect you and your children to hide yourselves under these furs. I would ask that you also hide these weapons and powder. Is that understood, Mrs. MacEwan?"

"No, Mr. Alden, it is not understood. To what purpose?" asked Elspeth.

"Do as I say, Mrs. MacEwan, or I will give one of your children to this Indian," replied Alden casually.

Elspeth gave a short gasp and darted a look at Broken Tree. He stared back at Elspeth with his usual impassive look.

Alden said, "I could also shoot one of them if you would prefer, Mrs. MacEwan. That might be more merciful given the cruelty of these Indians."

Elspeth looked at Alden and considered. *Did he mean this?* she thought.

Then slowly nodding assent, she said, "We will do as you ask." She spat her words out like poison.

"Very well then. It will not be long before our escort arrives. When they do, cover yourselves and these supplies. Stay quiet, all of you." He then turned and made his way down the road.

"Do not mind him, Mrs. MacEwan," said Broken Tree. "He is far less a man than he appears. Goodbye to you and to you as well, little ones. I will miss your company."

"Goodbye, Broken Tree," answered Elspeth carefully.

As they watched the tall lame Indian ride away, Aelwyd began to cry softly. Elspeth gathered her up in her arms and slowly rocked side to side. "Now, now, why do you cry, Aelwyd?"

The little girl wept on her words. "I am afraid of the Indians, Mother."

"Well, as you see, they are gone now," said Elspeth with a wide smile. "You needn't be afraid anymore, dear heart."

The drum of marching boots came up the road and with it sharp commands of British military order. Canteens, short barrel muskets, ammunition tins, and bayonets created an unfamiliar racket that brought a new fear to the children. Elspeth had to settle them down, and so she made a game of covering the supplies, and as added fun, they would also hide under the beaver and racoon hides. Alden came alongside the wagon.

"You must conceal yourselves now, Mrs. MacEwan. I will let you know when it's safe to come out."

Elspeth carefully covered herself and the children under the rancid hides as instructed. The scent from the beaver skins was particularly harsh.

Several soldiers arrived, surrounding the wagons. At one command, a few of the men tossed their haversacks into the wagon, landing heavily on Elspeth and the children. Aelwyd let loose a sharp cry that Elspeth was forced to stifle with a firm hand. She spoke softly and quietly, reassuring the children that all was well and that they would be safe and sound once the wagons came to a stop.

It was hot under the animal hides, and the twins started to fuss. Elspeth lay on one side of the boys, with David and Aelwyd on the other. Elspeth's calming words finally settled things as the wagons began crossing a wooden bridge. The weight of the heavy wheels rattled noisily over the wooden planks, bringing another eruption of whimpers and cries. They traveled on farther into the city. Peeking out from the heavy pelts with exaggerated relief, Elspeth looked about as the wagons proceeded through the city. Shops lining the broad streets were dark and colorless. There was trash piled up along the avenue in great quantity. Redcoats could be seen everywhere, all carrying Bess muskets.

There were few citizens other than the occasional ragged figure loitering beside a building. Those who cared, too, stared openly at the passing wagons, their faces displaying mild curiosity. They appeared bereft of emotion, no hostility, pity, or joy, just a passing interest as if an odd-looking cloud had floated by in the afternoon sky.

The four- and three-story structures that stood on either side of the street blocked the waning sun. Soon it would be night. They continued into a poor part of the city. Here were no grand buildings, barely a soul to be seen.

The wagon rolled to a stop in front of a ramshackle clapboard building in bad need of paint and repair. Elspeth threw back the furs, taking a breath of fresh air. Two soldiers waited on either side of the steps leading up to the door. Standing on the small porch in front of the door was a large woman wearing a simple brown dress. She held a candle in her grip.

"Good evening, Mrs. Weatherly," called out Alden. "Is everything ready?"

"Yes, sir, quite so. We done what was asked. The back room is all set up."

Alden turned to Elspeth. "Mrs. MacEwan, please exit the wagon and follow Mrs. Weatherly inside. You are to stay here until I return. Is that understood?"

Elspeth gave no reply, too tired to speak. Climbing out of the wagon took some effort, having been so long in a cramped position. David came next and then Aelwyd and the twins. They were all exhausted.

The children looked over the strange environment. Staring up at the two-story house, David said, "It's as tall as a tree, Mother. Do people live in there?"

"Yes, David, people do."

"This way," commanded Mrs. Weatherly. "I have one room in the back that should be enough for the lot of you. I don't care to have rebels in my house, but if Captain Alden says you must stay, then I suppose you must."

Elspeth took hold of the twins' hands and marched resolutely up the steps. David and Aelwyd followed. It was warm inside. As they passed a large open room, Elspeth spied four men standing silently, hat in hand. A small fire burned in a fireplace, with a large black pot hanging from a hook just above.

Mrs. Weatherly turned. "Follow me."

They walked a long dark hallway to the center of the house with doorways left and right. All were closed. Farther down was an open parlor. The voices of men and women could be heard. Near the end of the hall, the old woman unlocked the last door and opened it. Elspeth and the children examined the surroundings with some unease. The inside of the house, much like the outside, was in desperate need of repair and a coat of paint. The floorboards, loose underfoot, creaked loudly as they entered a dark room.

"You stay here," said Mrs. Weatherly briskly.

As the little group looked about the room, the old woman passed Elspeth the candle she was holding.

"You get one candle a week, that's all. This door stays locked till morning. I'll be back at sunrise."

"Food, water?" asked Elspeth.

"You're too late for that. You'll have to wait till morning. Don't be making any fuss here, Mrs. And mind these children of yours. I'll not have them running through my house."

Weatherly turned, slamming the door behind her. The lock was heard clearly as it engaged.

"Well," said Elspeth, "we are here. Let us make the best of it."

"I'm hungry, Mother," said David.

Eleventh Virginia

"Can you see them?"

The four young men stood atop a hill just outside the city of Philadelphia. William was pointing to a train of wagons entering the city over a broad wood bridge that crossed the Schuylkill River.

"Hard to say, William. There is a line of wagons down there now, and night's coming on. The only one it might be is that one up front with the escort. I see no one riding in the wagon though."

"I'll go down to take a look," said William.

"You cannot," answered Timothy. "The British are entering the city in force. Those redcoats down there will take you for a rebel. They can't hit much with those muskets, but they do get lucky at times."

"How else will I know?"

"We must see the colonel," said Timothy simply. "He'll know what to do."

"I cannot delay, Timothy. I must know if my family was brought here or they travel with the Shawnee."

"It's too late to know if they're with those wagons, William. I'm afraid that's all there is for it."

William looked about, unsure what he should do next. His friend Timothy Murphy felt a wave of pity for William. He could only imagine losing his own family, not caring for the thought in the least. "Come," he said. "I know where the regiment is camped. It's a way up that trail into the hills. We must hurry while there is still light."

As they approached the regiment campsite, an array of small fires glowed softly through the darkening hills. There were many. Walking along the trail that entered the camp, two men emerged from the shadows, each holding long rifles. A sharp query followed. "Who goes there?" called the voice clearly.

William, Timothy, and the Fallon brothers stopped short.

"It's Tim Murphy. I come back with horses and recruits."

"Tim!" cried the man on the left in obvious welcome. "Howdy-do there? By god, it's good to see you back."

"Who's that then?" asked Timothy, squinting through the shadows.

"It's me, Billy Pike," replied the voice.

"Well, hello, Bill Pike."

"Who's these fellas with you, Tim?"

"New recruits. I have three horses as well. Listen, Bill, I have something important for the colonel. Can you tell me where he is?"

"Sure can. He's down that path about five hundred yards or so. It takes a fork left. Just follow that, and you'll come to the big house. Colonel's headquartered there."

"Thanks, Bill."

Following the path, all four men dismounted and led their horses along on foot. As they came into the camp proper, a mass of men could be seen wandering about. Cooking fires were burning as the evening fell to full darkness. The scene that came to William was one of sheer chaos.

Officers dressed in dark blue jackets with a wide white sash across their breasts bellowed out orders in brisk fashion. The men were busy tending horses, cleaning long rifles, and packing powder and ball. More blue-coated officers inspected the population one campsite at a time, leaving no one unattended. Several men recognized Timothy as they passed by. Many called his name in greeting.

"By god if it aren't Tim Murphy," said one exceptionally large fellow, slapping Tim so hard on the back that he nearly bowled him over.

"Good to see you, Tim. Will you have a drink with me then?" he said, holding out a bottle.

"I'll have to come back for that, Michael," answered Timothy. "I have to see the colonel just now."

William looked about amazed at the number of men and burning fires making up the encampment. As night came on, the fires scattered all around defied the darkness. The general mood of these men was one of boisterous camaraderie—mostly.

An argument broke out in one group, obviously drunk. A fight followed between three or four of them. It was hard to tell who was winning given the tangle of men and those trying to break it up. Most of the witnesses to the scrap looked on with mild interest. It seemed disagreements were common among these men. Timothy paid no mind. These were rough men. They came from all walks of American life—hard-bitten hunters, farmers, Indian fighters, horsemen, blacksmiths, teachers, and river boatmen. Many hailed from Virginia, speaking in a folksy accent that William was unfamiliar with.

They wore heavy flannel britches, some of which were badly in need of stitching. Their hands and faces were filthy as bathing was near absent in their current situation. Leather jerkins covered their backs with threadbare shirts beneath. Some men wore cloth rags on their feet, while others had fine boots. Powder horns, much like William's, were slung over the shoulder to lay across the chest. They all carried a variety of hand weapons such as knives, hatchets, and tomahawks, the long rifle being the most common feature.

As William and the others traversed the length of the camp, it was clear a very large group of men made up a regiment.

"How many men are in this camp, Timothy?" asked William, surprised at the number he could see.

"A regiment carries about fifteen hundred souls as I understand, William. This is not the whole lot by any means."

William stopped short, gripping his horse reins tightly. He stared openly at two people standing beside a large cook fire. It was a man and a woman. The woman was tending a fair-sized cooking pot while the man carefully shoveled cut wood and kindling into the flame below.

Timothy looked back and stopped. The Fallons held up, nearly bumping into Timothy's rear.

"What is it, William?" asked Timothy.

"They are black Negroes," said William with wonder in his voice. "I have never seen a black Negro before. Are they slaves?"

"There are no slaves here, William, only freemen. That is Mr. Moses and his wife, Winifred. They bought their freedom from the colonel, and the first thing they did was join up."

"The colonel is a slave owner?" asked William, surprised.

"He is, but he treats his people fair, just as he would an indentured soul. After a turn, he sets them free. Usually, they pay their way out with the money earned while working his land."

"My mother says slavery is a sin, as bad as any. She's not much for indentured either."

Mr. Moses stood up and, seeing Timothy loitering with a small knot of young men, called out as he waved, "Hello, Mr. Timothy! You are back with us again, sir. I am happy to see it. The colonel will be right glad to have you back again as well."

"Hello to you, Mr. Moses, Miss Winifred." Timothy tipped his cap to the lady. "I'm off to see the colonel just now."

"Well then, say hello for me and take my good wishes."

"I will, Mr. Moses. Good evening to you, sir, Miss Winifred."

As they approached the house that headquartered Col. Daniel Morgan, it was plain to see a good deal of activity underway. The place was a veritable beehive of commotion. William and Timothy handed their reins to the Fallons. Timothy asked that they wait for his return.

"I'm hungry, Tim," said Myles.

"Don't worry about that. We got plenty."

Two soldiers in blue jacket uniforms with white lapels stood outside the front door, rifles at the ready. Two others lingered at the corners of the house with short-barreled Brown Bess muskets, bearing bayonets. Every window in the house was alight, and William was amazed by the sight of real glass in the frames. Uniformed men rushed in and out the door. Six horses tied up on the long hitching post just off the porch stood patiently. William could tell they were fine mounts, as fine as he had ever seen.

William and Timothy stepped up onto the porch, and the two uniforms crossed their rifles, preventing entrance.

"Hello, Tim," said one casually. "No entry now, officer meeting."

"Well, Ezra Hand, I think you better go inside and tell the colonel I have urgent news for him, most important." Then he winked at Ezra.

Ezra looked over at his companion, who nodded. He then turned and entered the house. After a few seconds, he stepped out. "Colonel said go on in."

The house was warm and covered in good light. There were candles and lanterns posted everywhere around the space. Maps seemed to be everywhere as well, some nailed to the walls while others were spread out over the floor. Still others covered the top of a large table sitting in the center of the room.

Four officers, all in uniform, stood beside the table. They peered intently at a map lying atop a scattered heap of yet more maps.

The uniforms varied from man to man, suggesting their different ranks. He had no idea what they were. Each man held a cocked hat under his arm, rendering the limb useless for anything else. Two of the officers had powdered wigs of white pulled tight on their scalp.

One gentleman wore a dark blue jacket with enormous brass buttons and a high collar trimmed in white. The collar was nearly touching his ears. His jacket was adorned with fine gold thread, a swirling pattern covering the lapel. He wore loose white britches wrapped in a red sash that bore an ornate buckle.

A black velvet scarf tucked neatly under his chin exposed the top of a frilled shirt, also white. The man's dark eyes darted about the room, examining everything. His face was thin with a long straight nose. His complexion was quite pale, almost wig white.

The light from a close lantern accentuated sharp angles of the officer's face. He turned his gaze on Timothy and William. As William studied the man, he realized he was not much older than himself.

Behind the big table set against the wall sat an enormous fellow dressed in a blue uniform jacket with wide tan lapels and a small black string tie. Epaulets adorned both shoulders. He wore no wig. His hair was nearly as white as those that did. His black mirrored boots rested firmly on the table edge as he leaned back, hands locked behind his head. A broad smile crossed his face when he saw Timothy as he and William approached.

"Tim Murphy!" cried the large man. He kicked his feet off the table and stood up.

"Gentlemen," he announced in loud command, "your attention if you will."

Every man in the room looked up, except for the well-dressed young officer. His eyes never left William.

"I would like you to meet my finest rifleman, Mr. Timothy Murphy. By god, it's good to have you back, Tim," continued the big man. "How did your mission go?"

"There was good and some bad, Colonel," answered Timothy, shaking his head.

"Let us hear it then."

"I could only gather three horses and two recruits, sir."

"And what of the rifles?"

"My father is in possession of the rifles, sir. He intends to let them out as you instructed."

"Good, good. And this fellow with you? A new volunteer?"

"No, sir, this is William MacEwan, a friend and neighbor."

"MacEwan? Well, I know that name." He turned to William. "Are you kin to Ian MacEwan?"

"I am, sir," answered William. "Ian MacEwan is my father."

"Well, that's fine, just fine. Have you come to join up then?"

William began, "I . . ." Then he stopped and turned, giving Timothy a pained look. "What am I to say?"

Timothy said, "William is trying to find his family, sir. The MacEwan homestead was attacked about five weeks ago by a band of Shawnee and British. Mr. Ian MacEwan was killed and William's family taken. The homestead was burned to the ground. We buried those we found.

"Some days later, my father and I returned to see if we could find the rifles Mr. MacEwan had secured. That's when we came on William, among the ashes. William believes, as do I, his mother and other members of his family have been taken either by the Shawnee or the British raiders. The Shawnee are moving fast north and east. We decided to follow the British wagons, hoping to catch them before they reached the city. We were unable to do so."

As Timothy told the tale, Morgan's face grew dark as if a storm were gathering over the man. Every eye was now focused on Timothy.

As Timothy explained, William felt the impact of each word. Simply hearing his father's name caused him to drop his head. Timothy finished, waiting on Morgan's response.

Morgan looked at William. "As I see your situation, Mr. MacEwan, you need to discover if your family was taken by English raiders to Philadelphia or by the Shawnee heading north. Do I have that correct?"

"Yes, sir," answered William.

"The wagons you followed, do you know where they came into the city?"

Timothy answered, "The north road, sir, over the Schuylkill Bridge."

"Corporal Hand!" shouted Morgan at the closed door.

The door swung open. Ezra Hand poked his head in. "Sir?"

"I want you to gather every scout we have watching the north road, the ones keeping an eye on the wagons entering the city over the north bridge. You understand?"

"Yes, sir."

"Bring them here quick as you can. Go."

"Yes, sir."

Morgan then spoke directly to Tim. "You gentlemen go around back and get some food. You must be hungry. Tell Mr. Bishop to fix something up for you. As soon as you're through, come back here. We'll find out if any of my men have seen your family being brought into the city by wagon or otherwise. Have no concern, Mr. MacEwan. We will know within the hour whether your family was seen entering Philadelphia."

"Thank you, sir," answered Timothy. Not knowing how to answer, William simply nodded.

William stopped as he was leaving. He stared openly at a large square painting mounted on the wall near the door. It was a simple landscape of a pond, a small house on the far side of the water surrounded by a copse of trees. A brace of ducks flew low over the water. The sky was brilliant blue with puffy white clouds that seemed so real that William felt as though he could see them traveling across the painted blue sky. He reached out his hand.

The well-dressed thin officer with the high-collared uniform stepped behind William. He had a noticeable limp. He asked quietly, "What is it you see, M. MacEwan?"

William turned. "It is a painting, sir. It is beautiful."

"Have you never seen a painting before?" asked the incredulous Frenchman.

"No, sir, not like this. The colors! You can almost hear the birds. And the pond! It looks so very real."

The young officer looked over at Morgan with a question on his face.

"William, may I introduce General Lafayette. The marquis has thrown his heart and soul into this fight we have with the British. He has volunteered to join us."

"A pleasure to meet you, sir," said William, shaking hands with the Frenchman.

"The pleasure is mine, M. MacEwan."

"It is not uncommon, General Lafayette," continued Morgan, "for a young man living in the western frontier to have never seen a painting like this before."

"I'm amazed," answered Lafayette.

"It looks as though young William is also amazed. You gentlemen go now and eat," said Morgan.

Outside, William and Timothy explained to Ezra about getting food. He directed them to the opposite side of the house. "Ask for Mr. Bishop. He runs the officer's mess."

A white overhead tent stood at the back of the house, inside of which was a long wooden table with loose benches arranged beside it. A short stocky man with very little hair on his head stood by a cooking fire with an enormous grill laid over the top.

"Kitchen is closed, gentlemen," called the hairless man over his shoulder.

Timothy said, "Colonel Morgan told us to come and get food. We are to ask for Mr. Bishop?"

"Is that so?" replied the cook. "And just who would you be that you deserve such consideration? You're not officers, that's certain."

"I am Tim Murphy, this is William MacEwan, and these two young gentlemen are new recruits, the Fallon brothers."

"So now I cook for recruits." It was not a question.

Timothy walked up to Mr. Bishop. "The colonel ordered us here, and I always follow my colonel's orders."

"I guess old Morgan knows what he's about," answered Bishop. "I do know your name, Mr. Murphy. The widow-maker? Come sit, and I'll fix up some catfish and corn cakes. You may go over to that barrel and get yourself some ale. Cups are on that barrelhead. You will clean every cup and dish before you leave."

"Yes, sir," answered Timothy. They sat at the table.

Myles looked at Tim and asked, "Why'd he call you the widow-maker, Tim?"

"It's what the redcoats call us riflemen. The long rifle can hit its mark at five times the distance of the English musket. We are the first in the field. Our orders are to pick off as many British officers and cannon crew as we can. When the British charge, we hightail it back behind our lines.

"Colonel says we're too damned important to get killed or captured. If the English ever did capture us, they'd hang us there and then. I do say this—we scare the devil out of those British officers and infantry. They never know when one will take a ball."

Mr. Bishop arrived just then with an enormous platter of catfish and corn cakes. In less time than it took to prepare, there was little left but bones and crumbs.

Alden

ALDEN MADE HIS way to regimental headquarters in a foul mood. The horse he rode was as beat as a drum, sway backed, and favored its left hindquarter. He had not had a bath or a glass of decent whiskey in nearly three months. As he entered the compound, a sergeant dashed up with a sharp challenge.

"I'm sorry, sir. No civilians allowed here."

"I'm delighted to hear it, Sergeant," snapped Alden. "I am Capt. Johnathon Alden of the Twenty-Third Light Dragoons. I am on special duty. I need a bath and a shave immediately. Where is General Howe?"

The sergeant looked Alden over with a curious eye. The man before him was dressed in wilderness attire, moccasins, beaver skin cap, and buckskin coat. He carried a military Brown Bess slung over his shoulder. He was filthy head to foot, and the animal he rode was broken down. The sergeant decided to ask a question of the supposed officer.

"General Howe just whipped Washington at a place called Brandywine Creek," said the sergeant. "Have you heard, sir?"

"No, I have not. Splendid news that. Now about the bath," said Alden testily.

"I'll have to check with the officer of the day, sir. Please wait."

Alden climbed off his horse and stretched his legs. He was tired, hungry, and thoroughly put out. His mission complete, Alden now only wanted a return to civilization. He needed a drink and, most of all, a woman. As he drew on his memory of the ladies he had taken to Philadelphia, the image of Elspeth MacEwan came to him.

The first time Alden laid eyes on Elspeth, he was drawn to her. For one thing, she was extraordinarily beautiful. When she turned her large brown eyes on him, he felt a jolt of desire. The more he saw of the beautiful Welsh woman, the more he wanted her.

When they met, her hair was combed back, pinned just so, framing her face. Alden found it quite fetching. She had been wearing a thin blue linen dress that was clean and well made. Held with a thin brown belt, it displayed her figure wonderfully. When she spoke, the words came in that sweet Welsh accent he found so enchanting. He smiled at the memory.

Elspeth had been polite but not overly so. When she smiled, it struck Alden. Her face simply lit up with the effort. Even Elspeth's eyes seemed to shine as she smiled. Alden shook his head in frustration. A captain of the Twenty-Third approached Alden as he stood holding the reins of his horse.

"May I have your name and rank, sir?" he asked politely.

"Capt. Johnathon Alden, Twenty-Third Light Dragoons. I have been on special duty."

"Alden?" queried the officer, looking into Alden's bearded face.

"Yes," answered Alden impatiently.

"It's me, John," said the captain. "Elliot Caversham! By god, man, where have you been? General Howe is most anxious to speak with you. He has sent a corporal every morning, inquiring after you." Caversham studied Alden carefully. "I say, are you well?"

"Yes, of course, Caversham, my apologies. I did not recognize you. I am merely tired. I simply must have a bath and shave. Can you help?"

"Of course, John."

After an hour, the sergeant drummed up a barber and a very hot bath. Alden began to feel human again.

Addressing the officer's valet, Alden barked, "I have no uniform here. All my personal belongings are still in New York. Can you find a uniform for me?"

"Yes, sir," replied the valet.

Twenty minutes later, the valet returned with the sergeant at arms.

"I am sorry, sir. It appears we have no spare uniforms here. We'll have to wait for the rest of the army to arrive."

Alden was too tired to argue. "Fine! The least you can do, Sergeant, is to find some decent clothing for me to wear."

The sergeant came back, again empty handed. "I am sorry, sir, but there is nothing available at this moment. Perhaps—"

Alden cut the man off, "Never mind, Sergeant."

Alden settled for civilian attire borrowed from Caversham. After dressing, he studied himself in the mirror. Pleased with the image, he slowly turned left and then right as he peeked over his shoulder. He never considered himself a dandy, but he also knew that a well-cut suit could turn a lady's head, just so.

The suit was the very latest style, light gray cotton with a split-tailed coat and a gold-colored vest. The shirt, pure white, carried lace ruffles running down the front as well as surrounding the shirt cuffs. They were a bit frivolous for Alden's taste but not too bad. The coat was trimmed in gold thread with many buttons arrayed down the lapel. Black shoes and white stockings completed the outfit. A dark blue ribbon tied his hair back with a gold cravat tucked neatly under his chin. He wore no wig.

The directions he received from Caversham for Howe's current location took him to a large Philadelphia mansion called Potstead House. As he marched down the quiet street, the eyes of posted redcoats followed him. He was relaxed and confident in his step.

As he approached the grand house, the sounds of music could be heard quite clearly. Caversham had confided in Alden that Howe had sent ahead for Mrs. Elizabeth Loring. Mrs. Loring was well known to most of the officers under Howe. She was a beautiful young woman much admired by the British officers on Howe's staff.

Mrs. Loring had left her husband, Joshua, behind in New York. Apparently, her cuckolded husband was content to remain in New York and profit from his new appointment. Howe had awarded Loring the lucrative commissary general position. It was a plumb appointment.

As Alden entered the mansion, a vast ballroom came into view on his right. The room itself took up most of the south end of the great house. Alden checked his appearance briefly in the entranceway mirror and carefully stepped into the ballroom.

Regimental officers occupied the dance floor along with a variety of well-dressed young ladies. The officers were the initial contingent entering Philadelphia upon Howe's arrival. It appeared they were settling in nicely. The musicians played an allemande as the dancers circled about the floor. This was followed seamlessly by a fancy minuet. Alden spied Howe's chief of staff in among a gaggle of ladies, half of whom were fanning themselves vigorously but perspiring nevertheless. Beside the chief of staff stood Gen. William Howe.

Alden passed within sight of General Howe. The man looked up and immediately realized the well-dressed civilian standing alone beside the punch bowl was Capt. John Alden. After several minutes, Howe disengaged himself from the ladies, making his apologies. As he walked toward Alden, he pointed to an open door on the opposite side of the ballroom. Alden nodded and followed.

Howe walked over to a small table and poured two large brandies. This was a courtesy few general officers afforded their juniors. Howe knew well that Alden had powerful friends and family.

"How have you been, Alden? Please have a seat," said Howe. "I imagine you would fancy a good brandy just now?"

Alden bobbed his head in agreement, taking the offered glass.

"Where is your uniform, Captain?" asked Howe, squinting at Alden's outfit.

"My auxiliary trunk is in New York, sir. I will have to wait for it to be delivered."

"See to it."

"Yes, of course, sir."

"Now, Captain, your mission?"

Alden began to describe how he fell in with a group of settlers heading west, one of whom was Ian MacEwan.

Howe held his hand up, halting Alden's discourse. "Please, Captain, spare the details. I have no time for anything more than principle points." The general continued, "Were you able to transfer the plans to the rebels?"

"Yes, sir. The documents were stolen by a man named Stevenson, a friend of Col. Daniel Boone. I observed him taking the papers from my belongings."

"Are you certain this Stevenson took them to General Washington?"

"Oh yes, sir, most definitely. He would have them in rebel hands very quickly indeed."

"Splendid. Now what of the rifles?"

"I'm afraid the rifles were destroyed, sir."

"What? By whom?"

"The Shawnee," replied Alden, averting his gaze. "They attacked the MacEwan homestead, killing everyone and burning the place to the ground."

"Good god! They were only supposed to help retrieve those weapons. What the devil happened?"

"When dealing with savages, sir, you never know what they'll do," said Alden, feigning ignorance.

"Bloody Indians," declared Howe with some frustration. "I wanted those rifles. I intended to send some of them to Lord North in London to demonstrate the accuracy and distance they are capable of. These damned widow-makers are picking my men off one by one."

Howe was losing his temper. "We lose two or three men a week. Officers!" he shouted. "Lord North and Skelton are dismissive of my concerns. I have explained time and again the clear danger of these long rifles, but do they listen? No."

"Perhaps you could send a few of these widow-makers to England instead of rifles, sir," said Alden casually. "They could demonstrate the weapons capability to Lord North, and the Crown would have the added pleasure of hanging the buggers."

Howe looked at Alden and raised an eyebrow. "Now that is a clever thought, Captain. We would have to capture some of them surely but, yes, a very clever idea, Captain."

Alden swirled his brandy glass in a lazy fashion, appreciating the aroma he had so missed. Yes, he thought it was indeed a clever idea—and one that may serve well.

Colonel Morgan

WILLIAM WALKED BESIDE Tim as they went in search of Lieutenant Pinch, the recruitment officer. Myles and Dermot lagged some few steps behind, gawking at the array of fighting men cleaning rifles, pouring molten lead into shot casts, and cutting strips of fine cloth patch for packing. This was a quiet, earnest effort that never seemed to cease.

The Eleventh Virginia regiment held twelve hundred men currently, five companies of volunteers from various parts of Virginia and neighboring colonies. Morgan's company of independent riflemen made up the remainder, almost all from the commonwealth of Virginia.

Regular volunteers carried the Brown Bess. This weapon could mount a bayonet and was quick to load. The Pennsylvania rifle, on the other hand, was slow to load and unable to hold a bayonet. For this reason, Morgan developed a stratagem that placed his riflemen on the front line at the beginning of a battle. After picking off several of the British officers and infantrymen from two hundred yards or better, they withdrew back to the American lines, reloaded, and stood their ground with the rest of the deployed regiment. This maneuver worked well.

"Where are we going?" asked William impatiently.

"I want to take Myles and Dermot to Lieutenant Pinch," replied Timothy. "He's our recruiting officer, and he'll need to take charge of them. Then we'll head straight back to the colonel."

William was silent at this. Still, Timothy could see that his friend was more than anxious to get back to Morgan and discover what the colonel had found. Evening fires were cooling now, with most of the men heading to their beds and homemade lean-tos. The camp was settling for the night.

"There's Lieutenant Pinch," said Timothy, pointing to an overweight officer leading a small group of men.

"I have two more for you, Lieutenant!" called Timothy.

Pinch turned and peered at the group of young men descending on him. "Is that you, Murphy?" asked Pinch.

"Yes, sir, Lieutenant. A couple of my neighbors here are joining up. These fellows are the Fallon brothers, and you will find them to be fine shots with a long rifle."

"I'll be the judge of that, Mr. Murphy. You two line up with these other men and follow me. We'll feed you and get you a bed tonight. In the morning, we will test Mr. Murphy's judgment of your shooting skill."

Myles and Dermot looked at each other and smiled—more food, and they get to shoot in the morning. They were delighted.

Back at headquarters, Ezra Hand was once again attending the door. "Colonel says go right in, Tim."

"Gentlemen!" exclaimed Morgan at the sight of William and Timothy. "Do come in."

Along the wall stood a line of six men, each leaning on a long rifle, hat in hand. They looked Tim and William over closely but said nothing. Beside Morgan's desk stood the tall narrow Frenchman, Lafayette.

Morgan stood up. "I have asked these men what hours they stood on the north road. They all agree they were assigned the watch from noon to dark. Is this the time that interests you, Mr. MacEwan?"

"Yes, sir," answered William.

"Well then, ask your questions."

"Have any of you seen either a woman or small children in the wagons entering the city?" asked William hurriedly.

Appearing mildly confused, the four men traded looks until one piped up, "Aye, I did see a woman come through about dusk. She was sitting high up with one foot on the buckboard, so I had a good view."

"What did this woman look like?" queried William, interrupting the man.

"Heavy," he said simply.

"Surely, you can do better than that, Private," said Morgan sternly.

"Well, sir, she was big for a lady."

A few chuckles followed this as a second man chimed in, "My name's Patterson, sir, and I, too, saw this woman just about that time."

"Well, that's fine, Mr. Patterson. Can you provide a more detailed description of this woman?"

"Well, sir, she wore a gray dress of sorts. She looked rough for a lady, that's for certain, and her hair was salt white. She had one boot up on the wagon buckboard, as Benjamin here said, and the other slung over the side of the wagon. She was driving the horses."

"Would this be your mother, Mr. MacEwan?" asked Morgan.

William wagged his head in disappointment. It was clearly not Elspeth.

"Did you see any children?" continued Morgan.

"None, sir," answered one as the others shook their heads in unison.

"Did you notice anything strange as the wagons passed?"

"There were two wagons that looked a bit out of place, sir," answered Patterson hesitantly. "They seemed to be hauling a load of hides, but they were escorted by a British platoon. I thought that odd, sir. I told my lieutenant so."

"Yes indeed. However, the British have been smuggling goods into the city regularly. Those wagons are frequently protected. Is there anything else you wish to ask, Mr. MacEwan?"

"No, sir," answered William sadly, "there is not."

"Well then, it is settled," said Morgan. "The Shawnee have your family, Mr. MacEwan. I expect you will want to go after them."

"Yes, sir. May I ask the loan of a horse, Colonel?"

"Of course. I'll have one ready for you first thing in the morning."

"I wish to leave now, sir," answered William sharply.

Morgan ignored William and turned to the scouts. "You men are dismissed."

After the scouts filed out, Morgan turned to William. As gently as he could, he said, "I know your desire is to leave now, Mr. MacEwan, but I would no more send you out alone, or even with Timothy here, after a full band of Shawnee warriors than I would send my own son. For one thing, both of you are flat on your feet. A blind man can see that. For another, if you wish to use one my horses, you can at least have the courtesy to heed my advice, and my advice is for the both of you to get a night's rest. I have long-range scouts out west and north of here, and I receive daily reports from them. You will want to know which way the Shawnee are traveling, would you not?"

"Yes, sir," admitted William reluctantly.

"I am able to loan M. MacEwan a horse, Colonel," offered Lafayette. "I have three here. You are welcome to any one of them, sir."

"Very gracious of you, General, but unnecessary. I will provision Mr. MacEwan and provide a good animal. I only ask that he rest first and, if possible, wait for more information.

"As I turn this matter over in my mind, I am considering Mr. MacEwan's situation. It would not be beyond my power to provide four good men to travel alongside Mr. MacEwan. I have had more than one experience with the Shawnee, General Lafayette. They are exceedingly dangerous."

William looked up at Morgan, resignation crossing his face.

"What say you, Mr. MacEwan? Will you wait until we have more confident information?"

"I will, sir," answered William reluctantly.

"Good, good," said Morgan. "And now, gentlemen, I would offer you a drop of General Lafayette's French Brandywine. He carried it all the way from his homeland as a gift. And I thank you for it, sir. It is very fine. What do you say, gentlemen?"

Timothy Murphy took a step closer to Morgan. "No need to ask me, Colonel. I'll take whatever you allow."

"And you, Mr. MacEwan?"

"Why, yes, sir, I could use a bite," answered William clearly.

Each man was given a tumbler. Morgan poured the golden liquid into their cups. They all agreed it was the best whiskey they had ever had. Lafayette smiled broadly, nodding his approval.

"How long will you wait for General Howe to emerge from the city, Colonel?" asked Lafayette casually.

"As long as it takes, I imagine," answered Morgan. "It is vexing to sit and wait like this. There is little choice otherwise. I only wish I knew what the British were planning. I know my boys will fight given the chance. They are best in a fight. This sitting and waiting is more difficult on them than the havoc of battle."

William placed his cup on the desk and watched it tumble on its side. "I may have knowledge of British plans, Colonel," said William with a slight hitch in his voice.

"What did you say, Mr. MacEwan?"

"I had forgotten to give these to you, Colonel. I do not know if they are true or false."

"Speak plainly, Mr. MacEwan. What do you know of British plans?"

William reached into his pack and withdrew a leather wallet. As he passed it to Morgan, a colorful feather fell to the floor.

Morgan took the wallet and carefully opened it. As he studied the papers, he let out an audible bark. "General Lafayette, come see this."

Lafayette leaned in close to the documents and began reading. He looked at Morgan with a small smile, and then both men turned on William.

"Where did you get these, Mr. MacEwan?"

"From a man named Stevenson, sir. He stole them."

"Do you mean Olaf Stevenson, the longhunter?"

"Mr. Stevenson is my friend. When we traveled to the Cherokee village, it was with a man named Alden. This Alden had been sent to the village to arrange a treaty between the British and the Cherokee. As you can see, he succeeded."

"So Stevenson stole these papers from a man named Alden?"

"Yes, sir."

"Why didn't Olaf bring them to me?"

"Mr. Stevenson was wounded during a fight between the Shawnee and Cherokee. He gave the papers to me and asked that I bring them to my father. When I returned home, I found my father buried and our home burned to the ground. I have carried these papers ever since. I had forgotten about them entirely."

"Why do you say they may be false, Monsieur?" asked Lafayette.

"I believe the man who carried them was himself false. He lied to us. He signed a treaty with Black Feather and yet ran away when the

Cherokee were attacked. The man was a liar and a coward. I could never trust the word of a man such as this."

Morgan and Lafayette looked at each other.

"A British spy, you think, Lafayette, meant to deceive us with these documents?" asked Morgan.

"Yes," replied Lafayette, "it is possible. The British are adept at deception, especially in war."

"William, you said the treaty with the Cherokee was real, did you not?"

"Yes, sir, as I understood from Mr. Stevenson."

"Well then, we must assume these plans are real as well. Stevenson would not miss such a fact. Wouldn't you agree, General Lafayette?"

"Not necessarily, Colonel. These plans could be a ruse while the treaty lends validity to them. It is something General Washington has cautioned us about in the past. A half-truth works better than a full lie, no?"

"Yes, George is wily about such things," said Morgan as he scratched his chin in contemplation.

"What do you say, William?" asked Morgan.

"I would trust nothing from Alden beyond the fact that he exists. For all I know of the man, his name may not even be Alden."

"Private Hand!" bellowed Morgan.

Ezra darted into the room, the ever-present rifle clutched in his fist. "Yes, sir."

"I need a messenger, Private, quick as you can."

"Sir," answered Ezra, turning about and disappearing into the night.

The Murphy Clan

"WHY DO WE leave this place, Stevenson?" asked Little Cornstalk. "Our shadows grow longer. William will come to his home soon."

They were traveling north of the MacEwan homestead. It was early morning. The sun, just beginning to rise, cast tall shadows across the well-worn path. Fall was coming, and it looked to be a cooler day.

"Yes," answered Stevenson as he thumped along the trail. "Fall is coming. We cannot wait here any longer. I must know what happened at William's home."

"We will find, William?" asked the girl.

"I hope to, yes."

"What is this place we go to?"

"The Murphys'," replied Stevenson shortly as he continued along.

"I do not know this tribe, Murphys. Are they fierce people?"

"You could say that," answered the older hunter.

After crisscrossing the MacEwan property and finding five fresh graves, Olaf Stevenson turned his mind to a range of possibilities. He concluded that some of William's family had been killed, others taken. This he based on the small information he had of the MacEwans and the many tracks surrounding the ruins. The discovery of a three-pound ball from a small cannon was a mystery to the seasoned hunter. He had never known Indians to use cannon.

Stevenson had no idea if William was alive or buried in one of those five graves. From their time on the trail together, Stevenson had grown fond of William MacEwan, and so he held this unhappy thought to himself. He had no wish to upset Little Cornstalk with such ideas. The notion of it was unsettling enough for him, never mind the girl.

They spent five days waiting for William, but not one soul came up the eastern trail—no hunters, trappers, settlers, or Indians. It was the same from the direction of the western gap. Although he had never been to the MacEwan homestead before his visit with Daniel Boone, he knew this was unusual as the MacEwan place was popular among such men.

"Do we travel far, Stevenson?" asked Little Cornstalk.

"It is some miles. We should be there midday tomorrow."

"If you were not so fat and slow, we would be there quick."

Stevenson stopped in his tracks and turned on the girl. "Do you wish to find William?" he asked angrily.

Little Cornstalk looked up in surprise at the longhunter. She nodded. "Yes," she answered.

"Then you will have to trust this fat old man."

"Yes," she repeated.

***

The Murphy settlement was built much the same as Boonesborough, the fort that Stevenson's good friend Daniel had built in spring 1776.

Murphy had designed his settlement to withstand attack and was well built to do so. On more than one occasion, the Shawnee chief, Blackfish, had tested the Murphy Fortification and failed in every attempt. Knowing this, Stevenson held fast to the idea that if anyone knew about the assault on the MacEwan place, it would be Connor Murphy.

As they moved along the trail, Stevenson could plainly follow the tracks of horses and men. They were days old and traveled in both directions, north and south. He picked up his pace. Little Cornstalk took notice of the increased stride and felt a surge of affection for the longhunter.

"I am sorry, Stevenson," said the girl.

Without turning, Stevenson said, "No need. Just keep up."

Little Cornstalk smiled to herself.

"Seamus Murphy!" hollered the big woman in the green linen dress. "Stop whacking your sister with that stick and get to those pigs as I told you!"

The boy quickly dropped the offending rod and dashed in the direction of the Murphy pigsty.

Murphy-Borough, as the residents of the settlement took to calling it, was perched atop a fifty-acre wide, sloping plateau roughly the shape of a square. The compound enclosure ran along the perimeter of the flat top hill more than seventy feet above the surrounding narrow valley. A swift running river ran just to the east.

The inner ring of the settlement was surrounded with a heavy stockade three timber thick and fourteen feet high. Beyond the valley lay dense forest packed with trees barely wide enough to allow a horse to pass. Two wide paths leading north and south wound up the slope in lazy fashion, allowing carts and wagons to pass into the settlement. Any unwanted visitors emerging from the tree line could be seen and immediately challenged. The elevated platform that ran along the stockade was manned by twelve vigilant watchmen at all hours, day and night. To ensure the safety of the Murphy-Borough folk, Connor Murphy had come into possession of two navy swivel guns that had once resided on a British man-of-war. They were mounted on posts along the stockade.

Bustling activity was near constant in the settlement. There was a trading house, a tavern, a blacksmith, and three large shelter barns. Smokehouses and privies lined the outer enclosure. Small tidy cabins stood against the inner wall of the enclosure each with a low, slanted roof tilting inward toward the center of the fort. Here was a total of forty-three families, making up the bulk of the population of Murphy-Borough, which at times held just under one hundred souls.

Most of the occupants were farmers transplanted from the east. The surrounding fields displayed this. Their constant tilling and tending produced large vegetable gardens and row after row of corn, wheat, barley, and hay. It all lay across the outer boundary of the settlement.

The livestock consisted mostly of chickens, pigs, milk cows, horses, a small flock of sheep, and four goats. Beef cattle were driven in from the east on occasion, but most of the meat consumed in Murphy-Borough was hunted locally or slaughtered from their thriving stock.

As Stevenson and Little Cornstalk came out of the trees, walking toward the main gate, a single rifle shot rang out. Little Cornstalk ducked down, scanning the landscape.

"It is all right, Little Cornstalk," announced Stevenson. "They are just letting folks know someone is approaching. They will not harm us."

The girl was not so certain. She stood up with some apprehension and continued to look about anxiously. Stevenson wisely held his rifle aloft and called out his own name as this was the preferred method of hailing the fort. Several faces appeared between the sharp-ended stockade timber. Two or three loud greetings came from behind the wall, and the main gate began to open.

As they came into the enclosure, a group of hunters stepped up and openly greeted Stevenson with a loud series of hellos and back pounding. Stevenson was a regular visitor here in Murphy-Borough as well as Boonesborough.

Little Cornstalk looked around the closed-in space and immediately felt confined in a way she had never experienced. Every direction she looked, there was a wall of timber. A loud clang erupted from her right, and she jumped suddenly at the unfamiliar sound. No more than twenty yards away stood a large heavyset man wearing a leather apron, swinging a mallet, and striking it down onto a piece of steel trapped between large pincers and a flat anvil. Sparks flew with each blow of the hammer. Once again, Little Cornstalk jumped at the ringing sound.

"He is a blacksmith, Little Cornstalk. There is nothing to fear from him," said Stevenson, attempting to calm the girl.

Standing on the wide porch outside the tavern, the woman in the green linen dress called out to Stevenson, "Lord save us, if it isn't Olaf Stevenson come back. You are just in time for food as usual. I'm putting it down now, fat sow belly and panned cakes, plenty of it too. Come in, come in."

"Hello to you, Mrs. Murphy. I do have an empty belly," said the old hunter. "And we have had a long walk."

As Stevenson and Little Cornstalk approached, the earsplitting clang continued behind them, forcing the girl to flinch with each blow. She walked two steps behind Stevenson, so close that she bumped into him when he halted in front of the tavern porch.

"Now who is this with you, Olaf?" asked Kathleen Murphy. "Don't tell me you have taken a woman?"

"No, Mrs. Murphy. This is a friend. Her name is Little Cornstalk. She is the daughter of Chief Black Feather of the Cherokee clan."

Kathleen Murphy smiled at Little Cornstalk. "Come in then, child," she said and waved her arm at the two visitors, suggesting they should follow.

Little Cornstalk peered in wonder at the white man's fort. Clean, wide paths wandered throughout the settlement, occupied with busy people performing all manner of activity. Men pushed wheelbarrows loaded with corn, wheat, and enormous carrots. Harvest season had just yet begun. This year's crop would be a good one. Soon it would all be pulled from the earth. There would be aplenty for the winter and beyond. There was much to do yet and many hands to do it.

Children played in the open grassy sections between the cabins and paths. The young girls ran about, twirling sticks with bright ribbons attached and squealing in delight as a host of little boys chased after them.

Stepping inside the warm tavern, a group of men greeted Stevenson once again. One passed the old hunter a tankard with rum and cool water. He thanked his fellows and took a large swallow. One drunken hunter sidled up near Little Cornstalk, studying her frankly.

"I know this girl," stammered the drunk as he sloshed his rum on the floor. "They call her Little Mother. She's a Cherokee witch and a pretty one too. Stevenson? How is it you come by her?"

Stevenson ignored the drunk and addressed Kathleen Murphy.

"I would have a word with Connor if it's not too much trouble, Kathleen. It is most important."

"Is it now?" replied Kathleen. "If I'm not mistaken, he's serving the bar round back, Olaf. I'll put your Indian girl at a table and bring her some food."

"I thank you, Kathleen. Round the turn, you say?"

"Aye."

Stevenson walked past the long serving bar as it turned near ninety degrees, continuing the length of the building and ending at the far wall.

This was the largest tavern in western America. Connor Murphy was adamant about that when he built the place. Back in Ireland, the public house of his youth was tiny in comparison, barely able to hold more than ten drinking men. Murphy's Tavern would be no hovel half buried in the ground. The ceiling was over eight feet high, studded with crossbeams that hung several candle mounts from heavy hooks. The large room could easily hold forty or even fifty in a push, good for the customers and good for business.

Connor Murphy scrubbed the bar top with a rough cloth, singing along with the effort. Stevenson could not understand the Gaelic, but he appreciated the tune.

Looking up, Murphy stopped scrubbing and singing. "Olaf, you old gun. Where have you been keeping this long summer? We have missed your company. Have you seen my Kathleen?"

"I have, Connor. How are you and yours?" asked Stevenson politely.

"Fine, fine. What brings you about, Olaf?"

"The MacEwans," answered Stevenson simply.

"Aye, that was a bad one. Shawnee it was with a band of city highwaymen. Bad lot that."

"Well, that explains the cannonball at least," muttered Stevenson.

"The British hand out small cannon to the loyal militia. Even the bad ones get them."

"What happened, Connor?"

"Two Catawba Indians that trade with us came along and told the tale. Shawnee and some British irregulars attacked the MacEwan place, killing everyone and burning it all to the ground.

"Naturally, I rode straight down there. I knew Ian had brought back rifles from Philadelphia. He and I were to set them out among the men willing to fight with Mr. Washington and his army. When I got there, I found Ian dead and scalped in front of his burned-down cabin. There were four other bodies there as well, but we couldn't identify them too good. They were badly burned. Anyway, me and my boys buried them best we could, put up some crosses, and laid heavy stone atop the graves. It was all we could do. I looked for the rifles but found nothing. There was a small hide up on the side of a hill covered in scat and manure, but it was empty. After that, we came back here."

Stevenson listened intently to his friend and realized that Murphy could well have buried William without knowing who it was he had put in the ground.

"Was there no one else that came along?" he asked anxiously.

"Well now, when I got back home here, I kept thinking on those rifles, so I decided to go back and take another look. That's when we ran into William. The boy nearly shot me!"

"William!" cried Stevenson aloud. "He's alive?"

"I'll say he is. Him and my boy Timothy are tracking that pack of cutthroats. The hand of God could not restrain William. They took three of my horses and two of my neighbor's sons, heading for Philadelphia."

Stevenson smiled broadly, his frame suddenly relaxing. He placed a hand on Murphy's shoulder, saying, "I need a drink, Connor. Whiskey or rum will do."

Kathleen Murphy sat Little Cornstalk down at a rough top table.

"Do you speak English, deary?" she asked.

"Yes," answered Little Cornstalk. "My father and mother learned this to me. I have good English. I have new words every day." She smiled at Kathleen.

"Well, you sit right here, and I'll bring some food. Are you hungry?"

"Yes, I am hungry."

"I'll be back quick as a turn. You just wait here, deary."

Two hunters who were bunched up along the tavern bar stared at Little Cornstalk, studying the girl intently. One pulled his cap and began strolling toward the table where she sat. He approached slowly, placing his tankard down on the hardwood.

"What's your name, girl?" asked the hunter.

Little Cornstalk did not answer.

"I asked your name, Indian girl. Your Cherokee, that's certain. My name is Polk. I am a hunter hereabouts."

The man took two steps closer and leaned in over the table, placing his face close to Little Cornstalk's. "Don't you speak English, girl? I heard you talking to Mrs. Murphy. Come now, I only ask your name."

Little Cornstalk stared straight ahead, ignoring the man. She could barely stand the odor of this person. He reeked of whiskey, animal skins, and human waste. She would not speak to this person. Suddenly, the hunter banged his fist on the table, startling Little Cornstalk. "Speak, damn you. You have nothing to fear from me."

The blade appeared in the girl's hand so swiftly that the smelly hunter barely had time to register the event. Little Cornstalk swung the knife downward, driving it into the tabletop with a solid thunk perilously close to the man's hand.

"Go away, white man," said Little Cornstalk softly.

"You heard the girl, Polk," said Kathleen. She stood behind the man and, being nearly six feet tall, towered over him. "Go back to your rum while you still have all your parts."

The man grabbed his tankard and retreated to the bar as swiftly as he could, mumbling to himself about wicked women and mad Indian girls.

Kathleen placed a plate of fried pig belly and panned cakes in front of Little Cornstalk. The girl deftly pulled the knife from the table and slid it into the leather sheath tied to her belt. She smiled again at Kathleen, nodding her approval. Picking up a slip of bacon, she chewed it gratefully. As she moved to place another piece in her mouth, she suddenly looked up at Kathleen Murphy with surprise and promptly threw up over the plate of food and table.

"God in heaven, girl, what ails you? Come," said Kathleen, taking Little Cornstalk by the hand and pulling her toward the kitchen.

As Kathleen and Little Cornstalk approached Stevenson and Connor Murphy, the women found the two older frontiersmen laughing aloud and swallowing great gulps of sugar buttered rum.

"Olaf Stevenson!" shouted Kathleen. "What in god's good name have you done to this girl?"

Stevenson turned and with a bewildered expression asked simply, "What?"

"You heard me. What have you done with this young woman? I cannot believe a man of your standing would stoop this low and at your age!"

Kathleen was in a fine lather, that was clear, but Stevenson had no clue about what the woman was railing on.

"How could you do such a thing?" hollered the tall Irishwoman.

"What the devil are you barking about, Kathleen?" shouted Stevenson in return. "I have done nothing to this girl, nothing."

"Then how did she become pregnant, Olaf Stevenson? Immaculate conception?"

Stevenson's jaw dropped two inches as he turned on Little Cornstalk, who was smiling broadly at everyone.

"Good lord, you don't think . . ."

"What else is there to think? You come among us with this girl and she pregnant. Men such as you should be horsewhipped."

"Now just wait right there, Kathleen Murphy. I'll have you know I have done no such thing with this girl. Little Cornstalk is here to find William MacEwan. And if anyone is responsible for her condition, it is he and he alone."

"William," repeated Little Cornstalk gleefully. "He is coming?"

"William MacEwan, you say?" said Kathleen, scratching the back of her head. "Is he even old enough?"

"I would have to say yes, Mother, considering the circumstance," piped up Connor Murphy.

"Yes, William MacEwan," repeated Stevenson firmly. "And before you consign me to the devil, Kathleen Murphy, I would get the straight of things."

"William," repeated Little Cornstalk, still smiling.

The Weatherly House

ELSPETH BEGAN EXPLORING the room. Morning light filtered in through a small window. The view overlooked a patch of ground at the rear of the house, grading downward at a steep angle toward the river. The property was enclosed by a tall white slat fence. Two British redcoats lazily wandered the perimeter, shouldering muskets. Occasionally, they would stop and drink from the water barrel along the side of the house. Once in a bit, they would have a short chat between rounds, each taking a turn every thirty minutes or so. They seemed to have little interest in their duty.

The house was quiet now. The night before, loud music and even louder conversation could be heard from nearly every corner of the building. Elspeth realized the house was essentially a brothel. Loud thumps, breaking glass, and an almost continual peal of laughter rang throughout until the early morning. A drunken brawl broke out at one point, but it quickly ended. The belligerents were ejected with a slam of the front door. Elspeth heard the entire exchange.

It seemed the place catered to British soldiers as well as civilian customers. This type of house was not unfamiliar to Elspeth. She had seen a few in her life. She felt pity for the women and shame for the men.

Elspeth had not slept the night as she considered her situation. The children were cold, and the hardwood floor afforded no comfort. She found a small door along the back wall of the room near the window, revealing itself in the morning light. She discovered two thin blankets stored within the small space. As she pulled the blankets out to cover the twins who were sleeping, a loud rap came at the door, and it swung open with a bang. The old Weatherly woman stood in the frame.

Elspeth tried to hide the blankets, thinking she might take them away.

"Why are we held prisoner here?" she asked Weatherly sharply.

"Couldn't say, missy," answered the older woman casually.

"What do you mean? You have no idea why we are held here against our will?"

"All I know is you and yours are rebel trash. Captain says to keep you penned up here until he comes back. And that's what I'll do. I'm well paid to hold you, and I intend to earn my money. Fact is I would have done it free if I'd known you was rebels. One of your bloody soldiers killed my Gerald. I'd see you all hanged if I had my way. That's a wish I make daily."

The venom that spewed from the old woman's mouth startled Elspeth. She was not used to such. Elspeth was on her hands and knees after laying the blanket for the twins. She stared intently at the old woman. Suddenly, she jumped to her feet and aimed straight for the hag in the dark brown dress.

Quick as wink, Mrs. Weatherly pulled a pistol from her dress pocket and backed up two steps. "You stay back, missy," she said, pointing the barrel directly at Elspeth's chest.

Elspeth stopped looking down the black barrel.

"You might get past me, missy, but you'll not get by those soldiers outside. Captain killed your husband, and if you go the same, who'll care? Your little ones, heh?"

Elspeth bowed her head and tried to calm herself. David was standing by the twins, bobbing his head between his mother and the woman filling the doorframe. Aelwyd sat along the back wall with a confused look. The old woman reached out with her left foot and pushed a small bucket into the room, all while holding the pistol on Elspeth.

"Cooked potatoes and a few pieces of bacon here. This is all you get. Any more food you want while you are here will be worked for, understood?"

Elspeth slowly nodded.

"Can the two older ones work?" asked Weatherly, indicating the children.

"David can. Aelwyd can do some chores, but she won't be able to do heavy work. She's too young."

"And what about you?"

"I can clean, launder, and cook if that is what you mean."

"I have a room upstairs if you like," said the old woman with a wily sneer. "You look to have a fine body and a comely face. The men would like you." She laughed.

Elspeth slowly walked toward the open door. "That would not be to my liking, thank you. I am a married woman."

Weatherly laughed again. "Suit yourself, missy. Half the women here are married, not that I care one way or the other. I have a laundry downstairs. There are two Negro slaves doing the work now, and they are poor at it, keep getting things mixed up. If you take care of that, I'll see to it you and your children are fed at the least."

"I can do that," answered Elspeth.

David was given the job of hauling water and supplying wood for the fireplaces throughout the house. He was required to split wood and kindling and then to clean the fireplace gratings and pile in new wood as needed. The ash would then be used for the making of soap. With the weather just turning cool, it was light work for the boy.

Mrs. Weatherly instructed Elspeth to head down to the laundry as soon as she was finished eating. Every bit of food was consumed in short order. Afterward, Elspeth told Aelwyd to mind the twins while she was away. The door to their room was now unlocked. As Elspeth opened it, a young Negro woman stood directly across from her in the hall.

"Mrs.," said the young girl, nodding, "you to follow me, please."

Elspeth was taken down to the laundry, where she found three huge wood tubs, one hot and two cold. The smell of lye soap filled the air, pinching her nostrils. Alongside the lye was store-bought Castile soap, but this was used sparingly due to the expense.

The lye soap was manufactured in a small shed in the back of the yard. Lye was being leached out of hardwood ash that David supplied when mixed with a concoction of oil or spoiled butter. The slurry was then poured into molds and left to harden.

Dozens of uniforms and civilian garments were spread over a long wooden table. Simple waxed marks identified each as it passed into first the hot tub, then a cold one, and finally the last cold rinse tub. Vigorous scrubbing by the two Negro girls was performed throughout the process. The uniforms with matching britches and shirts all hung on a thin rope just outside the door to the yard.

Mrs. Weatherly entered the space. "These Negros keep getting the uniforms mixed. I have tried to remedy this, but it seems an impossible task. They simply cannot do it properly," she complained.

Elspeth watched the process for a few moments, leaned over, and picked up one of the uniforms marked with wax. She carefully turned the coat over, examining the interior for identifying features. She walked down the long table and picked up one uniform jacket after the other, doing the same.

Turning on Weatherly, she asked, "Can these women read letters?"

Weatherly stroked her chin. "I would think not. Whatever difference could that make? I am asking them to wash these clothes, not read them."

"The wax marked on these uniforms melts off in the hot water. See here," said Elspeth, showing Weatherly a pair of britches. "These uniforms are marked by the owner. Some have a simple thread sewn in as an initial or a pattern of their own making. Soldiers are required to mark their clothing for just this reason. If these women could read letters, they would be able to separate them properly without getting them mixed up. The wax they mark with becomes unusable. Little wonder they are confused."

"So do something about it," said Weatherly sharply.

"I will do my best."

Within two hours, Elspeth had all the uniforms and linen smallclothes properly arranged and sorted. She showed the two laundresses the identifying marks and explained their meaning.

"I don't read any, Miss. Never did," said one girl named Bell.

"Well, we can deal with that later. For now, I just want you to recognize the marking inside the woolen jackets and match them with the britches, shirts, and small clothes. Do you understand?"

"Yes, Miss."

David walked back into the steaming laundry room and dropped the empty bucket he had filled with hardwood ash. He looked up at Elspeth.

"Mother, is Father dead?" he asked simply.

"This is not the time, David. We can talk about it when we get back to the room."

David shook his head in negation. He screwed up his face, giving his mother a hard look.

The Shawnee Trail

WILLIAM HAD BEEN riding two days over hard ground. The mare was tiring, slowing her pace to a lazy walk. William tried to persuade the animal to a livelier trot, but she was just too worn. If slowing up did little to help his horse, it at least allowed his four companions to catch up.

The four men whom Colonel Morgan sent along with William were all volunteers. Colonel Morgan chose the best long-range scouts in his company. Although able, not one turned down Morgan's request.

Arron Pendleton was the oldest. At forty-two years of age, he carried scars from a number of Indian encounters as well as two hot fights with the British. Arron had faced off time and again against the Abenaki, Algonquin, and Shawnee in his earlier years. He was a seasoned fighter, one of many making up the backbone of Morgan's riflemen.

Next in age came Peter Small, a westerner from the Kentucky territory, born not far from the MacEwan homestead. Peter was new to the army. Still, he took to it readily. He could sit the saddle for days at a time without complaint. His bright blue eyes seemed to catch everything. He was a crack rifle shot as well. Wearing a constant smile, he chattered on continually. As far as William was concerned, he was the wordiest man he had ever met.

"That man's mouth goes like a duck's ass," mumbled William after meeting Peter.

Wallace Grant and Bowling Miller were two Virginians. Each man was tied to Morgan through family. They followed the colonel wherever he led. It looked to William that Wallace and Bowling were near to being permanently attached to each other. You never saw one without seeing both.

William walked his horse just east of the north trail, studying the ground closely for sign. The five men had cut the Shawnee trail twice so far, but the tracks were getting old and fading quickly. It was clear the

Shawnee were at least four days ahead and traveling fast. Arron trotted up to William and pulled his cap.

"The others are coming up back of us. They look to be in a hurry. We should tuck ourselves in those trees for a bit. Have some food and a little shade. It will do no harm."

"What do you make of these signs, Mr. Pendleton?" asked William.

"They are heading north for certain. I'll send Wallace and Bowling up ahead. They're good at sign. That Bowling could track a racoon through treetops."

As the two men waited inside a thick hammock of pine and brush, Arron chewed noisily on a lump of pemmican, a mix of tallow, dried meat, and berries. William liked pemmican, but he could never eat it uncooked like Arron. He had to have his pan-fried at the least.

"How long have you been looking for your family, William?" asked Arron with a full mouth.

William looked at the soldier and bowed his head. He thought about the question as Arron patiently waited, chewing the tough ball of pemmican with intensity.

Arron Pendleton was thin as a blade of grass with low-cut moccasins and heavy leather trousers. His shirt was cotton white with delicate string ties to fasten. He wore a buckskin jacket held together with long strips of black leather. His face, thought William, was as sharp as a knife. A scruff gray beard filled in his hollow cheeks. He appeared dreadfully thin. His brown eyes were rheumy and stood wide open as he waited with anticipation on William's reply.

"I am uncertain of the date, Mr. Pendleton. I would guess it has been several weeks and a bit. I have not counted the days."

"You will," said Arron, nodding. "I have spent many a day chasing Indians. They are dirty creatures without the soul of a white man. They are much like the beasts that roam these woods. They'd just as soon roast and eat you. That's not the worst of it."

Thinking of his family, William winced at the words.

Wallace and Bowling came up over the rise, quickly followed by Peter blue eyes. Arron waved the two Morgan relatives on, urging them to take care and stay with the Shawnee tracks if possible.

Peter pulled up and began a nonstop dialogue that included not only the fact that a rider was coming up from behind them but also the morning weather, the tree line north, and the direction the birds were taking. He took a sharp breath, ready to begin again, but Arron pointed a crooked finger at him, saying, "How many riders, Peter, and are they white or Indian?"

Peter looked down the barrel of Arron's finger and swallowed. "Just the one, Arron. No need to get snappy, and he is a white man. In fact, it looks like Tim Murphy from the way he's riding. I—"

William interrupted, "Tim Murphy, you say?"

"Looks like," repeated Peter, nodding in affirmation.

William climbed his horse and took off in the direction of the coming rider.

At five hundred yards, William knew it was indeed his friend Timothy Murphy. As the two young men closed on each other, each raised a hand in greeting. Timothy sidled up to William, wearing a broad grin. Their horses were rubbing alongside each other, bumping both men in welcome.

"What news?" asked William. "Did the colonel send you?"

"Yes," answered Timothy. "And I do have news. We know where the Shawnee are heading. Colonel received a report from General Washington. Their heading east and north."

"Trail here says they are heading north, Tim."

"They'll be cutting east soon if they haven't already. As I said, the colonel knows where they are going."

"And where is that?"

"New York," answered Tim. "Your horse looks worn, William. Mine as well. We should walk these animals. My tailbone could use a rest as well." He laughed.

The two men walked up to Arron, who stood alongside his horse, still chewing the pemmican knob.

"Well hello, Tim Murphy," said the older man. "Have you come to join our little adventure?"

"There is no adventure here, Arron. The colonel is on his way. We're to meet east of here on the main road that runs north to New York."

"New York?" queried Arron. "Why New York?"

"The British. The British are marching down from Canada. General Burgoyne commands an army, invading from the north. They have already taken two of our forts. Ticonderoga is one of them. They have also taken several small towns and cities. General Gates has been ordered to halt Burgoyne or at the very least slow him up before he reaches Albany."

"What have the Shawnee to do with all this, Tim?" asked William, confused.

"They fight with the British along with the Iroquois, Algonquin, Mohawk, Seneca, and Delaware. That is how Colonel Morgan knows their destination. Burgoyne is low on supplies. He awaits reinforcements from General Clinton, but he cannot wait long.

"General Gates wants to catch Burgoyne before he is reinforced. Half Burgoyne's army are Hessian troops, and they say more than a thousand Indians are also with him. Should be a good fight."

"Does the colonel have a plan?" asked William.

"Oh yes, most definitely."

"And that is?" prompted William.

"Kill as many British as possible," answered Tim simply.

William was getting agitated with the circular conversation and stopped in his tracks. "I do not see how this will help me find my family, Timothy."

"Ah, but it will, William. When we defeat the British, we will be taking many prisoners, among which will most certainly be Shawnee warriors. We will question them to find out where your family was taken. The colonel promised that he would help retrieve them once we know where they are. The way the colonel sees it, he can trade the captured Shawnee prisoners for your family. It's a good idea. I think Colonel Morgan likes you, William. He seemed determined to help."

William looked at his friend. "And what if we don't defeat the British?"

"Colonel says we'll be wearing British tricorns when we're finished, and if Colonel Morgan says so, then it is so."

"Do you think it will work?" asked William.

"I would put a hefty wager on it, William," answered Timothy with a broad smile.

Wallace and Bowling cantered up over the rise, reporting that the Shawnee trail had inexplicably turned east instead of continuing north to west as expected. They had no explanation for the change in direction.

"Hello, Wallace. Hello, Bowling," said Tim. "Colonel sends his greetings."

Both men smiled broadly.

"As you say, we are now heading east, gentlemen," continued Timothy. "We will meet the colonel and the Eleventh Virginia just south of our destination."

"Which is where precisely?" asked William.

"Some place called Saratoga," answered Timothy.

Philadelphia

ALDEN PACED THE floor silently. The home commandeered from an absent rebel family was spacious, warm, and comfortable. It was not to his standards, of course, but it was clean and well placed in the city, allowing ready access to Howe's headquarters and the busy Philadelphia docks. He was angry with himself as he paced and turned, tapping the wall with little flicks of his fingers like a tiny drumroll. *What can be done about Elspeth and her children?* he wondered.

He was satisfied with his decision to take Elspeth. But her children? They were now firmly in the way. Was it wise to bring them along? He was truly baffled at the refusal of Tenskwatawa to take the children. He had never heard of the Shawnee declining such an offer—four young white children.

He wanted Elspeth so badly that he could taste it—to hold her in his arms, to make love to her. How to deal with these blasted children, that was the problem. He could have that old witch Weatherly spirit them away somehow, perhaps sell them as slaves or indentured? He would have to pay Weatherly, of course. But it would be worth it.

The other problem was Elspeth herself. He would have to be very careful. After all, she had pointed a pistol at his chest and pulled the trigger with full intent. If the powder had been dry, he would be dead now.

He had never taken a woman capable of such a thing. It was her strength that intrigued him the most. That resolve in her eyes as she pulled the trigger, it had truly frightened Alden, he had to admit. It affected him in a way he could not fully understand. He had never seen a woman with such fire in her heart. He laughed aloud and wagged his head in simple wonder. It was as if he had captured a wild animal.

He needed to shake these thoughts from his mind. Within the hour, he was to report to General Howe. The order had been brusque. Howe had questions.

Elspeth came into the room bearing an armload of food. Mrs. Weatherly seemed pleased with Elspeth's efforts in the laundry and so rewarded her with extra bacon, beans, and potatoes. There was also a loaf of dry bread, which she broke up into small pieces for the twins, soaking the brittle bread in bean gravy and bacon fat.

Sitting on the floor, completely exhausted, she watched as her broken family consumed every morsel. David ate in silence, looking up occasionally at his mother.

"Come sit by me, David," said Elspeth, noticing the boy's sullen mood. "The rest of you, gather round."

The children shuffled closer to their mother.

"I know you are frightened, and you do not understand what is happening. I also want you to know that I will not let anyone or anything harm you. Do you understand this? We are safe here as long as we stay together."

"Is Father dead, Mother?" asked David sharply.

Elspeth hung her head, holding her tears. "Yes, David. Your father is dead. He was killed by the Shawnee."

"What of Mary, Mother?" cried Aelwyd.

"I am sorry, Aelwyd. Your sister Mary was also killed." Elspeth cleared her throat to steady her speech. "It is just us now. And we must hold together as a family to protect one another. Do you understand?"

"But what of William, Mother?" asked David.

"I do not know where William is, David. But I am certain he is looking for us."

"Will he find us, Mother?"

"If anyone can," replied Elspeth.

Aelwyd began to cry quietly, sniffling as she pulled her dress sleeve under her nose. David gave her a little shove. "It will be all right, Aelwyd, you will see. William will find us and bring us home."

"Do we still have a home?" she asked nervously.

"Of course," answered Elspeth with a smile. "No one can take that from us. Soon we will all go back. You can feed the chickens, David will hunt with his brother William, and the twins will help me in the field. You'll see. Everything will be just the same when we go home."

David gazed at his mother steadily. "Nothing will be the same again, Mother."

Alden walked into Howe's headquarters, dressed in the uniform of a dead captain from the Sixty-Third Foot. A small hole in the jacket just below the left breast revealed the cause of the captain's demise. Alden did not know the man, nor did he care. The hole was patched efficiently. That was enough. You could barely see it.

The day orderly looked up at Alden. "The general is expecting you, Captain. You may knock, sir."

Alden did so and was answered with a single "Come in."

Howe sat behind a great polished oaken desk, black and brown. Two officers stood beside the desk, hat in hand. Alden swept the tricorn from his head and bowed slightly.

"General, gentlemen," he said, nodding in acknowledgment to the officers.

"You are dismissed, gentlemen. Please check your supplies before heading north. I do not intend to be left destitute again in the wilds of America. Is that understood?"

"Perfectly, General," said the senior of the two. They left the room.

"Have a seat, Alden."

Alden sat down in a plush blue cushioned chair facing the general's desk. He placed his tricorn on the small table at his side and casually brushed lint from the dead captain's jacket, hoping to obscure the patched bullet hole.

Speaking more to himself than to Alden, Howe's gaze wandered to an open window. "I have been forced to hang three of my men, two Hessians and a British corporal, for murder and theft. It appears my standing order of execution for plundering American civilians has been largely ignored. The Hessians murdered and raped a woman south of Brandywine Creek. The bloody corporal lopped off four fingers of some poor woman to steal her rings for god's sake. Can you imagine such a thing? I fear this war will be our undoing."

Alden did not answer as he watched Howe rise from his desk and walk slowly across the room.

"My brother and I have warned Lord North to the consequences of this war. Our words have fallen on deaf ears."

"What choice did we have, General Howe?" answered Alden sympathetically.

Howe turned about and looked at Alden as if seeing him for the first time. "We had a choice, Captain."

"Well, yes, sir, I suppose that could be true. But you, of all people, understand the vagaries of war."

Howe looked at Alden as if his head had just popped off. "Vagaries, Captain?" he asked angrily. "You could reduce such gruesome events to the whims of war? What nonsense. This whole affair is beginning to spiral out of our control."

He stared down at Alden, and a question came to mind. "Why are you here, Captain?"

"You sent for me, sir," answered Alden carefully.

"Ah yes. I have gone over your report, Captain Alden. It appears you have omitted some rather critical information."

Alden looked perplexed. "What information would that be, General?"

"Apparently, your mission west included the kidnapping of this fellow, MacEwan's family. Would you care to enlighten me about the reason why?"

Alden was surprised at this but prepared nevertheless. He had a ready answer.

"I was hoping to keep that quiet, General. Obviously, your intelligence is well placed. Am I being watched?"

"Certainly not, Captain. But you must realize there is very little I am unaware of in my command. A general should know what his officers are up to. Don't you agree?" said Howe. "So tell me, Captain, why kidnap these people?"

"For two very good reasons, General—common decency, sir, and information," answered Alden flatly.

"Decency and information," repeated Howe.

Alden continued, "I couldn't very well place a widowed mother and four children in the hands of the Shawnee, and more importantly,

Mrs. MacEwan knows where those rifles were going. She also knows the names of every rebel leader in the west and the location of their strongholds. With this information, we can attack western redoubts using our Indian allies while you destroy Washington's forces here in the east." He finished with a confident look.

"And this woman's children? Are they part of your plan to extract information?"

"What better leverage to gain the information I want, General?"

"You would threaten these children, Captain?" asked Howe, his voice rising.

"In word only, General," Alden quickly assured. "I would never bring harm to a child. Still, with the advantage I hold, it would be a simple matter to question the mother with an implied threat. Wouldn't you agree?"

"Yes, I suppose that could be an advantage—a rather distasteful one, I might add. It strikes me as improper, even immoral. And of course, withholding something like this, Alden, especially from your senior officer, reflects badly on your intentions."

"To put it plainly, sir, if the rebels discover I have this woman, they would be forewarned. We would lose what advantage I might have if that were to occur."

"And once you have gained your information, Captain, what happens then to this woman and her children?"

"We . . . send them home," answered Alden simply.

Howe noted the hesitation in Alden's statement. He looked Alden over, studying the man closely. Alden's explanation made sense in a way. Still, he was uncertain about his intentions. *Why did he keep all this to himself?*

It appeared Alden enjoyed ignoring the rules of decent men as far as that goes. Stealing women and children to garner information was more than distasteful to Howe. There were things in war that Howe detested—the loss of good men, pain, sickness, pitiful suffering, but the worst was dealing with men like Alden, a necessary evil in these times.

"You are dismissed, Captain," said Howe, clearly disgusted. "Revise your report before you leave. Be sure to address it to General Clinton. He will be taking command here in Philadelphia while I return to New York. Make sure you include every detail, Captain. I do not believe General Clinton would appreciate your lofty machinations any better than I do. Do we understand each other?"

"Oh, yes, sir, quite understood," replied Alden with a thin smile.

Early next morning, Elspeth quietly left the room and began padding down the long hall that separated the house from the kitchen, laundry, and bedrooms. She was heading to the laundry for another day of fatiguing effort. At the other end of the hall, Mrs. Weatherly could be seen talking to a rough-looking tall man. The man turned and spied Elspeth. He pulled his hat from his head for a better look. Suddenly, he strode down the hallway toward Elspeth. She recognized this man instantly. He was with the wagons that had taken Elspeth and the children into Philadelphia. This man was the tormentor. He had pulled at Elspeth's dress, teased, and made horrible sounds and faces at the children. At five yards, Elspeth could smell him, reeking of alcohol, filth, and sweat as he closed in. His hair was lank, oily, and long. The strands hanged down in streaks of black along either side of his head. He smiled, revealing shattered and yellow-stained teeth. He wore a scruffy beard and walked with a rolling gait.

"Remember me, little mother?" he rasped.

"Yes," replied Elspeth stonily.

"Work here, do you?"

"I do laundry," answered Elspeth flatly.

"She's no whore, Mr. Evens," said Mrs. Weatherly as she stepped up behind the man.

"It's a whorehouse, is it not?"

"This woman and her children are here on the order of Captain Alden. She works the laundry, and that is all. If you have any complaint, take it to the captain."

Evens snapped his head round and glared at Weatherly. The woman stood six inches over him with one hand in her dress pocket. Weatherly's steady gaze never faltered as she matched the menace in Evens's eyes.

The drunken wagoner backed away from Elspeth, knowing full well the old hag was ready to pull her pistol if necessary.

"Day to you, ladies," he mumbled as he made for the front door.

He pushed his cap back on his head, turned, and sneered at the two women as he left the premises.

Little Cornstalk

"YOU CANNOT LEAVE without me, Stevenson," said Little Cornstalk firmly.

Stevenson shook his head in frustration. They had been through this same argument at least four times, and the hunter was weary of it.

"I will not take you along," replied Stevenson, frustrated. "You are having a baby for the love of god! How am I to deal with that on the trail to Philadelphia? You cannot go. You will only slow me down."

Little Cornstalk looked at Stevenson doubtfully. "It is you who will slow me down," she answered, nodding to affirm the statement.

"By god, what am I to do with you?"

"You are to take me with you."

He looked at her, flummoxed. "I have told you time and again if we wish to find William, I must go to Philadelphia. Mr. Murphy was plain in his knowledge that William and his son Timothy were heading for Philadelphia.

"It is a long distance, Little Cornstalk. We cannot expect to see William anytime soon. It could be many weeks before William returns. Therefore, I must go alone to discover his whereabouts. I must also seek information about William's family. For me to do this, I must travel alone. Don't you see that?"

"No," answered the girl flatly.

"God in heaven, girl!"

"Who is this god in heaven?"

"You speak with the Mother Spirit, do you not?"

"Yes, every day, Stevenson. You know this."

"Well, I speak to the Father of the Mother Spirit."

"I do not know this father," replied Little Cornstalk petulantly.

"Perhaps you should just shoot her, Olaf," said Connor Murphy mildly. The Irishman was slumped over the tavern bar top behind Stevenson, sipping a flagon of water and rum.

"Keep talking in like manner, Connor Murphy," scolded his wife, Kathleen. "And you may find yourself sleeping in the corn bin."

Murphy smiled at his wife.

"Little Cornstalk," said Kathleen, taking the girl's attention away from the two men, "it would be a great help to me if you stayed here. As you see, my hands are always busy. I have a gaggle of wild children, a simpleminded husband, and a tavern to run. You have been helpful to me. I have no notion what I would do without you."

Kathleen Murphy was a wise woman, nothing less. If she knew anything about Little Cornstalk, it was this. The girl took responsibility to her bosom. With children, she was patient, with friends and neighbors kindly. She worked morning till night and was quick to help any man or woman in the community if she saw the need. Over the last week or so, Little Cornstalk had made friends with nearly everyone in Murphy-Borough. She was a handsome girl with sparkling gray eyes, high cheekbones, and a brilliant smile. The gentlemen of Murphy-Borough were only too happy to stop and chat with her. The ladies were less friendly but still respectful. Even so, they could not help but like the girl. So lively, cheerful, and helping was she.

Stevenson had known Little Cornstalk since she was a child. He mentioned to Kathleen one time that the girl was often called "Little Mother" by her Cherokee family. It seemed almost a joke to Stevenson, but Kathleen knew better. She knew what Little Cornstalk wanted—nothing more than to be needed. Kathleen herself had often felt this way.

Little Cornstalk softened her expression and then dropped her eyes in resignation. She was happy that Kathleen needed her but unhappy at being left behind in the search for William. It was a conflicting emotion and unsettling.

"You will come back, Stevenson?" she asked the old hunter.

"Of course, Little Cornstalk. I will be back in two moons and a bit, no more. Kathleen will count the days with you. Isn't that right, Mrs. Murphy?"

"Why, yes, we'll count the days together, Little Cornstalk," said Kathleen with a confident smile.

Little Cornstalk turned on Connor Murphy. "You will not shoot me, Connor Murphy," she said sharpish. "Little Cornstalk is your friend."

"No, I would not shoot you," said the stocky Irishman, wagging his bushy head and chuckling. "I don't believe Kathleen would allow that."

"Words that cross your lips, Mr. Murphy," said Kathleen as she glared at her husband.

Four rowdy children burst into the tavern, scrambling furiously for Kathleen's skirts. Two girls hid behind the tall woman's blue dress as the two boys chasing them stood cautiously off a short distance. They were all breathing like a worked horse.

"Stop!" shouted Kathleen. "What is this fuss now?"

Seamus pointed a dirty finger at his sister. "She pitched dirt right to my face, Ma."

"Emily, you are not to throw dirt at your brother. And, Seamus, you go out right now and wash that dirty finger of yours along with the rest of your hands, or I'll give you reason to regret. Now, all of you, out!"

"I will take them," said Little Cornstalk. The two girls each grabbed a hand from Little Cornstalk and slowly walked toward the tavern door, chins up, heads held high. The boys backed carefully out of the way, giving wide berth to the three females.

"The back of your head is a treat," called Kathleen as all the children piled out the door.

Connor Murphy plunked his tankard on the bar and pushed it toward Stevenson.

"If you plan to head east, Olaf, I would remind you of Blackfish. That damn Indian has assaulted us three times this year alone. He's a stubborn bugger. After Boonesborough, he takes the notion this place will fall the same."

"I will be fine, Connor."

"You be certain to head south first toward MacEwan's and then east. Blackfish and his Shawnee devils stay clear of the south as you well know."

"I am aware, Connor."

"Just making certain, Olaf. No offense."

"I take no offense, my friend. I do ask a favor, however. I would take it kind that you and Kathleen look after the girl. I have known her and her family for years. If any harm were ever to come to her, William and I would take it hard."

"She'll be fine, Olaf," answered Kathleen. "Besides, I have the sense she's able to hold her own, if you get my meaning."

Stevenson picked up his rifle and slung his pack. He grabbed hold of Kathleen and gave her a mighty hug, sweeping her off the floor.

"You can leave go of my wife anytime now, Olaf," said Connor, frowning.

Stevenson ignored his friend.

"Goodbye, Kathleen. I'll bring some black tea back for you."

"Bring yourself back and in good health, Olaf."

The dappled horse that Murphy gave Stevenson was slightly swaybacked but with good stout legs, high withers, and a fine set of teeth. Her belly was a little swollen, but she walked fine. Murphy swore by the heavens it was the finest horse he had. Stevenson doubted that, but still, it was a good horse and would make a welcome conveyance on his way to Philadelphia. If he covered twenty-five miles a day, he would make the city in just under a month.

The trail south was well worn and easily traveled. White men and wagons made their way along this route as well as Indian foot and horse. It was a cool September morning when Stevenson set off, and the trail was quiet. The only sound heard was the creak of his saddle and the gentle padding of his horse as they made their way.

This part of the year was Stevenson's favorite. The trees were just beginning to turn. He always loved the amazing colors of fall and the fragrance of the crisp air, all provided by the fading red, yellow, gold, and purple leaves that fell from the trees. *This is a present from God*, his mother used to say, *the colors of a rainbow painted through the trees.*

A man would have to be a fool not to appreciate it. His thoughts turned to William MacEwan and Elspeth. He had no idea what he would discover when he arrived at Philadelphia, but for some odd reason, the nascent color in the trees provided a ray of cheerfulness.

Little Cornstalk walked through the field with thoughts of her mother and father. Young Seamus Murphy followed a few steps behind as she wandered among the striped cornstalks. She thought about her brother, Shadow Bear. She knew he was safe in the arms of the Mother Spirit and waited alongside Adsila for Little Cornstalk to join them. She looked about the compound. Here, she saw only white faces. She stared down at her hands. For the first time in her life, Little Cornstalk felt alone, separate. This was a new feeling for the girl. She had always thought of herself as independent, strong, never needing anyone or anything. Now, though, she could feel the loneliness creep inside her like an illness.

"Are you sick?" asked Seamus.

"No," she answered quietly. "I am good. It is the baby inside."

"Can I help?" queried the boy, concerned.

She looked up and smiled at Seamus. "I am collecting dry corn for something to eat. You can help find more."

"You mean like seed corn?"

"I do not know this seed corn, but dry corn is best. It can make a Cherokee food you have never seen. It is wonderful."

"I can help with that," said Seamus eagerly.

He began dashing among the stalks, collecting small kernels of dry corn scattered along the ground and empty stalks. Little Cornstalk showed Seamus how to pick out just the right kernels. After a time, they had collected a fair-sized sack and headed back to the Murphy Tavern.

That afternoon, Little Cornstalk explained to Kathleen what she needed—a large deep-cut, flat pan with a good cover. A cook fire with a large grate over the top was prepared by Seamus, and as the early fall sun began to descend, the Murphy brood gathered about the kitchen, looking on with curiosity.

Little Cornstalk rubbed the pan bottom with pork fat and watched as the heavy metal melted the fat until sizzling. She tossed in a handful of dry corn and quickly covered the pan. She took hold of the handle with a thick cloth and began shaking the pan with vigor, scraping it over the grate, constantly moving back and forth, side to side. After a time, a popping sound could be heard from within the covered pan, and the curious children leaned in closer to listen.

"What's happening?" asked Seamus, thrilled without understanding why.

Little Cornstalk just smiled and continued shaking the pan with renewed energy.

When the popping sound ceased, Little Cornstalk lifted the heavy pan off the grate and placed it on a metal plate sitting on the large wooden table. She pulled the top free, and the aroma of freshly popped corn filled the kitchen space. Reaching in she, grabbed a handful andstuffed it into her mouth.

At first, the children shied away, unsure of the snowy mound of corn. Seamus watched Little Cornstalk carefully; he reached over the table and took a few popped kernels in his hand. They were still warm. He began to chew. A wide smile crossed his face as he reached for another handful. At this, the remaining children all took some to hand, tentative at first. Then in a wild rush, they assaulted the great mound of popped corn and began eating and laughing simultaneously.

Kathleen watched her children, clearly amused. She gathered up a bowl of the snowy corn and brought it into the tavern.

"Try this, Mr. Murphy," she said as she passed the bowl to her husband.

Connor Murphy looked the bowl over with suspicion. He picked up a few pieces and popped them in his mouth. He began nodding.

"Good," he managed to say over the dry corn.

He passed the bowl to several tavern patrons. They gobbled it up.

Bringing the bowl back to Kathleen, he said, "Can you fill this again, Mrs. Murphy? This time, add some of that fine salt we have."

"My good salt? Whatever for, Connor?"

"Salted men drink, Kathleen. That's whatever for."

The words "popped corn" flew through the small community of Murphy-Borough like a winged bird. It became a favored food of the small community.

New York, South of Saratoga

MORGAN'S COMPANY OF five hundred moved along the narrow road to northern New York at a quick pace. They carried no cannon, only swift wagons of powder, food, and shot.

The men were in high spirits after their long wait in Philadelphia, singing and chatting as they passed the homesteads and farms lining the road. Occasionally, a resident would appear and offer food or well water to the marching men. Some came out only to stare at the marching riflemen as they passed along. Their boots, wagons, horses, and in some cases bare feet kicked up a cloud of dust that surrounded the long line of men.

The pace that Morgan set was quick march. Each man in the company carried light. A rifle, small pack, and hand weapons were all that was needed. Some walked along, cradling their rifle, while others balanced the long gun over their shoulders. Many walked with long staffs to be used as a cudgel in the hand-to-hand fight sure to come. Stragglers were uncommon, but there were a few. Mounted officers occasionally dropped back to prod along the slowest.

"Morning, Mr. Bishop. What's this you have in your wagon? Are they apples?"

Trailing the line of marching men, Bishop, the cook, drove a short flatbed wagon with tall rails running along the side. The wagon was fully packed. Two horses pulled. In the back were two large open barrels loaded with apples.

"Good morning to you, Lieutenant. Yes, sir, Dutch apples they are. I have been collecting them from folks along the way. They have been very generous, sir."

"Do you have enough for a jug of cider then?"

"I do, sir."

"The colonel is fond of cider, Mr. Bishop."

"Yes, sir, I am aware. I will see to it."

"Thank you, Mr. Bishop."

As the lieutenant turned his horse, he spied a lone straggler trailing behind Bishop's wagon. The man wore little more than rags on his feet as he shuffled along in the dirt. He carried an older rifle with a thin stock and squared-off barrel. A small pack hung from his belt that slapped rhythmically against his thigh as he walked along. A battered cap sat at the back of his head, exposing a bald pate that tapered down to thin strands of black and gray hair. He was old.

The lieutenant held up until the man came alongside. "I must ask you to quicken your pace, soldier. The colonel is expecting all of us when the fighting starts. You must take a broader stride, sir."

"I have no difficulty with my stride, Lieutenant. It is my feet that desert me," said the man.

The lieutenant looked down on the older man's rag-bound feet.

"Where are you from, soldier?"

"Maryland, sir."

"How old are you?"

"I will be sixty-two next spring, sir," answered the old man, nodding.

"Mr. Bishop!" called the officer loudly.

Bishop turned on the buckboard. "Sir?"

"Hold your wagon a moment. I have a rider for you."

The old soldier looked up at the lieutenant and smiled, "Bless you, sir. I am grateful."

West of Saratoga

"ARE YOU THINKING of your Indian maiden, William?" They had halted to water the horses. After a time, the group of five men walked their animals to a bald hill covered in dry grass. The horses grazed.

William looked over at his friend Timothy and bobbed his head in confirmation.

"My family as well," answered William.

"We are close now," continued Timothy. "Another day at most, and we will be with the company. We will find your family, and when we do, you can go back to your home and marry your Indian princess."

William looked shocked. He loved Little Cornstalk, and he wanted to be with her always, but marriage? The thought had never entered his mind. Timothy could see what his friend was thinking. He laughed aloud.

"Yes, William, marriage. You can rebuild your family home again and marry your Cherokee maid. Raise a family of your own. By god, you'll have your own tribe, William. Is that not a wonder?"

"You talk too much, Timothy."

Tim laughed again, whacking his leg in the process. William smiled at his friend.

They were separated from Morgan's rifle company by little more than seventeen miles. Timothy assured they would meet up with the colonel by the next day at most. Wallace and Bowling had ridden ahead, scouting the trail that now turned eastward.

William and Timothy ambled along on foot through a thick wood, chatting idly as they wound themselves through the tall trees. The air was quiet and seemed especially silenced among the great oaks, spruces, and white cedars. William missed his friend on the long ride north. He hadn't realized how much until now. It was a comfort lost to him, returning only through his friend's company. He smiled to himself. As

William and Timothy emerged from the trees, they came out onto an open meadow at the base of a bald hill. They began to climb.

When they reached the top, they viewed a valley below that carried a slow-running creek straight through its center. The valley was narrow, surrounded by a series of hillocks and berms bordered by a thick tree line. The grass was a golden blond color well suited for man and beast. The distant tree color was just beginning to turn. Soon the entire valley would blossom into an array of brilliant colors.

The two young friends waited patiently at the top of the hill for Arron and Peter to catch up. The older rifleman had trailed behind them some one hundred yards or so. Peter held reins in one hand while waving the other about in animated speech. Sitting a saddle for nearly three weeks had taken a toll on Arron. He was only too happy to walk his horse the remainder of the day, but after listening to Peter for several minutes, he climbed his animal and trotted ahead.

Timothy took the opportunity to examine his rifle, ensuring the pan was clean and both barrels fully loaded. Timothy had saved his money through years of hard labor. He accomplished this for the sole purpose of acquiring a special rifle from Isaac Worly, the famous Pennsylvania gunsmith. The fee was an incredible twenty English pounds. The rifle was one of a kind, the only two-barrel rifle William had ever seen or even heard of.

The stock was dark wood with a brass plate held in place by three flat screws. The brass was polished to a shine. The plate itself was in the shape of a bishop chess piece. Alongside the plate was a series of scrimshaw-like carvings. The trigger guard was thin and delicate, made up of ornate curls, polished through the constant attention of its owner's hand.

Because of the square-rifled barrels, the weight of the weapon was considerable, nearly the same as two rifles. This forced Timothy to constantly shift the mass from shoulder to cradle and back again. He would often use two arms to cradle the piece.

The advantage to this rifle, of course, was that Timothy could fire two times before reloading. In consideration, he believed this weapon saved his life on more than one occasion.

"Hello," said William with some urgency.

"What is it?" asked his friend.

"Two riders coming over the top of that far bald hill. It looks to be Wallace and Bowling. And they're riding hard."

"By thunder and earth, William, how is it you can see that far?"

William smiled shyly and said, "I do not know, Timothy, but it is a gift I cherish. I only wish I could hear with the same ability. My father was always best at that."

"Are they alone, or is someone in pursuit?"

"I see no one else."

"Well then, I for one am not waiting."

At that, Timothy slung his two-barrel rifle across his back, leaped on his horse, and took off toward the two cousins. William hesitated for a second and then did the same.

As Arron looked on, it occurred to him that something was amiss and reluctantly spurred his horse as well. He made for the top of the hill and saw with his own eyes that two riders were sailing over the grassy mounds at breakneck stride. Although he could not see clearly who the riders were, he nevertheless pounded after William and Timothy as fast as he could, spitting out a mouthful of pemmican. Peter followed in silent pursuit.

Timothy pulled his horse to a stop, waiting the few seconds it took for Wallace and Bowling to arrive. When they did, the two cousins were all grins.

"We're close to the company," said Wallace, gulping air.

"You can see their dust from the road as they travel," said Bowling happily.

"There are company scouts out as well. We spoke with them not far ahead," said Wallace.

"They're tracking the British," said Bowling.

"The first thing I am going to do is get a tall drink of rum!" continued Wallace.

There was silence.

Timothy and William glanced at each other. "Who's turn is it to speak next?" asked Timothy, turning his head from Wallace to Bowling.

Wallace and Bowling looked at Timothy with a question in their eyes. William laughed out loud as he realized Timothy's joke.

Arron came up on the group. "What is it?"

Suddenly, Wallace broke into a sputtering horselaugh. He pointed a finger at Timothy. "You are a rascal, Timothy Murphy. Yes, you are."

Arron frowned at the laughing men, looking confused. "What is it!"

The Weatherly House

BRIAN STOOD ON Duncan's shoulders, peering out the lone window of the gloomy room. It was raining lightly with the feel of approaching cool weather. Elspeth looked on as the twins held their unsteady position at the window. Duncan was getting a little fidgety under his brother's feet as they dug into his shoulders.

"You see, Mother," said Aelwyd, hands on her hips. "This is what they do all day. If they are not at the window, they are pitching wood chips and trash in the waste bucket. It's so dirty."

The twins were a handful, all right, and Aelwyd's complaint was a fair one. Mary had often complained in a similar manner when asked to watch the boys.

Brian turned abruptly and announced, "Red soldiers, Mama!"

"Yes, Brian, there are red soldiers, but you needn't worry about them. They are just watching."

"Father will shoot them," he answered, rolling his words for emphasis. "He will shoot them."

It seemed that the twins had not accepted the fact that Ian was dead. Their father was simply away as he often was. The concept of never seeing him again was too foreign for their young minds. Father was just away again.

Elspeth worried about the twins, knowing they were least able to care for themselves. Still, Brian and Duncan were as one, a single person. They were in constant company with each other, and so their strength and certainty were equally constant. They communicated with each other on a level only they understood. Their support for each other was also constant. It amplified their confidence to the world around them and provided a certainty found nowhere else.

Elspeth recalled one early spring morning, about ten months ago, when she had asked David to kill one of the chickens for the supper plate. When the twins heard the request, they took it on themselves to do the job. David was hesitant to employ their aid, but he thought if the boys could just corner one bird, then David could easily catch it.

As this adventure evolved, Ian stepped out from the cabin and began watching alongside Elspeth. As husband and wife looked on with interest, the two boys gamboled about the yard, chasing several chickens. The action soon became more and more amusing. Each time one of the boys had a bird cornered, the chicken simply flew over the head of the approaching twin, scrambling around the other. The boys were getting frustrated.

Then as Ian and Elspeth watched, Brian and Duncan put their heads together and came up with a plan. Ian was certain it was Brian's plan, but Duncan was right there with him. Brian went over to the fence rails and picked up a good, sturdy stick as tall as himself. "Ready," he announced.

With that, Duncan rushed one bird and cornered it against the cabin; and as expected, the bird flew in the air over Duncan's head. That was when Brian stepped up, swinging his stick with all the energy a small boy could provide, and smacked the bird hard to the ground, killing it instantly.

Ian and Elspeth looked on in shocked wonder as the two boys danced about the dead bird, calling, "Mama, Da, come see! Look, look!" They were delighted with their effort.

"Well," said Elspeth, smiling, "I should go put the pot on."

"I swear, Elspeth," said Ian, "our little Brian is the devil himself."

"Yes," answered Elspeth quietly, "and Duncan his advocate."

David was livid. "You killed it!"

It was a pleasant memory and would have been more so had her beloved Ian survived. Still, Ian was alive as far as the twins were concerned, and this thought gave Elspeth a tiny comfort.

Mrs. Weatherly knocked on the door and unlocked it as she did every morning. Her feelings toward Elspeth had not changed despite her help in the laundry.

This woman of the west thought Weatherly was strong willed and too smart by half. She would keep a hard eye on this one. The captain was becoming impatient about the children. They would have to be dealt with. *Remove them,* he told Weatherly. *I care not how. Do it, and I will reward you well, old woman.*

"I have two heavy buckets of food for you down at the kitchen. Who wants to carry them?" said the older woman, smiling at the children.

"I will," answered David.

With that, David dashed out the door and headed for the kitchen.

"I will too!" cried Brian. The twins ran after their brother.

"Thank you, Mrs. Weatherly. The extra food is most welcome."

Elspeth was gathering up the blankets on the floor, cleaning the room best she could.

"It looks to be cool weather coming, Mrs. Weatherly. Could I ask that you spare another blanket or two?"

Weatherly's face turned grim, and then she suddenly smiled. "Take what you need from the laundry. The girls have plenty."

The three boys trundled back into the room, hauling two buckets loaded with bacon, apples, potatoes, and bread. It was more than they could possibly eat at one sitting, and so Elspeth set one of the buckets aside and told Aelwyd to cover it with a folded blanket.

"Don't let the twins into that, Aelwyd."

"Yes, Mother."

"Would you care for a cup of tea, Mrs. MacEwan?" asked Mrs. Weatherly.

Elspeth was surprised at the offer from the old woman. She was unsure if she should accept. Mrs. Weatherly's look softened some. Still, Elspeth was wary of her intentions. Nevertheless, she decided to accept. The more she knew of things, the better. As she passed by the open bucket, she pulled an apple out and trailed behind Mrs. Weatherly to the small kitchen.

"I was married once," said Mrs. Weatherly softly as they each took a chair at the thick-topped wooden table.

The kitchen was a good size with a large fireplace and a long wooden table for preparing food. Three windows looked out on the backyard area, letting in plenty of light on sunny days. A rack of thick, cooked bacon lay in a flat pan at the end of the table along with a great pot of simple beans. An array of ripening apples lined the windowsills, adding a sweet aroma to the room. Woodsmoke lingered.

Elspeth was trying to understand the reason behind this polite invitation. Was the old woman just lonely or trying to cull information from Elspeth? Elspeth did not know. She continued to chew on her apple in silence.

Mrs. Weatherly continued, "Gerald was a good man. That was my husband," she added. "We kept a clean house then, well respected by our neighbors too. Look at my home now, full of soiled women and men with nothing but lust on their minds and sin in their hearts."

"Was this situation forced on you then, Mrs. Weatherly?" asked Elspeth, curious.

"When the war began, Gerald wanted to fight the rebels alongside the British. I warned him. Men who fight for ideas cannot be changed, only killed. Why is it men do such things, do you think?" she asked Elspeth.

"I do not know myself," answered Elspeth cautiously. "Perhaps they feel they are protecting us in some way. I can only say that my Ian was the same in nature. I knew he would do whatever was needed to protect us, and so he did. Nothing could change that. Do you have children yourself, Mrs. Weatherly?"

"No. Gerald and I were never blessed with children," she said, shaking her head. "Anyway, when Gerald was killed, I had to have some way to keep my home and feed myself. That was when I started the laundry. Soon after, a young girl came asking to rent a room. I took pity on the poor thing and did so. I thought it was a godsend really. The house is large and I the only occupant. I needed the money as well. I had no idea she entertained gentlemen, but to be frank, I doubt it would have made much difference. I was desperate then. It wasn't long before word spread, and before I knew it, I was renting rooms to six women."

Elspeth simply nodded, remaining silent.

Mrs. Weatherly had told this same story a hundred times. It was a lie, of course, but it served. The authorities were sympathetic and mostly left her alone. The fact that these same authorities were frequent customers at the Weatherly house helped enormously. It made little difference to the old woman who ran the city. Yankee rebels or bloody British, they were all the same.

Mrs. Weatherly continued, "For the first time in a year, I was able to save money and gave in to the whole notion. I renovated the house, upstairs and down. The girls give me a small percentage of their earnings for rent, and so the money just keeps coming. They appreciate the safety this place affords them. Everyone is happy.

"When the British entered the city, I thought little of it. Then Captain Alden came, threatening to close the house and burn it to the ground if I did not do as I was asked. Now I worry all the time," she finished sadly.

"I see," said Elspeth, considering the old woman's words. "I am no one to judge, Mrs. Weatherly. I have worked and struggled in this life as we all do. You do what you must to survive. I hold no animosity toward you, Mrs. Weatherly. Nevertheless, I would happily shoot your captain Alden given the opportunity."

Weatherly barked a laugh. Elspeth grinned.

"I must go to my work now," said Elspeth, starting to rise.

"No, please stay a bit longer. I want to talk to you about your children."

Elspeth suddenly became apprehensive. The hair on her neck was rising with a chill. "What of my children?"

"I was thinking. Might they be better situated at the church or possibly the ministry? Wouldn't you agree? This is no place for young children, Elspeth. I could carry them over to the Methodist preacher. He's just down the street. His ministry is always caring for children, you know. It would just be until you are on your way home, of course, no more than a few days."

Elspeth gave Weatherly a stony look. She said flatly, "My children are right where they belong, Mrs. Weatherly, at their mother's side."

"Call me Emma. That is my given name." The old woman displayed a crooked smile. "At the least, you should consider what I said. This really is no place for children."

Standing from her chair, Elspeth stared down at the old woman. "This is no place for anyone, Mrs. Weatherly. And I will not be separated from my children for any reason."

With that, Elspeth turned and headed for the stairwell down to the laundry.

Weatherly sneered at Elspeth's back as she descended.

***

David was popular in the house. This was due to his constant replenishment of water and firewood, required daily. That was David's job at the Weatherly house, and he did it well.

The young ladies plying their trade were happy to see the young boy hauling in a bucket of cold water for them or an armful of dry wood. They would give him a smile and, on a few occasions, a coin. David had never really possessed money before. He knew what money was, of course, but in his world, there was no need for such a thing. David would take the money gratefully and give it to his mother. There were King George III halfpence, French silver coins, and Dutch halfpence. One girl had given David a Mexican real, called a pillar dollar. The girl was thoroughly drunk when she pressed the silver coin in David's small hand. Elspeth made him return it. When he did, the young prostitute gave him five French pennies in return.

The two Negro girls who worked the laundry were the most delighted to have David's help. Bell and Gwinn were grateful for David's daily assistance. They no longer had to haul water buckets from the river or carry cords of heavy wood for the huge cauldron used to boil the garments. David's help made a grinding day far more pleasant for the two hardworking women.

As Elspeth headed down to the laundry, David dashed through the kitchen, dropping a load of firewood in the woodbox. Mrs. Weatherly's gaze followed the boy as he strode through the kitchen and out the door.

"I must admit," said Mrs. Weatherly loud enough for Elspeth to hear, "your David here is most welcome. His addition has pleased the ladies greatly. He is a good and happy child. You are lucky to have such a son. 'Tis a shame, really. He could be treated as a rebel, you know. He is old enough."

"Mrs. Weatherly," said Elspeth, poking her head up from the stairwell, "I would argue that your captain Alden is a bold liar indeed. Neither I nor any of my children have ever taken the rebel cause. I believe that Alden has some other purpose in mind. Perhaps you are aware of his intentions?"

Mrs. Weatherly gave Elspeth a worried look. "You have an older son as well," said Weatherly suddenly.

"Yes, David's elder brother, William," answered Elspeth guardedly.

"Captain Alden has described him to me. I am to keep an eye out for him as instructed, a tall boy with broad shoulders, reddish-blond hair worn long in style and tied as a horse's tail. The captain declared he would be dressed as a savage Indian carrying a long rifle and bearing a tomahawk."

"Yes, that is my William," said Elspeth, slowly nodding. "I know nothing of Indian tomahawks, but he will surely be carrying a long rifle."

It was near mid-September now. The days were shortening and the evenings cooler, making Mrs. Weatherly's house a welcome place for those who sought such comfort. A continual line of men and soldiers marched through the house from nighttime till morn. The leaves were turning. Their addition to the landscape lent some small color throughout the city. There was another advantage to the cooler temperature—the smell from the trash in the streets subsided considerably.

One thing Elspeth did notice was that the number of British soldiers coming to the Weatherly house was markedly reduced. Their number had diminished over the last few days. She wondered about that. As dusk came on, Elspeth returned to her room, tired from the long day of working the laundry. Giving Aelwyd a hug and scolding the twins for their continued mischief, she went about distributing the remaining food in the second bucket. David carried the waste bucket away, and as he did so, Elspeth instructed him to return the empty food bucket to the kitchen as well.

They still had only a single candle for the room, but it was enough. Fading sunlight filtering through the window helped. Mrs. Weatherly, true to her word, allowed Elspeth to bring three or four more blankets into the room. She began spreading them out along the wall so each child would have good covering for the night. The door to the room opened, and Elspeth looked up, expecting David. It was not David. A tall swaying man stood in the doorway, glaring at Elspeth. It was the tormenting wagoneer, Evens.

"What do you want here?" asked Elspeth, knowing full well what the man wanted.

"I'll have some of that quim, Mrs.," said Evens in his raspy voice.

Elspeth knew this word. "Stay away from me," said Elspeth urgently. "You stay away."

Aelwyd and the twins backed into the corner of the room away from the window. They were frightened by this strange man. Aelwyd began shaking visibly.

Evens placed his rifle against the wall by the doorframe and pulled his dirty coat off, dropping both hat and coat to the floor. He began walking unsteadily toward Elspeth, creaking the floorboards with his weight. Elspeth had secreted a kitchen knife in her dress some weeks ago. She slipped the weapon out now, holding it toward Evens as he approached. She was prepared to use it. The man smiled. Elspeth continued backing away.

"Come here, Mrs. Pull that dress up, or I'll tear it from you."

Evens neglected to close the door, and without notice, David entered silently, carefully placing the empty bucket on the floor. The boy quickly took in the scene.

Elspeth swung her blade, and Evens pulled back some. He laughed.

"I should take that little knife from you and cut your tits off, bitch."

David began to panic. He looked about and discovered the leaning rifle. He picked it up.

"Back away, sir, or I will cut you!" shouted Elspeth desperately. She could not see David for the vague light and the towering figure of her assailant.

David checked the rifle pan. It was empty. A small powder horn hung from a hook on the rifle trigger guard. He swept it up and pulled the wooden plug with his teeth as his father had taught him. His hand trembled as he poured the black powder. He could hear his mother pleading for the man to stay away as he tried to concentrate. He poured a small amount of powder into the pan.

Aelwyd began screaming in a high-pitched wail that filled the room. The twins began shouting, "Go away! Get away from here!"

Brian took two steps toward Evens as if threatening.

Evens turned on the boy.

"Keep your rats away, Mrs. I'll hurt 'em."

"Get back, Brian! Stay back!" called Elspeth in a shaken voice.

Evens reached out with his left hand as if to grab the knife from Elspeth, and as she turned to avoid the attempt, he threw a short punch with his right hand, smacking Elspeth on the side of her face. She slammed back against the wall, striking her head and sinking down in a sitting position. Evens advanced, stepping toward Elspeth as he slipped off his trouser belt. Elspeth was barely conscious, sitting propped against the wall, stunned from the blow.

David leveled the rifle at Evens and pulled the hammer back. With Aelwyd screaming and the twins shouting, the sound of the hammer could barely be heard, but Evens knew that sound well. He heard it. He turned and faced David.

David had no idea if the rifle was fully loaded, he knew only that the pan had been clean. As he gripped the rifle, the long barrel wavered ever so slightly left and right. He expected the man to back away from the muzzle, but he did not. Instead, Evens pulled a long blade knife from his undone belt and pointed it at David. He hitched his trousers up with his free hand. Evens knew very well that his rifle was loaded, but he also knew the pan was empty, rendering the weapon useless.

"Steal a man's rifle, would you? What do you expect to do with it, boy?"

"Shoot you," said David simply.

Through the flickering candlelight, Evens saw the determination on David's face; he hesitated a step. The cold light reflecting in David's eyes told Evens this boy was serious. Still, knowing his rifle was harmless, Evens advanced in three quick steps; and as he did, David pulled the trigger.

The rifle kicked David back with a great roar of thunder. A cloud of burnt powder filled the room. The ball struck Evens just below the breastbone, smashing through his upper spine, exiting the man's back, and placing a small round hole in the wall beyond. Blood sprayed out across the space, splattering the walls, showering over Aelwyd and the twins.

The look on Evens's face was stunned surprise. Striking the hardwood with both knees, he fell forward, smashing his nose with an audible crack as his face struck the floor. The body bounced and settled. Aelwyd's screams grew frantic, mixed with labored sobs. The twins looked on in silent amazement. David looked down on the man he had killed, still holding the smoking rifle in his hands.

Two drunken men burst into the room, banging into each other as they tried to enter simultaneously.

"Who's shot?" blurted one of the men, slurring his words.

"Look," said the other. "It's Tom Evens. That's Evens for certain."

The first man ripped the rifle from David's hands, pushing the boy to the floor. The next person to enter was Mrs. Weatherly. Elspeth slowly began to rise from the floor, still very much stunned from the punch she took.

"What goes here?" cried Mrs. Weatherly. Her pistol in hand, she swung it from one man to the other.

"The boy . . . the boy shot Evens!" said the second man.

"Nonsense," said Weatherly. "You're the one holding the rifle."

"I just took it from this boy," said the first man, pointing down at David. "He shot Tom for certain."

"Get out of my house," declared Mrs. Weatherly. "The both of you, get out—now."

"We'll call for the magistrate," declared the first man.

"Call whoever you like. Just get out of my house." She waved her pistol for emphasis.

A large pool of blood gathered on the floor beneath and around Evens. It slowed to a stop as it soaked into the dry wood, making a large black spot on the floor. David stood up and continued to stare at the dead man on the floor. Elspeth wobbled over to her son, wrapping him in a tight hug.

"Don't look, David," she whispered. "Don't look, dear."

Aelwyd ceased her screaming, not for lack of want but more for lack of air. The little girl was shaking like a leaf and gasping from her gathering sobs. The twins walked slowly over to the body and peered down in wonder. They had never seen a dead man before.

"What happened, Elspeth?" asked Weatherly. "Did you shoot Evens?"

Elspeth looked down on David and nodded firmly. "Yes," she answered, "I did."

David snapped his head up and looked into his mother's eyes. Elspeth held a warning on her face and shook her head the smallest bit.

"I shot this man, Mrs. Weatherly," said David. "He was attacking mother, and I shot him. I would have shot him anyway. He killed Father."

Weatherly stared down at David and slowly wagged her head. She bit down painfully on her lower lip, not knowing what to reply. Just then, Brian stepped closer to the body and delivered a swift kick to the side of Evens's head, rocking the body slightly. David threw up.

"Brian, Duncan, get over there with your sister and do not move until I tell you!" shouted Elspeth shakily.

"Those two drunken fools are partners to this man, Evens. The whole lot are a bunch of cutthroats, nothing less than murdering thieves. If they go for the magistrate, there could be trouble for you and the boy."

Elspeth, clearly shaken, looked at the older woman. "What can I do?" she asked.

Mrs. Weatherly was taken aback. She had only seen a stiff back and burning pride from this woman. Was Elspeth about to break? Several of the girls had come out of their rooms and were gathering around the open door. They all gawked at the body.

"Why, that's Tom Evens, dead. He just had me not more than an hour ago."

"Did he die happy, Emily?" One of the girls laughed.

Grasping the situation thoroughly, Mrs. Weatherly took matters in hand.

"Emily, go down to the laundry and fetch Bell. Bring her straight back. The rest of you, go to the parlor."

The Negro laundress Bell arrived quick as a flash, a question on her face.

"Go out to the front of the house and send one of those soldiers in here," said Mrs. Weatherly.

A moment later, one redcoat stepped into the house.

"What is it?" he asked brusquely.

"You must go and find Captain Alden immediately. This woman and her children were attacked." The soldier stuck his head in the doorway to the room and spied the sprawled body of Tom Evens.

"Is he one of our soldiers?"

"No," answered Weatherly. "He's just a drunken fool."

"Why would the captain have any interest in that?"

"These people are the captain's prisoners as you know. I am certain he will want to know what happened."

The soldier thought about this for a few seconds.

"All right."

***

Alden had been preparing to travel. He packed what few belongings he possessed—a small pocket diary, a wicked two-edged knife with a deer antler handle, and some small cloth undergarments he had purchased recently. He had been able to borrow a second officer's coat without a bullet hole and a new pair of boots. Everything he owned was easily packed in a hand carry.

He was heading for New York to collect his proper belongings. The trip wasn't necessary; it would have been simpler to send for his things. Still, he would have an opportunity to see his cousin Jeremy as well as get away from the squalid odor of Philadelphia, which was so disagreeable. He would not miss the rotting piles of trash and waste.

He was to board the *Hermione* at midnight, joining General Howe and his staff. Howe was preparing to resign as commander of the British forces in America, turning his duties over to General Clinton. When

Howe told Alden of his plans, the general seemed pleased. It was the happiest Alden had ever seen the man. It was clear that Howe's heart was not in this fight. His failure to prosecute the war after his defeat in Boston was noticed by all. The loss of over a thousand of his men to American rifles had diminished Howe's desire for this contest. The plain fact was Howe did not believe in this war. Destroying the American colonies would only end in disaster for England. He was certain of this.

When the pounding came to his door, Alden barely looked up from his task. A near-constant stream of messages was delivered daily from headquarters. Alden read them all but with little enthusiasm.

"Come in," answered Alden.

The orderly entered and handed Alden a note. "Urgent message for you, Captain," said the man. He quickly left the room.

"Weatherly house, urgent. come immediately."

Alden read the short note twice. "Orderly!" he shouted.

The man returned through the open door, "Sir?"

"Bring my horse round and saddle it. I must leave right away."

Alden could not imagine what the urgent matter might be, but his concern for Elspeth rose by the minute. He knew Mrs. Weatherly despised Elspeth MacEwan, but recently, it appeared the two women were getting on. *If anything happened to Elspeth*, he thought, but he shoved this notion aside. *Wait, wait, and see what the matter is.*

Arriving at the Weatherly house, he acknowledged the two British guards and bounded up the steps to the front door. Mrs. Weatherly stood to greet him.

"What has happened?" he asked Weatherly.

"A man was killed, shot through the breast. He came in with your wagons. His name is Tom Evens."

"Why should I give a damn about that?"

"He was attacking Mrs. MacEwan when he was shot."

Alden looked alarmed. "How is she? Elspeth, I mean. Is she all right?"

"Evens struck her a blow to the head. She has a nasty bruise on the left side of her face. She'll be all right. She's in the kitchen."

"Did she shoot this Evens?"

"It's not clear who shot Evens. I only know he's dead. Two of his friends went for the magistrate, claiming that Mrs. MacEwan's son David shot Evens."

"The boy?"

"Yes."

Alden considered this for a moment. If the boy did kill Evens, then to protect her son, Elspeth would take the blame. That was certain. If the magistrate came into this, they could take the boy and most likely hang him. If Elspeth took responsibility for the shooting, they would surely hang her. The question was, could Alden use this situation to his advantage? He could protect them both, claiming martial law. After all, they were his prisoners; and as far as the military was concerned, he had good reason to keep them under lock and key. It was all for the benefit of the British Empire and the execution of the war. He made a quick decision.

One of the guards appeared in the doorway.

"The magistrate is here, Captain. What do you want me to do, sir?"

"I'll be out to speak with him momentarily. Do not allow him to enter."

Alden walked the length of the hall, passing the large parlor where customers would normally queue up for a night's dalliance. His boot strides were the only sound in the unfamiliar silence of the house. Several of the ladies were quietly fussing over the MacEwan boy David. The young girl, Aelwyd, and the two twin boys lingered in a corner near the fireplace. A barely dressed prostitute leaned over them, offering cups of water. There were sniffles and murmurs of soothing words among the group. It was a strange scene for the usually boisterous Weatherly house.

Alden studied the boy David carefully and realized with growing conviction that the boy must have been the one to shoot Evens. He had no idea how David accomplished this, but he was certain of his conclusion. The boy shot Evens, protecting his mother. That made sense. This was working out better than Alden had hoped. He continued into the kitchen.

Elspeth sat in a chair at the end of the table, drinking a mix of water and whiskey Mrs. Weatherly provided. She gingerly touched her face where a large welt had risen, obscuring her vision in the left eye. As Alden entered, she looked up at the man.

"Are you all right, Mrs. MacEwan?" asked Alden gently.

"As right as a woman can be after being attacked by a drunken madman. You placed us in this situation, Mr. Alden. Did you expect anything less?"

"The magistrate waits outside, Mrs. MacEwan. He is here to take your son."

Elspeth looked up, fear in her eyes. Alden stood by the table patiently. He knew he had her. Elspeth was no fool; she also knew what Alden was thinking. He waited, staring down at Elspeth. Then in a single motion, he removed his hat and sat down at the opposite end of the table.

"Can you save him?" asked Elspeth.

"Yes," answered Alden simply.

"What do you want from me?"

"Only your cooperation. You knew of your husband's activity. You know where those rifles are, and you know where they are going. If you expect me to help you, I will need the names of everyone involved in distributing those rifles, everyone's name. If I can show my superiors that you have cooperated, then I will have more freedom to deal with your, eh . . . problem."

"Is that all you want?"

"I am leaving for New York tonight. I will return in a fortnight. If you agree to have dinner with me when I return and you provide that list of names, I will step outside and invoke martial law, Mrs. MacEwan, sending the magistrate away. It would be to your benefit," he finished, tilting his head just so.

Elspeth had no idea to whom Ian was bringing the rifles. It was most likely Daniel Boone and his companions or possibly Connor Murphy. But could she name her neighbors to save her son? She knew she would if it came to that. She understood fully why Alden invited her for dinner. To be defiled by a British dog was a small price for the life of her son. Still, she could not trust this man. Would he do what he promised? Elspeth put no faith in that notion. Just now there was no other reply for her to give. She would have two weeks to discover another solution.

"I agree to your terms, Captain. I will provide the names as you request, and I will attend your dinner. After all, I have no choice in the matter. Do I?" she said sadly.

It was the first time Elspeth had addressed Alden as "Captain." This and her ready acceptance thrilled Alden in a way he could not contain. He smiled. Elspeth MacEwan would be his greatest conquest.

"Then we agree, Mrs. MacEwan?"

"Yes, yes," answered Elspeth shortly, "as long as my children are safe."

"I assure you they will be," answered Alden with a smile. He came around the long table, leaning down, brushing the back of his fingers along Elspeth's swollen cheek. "Now if you will excuse me, I must attend to the magistrate." He replaced his tricorn to his head and walked out. Elspeth remained quiet, considering Alden's words.

The magistrate stood waiting just at the foot of the steps that led into the Weatherly house. He was familiar with the place and had been here both as customer and constable. Since the British had occupied the city, he was less inclined to visit. When he heard of the shooting from those two half-drunk miscreants, he was forced to go and not happy about it. Alden stepped out of the house, alerting the two British guards, who snapped to attention. The magistrate involuntarily straightened up a bit too.

Alden was polite, insisting the matter to be strictly a British army concern. Martial law was invoked, allowing Alden to deal with the shooting as he saw fit.

"Well, that's fine with me, Captain," declared the magistrate happily. "I will leave this matter in your capable hands then."

With that, the magistrate and his deputy simply walked away.

Alden had the two guards remove Evens's body, instructing them to throw it in the Schuylkill. In a month, no one would remember this ever happened.

Olaf Stevenson

STEVENSON HAD BEEN traveling for nineteen days. He was in good humor as he moved steadily along. Tramping through the woods unaccompanied was a joy without measure to the hunter. A mild wind blew from the east, rustling his beard. It was a sweet breeze filled with the scent of surrounding dogwood, serviceberry, red maple, and oak. His tread was silent on the narrow Indian path he followed, leading his horse down into a shallow valley.

He found the horse to be a good mare. Over the last weeks, he discovered that she was decent natured and steady on her feet. A little fat in the middle and just slightly swaybacked, she held up well throughout the long journey, maybe not Connor Murphy's best mount but a good animal nonetheless.

On one passing morn, an Irish farmer popped out of the trees, offering to sell Stevenson fresh carrots, cabbage, and apples. The produce looked good, and so he bought some carrots and a few apples, knowing the fresh food would be a welcome change from his dry provisions. When he offered a carrot to the mare, she gobbled it up, doing a little prance to show her delight. Stevenson's fondness for the horse grew daily.

Along the way, Stevenson crossed paths with few people. Those who appeared were mostly hunters and local farmers. From these persons, he learned all the latest news concerning the American forces as well as the British. Who was winning, who was losing, and who was where? Entry into Philadelphia, he was told, was blocked by the British occupation. Admission to the city was difficult. The British allowed walking beef and fresh produce and that only through local farmers sympathetic to the Crown. He also learned that several bands of patrolling British redcoats had plundered farms hereabouts, killing livestock and stealing anything of value. In some cases, they burned the farms out, depriving the American Army a source of supply.

As he walked out of the trees into an open field of dry grass, he came on two men camping by a small stream. The look of these fellows brought Stevenson up short. They both sat squat by a healthy fire, seemingly in deep discussion. Alongside them was a beaten-down mule hauling a two-wheel cart. The cart was packed with an assortment of belongings, clothing, chairs, boxes, animal skins, and even a large mirror. Hanging from the mule cart were three human scalps. The men themselves wore good boots and heavy jackets for weather. They appeared well provisioned.

"Hello, the camp!" called Stevenson as he approached.

The two fellows bolted up quick as a wink, each swinging a Brown Bess round. Both men aimed their guns at Stevenson.

"Hold your weapons, gentlemen!" cried Stevenson, raising an open hand. "I am a hunter on my way to Philadelphia for stores."

"Who are you then?" asked the taller of the two.

"My name is Stevenson, sir. I have business in the city and wish to do so without injury."

"If you don't want to get yourself shot, then don't be sneaking up like that."

"My apologies, gentlemen. I did call the camp."

The two men took stock of Stevenson, looking him up and down. He appeared to be as he stated, a hunter or trapper of the western woods. Stevenson carried a long rifle and wore an animal hide cap with moccasins on his feet and a deerskin jacket held up with rawhide string. Deciding the older hunter was no threat, they lifted their guns and resumed their position by the fire.

"If you have no objection, I will water and graze my horse."

"Please yourself. There's plenty a grass and water, but we have no food to share," answered the shorter of the two.

"I have some carrots and apples. If you like, I am willing to share."

"Do you have jerked meat?" asked the tall one.

"No, I am afraid not, just dry corn and a few pemmican biscuits," answered Stevenson.

"Pah, can't stomach pemmican. What else you have?"

"Nothing," replied Stevenson matter-of-factly.

Stevenson walked the mare over to a small stream that ran through the valley. Holding her reins loosely, he allowed the mare to drink her fill. He never turned his back on the two men by the fire.

"You gentlemen appear to be moving your belongings. Are you traveling far then?"

They did not reply.

"I am looking for the American Army as well. I was told they are just east of here."

"Better to stay clear of them. They'll take your horse and pay you nothing," said the tall one. "Are you a soldier then?"

"No," answered Stevenson. "I am searching for two friends who passed by here about a month or so past. They would be riding horses from the west. Have you seen anyone of that sort?"

"I thought you were on your way to Philadelphia for stores?" asked the tall one suspiciously.

"I am, but I made a promise to my friends I would pass along some letters. Their boys joined the American Army, you see."

"That's a mistake for certain," said the tall one.

"You have letters, you say?" asked the other. "Are they worth anything?"

"Only the words they carry. I imagine you get letters just the same."

"Can't read," said the small man. "As I said, if you wish to keep your horse, I would pass the Americans by. They'll just take your animal and pay you nothing! Stick to the north road, and you'll pass around them."

"I thank you for the good advice. I will do as you say. I certainly do not want them to take my horse. She and I are old friends."

The tall man chuckled. "He's a simple one, isn't he?" He jerked his thumb at Stevenson as he spoke.

"Well, I will be on my way then, gentlemen. I thank you again for your advice."

Stevenson climbed up on the mare and headed for the north road at a leisurely pace. When he was well out of sight of the two, he cut back south and once again took to the Indian trail.

Stevenson had come across men such as these before. They were scavenger thieves. Too cowardly to kill, they would wait out the bloody outcome and then descend on the burned-out farmstead like vultures, stripping the dead and taking anything of value. These men had no soul as far as Stevenson knew. They existed like an animal in the wood, only worse. He decided it was best to avoid them as he knew full well they would follow and steal his mare sometime in the night.

Stevenson traveled well into the late hours, and although he did not carry a timepiece, as most hunters, he knew the time when needed. Sometime after midnight, he felt he was far enough away from the scavengers to safely rest the remainder of the night. Hobbling the mare, he sat down by a large oak, leaned back, and fell fast asleep.

Morning came early for Stevenson. The mare was nickering and bobbing her head as she rubbed the oak with her flank. Stevenson rose and gave the horse the last carrot he had. When he tried to mount the animal, she refused. Backing away in a tight circle, she simply would not allow him to climb the saddle. He finally relented, and the two continued down the trail, walking as Stevenson muttered under his breath about ungrateful horses.

At midday, he came on a small pond that lay between a series of low hills. As he approached the water, he saw a man fishing the opposite bank. Stevenson wound his way round the water's edge. The fisherman was young. He wore blue cotton trousers, a broad belt with brass buckle, and a new tricorn hat. A white linen shirt covered his breast. He was barefoot.

"Hello, sir!" called Stevenson as he waved a friendly hand.

The young man turned and replied with a greeting of his own.

"Hello to you, sir."

The two stood some twenty yards off each other as they looked each other up and down.

"I am seeking the headquarters of the American Army," said Stevenson. "Can you oblige me about the location?"

"Yes, sir, I believe I can," replied the younger man.

Stevenson's mare began backing up suddenly. He turned about and swept up the reins, halting the animal from wandering off. When he turned back to the fisherman, he found the man had donned a dark blue jacket overall with white trim. He cradled a Brown Bess musket in his arms, aimed directly at Stevenson's belly.

"I do apologize, sir," he said politely. "But as ordered, I must take you to my commanding officer and requisition your horse."

Stevenson was surprised at this, but he felt no real threat from the young man. Apparently, the fisherman was an American soldier.

"As to that, young man," said Stevenson, "I wish to see your commanding officer, but I cannot allow you take the horse. I only have the loan of her. Besides, she and I have come to an understanding."

The young soldier looked past Stevenson and began studying the mare. He tilted his head this way and that. He walked toward the horse, closing the gap between the old hunter and himself. As he passed the bewildered Stevenson, he calmly placed the Brown Bess in the hunter's hand and continued onto the horse.

As he approached the mare, he removed his tricorn and slid it behind his back. He placed a gentle hand on the animal's neck. Examining her flank, he ran his hand the length of her body over her rump and back down under her belly. With the hat still behind him, he came up alongside the mare's neck and mane and whispered something in the animal's ear. She replied with a twitch of her head and a firm nod.

"If you think me a British spy, sir," announced Stevenson, "I assure you that I am not. In fact, I am a good friend of Colonel Morgan's. He will vouch for me."

Walking back to Stevenson, the young soldier simply held out his hand for the return of the Bess. Stevenson complied.

"No, sir, I do not believe you are a British spy," answered the soldier. "You can rest your mind concerning that. And I will not be taking your horse."

"Well," said Stevenson, "I am happy to hear that."

"You are certainly no spy. You look to be a westerner. As to that, I do not believe a spy would be fool enough to infiltrate an enemy camp on a pregnant horse."

Stevenson stood dumbstruck. He looked up to the sky and wagged his head in frustration. "If ever I see you again, Connor Murphy, I swear to heaven . . ."

Stevenson sat alone in the room. It was the same house Morgan used for his headquarters. In front of him stood the same wide table with a similar pile of maps stacked one on top of the other as before. The room had good windows of real glass and was well lit with sunlight. He looked around.

When the door opened, Stevenson stood up and turned. An American officer strode across the room, removing his cape and tricorn as he did so. Draping the cape and hat carefully over a wood post that stood off the wall, he stepped over to the empty chair beside the table.

"Your name, sir?" he asked abruptly.

"Olaf Stevenson."

"What business do you have with the American Army, Mr. Stevenson?"

"I am looking for two young men, William MacEwan and Timothy Murphy. I believe they came this way and would certainly have contacted someone in the army, most likely Colonel Morgan."

Pulling the chair away from the table, the officer sat down, heavily stamping his feet as he did so, explaining, "These boots are too damned tight for my oversize feet."

He was a man of average height with broad shoulders and a thin waist. His hair was shot through black to gray. He wore no wig. His boots came near to the knee and were highly polished. They looked tight.

He continued, "Have a seat, sir. I am Maj. John Clark, attached to the Eleventh Virginia. I have seen the men you are asking for. However, I am not at liberty to tell you more than that. What purpose is it you have in seeking these men?"

"I am a friend of the MacEwans," said Stevenson simply. "William MacEwan went in search of his family. He believed they were taken in an Indian raid on the MacEwan home near the gap. Both young men have been gone some time without any word. The Murphys and I became concerned, and so here I am, seeking their whereabouts."

"Your name is familiar to me, Mr. Stevenson," said the major, scratching his head. "In fact, I have heard that name in connection with the men you seek. Unfortunately, I cannot help you, sir. I do not know who you really are. Since your inquiry concerns the army, I am compelled to silence on the matter."

"If you have a doubt about who I am, please contact Colonel Morgan. He knows me well and would certainly vouch for me."

"I am afraid the colonel is away just now. Would you have some other means of confirming your identity?"

"I am good friends with Colonel Boone, Daniel Boone. We have known each other for over twenty years. He would speak for me."

"I have no idea where Colonel Boone might be, but that does give me an idea. Do you know a man by the name of Gunnarsson?"

"Dag Gunnarsson? Yes, I know him well."

"Orderly!" called the major.

The door flew open, and a young soldier stepped inside. "Sir?"

"Send for Captain Gunnarsson. I would like to see him immediately."

"Yes, sir."

While they waited, the major offered Stevenson a mug of stale coffee.

"You say you are a friends to the MacEwans. Do you know them well?"

"Very well. Why do you ask?"

"A man by the name of Stevenson gave some papers to young Mr. MacEwan. They were secret British plans."

Stevenson looked at the major and slowly bobbed his head. "You know about the plans?"

"I do, sir. I also know they were false plans intended to mislead General Washington. What do you know of this?"

"False, you say?" Stevenson looked baffled for a moment and then shook his head. "I cannot say if the papers are true or false. I can only say that I am the man who gave William those papers. I stole them from an Englishman named Alden."

The door opened, accompanied by a loud knock. "Captain Gunnarsson, sir," announced the orderly.

A giant of a man appeared in the doorframe. As he entered the room, he was forced to duck down and turn slightly as he passed through.

Dag Gunnarsson stood fully upright as he entered. At six feet five inches, his pointed tricorn just cleared the overhead beams. He swept the large tricorn from his head. His hair was long white-blond pulled back in a tight queue. His beard, also blond, was full and neatly trimmed. Standing in the room center, he appeared every inch the Viking of his heritage. Dressed in full uniform, he looked more like a park statue than a living man. He addressed the major. "You sent for me, sir?"

Major Clark simply pointed at Stevenson. "Do you know this man, Captain?"

Stevenson turned in his seat, standing up slowly as he did so. A broad grin crossed his face as he looked up at his friend, locking eyes with the giant. "Howdy-do, Dag?"

"By god and thunder, if it isn't Olaf Stevenson." Gunnarsson laughed aloud, shivering the windows with the volume. "Yes, Major, I know this man. He is an old friend and a true patriot."

The two Swedes approached each other. Grasping hands, they began pumping vigorously, laughing all the while.

"I take it you vouch for this man, Captain?" asked the major.

"Most certainly, yes, sir. Olaf is an old friend, Daniel Boone's as well. We have known one another for many years."

"Yes, Mr. Stevenson claimed to be familiar with Colonel Boone. The first person I thought of was you, Captain. You have told me many times of your adventures with Boone."

The major turned to Stevenson. "What do you wish to know, sir?"

"Where is William and Timothy?"

"My information is they are approaching New York. They may have already arrived," said Clark. "MacEwan and Murphy had been following British wagons to the city. It was determined that the young man's family was not with the British. Colonel Morgan was good enough to provide MacEwan with a horse and supplies as well as four scouts to pursue the Shawnee. They now believe the Indians have the MacEwan family."

"New York, you say?"

"Yes, in fact, Colonel Morgan and his rifle company followed only two days later. The colonel expected to meet up with MacEwan, sending

Murphy ahead. Colonel Morgan has every intention of aiding MacEwan in the recovery of his family. But there is something the colonel does not know, something perhaps you should be made aware of."

"What is that?"

"We have patriots in the city. I receive daily reports from them. I am charged with command of local intelligence in this sector. Four days ago, there was a shooting at one of the local bordellos. A man was killed. The magistrate was called out to make an arrest as usual for such a case. It was soon discovered that the victim was shot by a woman, not unusual for this type of establishment, of course. However, the woman in question had four children under her care. When the magistrate attempted an arrest, he was sent away by a British officer. Naturally, this attracted our interest. We have been watching the place ever since. The house, it appears, is under constant guard. We believe the English are holding this woman and her children prisoner there. Could this be the MacEwan family the young man searches for?"

Stevenson stared out a window for several seconds in silence. "Is there a way to discover if it is the MacEwans? Can any of your people help?"

Major Clark looked over at Dag Gunnarsson. "What do you think, Captain? Could we get someone inside the house to discover who this woman is?"

"I have just the fellow, Major," answered Gunnarsson. "Richard Bennett. He was the man who sent in the report on the shooting at the house. He is well known there and trusted by the folks therein."

"You're not referring to that drunken sailor?"

"Yes, sir, the very same."

"He strikes me as somewhat unreliable, Captain. Are you certain he will do?"

"Quite certain, sir."

***

When Bennett stepped into the parlor, a small fuss took place. He was quickly smothered in ladies. Richard Bennett was considered the unofficial guardian of the Weatherly house, not that he intended to be. It was more happenstance than deliberate, a happy annoyance really.

One evening the Weatherly house parlor was full of customers, one of whom was Bennett himself. Two other fellows, obviously in their cups, began getting a little too rough with the ladies they were negotiating with. One man became so belligerent that he struck the defenseless girl across the face, knocking her to the floor. Then he followed with a kick to the side of the young woman's head.

Amelie, sitting comfortably in Bennett's lap, was lifted straight into the air and gently placed back down on the seat, whereupon Bennett closed in on the two miscreants, drumming each with a solid blow and knocking them cold. After that, Richard was considered a hero of sorts at the Weatherly house. He spent his money generously and without favor. He was always welcome.

Bennett knew which room he had to get into. It was just down the hall nearer the kitchen and out of sight to the parlor. When he passed by the door, he quickly tried the doorknob but found it locked. Meandering into the kitchen, he saw Mrs. Weatherly peeling some apples at the sink. He came up behind the old woman and grabbed her round the waist, lifting her into the air, laughing, and jiggling her about. He set her down smoothly. She turned.

"Why, Mr. Bennett, are you always this rude with the ladies?" She barked a laugh.

"Just admiring your full figure, Mrs. W.," said Bennett. "I do admit I am cheered with rum, but then your home always brings the best from me."

They both laughed, and Bennett made his way back to the parlor. The key he slipped from Mrs. Weatherly's pocket was held firm in his grip as he passed it unnoticed to his own pocket.

Bennett spent some time with Amelie, drinking rum and spouting tales. Then he took up a candle and excused himself. Stepping into the darkened hallway, he could see one or two people milling about the kitchen. What he did next took some theatrics on his part, but he played it well.

Bumping along the hallway wall, he appeared very drunk. Bennett feigned a bowlegged walk in the extreme and was known for this. He waddled to and fro, knocking along the walls of the hall as if he was strolling the boards of a rolling ship at sea. His timing was perfect.

Bouncing off the opposite wall straight into the doorframe, he slipped the key in the lock, releasing the bolt. Opening the door with a slam, he fell inside on one knee, mumbling incoherently. He held the sputtering candle up and outward.

Elspeth did not scream. She knew if she did so, the children would wake, and she did not want that.

"Get out," she whispered as loud as she dared.

Bennett held the candle higher. "Who are you?" he asked clearly.

A figure nestled in the corner rose and walked toward Bennett. It was David.

"David, get back!" called Elspeth.

"Stay back," she spoke urgently.

Bennett looked at David, clear in the candlelight. "What is your name, boy?"

David did not answer. He simply stood his place in front of Bennett. Elspeth rushed up to her son.

"Stay back, David. This man is leaving—now."

Heavy footfalls were coming down the hall, and Bennett knew he would soon be discovered. He snapped his head up at Elspeth. "Is your name MacEwan?" he asked urgently.

Elspeth drew in a startled breath. She looked over at David. "Yes," she answered hesitantly, turning back to the strange man.

"Who are you?" asked Elspeth.

Just then, Mrs. Weatherly came through the open door, pistol out. She looked down on Bennett, who was still perched on one knee. He wagged his head slightly.

"You have moved the privy, Mrs. W.," said Bennett, slurring his words.

"Why, Mr. Bennett," said Weatherly, surprised. "How in the world did you get in here? I locked this door myself not more than two hours ago."

She reached in her pocket and discovered the key missing. She looked down at the door lock. There was the key, fixed in the lock as if it had been there the whole while.

She quickly pulled the key and turned to Elspeth. "I am sorry, Elspeth. I must have left the key in the lock." She reached down to assist Bennett in getting to his feet. David silently helped.

"This is Mr. Bennett. He is one of our favored customers here at the house and in most cases a perfect gentleman. We consider Mr. Bennett a friend. Don't we, dear?" she said, addressing Bennett as he picked himself off the floor.

Bennett stood up as straight as a drunken man with lopsided knees could; held the candle up, illuminating Elspeth's face; and announced loudly, "I am indeed a friend. Hiccup!" Bennett giggled.

Slipping a wink to David, he turned to Weatherly. "Mrs. W.?"

"Yes, Richard, dear, what is it?"

"Where have you moved the privy?"

Saratoga

WILLIAM AND TIMOTHY came up on Colonel Morgan and his rifle company just south of Saratoga, New York. They were bone weary but happy to be back in the company of friends. Wallace, Bowling, Peter, and Arron went straight for the supply wagon. They had missed their issue of rum and would be looking for every drop owed. Peter was naturally chattering away.

Colonel Morgan was delighted to see Timothy and William again. Once the camp was set, they were told to come to Morgan's tent. As the day began to fade, the company settled into their positions for the coming battle. It was a long walk from Pennsylvania, and every rifleman was eager to put his feet up. Rest would come but not before orders were carried out and the men fully settled.

William and Timothy unsaddled their mounts and turned them out to the makeshift corral. Once fed and watered, the animals would be returned to the American cavalry for the coming fight.

As they walked back toward the colonel's tent, a rustling sound up in the trees caught William's attention. It was unusual. The peculiar din appeared to come from the west, heading straight for them. Suddenly, the trees overhead erupted in wild commotion as screeches and squeals echoed through the dense limbs. Thousands of leaves and small branches began showering down on the men from the treetops. Overhead, an enormous raft of gray squirrels sailed from branch to branch through the trees at breakneck speed. The raft was thirty yards across and more than sixty long. There were hundreds of them.

Several riflemen, just settling in, began firing straight up into the mass of gray fur flying overhead. Dozens of dead and injured squirrels fell to the ground. Officers began shouting for the men to cease firing, and for a few moments, pandemonium reigned. Moving with incredible speed through the branches, the squirrels passed farther east; and just as suddenly as they appeared, they vanished. Men were running about, laughing, and shouting as they gathered up handfuls of squirrels, singing, "Squirrels to roast! Supper tonight!"

William, awed at the scene, twisted his head up and around as he followed the swirling activity. The two friends had to dodge fleeing squirrels falling uninjured at their feet. The small gray rodents scrambled like mad through ground leaves, shooting up the nearest tree.

"Have you ever seen such a thing, Timothy?" asked William, tilting his head back in wonder as he peered up into the trees.

"Yes, once in the Ohio, chasing Indians. I witnessed such a thing. The raft of squirrels that flew overhead that day was even larger than this. We had squirrel stew for a week."

As the two young men approached Morgan's tent, a continuous line of officers and enlisted men could be seen flowing in and out, rushing in every direction. William and Timothy found Morgan sitting on an elevated chair, tossing out orders at a rapid pace.

"Gentlemen!" shouted Morgan when he spied them standing at the tent opening. "Please take a seat by my cot. I will be with you momentarily."

Timothy and William did so. It turned out to be a fine perch to witness the mayhem of battle preparation.

Morgan placed a heavily scarred hand down on a low table containing a map. Addressing the captain standing before him, he declared, "I need your men to cover this area. It is just right of your current location. Is that understood, Captain?" The man nodded. "How many do you count in your command?"

"I have fifty-three men in good order, sir."

"That will do. Colonel Arnold has directed us to cover the entire flank this side of the heights. He expects the British to break through here. We cannot allow that. Take the cannoneers first, then the officers. If the British break our right flank, then we are done. Do you understand? They must *not* get through."

"I understand, sir. They will not break the line."

"Good. Now go."

Morgan stood up and stretched his legs. He poked his head out the tent opening and reviewed the bustling mass of men who seemed to move in every direction at once.

"Mr. Hand!" shouted Morgan.

Ezra Hand popped up out of nowhere. "Sir?"

"Fetch my horse, Mr. Hand. I will be riding the line."

"Yes, sir," answered Hand, disappearing into the chaos.

Turning back inside, Morgan addressed his two visitors.

"Mr. MacEwan," said Morgan, "do you trust my judgment?"

William looked over at his friend Timothy, who simply nodded, and then back at the colonel. "Yes, sir, I do."

"You realize this is only a chance—a chance that may fail. If we win the day, and I say if, we will be taking prisoners, some of whom will be Shawnee allies of the British. If we capture a few of them, possibly some leaders, we can trade them. The Shawnee will exchange your family for these prisoners. Do you agree to this?"

"Yes, sir, I do," answered William enthusiastically.

"Fine. Timothy," said Morgan, addressing his rifleman, "you know well what is ahead of us tomorrow. Mr. MacEwan will stay at your side throughout. I expect you to do your best to keep him from harm until we complete our defeat of the British. He is a civilian after all. Is that understood?"

"Yes, sir. It is."

Ezra Hand stood before the tent, holding the reins of a saddled horse. "Your horse, sir."

"Until the morning, gentlemen," declared Morgan, pushing his hat down firmly on his crown. He stepped outside and climbed his horse.

William and Timothy were idle for a time as they wandered through the mass of men. Some were already skinning squirrels for their upcoming meal. As they approached the top of the heights, the full American line came into view. Cannons arrayed just behind the ridgeline were rolling into position. As William reviewed the landscape, he found it an amazing sight. Grasping the enormity of what he was witnessing humbled the young longhunter. Acres of men aligning along Bemis Heights faced a large open field of golden grass. There were so many men that it was impossible for William to estimate their numbers. Across the field of grass, the British were maneuvering in similar fashion. The line of redcoats seemed to go on forever, disappearing over the rolling landscape.

The British appeared well organized as they aligned their forces. Their orders echoing over the field sent a chill through William. This was no Indian fight. The scale of it was overwhelming.

Timothy waved his arm along the field to the American left flank. "That's where the fight will start, William. Colonel Arnold believes the British will try to break through there. This is where the Eleventh Virginia will stand and fight. I may be called to assist in removing some of the officers and cannoneers, so keep an eye and stay close. We wouldn't want to lose you after all we have been through."

William looked concerned but nodded.

"The field guns will fire first. It is a god-awful thunder and rattle when it begins. Some men jump and run at the sound of it, so fair warning. It will shake your bones to the very ground."

Gunfire could be heard in the distance, and William turned to his friend. "Is it starting already?"

"No, that would be a skirmish around the edge of the field, just British and Americans bumping into each other. That will end when the sun dies. Things will get hot first thing in the morning, though, or shortly after. We should get some meat and drink along with a good rest before daybreak, Colonel's orders."

The evening seemed to come on slowly for William. He thought of his family. *Are they still alive? Will Morgan's plan work?* He wasn't certain. The vision of Little Cornstalk came to him then. He gently stroked the beaded pouch she had given him. Her beautiful face came to him in a rush of affection. He wondered where she could be now. Peering into the same sky hundreds of miles away, could she feel his heartbeat?

Trailing in Timothy's wake as they moved through the encampment, he begged off eating with the men. His stomach whirled about, leaving him unable to enjoy food.

After a dish of roasted squirrel and corn cakes, Timothy decided to spend some time with his fellow combatants. Rum and whiskey were passed along and liberally dispensed. After a time, the men began singing.

> Come unto me, ye heroes
> Whose hearts are true and bold,
> Who value more your honor
> Than others do their gold;
> Give ear onto my story,
> And I the truth will tell
> Concerning many a soldier
> Who for his country fell.

The tune was unfamiliar to William. It seemed melancholy, almost fateful. The coming fight for these men appeared to be ordained in some way. They would carry their fear into this fight, resigning themselves to fate.

As William continued to wander among the soldiers, he came on an open field back of the tree line. He found several soldiers lying on the ground, attended by a troop of men in white aprons. These men were wounded from previous skirmishes with the British. Some were badly injured. There were cries cast out for their mother, father, wife, or sweetheart. The white aprons rushed from one to the next. Bloody bandages were unfurled and replaced with clean white linen. As he scanned the scene, William recognized one person. He came on the man with a muted greeting.

"Good evening to you, Mr. Moses."

The former slave turned and smiled. "Hello to you, Mr. MacEwan. Have you come to help with the wounded?"

"I am afraid my mother would be better suited to the task, Mr. Moses. I know little of medical science."

"She must be a fine woman. I pray she will be returned to you safely."

William was astonished at this. "You know my family's predicament?"

"I do, sir. No need for concern. There is very little that is unknown in this company. Your tale of woe is familiar to us all."

William simply bobbed his head in acknowledgment. "Are you able to help these poor souls?"

"Many of them, yes. Others, I fear, are beyond the aid of man. They are in the hands of God now. My pardon, sir, but you look troubled. Are you well?"

William smiled weakly. "I am, sir. Thank you for asking. I am unaccustomed to . . . this. My life has always been quiet and small in comparison. Here"—he swept his arm toward the ridge—"is beyond my experience."

"Will you fight tomorrow?"

"I will do what I must to rescue my family, Mr. Moses. That is all I can say."

"My Mrs. and I will pray for you, sir. You will forgive me now. I must attend the surgeon. Farewell."

The morning came light and cool. William slept fitfully. When he woke, he was hungry. Timothy was already up and about, pulling his gear together.

"Come along, William. We have the devil's work today."

Morgan sat his horse near the top of Bemis Heights. One man wearing a brilliant red sash and blue jacket rode up alongside the colonel. The new arrival raised his right arm, pointing across the open field. Both men were in heated discussion.

Timothy turned to his friend. "That is Col. Benedict Arnold sitting the dapple-gray. You see his bandaged left leg? That is a wound received just recently. The man is fearless in battle. Colonel Morgan has fought by his side before, all the way to the gates of Montreal. A brave fellow to be sure."

"Has the battle begun then?" asked William.

"No." Timothy laughed. "You will know when it does."

Morgan turned his gaze toward William and Timothy no more than sixty yards away. He pulled his reins and headed straight for the two friends. He came up in a rush.

"Timothy."

"Yes, sir."

"Can you see that British officer? The one on the white?"

"I do, sir."

"Shoot that man."

Timothy looked across the field of rolling grass and began running in the direction of the enemy position. William followed close behind. Approaching a tall heavy-limbed oak, Timothy passed his two-barrel rifle to William. He climbed up to the first large branch. William passed the rifle to his friend.

Across the field, sitting a white horse, was a British officer in full regalia. A large black tricorn with silver trim sat on his head. His bright red coat with white and gold flash stood out in sharp contrast to the surrounding landscape. He held his horse in position as he directed his men in the field.

Timothy rested his rifle barrel on a sturdy limb and aimed carefully. William watched from the base of the tree. Tim fired. The officer's horse did a little kick and backed up, rocking the man slightly. He held his mount.

"You nicked his horse, Tim!" shouted William. "You are just low and to the right."

Tim fired his second barrel, but as he did, the officer's horse slipped to the right, and the shot missed clean. Timothy let out a string of profanity as he passed his rifle down to William for reloading.

"Pass up your rifle, William. That slippery bastard must have a bargain with the devil himself."

As William passed his rifle up to his friend, he added, "She shoots a hair left and down some. Gauge your wind."

Timothy grasped the rifle and gently placed it across the tree branch. He aimed; pulling the hammer back slowly, he fired.

The officer gripped his belly as he fell from the white. A scramble of men and horses quickly surrounded the prostrate officer, pulling him and his horse back behind British lines.

Timothy climbed down from the oak and handed William his rifle.

"That is a fine piece, William. She shoots true."

"Aye," said William, smiling at his friend.

Colonel Morgan cantered up to the two riflemen and removed his tricorn with a broad sweep of his arm. "Well done, Mr. Murphy. You have just removed Gen. Simon Fraser from the field, an excellent beginning to our fight." Morgan rode back to the ridge, laughter in his wake.

A great roar ripped through the air, the likes of which William had never experienced. A massive thunder echoed overhead, followed by a chain of several more. The ground beneath William's feet trembled with the sound. A series of musket and rifle fire followed, rolling over the low hills.

Timothy hollered over his shoulder at William, "Follow me and stay low!"

A fierce knot gripped William's belly as a second unbelievable shuddering of the surrounding air began. American cannons were answering the British salvo. What followed next was the crashing sound of iron balls passing overhead through the treetops, shearing branch limbs as thick as a man's waist. The falling timber cascaded down on the men with a tremendous thump. White and gray smoke filled the air as burnt powder exploded everywhere at once. The cry of command orders moved the men farther left as the British began crossing the open filed.

A vigorous breeze cleared sections of the field from the powder smoke, allowing William to view the advancing British line. Incredibly, a long line of redcoats three to four men deep began marching straight toward the company line of riflemen. They marched in good order as they traversed the open field. The riflemen held fire, many loading as they calmly watched the enemy advance. Orders were given to hold the line as ready riflemen crouched down and took aim.

The redcoats carried their Brown Bess muskets fixed with bayonets. They moved in a steady line of march, coming closer to the American lines with each step. American officers standing behind their men held swords aloft for the command to fire. When the British lines came within eighty yards, the swords swung down, and the command was given. It was a slaughter.

British soldiers fell in great numbers. The first line was completely decimated. Cries of the wounded carried through the air as the second row of American riflemen took their positions. The British continued on. A second volley of long rifles fired, wreaking havoc on the following British line. William was aghast at the sight as hundreds of men fell in the field without ever firing a single shot. The survivors incredibly continued onward.

Still well out of accurate range, the British gave their surviving front line the order to kneel and fire. Their barrage was ineffectual. A few lucky shots struck but did little damage to the American line. The second line of British behind the kneeling men fired, and then a great shout erupted from the English as they charged in a rush straight into the American rifles. The Eleventh Virginia's third line knelt and fired.

The British line stuttered in their advance and began falling back, retreating. By this time, the first line of American riflemen had reloaded and taken their place up front. Morgan's men fired at will. Fleeing British redcoats fell one by one as the Americans continued their deadly barrage.

Excepting the terrific thunder, the English cannon was doing little damage to the American lines and with good reason. Timothy knelt low to reload his two-barrel rifle. As the English cannoneers rolled their guns forward, a select group of riflemen took aim, Timothy included, and fired on the cannoneers. Before they even placed taper to cannon, they were shot down. With no time to align and aim the big guns, their barrage missed the intended targets by a wide margin, mostly over the heads of the advancing American line.

"Get your head down, William!" shouted Timothy. "In god's name, what are you doing standing there like an oak waiting to be cut down!"

It was the last thing William heard before the ball struck.

Offices of Lord Jeremy Skelton, Manhattan Island

"JOHNATHON!" CRIED SKELTON. "You are alive! How wonderful to see you again, cousin."

Alden pulled a silver-trimmed tricorn from his head and flopped down heavily into the cushioned chair beside Skelton's desk.

"No happier than I to see you again, cousin. How is it you fare?"

"Very well. Very well indeed. I only just now received word that Gentleman Johnny is rounding up the last of Gates's rabble northwest of here in Saratoga. General Clinton is on his way to assist in Gates's destruction. It is a happy day. So now tell me everything, cousin. I must hear all the gruesome details of your adventure in the wilds of America."

Skelton called for his orderly. "Tea and biscuits, if you will."

The two cousins smiled at each other in knowing fashion. As members of the elite, these men were rigidly schooled in the grandeur, majesty, and omnipotence of the British Empire. They'd had tea with the royals. Their families and friends were privileged members of Parliament, both houses. They owned vast tracks of land both in England and abroad. Ruling through the right of imperialism, they considered England master of the world, and they behaved as though it were so.

Alden began his tale.

He started by describing his scheme concerning the English invasion plans, how he watched as those same plans were being stolen by a rebel sympathizer named Stevenson. The inclusion of the Cherokee treaty, added to lend validity to those plans, was simply grist for the mill. The plans eventually wound up in the hands of the American general George Washington as intended. Specifically designed to mislead the Americans, it allowed for the preparation of Burgoyne's invasion from Canada. It all worked perfectly.

"When the Shawnee attacked the Cherokee village," said Alden, "I barely escaped with my life."

Skelton sat quietly, listening to his cousin. His eyes were growing ever wider as the harrowing tale was revealed.

"I stumbled upon the Shawnee west of the village," continued Alden, raising his voice for effect. "I thought I would be cooked over a fire! Thankfully, Tenskwatawa's brother Broken Tree realized who I was, so I then joined forces with the savages.

"I offered the rifles I had been following to the Shawnee, explaining where they could be found, the MacEwan homestead. Along the way, we came on my group of irregulars. They are British loyalists. Brave and steady men they are too. Unfortunately, the rifles were not discovered. The Shawnee then destroyed the MacEwan place, killing the owner and some of his family. After that, I made our way back to Philadelphia."

Alden hesitated, taking a sip from his teacup. "Now here is something you will not believe, cousin. I have taken the wife of MacEwan prisoner," he stated flatly. "She is incredibly beautiful with the form of a goddess."

"My word," said a flushed Skelton, "what a stupendous tale. We must send a letter to your mother, mine as well. They will simply love to know all this. You have taken this woman, you say? Remarkable. Do you intend to kill all your rivals in the game of love, Johnathon?"

"Pure happenstance, cousin. I assure you. Of course, I would have killed the man myself had I the opportunity. However, one of the irregulars did the job for me."

Skelton let out a barking laugh that echoed off the walls. "You are a scoundrel to be sure, cousin. I would wish no competition with you. I might get scalped!"

This time, both men laughed.

Murphy-Borough

IT WAS A small noise, no more than the riff of a cricket. Little Cornstalk sat up, twisting her head in the direction of the uncommon sound. She knew it was too cool for crickets. She swung her feet out and placed them lightly on the wood slat floor. Her belly, just beginning to swell, slowed her down somewhat but not too much. Her moccasins were silent as she traversed the space along the floor. She quietly ducked her head into the warmer kitchen, where the Murphy children slept on cool nights. She listened—nothing.

Connor Murphy snorted with a rattle and settled back to quiet. The man's snoring was infamous throughout the community. It rattled cabin timber. With the upper loft shutters open, he could be heard as far as the cornfield.

As Little Cornstalk approached the tavern doorway, the unmistakable bang and echo of rifle fire shattered the silence. The community bell immediately began ringing, followed by a cry of "Indians!"

Murphy-Borough came awake. The men standing the parapets called to arms as they fired down on the invaders. Blackfish with his Shawnee band were attacking once again. They had somehow made their way within yards of the protecting walls. Throwing long ropes with looped ends over the pointed tops of the pine barricade, they began to pull themselves up to scramble over the top. Four Shawnee braves were now inside the compound, running along the parapet.

Little Cornstalk watched through the open door as two braves jumped to the ground not more than thirty yards from the tavern. Connor Murphy with Kathleen close behind pounded down the short set of stairs that led from their bedroom above the tavern proper.

"Move!" shouted Murphy as he shoved Little Cornstalk aside and stormed outside. Murphy made straight for one of the navy guns. Little Cornstalk lost sight of the two Indians who had made it to the ground and anxiously scanned the area where they were last seen.

"Get back inside here, Little Cornstalk." It was Kathleen Murphy. She stood just behind the girl, holding a musket, ready to fire. Little Cornstalk shook her head in negation.

"Shawnee," she whispered hoarsely, continuing her search.

An arrow struck the doorframe, narrowly missing Little Cornstalk. She tracked it to the small smokehouse. Grasping the arrow, she snapped it off at the head, stuck it between her arm and body, and made as though she was hit, falling to the floor half inside the doorway. Squinting so her eyes appeared closed, she watched as the Shawnee brave trotted across the open ground toward the tavern. She gripped her knife close to her side.

The brave crept up onto the tavern porch and approached Little Cornstalk cautiously. He looked down on the seemingly dead Cherokee girl with an arrow protruding from her body. Ignoring his apparent victim, the brave pulled a long blade. A square-headed tomahawk adorned with red feathers was gripped in his opposite hand. As he made to step through the doorway, Kathleen fired, striking the frame and missing the Indian.

The Shawnee jumped back, momentarily hesitating. As he did so, a cry from some of the children rang out. Kathleen rushed inside, entered the kitchen, and took up a large carving knife. The brave began to follow, and as he stepped over Little Cornstalk sprawled in the doorframe, she sat up, whipped her knife around, and drove it through the Indian's foot, nailing it to the wooden floor. The brave screamed out in pain. Losing his balance, the Shawnee fell backward on his bottom.

Little Cornstalk rose, pulling her knife as she did. Before the Shawnee could bring his tomahawk up, she slammed her blade hilt deep into the right chest of the Indian. At the same moment, Kathleen dashed out the kitchen with her meat knife. The dying brave tried to sit back up. Kathleen was on him, thrusting the blade into the Shawnee's vitals. He let out a groan and collapsed. Blood spilled from the wounds in great quantity, soaking the surrounding wood and timber.

Little Cornstalk scrambled to the edge of the porch and began searching the barricade wall again, looking for the second Shawnee brave. As the first wave of Shawnee retreated, the girl spied the second

Indian as he came out from behind the smokehouse. Leaping up, he grabbed the edge of the walkway to make his escape. Little Cornstalk ran straight for the Shawnee, who was now hanging from the platform rim, his back to the girl. Her knife flashed in the half moonlight as she brought it down on the base of the Indian's neck, severing his spine. He died instantly, crumpling to the ground.

Little Cornstalk let out a bloodcurdling cry and began a shuffling dance beside her victim. Kathleen stood in the doorway with Seamus by her side, watching as the girl spun about, chanting and raising her arms to the moon descending in the night sky.

The navy swivel gun had done its work. Blackfish and his braves retreated, hauling off as many wounded and dead as possible. Four Shawnee braves lay dead outside the gates of Murphy-Borough, two inside the compound.

Seamus ran up to Little Cornstalk, and as he did, he grasped the girl's hand, halting her celebration. Coming out of her reverie, she turned on the boy. Blood was splattered over her white deerskin blouse.

"Are you all right?" asked Seamus at the sight.

Pulling air like a horse under full gallop, Little Cornstalk replied, "I am good, Seamus Murphy." Looking down on her bloodied white blouse, she made a small "ooh" sound. Seamus and Little Cornstalk walked back hand in hand toward the tavern. Kathleen, watching from the open doorway, stood over the body of the dead Shawnee, daring the Indian to rise. He had nearly made his way into her kitchen, where her children slept. She spat on the corpse.

When Connor made his way back to the tavern, he took in the scene of a bloodied Cherokee maid, a dead Shawnee brave, Kathleen, and young Seamus.

"Jesus, Mary, and Joseph," he declared, "what is this?"

"She saved us, Da. Little Cornstalk saved us. Did you see, Ma? Did you see her kill that Indian?" howled Seamus, pointing at the dead Shawnee.

"Little Cornstalk only stop Shawnee, Seamus Murphy," said the girl.

"Your mother kills this Shawnee," she announced proudly, nodding toward Kathleen.

"I kill that one," she said simply as she pointed to the dead Shawnee lying under the parapet.

"Good god in heaven, woman," said Connor Murphy, raising his voice. "How many times have I told you to bolt that door and stay with the children? You've no business being out here at a time like this."

"You pushed Little Cornstalk outside and left the door wide open, Mr. Murphy. And the next time you bellow at me like that, be prepared to take a good smack from my broom," Kathleen answered hotly.

Turning to Little Cornstalk, she quietly added, "Come inside. Let us get you cleaned up, dear."

"I will do," answered Little Cornstalk stiffly as she began pulling her blouse up over her head.

Connor and Seamus whipped around from the undressing girl, staring idly into the tavern. Kathleen roughly pulled the blouse back down. "Inside, please." She hauled Little Cornstalk into the kitchen and chased all the children out into the tavern.

Outside Philadelphia

"HAVE YOU LOST your reason, Olaf?" Dag Gunnarsson towered over his friend as Stevenson carefully linked two lengths of sturdy rope through the small strapped harness that looped over the steer's head.

"No," replied Stevenson as he quietly continued his task.

"Surely, there must be some other way to accomplish this. It is much too dangerous, my friend."

Stevenson remained silent.

"You would risk your life for this woman?"

"Yes."

Gunnarsson looked over at Major Clark. "Can *you* persuade him, Major?"

John Clark, looking tired and mildly bored, answered Gunnarsson, "Apparently not, Captain. I have depleted the bulk of my daily oxygen trying to do just that. After all, he is a civilian. I have no power over the fellow as you can plainly see. Perhaps your friend Bennett could assist in the matter, although I have my doubts on that."

"Now there is an idea, Olaf. We could ask Bennett to rescue your lady friend and her children. He knows every corner of the city and the people therein. I am certain he would have a better chance of success."

"I need no assistance from a drunken sailor," said Stevenson, nodding in affirmation.

Almost shouting at his friend, Gunnarsson said, "You do realize if the British find you out, they will have you before a firing squad. No one will save you!"

Ignoring his friend, Stevenson addressed Major Clark. "I thank you for the cattle, Major. I trust it will not cause too much grief with your quartermaster. The price was fair, and I do appreciate that."

"Well," answered Clark, "I thought it very clever of you to think of it. It will certainly gain you entrance into the city. The British are only too happy to see beef cattle walking their way. The Hessians are especially appreciative. I only hope your German friends are still in business. Many rebel sympathizers have already fled the city."

"They will be there," said Stevenson. "Ulli and Helmut would never leave their shop."

Stevenson was dressed as a country farmer. A broken, floppy straw hat sat on his head. His moccasins were replaced with a pair of well-worn wooden-bottomed shoes. The trousers and dirty blouse he wore were held together with a combination of rope and shoulder braces. He leaned over, plucked a tall dry grass blade from the ground, and then stuck it in his teeth. Smiling broadly, he asked the two American officers, "How do I look?"

"Like a fool," answered Dag Gunnarsson angrily, wagging his head. "You are going to get yourself killed, Olaf. That house has guards surrounding it, front and back. That is the information Bennett provided. Just how do you intend to gain entrance?"

"I have a plan, my friend," said Stevenson, still smiling. "I have a plan."

Approaching the Schuylkill Bridge, Stevenson dipped his head down to shadow his eyes with the straw-brimmed hat. The bridge appeared to be well guarded. At the far end sat two large cannon. Their placement was aimed directly at the entrance of the bridge where Stevenson walked. As he guided the two steers toward the bridge, a brace of redcoats held up their arms, brandishing silvery bayonets. The soldiers carefully eyed the cattle.

"Hold there, sir!" called one soldier on the far right. By his stripes, he looked to be a sergeant.

Stevenson stopped.

"What business have you here?"

Stevenson's Swedish accent was normally mild in nature, worn away by years of backwoods English. Now, though, he affected a deep Swedish tongue much as a local farmer might.

"I am Olaf Svenson," he answered, nodding with a broad smile. "I come for the butcher on Prince Street. He buys these steers. I get half pay for order. Now I bring dem, and I get full pay."

"Are you meaning the German butcher on Prince Street?"

"*Ja*, dat is da one."

The soldiers huddled up close and began speaking rapidly in hushed tones. One was shaking his head in negation. Another tapped his musket butt repeatedly on the wood planking of the bridge. Stevenson began to get nervous, wondering if he would even enter Philadelphia before being arrested. Finally, the tapping soldier turned back to Stevenson.

"Wait here," he demanded.

Stevenson was worried now. "*Ja*, I wait," he said nervously.

Stevenson watched as the soldier trotted the length of the bridge and began speaking urgently to the men guarding the cannon. The soldier turned several times, waving his arm in the direction of the patient farmer and his bovine companions.

As he waited, Stevenson nervously rocked from foot to foot, occasionally stroking the steers to keep them calm. The soldier hurried back. Coming straight up to Stevenson, he handed over a small sheet of rough paper.

"This is a note for the German butcher," declared the soldier loudly as if Stevenson was deaf rather than Swedish. "He is to set aside ten beef steak roasts for us." He waved his arm, indicating the soldiers standing by. "We will collect the meat when our duty on the bridge is complete. Do you understand what I say?"

Stevenson smiled at the soldier. "*Ja*, you want beef steaks from butcher, *ja*?"

"Yes," answered the soldier, smiling back.

It had been years since Stevenson had entered Philadelphia. He was not overfond of the city. It was simply too busy, and there were so many people. Still, the city did have its attraction. There were gardens with colorful flowers along the streets. Shops of every type crowded between houses. The homes that lined the thoroughfares were clean and well ordered, many built of solid red or yellow brick and stone.

Today as he moved down the lane, walking along with his beef cattle, there were few people. The homes appeared shabby now, many abandoned. There were no flowers to be seen. Trash of every sort was gathered along the walkways, lining the streets, piled as high as a man's shoulder. The smell was awful.

Although it had been years, Stevenson still remembered the way. Winding through one lane after the next, he could see what effect the war was having on the great city. It was not good. For the first time in his life, Stevenson felt sorry for the occupants of Philadelphia.

Slate gray clouds threatening rain blackened the late afternoon sky. No lamplight could be seen as he passed rows of windows that looked down on the street. Stevenson thought the rain might at least reduce the terrible smell. It could even send some of the uncollected trash flowing to the river. It was wishful thinking all the same.

When Stevenson came on Prince Street, he could clearly see his destination ahead on the left. The old wooden sign atop the shop doorway brought a quick smile to the hunter. "Deutsch Butcher, Becker & Rohs, Proprietors." Small colorful images of dancing beef cows, sheep, pigs, and chickens adorned both ends of the sign.

To the left of the large dark-stained shop door was an even larger bifurcated barn door. This was where livestock was held before slaughter. Ordinarily, the sounds of unhappy animals could be heard in the street, caterwauling day and night. Now only silence came from the empty barn. To the right of the door was set glass windows opaque with age, allowing only a view of shadows within. It began to rain.

Stevenson tried the shop door. It was locked tight with a handwritten sign posted, no meat today. He knocked heavily on the door again. He waited.

The building was two stories with living quarters located above the shop. His friends Ulli and Helmut occupied the rooms, and as Stevenson recalled, they were comfortable with a good fireplace, overstuffed chairs, and real carpet on the floor.

Watching through the cloudy glass, Stevenson could see a lantern marching down the stairs into the shop. The figure with the lamp made its way to the door.

"We have no meat today!" shouted the voice in a German accent. "Go away!"

"Open the door, Ulli!" shouted Stevenson in return. "A friend has come to visit!"

The door was quickly unlatched and swung open. Standing in the frame was a gentleman of medium height. He wore a long nightshirt open at the throat. It trailed down to his knees. He was barefoot. The round face was clean shaven with a rosy flush. His light green eyes twinkled in the manner of a child. He delivered a small crooked smile.

Ulli Becker threw his arms in the air, delivering a great shout. "Olaf Stevenson! My goodness, is that really you? What—"

Stevenson quickly held a finger to his lips. Ulli understood, going silent.

"Come in, Olaf," he offered quietly.

"Can I bring my friends?" asked Stevenson, holding up the rope attached to the steers.

Ulli scratched his balding head as he peered around Stevenson's bulk. Two beef cows stood patiently, swishing their tails in the rain. They looked up at the German with sad eyes. Ulli smiled and then wagged his head.

"I see you brought Helmut and me a gift. Give me a moment. I'll open the barn."

As he raced back inside the shop, leaving Stevenson in the downpour, Ulli called out for his partner, Helmut Rohs, to come down right away. "We have a surprise," he declared.

As far as Stevenson was aware, Helmut was the only person who could compare in proportion to Dag Gunnarsson. The quiet German measured six foot two in his stocking feet. He could easily fill a doorframe. Stevenson could hear the massive German pounding down the stairs at Ulli's call, generating both sound and vibration. The man weighed as much as a steer.

After the beef cattle were stowed away in the barn, all three men climbed the stairs, gathering in the living room loft, where the two German butchers lived. Ulli pulled a bottle of flavored schnapps from a cubby, pouring generous drafts for all.

Stevenson pulled off his sodden jacket and hat and sat down heavily on the sofa residing in the shared space. The room was well illuminated through a series of lanterns scattered about. A faded brown damask carpet sat under a low table positioned in the center of the room. A small fire burned in a soot-covered hearth. It was comfortably warm. Ulli and Helmut sat opposite Stevenson in overstuffed armchairs.

Ulli spoke first. "So tell me, Olaf. Why are you dressed as a farmer, walking two beef cattle through the streets of Philadelphia?"

"I have come to rescue a family held prisoner here inside the city. Like you, they are good friends."

Ulli opened his eyes, raising both brows. He tilted his chin upward after the fashion of a small bird. Always restrained, Helmut displayed little expression on his long clean-shaven face.

Stevenson continued, "I have come to you to ask your help. You know the city well and the people in it. It is almost certain to be a dangerous task, so I will understand if you refuse me."

"Refuse you," repeated Ulli, clearly insulted. "How can you say such a thing to us, Olaf? You, the man who helped two lost German boys when first we came to America. We will absolutely help you. Am I right, Helmut?"

"Ja," answered Helmut in his deep baritone, nodding for emphasis.

Ulli screwed up his face with a question. "What is it we are helping to do, may I ask?"

Stevenson quickly laid out his idea to the two Germans. They remained silent throughout, bobbing their heads occasionally as the details came forth.

"I know the house," said Ulli. "A woman named Weatherly runs this house. It is a brothel, you know. I have not been there myself, but I know people who have." He looked over at his partner, Helmut.

"It's a nice house," said Helmut simply. "It is painted German blue."

"I think the problem you have, Stevenson, is men," said Ulli, ignoring Helmut. "You will need several men to do this, men who can fight if necessary."

"I can fight," said Helmut, smiling.

Stevenson returned the grin. "No, I believe a fight would work against us. For this to work, we must be discreet. Musket fire would only bring British soldiers down on us. I do not wish to endanger the family in any way. There are small children involved. We would never make it out of the city. Do you think you can find good men for such a dangerous task?"

"Many, if not all, of the rebel sympathizers have abandoned the city, Olaf. Those who are left are with the English. There are few patriots in our city now. And those who remained are poor and most are women. Yes," pondered Ulli, stroking his chin, "getting good men for your idea could prove difficult."

A loud shuttered banging on the shop door halted their conversation. It was followed by a series of lesser persistent knocks. The three conspirators stopped their conversation. Ulli stood up. "Someone at the shop door," he announced unnecessarily. He headed toward the stairs.

"Wait," said Stevenson, pulling the paper sheet from a shirt pocket. It was soaked through but still readable. "The soldiers on the bridge gave this to me."

Ulli turned back, reading the note. "*Ja*, I understand."

Anticipating a group of hungry British redcoats, Ulli was surprised when he opened the door. Before him stood a sailor dripping water from his hat and heavy peacoat. He looked up at Ulli with a grin. "Evening to you, Mr. Becker," said the sailor, doffing his cap.

Ulli frowned. "Good evening, Mr. Bennett," he answered unhappily. "We are closed as you see," The German indicated the posted sign on the door.

"Oy, now? What's this then? I had word of two fat cows wandering into your shop not long ago. Alongside an overweight Swede maybe?"

Ulli raised his chin and eyebrows again. "If you want meat, Mr. Bennett, we have not slaughtered the beef yet."

"Don't be ill mannered, Mr. Becker. You can let me in out of this downpour at the least. I really must insist that I speak with your guest. He is here?"

Ulli considered Bennett's demand for a moment and then pulled the door wide, allowing Bennett to step inside the shop. He shook himself like a wet dog, spraying water about. Ulli frowned again.

"Who is there, Ulli?" called Helmut from the loft.

"No need to call your Alpine bear, Mr. Becker. I come in peace," said Bennett, holding both hands up.

"It is Mr. Bennett, Helmut. He is here to see Olaf," answered Ulli carefully.

The heavy steps of Helmut Rohs now echoed down the short stairwell. He stopped midway, bending half over the handrail to view their guest. He smiled. "Hallo, Richard! Come, come. We are upstairs."

Ulli shook his head in disgust as he followed Bennett up.

Entering the room, Bennett found Stevenson and Helmut waiting. Helmut reached out his hand and shook Bennett up and down till his hobnailed boots rattled the floor. Both men smiled broadly.

"You would be Stevenson, the hunter?" asked Bennett, shaking Stevenson's hand.

"I am Olaf Stevenson. And you are Mr. Bennett?"

"That I am, sir. Our common friend Dag Gunnarsson asked that I contact you. I can help. Dag was most firm about that," said Bennett as he plopped into the chair Ulli had vacated.

"You are soaking my good chair, Mr. Bennett," said Ulli unhappily.

"Oh my," said Bennett sarcastically. "I do beg pardon, Mr. Becker." He slapped his peacoat, sending water droplets in every direction.

Turning on Stevenson, Bennett continued, "I hear from Dag that you have some sort of strategy to rescue this MacEwan family? Tell me, Mr. Stevenson. Who are these people to you? Why are you risking your freedom and your life to save them?" He leaned in closer to Stevenson.

Stevenson sat back.

"They are friends, if you must know," said the hunter, surprised at the question. "I have visited their home and know their hospitality. I was friend to Ian MacEwan and his son William. Ian MacEwan was a patriot assisting the cause, bringing rifles west to frontier settlers. I have traveled and hunted with the eldest boy, William. He wrongfully believed his mother and some of the younger children were taken by Indians. He followed those same Shawnee north, all the way to New York as I understand it. He is there yet. It was only now I discovered the family was here, held prisoner in Philadelphia. William himself does not know this.

"He and I became close friends on the trail. I think it only right I do what I can to help, Mr. Bennett. Their home was burned to the ground, their livestock taken or killed, sir. Ian MacEwan was murdered on his doorstep. That left Mrs. MacEwan and the children. We don't even know which children are alive."

It was an impassioned speech Bennett could understand. The war, it seemed, was touching every life in America, leaving no one unscathed.

Stevenson continued angrily, "What I cannot understand is why? Why would the family be taken by the British at all? What possible worth could a woman and her children have to the English?"

"Yes," said Bennett. "I have been scratching my head over that myself. Did Mrs. MacEwan share any knowledge of her husband's activities?"

"Not that I am aware. Why would it matter? The rifles were found by another patriot and distributed as intended. MacEwan is dead, so he will not be bringing any more rifles west. That effort will fall to another. There just seems to be no reason for their imprisonment."

"Well," said Bennett, "if Mrs. MacEwan was to have information, she has not shared it thus far, hence her continued confinement. So, Mr. Stevenson, what do you intend now?"

"I will acquire a large wagon with horses, go to this Weatherly house, where the family is held. I will falsely identify myself as the city magistrate and pretend an arrest of the family for the murder of a fellow named Tom Evens. I believe that is the name. As I understand it, Mrs. MacEwan had recently been accused of killing this man. Once I have the family safely in the wagon, we will exit the city the way I came, over the Schuylkill Bridge."

Bennett looked down on his hands. They were calloused, rough, and scarred much like any sailor. He looked up at Stevenson.

"I must admit, Mr. Stevenson, you carry more brass than a monkey. You are going to get yourself killed, you know, and likely anyone you bring along."

Stevenson studied Bennett closely. He knew he needed help. That was certain. He had no wish to endanger his German friends, Ulli and

Helmut, but he seemed to have little choice in the matter. "You think this a bad plan then, Mr. Bennett?"

"Oh, the plan is fine," said Bennett. "It is the detail that is lacking. If you try this as you say, it will come to a bad end. I assure you."

"And what is it you suggest?"

Bennett slapped his hands together as if anticipating a hearty meal.

"First, you will need a wagon that looks like a magistrate transport wagon, not just any wagon, you see. It must be painted city green. Then you will need uniform jackets for yourself and the men you bring along for this false arrest. Everyone wears jacket uniforms these days, sir. Next, you will have to absent the real magistrate somehow. That may prove difficult. If he discovers what you intend, you are finished. Aside from that, the woman who owns the house, Mrs. Weatherly, knows the magistrate on sight.

"You will also need legal documents to press your case of arrest, the types of papers required for an arrest, a warrant or at the least instructions from a British command officer. It is possible to acquire counterfeit documents, but they must appear genuine.

"Finally, you cannot leave by the Schuylkill Bridge. When you do not arrive at the Walnut Street Jail, an alarm will be raised. In fact, once you leave the Weatherly house, your charade may be discovered at any time. If the alarm is given, the city will shut down quickly. You will have no avenue of escape."

Stevenson scratched his head absently. He had not considered anything like this. His notion of rescue was suddenly in jeopardy.

"Well then," replied the hunter simply, "I guess I will have to think of some other way."

"No," said Bennett, shaking his head. "As I said, your plan is a good one, very good, in fact. It only requires some refinement. We will need to assemble all I have mentioned to succeed. One thing in your favor—the officer in charge of the family's confinement is in New York City currently, a Captain Alden."

Stevenson suddenly shot up from his seat, knocking the bottle of schnapps, causing Bennett to reach out and save it.

"What was that name?" asked Stevenson menacingly. He absently reached for his knife.

Bennett and the two German butchers, startled at Stevenson's sudden leap from his chair, ogled the hunter.

"Alden," repeated Bennett slowly. "Captain John Alden? You know this man?"

"I do," answered Stevenson. "And if ever I see him again, I will kill him on sight."

"One more thing you should know. It was not Mrs. MacEwan who killed Tom Evens. It was her son, a young boy named David."

A Field of Wounded

WILLIAM FELT AS though he was in motion, as if he was on a horse or possibly a wagon. He knew he was moving. He was flat on his back as he began to struggle and rise.

A voice said, "Stop moving, Yank. It's hard enough hauling you about without you bouncing around on us."

The accent was distinctly British.

Another voice said, "Leave off, Archie. You're likely to get us shot."

William tried to open his eyes, but only the right cooperated. The left seemed to have something sticking the lid shut. With his one eye, he looked straight up and could see daylight filtering through the leaves above. The day was fading. Next, he tried lifting his head, but a shock of pain ran through his head, forcing him to close his right eye. He slowly laid his head back.

As the pain subsided, he opened his eye again and looked down toward his feet. The back of a redcoat soldier wearing a broad white band from shoulder to waist was all he could see. He tilted his head backward and stared up into the face of another British soldier. Each man held the handles of a litter, which was the instrument that William was traveling on.

Good lord, thought William, *have I been captured by the British?* Wounded on the field and collected after the battle, the only thought that came to William now was how to get away. How could he find his family as a prisoner of war? He wasn't an American soldier, but would they care? He doubted that. He began to struggle again despite the pain.

"Lay still, you bloody cracker, or you'll spill for certain."

"You there, lobsterback! Slow down, or I'll crack your head."

This voice was familiar to William. It was clearly Timothy Murphy. The British must have captured Tim as well. This was looking worse by the minute.

"William," said Timothy softly, "can you hear me?"

William could see his friend's face fading in and out as he bobbed up and down. It was difficult to focus. There was a ringing in his ears. Still, he was happy to hear a friendly voice.

"Yes, Tim, I hear you. I just can't raise my head much. It hurts something awful. Where are they taking us?"

"They are taking you to the surgeon's field. I am happy to see you talking again," continued Tim, smiling. "You gave us quite a turn. Colonel Morgan was angry as a bear when he found out."

"I am so sorry I got you captured, Tim."

Timothy began laughing aloud. "It's us that captured them, William. We captured the whole lot. We beat those bloody-backs and their Gentleman Johnny fair, captured them all. There must be five thousand of them. These two were taken as litter bearers, and if they don't stop jostling you round, I'm going to put a ball in each one. I have two ready barrels here, gentlemen, so pay heed!"

William's litter ride suddenly became smooth and even.

With the litter now settled to the ground, William managed to open his left eye with some difficulty. The view he found was bloodred and vague. He lifted a hand. Reaching up to his face, he discovered a cloth wrapped about his head, partially covering his eye. The bandage felt wet. Peering at his bloody fingers, he realized he had been shot. He felt desperately tired and weak. He fell to a deep sleep.

When William awoke, he heard voices mixed with the sounds of wagons passing, horses nickering, and the clanking of military gear and men traveling along. His right eye opened readily, but the left stubbornly refused to open. He pulled himself up on his elbows and looked about.

The familiar scene before him was the same large field he had visited earlier, again littered with men much as himself, lying flat and crying out in pain. Some lay on blankets while others rested on the litter that brought them to this place. The field was bursting with wounded redcoats. As before, several white aprons moved among the injured, administering aid, changing bandages, and offering water. The call for water was called from every corner of the field. William turned his head.

Beside him lay a British redcoat. He wore no hat. His arms splayed out from his sides. The left one was nearly touching William's shoulder. His white trousers were bloodied and torn. There was an enormous bandage wrapped about the soldier's right leg. The man coughed and then moaned in pain.

"Hello," said William softly. His throat was incredibly dry, making it difficult to speak.

He croaked out, "Are you all right?"

The moaning Englishman turned toward William and studied him. He was shaking visibly. He blinked several times before answering.

"Who are you to ask?" said the soldier.

"My name is William. Are you badly injured?"

"You bloody Yanks shot my leg off. It's the pain of the devil is what it is. Doctor says he'll come get me in a bit, and they'll cut it off complete."

"What's your name?" asked William.

"Walter Jones, if it's any business to you." He coughed again, shivering from the pain.

"That's a Welsh name, is it not?"

"And just how would you now that, Yank?"

"My mother is Welsh. Thomas was her maiden name. She married my father and changed it to MacEwan."

Walter softened his tone some. "Thomas is a good Welsh name, not a Jones or a Davies, mind you, but good."

"I am sorry about your leg," said William.

"And I as well," answered Walter.

"Me mom warned me not to join up. She'll be angry about this, that's certain. What is a man to do, I ask you? Stumping along with a wood post for a leg. I'll not be dancing with any ladies now," finished Walter sadly.

"Can I ask you something?"

"Don't know. What is it?"

"Why do you charge like that, straight into a line of Virginia rifles? You must have known what would happen. It was near-certain death. Do you do this for your king?"

"King and country," said Walter proudly. "Same for us all."

"He must be a great king to inspire men so. Still, I do not think I would throw myself in front of an American rifle for any man. I think it a poor choice."

"That's the problem with you, Yanks. You believe in nothing. You're all foolish with this idea of independence. Independent from what? Without your king, who would you follow?"

"I follow my own path," answered William. "The same as any longhunter."

"Humph," muttered Walter as he turned his gaze back to the trees and the leaves that hung above them.

With the conversation apparently over, William rolled his head back to a neutral position and closed his eyes.

He heard the voice but had some difficulty identifying it. William opened his good eye again and once more struggled with the left. A vague form of a man's head appeared before him. Focus was coming slowly.

"Hello, Mr. Moses," croaked William. "Water, please."

"How is it you fare, Mr. MacEwan?"

"Thirsty, sir, very thirsty."

"Here now, take a drop of this. I have water to follow."

William took a desperate gulp from the cup Mr. Moses offered. He immediately began barking like a pond duck. Mr. Moses swiftly poured water into the cup and offered it again. William took a cautious slurp.

"Ah, that is better. What in god's name did you give me, Mr. Moses? It nearly knocked my head off."

"Colonel sent this from his personal stores. It is a mix of whiskey and laudanum. Good for the pain. It will help you get some rest. Here now, take a little more." Moses began pouring another cup, but William held his hand up to halt the process.

"You have to take this, Mr. MacEwan. I must remove the bandage from your head and replace it with a clean one. It will be painful. The doctor wishes to view your wound as well."

William took another sip of the bitter elixir. "You may take the bandage at your leisure, Mr. Moses, but first, I would ask that you give some of this vile fluid to the man next to me."

"Colonel said this was just for you and not to pass it to anyone else. He was clear about that."

"Please, Mr. Moses. Walter here is about to have his leg taken. I would consider it a kindness if you gave him some. I think he will need it."

The black man looked down on William and slowly wagged his head. "I will do as you wish, Mr. MacEwan, but you must promise not to tell the colonel."

"You have my oath, sir."

Walter overheard William and Mr. Moses. "I thank you, Yank. Decent of you."

Mr. Moses refilled the cup and helped Walter drink it down.

William displayed a crooked smile.

Mr. Moses went to work. As he peeled the bandage away from William's head, the longhunter began to question his judgment on the whiskey-laudanum matter. He may have been a little hasty. Long blond, red hair pulled away along with the bandage as it unfurled. William thought his head might go along with it. He yelped whenever the wrap was pulled away close to the wound. Finally, the entire bandage came free, and William could feel cool air rushing over his unwrapped head. It felt good.

"I have clean water here. This will wash you up a bit," said Mr. Moses. "Hold on now. Should hurt some."

Ten minutes later, William's head, face, and neck were clean of blood and debris. He could easily open his left eye now with the sticky blood removed. A small issue continued lightly. The field surgeon followed this up with his thick fingers probing William's wound carefully. The examination caused William to wince painfully more than once.

"Well, I would say you are a very lucky fellow, Mr. MacEwan," declared the surgeon after his scrutiny. "The ball clipped your left cheek, leaving a furrow behind like a plowed field. Following that, it grazed the side of your skull. I would say you have a solid head, sir. I am sure it was a good knock though. How is your balance?"

"A little off when I raise my head, but it seems better," announced William. "Will I be all right, Doctor? I have much to do."

"I see no reason why not. You should try to get as much rest as possible. That should help your recovery."

The surgeon turned to Mr. Moses. "Apply a clean, dry bandage. Wind it tight to stem the blood flow. I washed the wound with alcohol. It is clean now, and the bleeding has mostly stopped. Head injuries can be unpredictable, so keep a sharp eye on him. Nevertheless, I believe this fellow will be fine. You may report to Colonel Morgan that his friend here will survive with little to no lasting effect."

"I thank you, Doctor," replied Mr. Moses, nodding his approval.

The surgeon left, passing on to the next wounded man.

William said, "Do you have news of my family, Mr. Moses?"

"No, sir, not yet."

"Were we able to capture any Shawnee? It is most important that I know."

"Oh yes, sir. We caught a bunch of Indians, all types. Not sure about your Shawnee, but we did collect a number of Indians."

"I am happy to hear it, Mr. Moses. Now if you will just assist me in getting up."

William attempted to sit up fully. The entire world began spinning about his head rapidly, clicking his eyes left and right. He slammed his lids closed, attempting to halt the effect. He lay back down on the litter slowly. The dizziness and laudanum were taking effect, making William nauseous. He retched. Closing his eyes again, William swiftly fell back to a deep sleep.

"You just rest now, Mr. MacEwan," said the ex-slave. "That's it."

Morning came with a mild breeze. The myriad colors in the leaves that hung above seemed out of place in this terrible field of wounded and dying. It was quieter now. Only the occasional cry could be heard echoing over the ground.

"Are you awake, Yank?"

William opened both eyes, which seemed quite normal now. The pain in his head subsided some but still throbbed considerably. He lifted himself on his elbows, testing the response. He was no longer dizzy from the effort. He turned to Walter.

"How do you fare, Mr. Jones," asked William.

"They took my leg," said Walter, visibly upset. "I do appreciate the whiskey you shared, Yank. That helped some. Oh, one of your fellow widow-makers come by whilst you slept. Said his name was . . . Murphy. He'll be back, so he said. Have you killed many British, MacEwan?"

"None," answered William, shrugging. "I never fired a shot."

"What?"

"I have not killed any Englishmen, Walter. And I am *not* in the Continental army as so many believe. I came here in search of my family. They were taken by Shawnee Indians who are fighting alongside your army here. That is why I came to this place."

Walter leisurely scratched his head in thought. "Well, I am glad you were not the one to shoot my leg off. I did wonder about that."

"Sorry to disappoint, Walter."

Walter laughed and then grimaced. "Here now, your friend is coming." He nodded in the direction of Timothy Murphy, marching straight for them.

Tim Murphy came up on William, squatting down beside the litter, balancing himself with the aid of his two-barrel rifle.

"How is it you fare, William?" he asked quietly. "Will you be right again?"

William ignored the question. "Do you have word of my family, Timothy?"

"Not I," replied the rifleman. "We do have a corral of Indians, including Shawnee. We've been guarding them day and night just for you, William."

"Where are they?"

"Over that hill, a mile off."

"Help me up, Tim."

"With pleasure," said Tim, hauling William up by his arm.

A flash of dizziness hit William. It quickly faded. His legs felt surprisingly weak, but he shook this off.

"Where is my rifle, Timothy?"

"It lies beside you here, William." Tim reached down and flipped the edge of the blanket that covered the litter. He picked up William's rifle hidden beneath and passed it to him.

"Been there all the while, William," said Timothy with satisfaction.

"How about that?" said Walter, scratching his head again.

Timothy passed William his powder horn and ball pouch.

"Farewell, Walter Jones," said William. "I hope you make it to home safely." William grinned at the Englishman.

"I wish you well finding your family, Mr. MacEwan," answered the soldier seriously.

The two friends walked side by side over the small hill, heading toward an abandoned corral meant for penning pigs or horses at one time.

As they moved along, the smell of dry grass and autumn leaves filled the air, clearing William's head of the rancid odor from the wounded field. His legs felt stronger now. Each stride pumped blood and determination to his limbs as he walked along.

As they approached the pig corral, a range of fiftysome Indians could be seen confined within its split rail fencing. Several American riflemen surrounded the little compound, walking in slow circles. The Indians gathered in separate groups, each to his own tribe—Iroquois, Mohawk, Lenape, Seneca, and Shawnee. A narrow entrance stood at one end of the pen, guarded by three familiar figures.

"William!" cried Bowling Miller. "There you are."

The two cousins, Wallace and Bowling, came on William like a small storm, grabbing his shoulder and pounding his back.

"Lay off that now," said Timothy, pushing the boys away. "He's still wounded, you know."

"Sorry, William. It is good to see you though. We thought you were gone for certain," said Wallace.

"It is good to see you as well," answered William, slightly ruffled. "Where are Arron and Peter?"

Silence followed.

Bowling cleared his throat. "Arron is just there by the gate. We lost Peter Blue Eyes in the fight, cut down with a dragoon lance. We buried him last night. God bless his soul. I would guess he's talking Saint Peter's ear off about now." He smiled unhappily.

William was struck by the news. He liked Peter. The young man was in a continual state of happiness no matter the circumstance. He told long stories to anyone willing to listen, always bringing a smile whenever he launched into one of his breathless tales.

"I am sorry to hear that," said William sadly. "We must message his mother."

"The colonel is handling that, William, as he does with all his dead and wounded. I doubt there is a man in the company he does not know by name," answered Timothy.

The five friends walked to the corral entrance. Arron stood just outside, cradling his long rifle.

"Good to see you, William," said the sour old man. "We got your Indians. Colonel says I can't shoot any till you talk with them. So I will wait."

William ignored Arron as he passed through the narrow entrance. He searched the group of silent Indians, his eyes falling on a tall Shawnee wearing the red headband so familiar to the tribe.

This man stood above the others and apart as well. He leaned heavily on a long thick staff gripped in his left hand. His hair, black as a crow's wing, was pulled back behind his head and tied in a knot. Two feathers jutted up from behind the mass of hair, one white, the other black. The front of his scalp was plucked clean as was common for the Shawnee. Red war paint covered his upper face from nose to crown. As William approached, the Indian looked up with a glint of recognition in his eyes.

Arron said, "They don't talk, just stare at you like a meal to be eaten."

The Indian did not move as William and Timothy came up to him. Wallace, Bowling, and Arron spread out slightly but held back. William stopped directly in front of the tall Indian and placed his rifle butt on the ground, grasping the barrel with both hands—a gesture of peace.

William asked in English, "What is your name?" When no reply came, he tried the same question in Cherokee.

The answer came clearly and with a decidedly English accent. "I am Broken Tree, brother to Chief Tenskwatawa."

"I will be damned," said Bowling, his eyes wide with surprise. "He speaks like an Englishman." The other riflemen were equally impressed but held their tongues.

Broken Tree continued, "You are the longhunter of the Cherokee, William MacEwan. The Shawnee know you well. You nearly killed my brother at the Cherokee village. Your rifle is feared by my people."

"If you know this," said William, "then you know where my family is. Do you?"

"Yes," answered Broken Tree simply.

"If you value your life, sir, tell me now where they are."

"They were taken by your British enemy."

William studied the man before him. He knew well that Indians could be just as deceitful as any white man, something he learned while living among the Cherokee.

"I do not believe you," stated William. "You could be lying to save your skin. I will ask you again. Where is my family?"

"I am not lying, Mr. MacEwan. I spoke with your mother many times as we traveled east."

"How many of my family are alive?" asked William, looking hard at the tall Indian.

"Your mother, David, Aelwyd, and the twins. Your family was smuggled into the city with the assistance of Captain Alden. He arranged everything."

William stood motionless at the sound of the familiar name. His face turned a ghostly white. In that moment, he knew this Indian was telling him the truth.

"What of Mary, my sister?" demanded William. "Did you kill her?"

"I did not harm your sister. She took her own life. Captain Alden witnessed this. Or so he said."

"Captain Alden," repeated William slowly. "Do you mean Mr. Alden?"

"Yes. He is a captain in the British army, the Twenty-Third Light Dragoons. He told me he was tasked with a special assignment seeking alliance with the tribes. Frankly, I did not trust the man. We came across the captain outside the Cherokee village as we retreated after the battle."

William wheeled on Timothy. "I need a horse, Tim."

Tim looked over at Wallace and Bowling, shaking his head. "There are no horses available just now, William."

The two riflemen looked confused and then began wandering toward the corral exit.

"I thank you for this information, Broken Tree. I believe you are telling me the truth."

"I would ask a token of you, William MacEwan," said Broken Tree.

William understood the request but not the reason for it.

"Why do you ask for this?" queried William.

"I do not wish to die. A token from you will keep me safe from your rifles. It is the Shawnee way."

William pulled his blade, widening Broken Tree's eyes. The Indian stood mute as the young longhunter pulled his own long hair over his shoulder and cut a rough handful. He passed the bundle to the Indian without comment.

Arron piped up. "Are you through with this Indian, William? Do you have what you need?"

Paying little attention to Arron, William simply nodded, digesting this new information from Broken Tree. Arron quickly stepped up between Timothy and William, pointing his rifle directly at Broken Tree's chest. As he pulled the trigger, William swung his own rifle up, knocking Arron's barrel skyward, sending the ball through the branches and leaves. Broken Tree stood perfectly still. His expression unchanged.

"This is Tenskwatawa's brother, William!" shouted Arron. "He should die with the rest of them."

"No harm is to come to this Indian. Is that understood?" said William forcefully. "I believe his words, Arron. He has told me the truth of things, and this may well save my family."

"Don't worry, William," said Timothy, glaring at Arron. "No one will harm your Indian. I promise you."

The three men passed through the pen's entry. Arron angrily reloaded his rifle.

Wallace and Bowling charged up just then, the two on the back of a reddish-brown mare. They jumped to the ground and held the reins out for William.

"What the devil!" cried Timothy. "Did I not say there are no horses to be had? William cannot leave now. He is injured."

Addressing William, Timothy continued, "You must take . . . what is the word? Conva . . . con . . ."

"Convalescence," finished William. "I am fine, Timothy. I must leave for Philadelphia immediately. I have wasted nearly a month chasing the Shawnee to New York while my family has been imprisoned in the city all this time. I must go!"

William marched briskly to the horse and climbed up.

Timothy strode up and grabbed the halter. "I cannot let you leave, William. You would be alone. We must stay with the company. Surely, you know that. We have our orders."

William jerked the reins, pulling the halter from Timothy's grip.

"And I have mine, Tim," answered William. "Tell the colonel I am on my way to Philadelphia and many thanks to him."

He spurred the horse and took off at a gallop.

"William, your hat!" cried Timothy. But the longhunter was already away.

"Where did you get that horse?" asked Timothy, turning on the two cousins.

"She was just outside the camp, grazing an empty field," answered Bowling.

"Well," said Timothy, resigning himself, "we must see the colonel. I am certain he will wish to speak with that English Shawnee Indian. He will wish to speak with you two as well."

"Why us?" asked Bowling.

"You just gave William the colonel's horse."

Seamus and the Blacksmith Witch

"YOU'RE NOT LISTENING, Da," insisted Seamus.

"Course, I am. I'm sitting right here, am I not? Now what is it you were you saying?" asked Connor mildly.

"Can you please stop working those papers, Da, and just listen?"

Connor Murphy placed his quill beside the brass inkstand, settled back in his hardwood chair, and glared at his son.

"All right then, what is it you wish to say?"

Father and son sat across from each other at the long serving table. The tavern was empty of patrons this time of morning. Murphy-Borough was just beginning a new day.

Seamus cleared his throat. "I need to ask you something, Da. It's about . . . girls."

Connor Murphy looked Seamus up and down, raising his eyebrows. Then he delivered a broad smile. "Well, you have come to the right man then, son. What is it you wish to know?"

"How do you get a girl to notice you, Da?"

Connor rolled his shoulders, grinned like a badger, and plowed right in. "Well now, there are some ways to impress a girl. You could give her flowers. Girls like flowers."

"I done that, Da."

"Oh," said Connor, scratching his left shoulder. "Well, you could help her with her chores then."

"Done that too."

"Hmm," answered Connor, trying to think. "What does the girl like?"

"She likes popped corn," said Seamus with a small smile.

"Everybody likes popped corn," answered Connor factually. "You could make extra just for her."

"She mostly makes her own," said Seamus, rejecting this notion.

"All right then, how about things she does *not* like?" asked Connor.

Seamus had to think on that for a minute. Then he brightened up. "She doesn't like the blacksmith."

"Mr. Cummings? I thought all you children liked Mr. Cummings. I have seen you all many times standing about, watching him swing that big hammer of his. The girls squeal like baby pigs and run around in circles when those sparks are flying. How is it your girl finds fault with Mr. Cummings?"

"That hammer is the very thing, Da. She doesn't like the clanging sound. It makes her jump near out of her skin."

"I'm afraid there is little you can do about that, Seamus. The man makes his living swinging that hammer."

Connor stood up and passed behind the bar. He grabbed a tall flagon and poured himself a warm ale, topping the lip.

"I could ask Mr. Cummings to stop. Do you think he would, Da?"

"Son, the only way you could get Mr. Cummings to stop blacksmithing is if you held a pistol on him. Even then, I would think it a difficult task."

Seamus simply nodded in agreement. "I suppose that's it then, Da. Not much else for it."

"That is true," said Connor, bobbing his head. He took a long draft of ale.

"I'm off, Da."

"Good luck to you, son." Connor chuckled as he turned back to the task. Then he began to think on things.

The stocky Irishman carefully reviewed the conversation in his mind. He stared down into the nearly empty flagon. *The girl jumps when Cummings swings his hammer. Now what girl would that be?* Connor tried to put his mind to it, and when he considered the idea, only one name came to him, Little Cornstalk. Murphy jerked his head up and looked out the open shutter of the tavern. There, walking across the compound, was Seamus, heading straight for the blacksmith with a flintlock pistol in his grip. Knocking over the flagon, Connor Murphy raced out of the tavern, nearly tripping up as he pounded through the door.

Seamus was already standing in the open frame of the blacksmith shop. Mr. Cummings already set a brisk fire under the forge. Black smoke bloomed throughout the small shop, obscuring both smithy and boy.

The forge was built of stone bricks arranged in a large circle some four feet high. It was much like any blacksmith forge. It held a heavy steel grate atop the brick. Beneath the grate, packed charcoal wood burned and would do so all day, throwing out heat and sparks as intended. A wide leather hand bellows was fitted to a gap in the bricks. When Connor made it to the shop, Seamus and Cummings were standing face-to-face. No one spoke. The boy held the pistol by his side. *At least he isn't aiming*, thought Connor with small relief.

"Seamus!" he called aloud as he stepped into the space. Both boy and blacksmith turned at the sound of Connor's voice.

"Leave go of the pistol, son!" growled Connor. "Right now!"

Seamus, looking somewhat sheepish, slowly raised the pistol to pass it to his father.

"Now, Seamus!" bellowed Connor impatiently.

Startled, Seamus whipped his arm up, accidentally pulling the trigger. The ball ricocheted off the round brick furnace, bounced up off a solid block of iron placed nearby, and lodged itself skin deep into the upper left leg of Connor Murphy. Connor's eyeballs looked as though they might pop from his head. A string of profanity, the like of which was rarely heard in Murphy-Borough, sailed out of Connor's mouth in English and Gaelic.

"Da!" cried Seamus, shocked at what he'd done.

Mr. Cummings pulled the pistol from Seamus's hand and laid it down on his anvil. He came over to Connor Murphy, who was now hopping up and down, still singing profane phrases, which included Jesus, Mary, and Joseph along with all the saints; something called a banshee; and the whole bloody world.

"I'm sorry, Da!" cried Seamus, staring at the blood oozing from his father's trouser leg. He began to cry.

By this time, Kathleen was running toward the blacksmith shop along with half the community. Little Cornstalk trailed in her wake.

"What happened?" demanded Kathleen as she entered the shop.

Connor, face screwed up in pain, pointed a finger at Seamus and said, "Your son shot me!"

Kathleen gave Connor a hard look. "I believe two of us were in the making of our son, Connor Murphy. Let me see your leg."

Kathleen poked a finger in the hole in Connor's pants and tore the cloth aside. She swept up her dress and wiped away the blood for a better look.

"Hold still," she ordered the fidgeting Irishman.

Leaning down, she pushed with her thumbs on both sides of the wound and squeezed the ball out. It fell at her feet in the dirt. Connor grimaced a moment and then went silent. Kathleen ripped a small portion of her dress and stuffed it into the hole. She stepped back and gave everyone a hard look.

"What goes on here?" she said with some degree of menace.

"It was no fault of Seamus. I hollered, he was frightened, and the pistol went off," answered Connor, wincing.

"What are you doing here with a pistol, Seamus Declan Murphy?" demanded Kathleen, turning on her son.

Seamus was still sniffling as he dragged a sleeve under his nose. "I was asking Mr. Cummings to stop using his hammer, Ma. Da said the only way he would stop was if I held a pistol on him."

"That is true, Kathleen," said Connor, bobbing his head up and down sadly.

"Bloody hell! Why would you do such a thing, Seamus?"

Connor answered, "It was for her." The Irishman jerked his thumb in the direction of Little Cornstalk.

Standing outside the shop, Little Cornstalk was swinging her head from one person to the next, trying to make sense of what was happening. She would not go inside the shop. Little Cornstalk was convinced the blacksmith was a witch.

"What did you say?" asked Kathleen, flummoxed.

Seamus looked on his mother as a wash of tears covered his face. In a rush, the boy told all. He loved Little Cornstalk. He wanted so much to impress the girl. He told of her fear of the blacksmith's hammer and its awful sound and finally his father's advice. When he finished, Seamus hung his head. He could look nowhere other than the ground beneath his feet. Little Cornstalk wanted to enter the shop to comfort Seamus, but she was too frightened.

Mr. Cummings neither smiled nor frowned. He looked down on the young boy and then across to Little Cornstalk.

Cummings wore a blue sleeveless cotton shirt with a heavy leather apron, dark trousers, and hobnailed boots. Tools of his trade resided inside a long pocket on the apron. They rang on occasion, the tools colliding with one another. Inside the tight space, the heat was rising. Sweat rolled down the sides of the blacksmith's face.

Kathleen spoke first. "Seamus, your but twelve years old, son. You're a might young for a girl like Little Cornstalk, don't you think?"

Seamus felt humiliated. If he hung his head any lower, it threatened to fall off.

Kathleen leaned over her son. "Go on the house, Seamus. We will discuss this later."

Seamus shuffled out of the shop, passing Little Cornstalk without a word. He could not look the girl in the eye.

Connor said, "She's too tall for the boy anyway."

"Don't you dare make light of this, Mr. Murphy," answered Kathleen angrily. "This is your fault!"

Connor rotated his head about and glared at his wife. "I beg pardon, Mrs. Murphy," he said sarcastically. "I'll just wait here and bleed to death until you decide what we should do next."

Kathleen looked over at Mr. Cummings, searching for a solution to this disaster. She had no wish to shame her son any further, and for once, she did not know what to do.

"I have a suggestion, Mrs. Murphy," said Cummings in a low, rumbling voice. "Bring the Indian girl inside. I have seen this kind of thing before. I think I know what to do."

Kathleen stepped outside, explaining to Little Cornstalk that no harm would come to her. She would be right there beside Little Cornstalk the whole time. After several minutes of coaxing, Kathleen led the girl by the hand as they both stepped inside the shop. Little

Cornstalk peered about at the strange collection of tools hanging on the walls. Almost everything looked like a vicious weapon. Then she turned her attention to the fiery pit.

Cummings took a long square bar of steel and placed one end into the fire. Little Cornstalk followed with her eyes closely. Then he took hold of the bellows handle. "This makes a wind that blows on the fire to make it very hot," he explained as he pumped the handle several times, raising the flames and spewing out glowing cinders. "Now watch the metal bar."

Little Cornstalk looked on with fascination as the bar began to turn a deep, glowing red. She squeezed Kathleen's hand tightly. Cummings pulled a large leather mitten off a hook on the shop wall. He took hold the cold end of the bar and turned it over. He did this several times along with more bellows pumping. When the bar glowed bright red, he pulled it from the fire and laid it on his anvil. He hoisted his hammer and showed it to Little Cornstalk. Then he struck the bar lightly, sending up a small spray of sparks. Little Cornstalk leaped back at the sound and tiny flecks of red-hot steel. Then Cummings offered the mallet handle to the girl. He nodded at the bar as if to say, *It is your turn now.* Little Cornstalk took the hammer. She was surprised at the weight of it.

Encouraging the girl to swing the mass of steel as he did, Cummings said, "Go ahead. Try it."

Little Cornstalk looked over at Kathleen, who simply nodded in affirmation.

Taking the hammer in both hands, she dropped it on the hot steel. It made a tiny ringing noise, and a few sparks popped out.

"Again," said Cummings. "This time, hit it hard."

Little Cornstalk gave him a smile, raised the hammer high, and brought it down with all the strength she had. A loud clang rang out, accompanied with a wide spray of sparks. Little Cornstalk squealed like a child. The softened steel yielded, spreading and flattening some. She struck the bar again and again with the same result.

Kathleen was smiling. Mr. Cummings was smiling too. They watched as Little Cornstalk pounded that bar until it was cold. Cummings had to stop her so he could place the bar back into the fire.

"Well, that's just fine," said Connor, clipping his words. "Can we attend to your bleeding husband now, Mrs. Murphy?"

"Go on with you, Connor," answered Kathleen, unconcerned. "That's barely the nip of rabbit. I have taken care of worse on you."

Kathleen and Connor left the shop, limping over to the tavern. They left Little Cornstalk, chattering away with Mr. Cummings. She was no longer afraid of the blacksmith witch.

Seamus stood in the doorway of the tavern, a sad figure.

"Ah, Seamus, me lovely boy," said Kathleen as she and Connor approached. "Love comes to us all, you know. Let's have a talk with Little Cornstalk later. You must consider her feelings as well, son. You need to know what it is that's in her mind."

"I know what's in her mind, Ma," answered Seamus sadly.

"You do?"

"William MacEwan," said Seamus with a tinge of jealousy. "That's what's in her mind—William MacEwan."

Rescue

STEVENSON SAT WAITING impatiently for Bennett. The man was infuriating. He seemed incapable of serious behavior. The more he learned of Bennett's plans, the less comfortable he felt about it. It all seemed too complicated. Stevenson was a man of modest thinking. You simply go straight at it and do what is needed. This plan of Bennett's was something altogether different.

Ulli sat opposite the agitated hunter; there was no conversation between the two friends. Helmut could be heard down in the shop, pacing to and fro as he marched across the hardwood floor, occasionally peering through the shop windows, searching for his friend Bennett. It seemed even the sun was unwilling to cooperate. They all waited impatiently for night to come.

As the day finally faded into darkness, Bennett arrived. He climbed the narrow stairway in a rush, Helmut close behind.

"Are we ready?" asked Bennett with his usual smile.

All three men nodded in uncertain silence.

"Why the long faces, gentlemen? You each know the task ahead. Is it a question you have? If so, ask it now."

Stevenson cleared his throat. "Explain again about this body we supposedly found."

"Oh, that," replied Bennett, nodding in comprehension. "We have little time left, so listen carefully.

"We need the redcoats guarding the Weatherly house to believe we are who we say we are. The information I collected from the ladies of the house will aid us in this. When the MacEwan boy shot this fellow, Tom Evens, your captain Alden intervened. Claiming martial law, he sent the magistrate away. Then he instructed his men to remove the body from the house and throw it in the Schuylkill River.

"We will inform the guards that we have recovered Tom Evens's body from the river, one mile south of Collier's Landing, a likely spot to dispose of a corpse by the way. The body has been reliably identified as Tom Evens. This is the reason for the warrant to arrest."

"But there is no body," said Stevenson.

"That is true," said Bennett.

"And they will believe this?" asked Ulli.

"Naturally. How else would we know the body was thrown in the river?"

Stevenson scratched his bearded chin.

"You look vexed, Mr. Stevenson. Is there something else that requires explanation?"

"No, I think not," answered Stevenson, bowing his head. "I trust you know what you are about."

"Yes, Mr. Stevenson, I do know what I am doing," answered Bennett passionately. "I am risking your lives and that of my crew to save a kidnapped woman and her four children. Have no doubt, gentlemen. This is a hazardous undertaking. However, we will accomplish what we are setting out to do—bringing the MacEwan family safely out of the city."

It was a walk to the Philadelphia docks, near three miles. Stevenson wanted to get there early to ensure that all was ready. Bennett, it seemed, had arranged everything. He acquired the wagon needed as well as blue jackets and hats from the magistrate's office. How was a mystery. The arrest warrant was written and in hand, complete with the magistrate's seal. There was also a letter from the military governor of all people. Stevenson had no notion about how Bennett accomplished these things, but he did. The ship he was to meet was a Dutch *hoeker*, the *Wind Maiden*. She was a 480-ton cargo ship, fully rigged.

Bennett explained, as a neutral country, Holland and the Dutch East India Company routinely hauled weapons and supplies to both sides of the American conflict. It was good money to be had. The *Wind Maiden* held a crew of sixty-two. Bennett had sailed her for three years. Although he was born in the British Isles, he considered himself as much American as any man in the colonies.

A forest of ship masts stood proud over the houses as Stevenson approached. The smell of tar pitch, salt water, and rope filled the air. It was getting close to Stevenson's time to arrive, and so the old hunter quickened his step.

As he came up on the ship, a line of men passing crates like a fire bucket brigade could be seen. The crates were being removed from a large canvas-covered wagon. The canvas read, "FIELDING CARGO," in large block letters. Standing alongside the wagon was Bennett. Ulli and Helmut stood opposite, watching the crates as they passed along. Bennett looked up at the approaching hunter.

"Good evening, Mr. Stevenson. Are you prepared, sir?"

"I am."

"Good. As soon as the remaining crates are removed from the wagon, we'll be on our way."

"I thought the wagon was to be painted city green, Mr. Bennett," said Stevenson, concerned. "This looks to be gray canvas."

"Look under the canvas," answered the sailor.

With a questioning expression, Stevenson stepped up to the side of the wagon and pulled the canvas cover aside. Peeking beneath, the wagon was clearly painted dark city green.

Standing behind Stevenson, Bennett said, "We'll pull the cover off when we near the Weatherly house."

Bennett held out a small scroll of papers. "Would you care to examine these as well?"

"No, thank you. I am sure they are in order."

"A man of honest words, Mr. Stevenson," answered Bennett, mildly surprised.

The last of the crates had now been removed. Bennett turned to the two German butchers.

"Helmut, Ulli, it is time for you to go. I expect to see you when we have completed our little adventure. You know where to be. We will meet you there."

Three of Bennett's crew members silently climbed into the wagon. As Stevenson peered inside, he could see them donning blue jackets and hats of the Philadelphia Magistrate's Office. They spoke in whispers. Each man carried a loaded Brown Bess and, from the looks of it, a small cudgel tucked in their trousers.

Bennett stuck his head inside the wagon. "Good luck to you, mates." The three men nodded.

"Reverend Pierce," called Bennett.

A rail-thin man walked slowly down the gangway of the *Wind Maiden*, running his fingers through a shock of salt-and-pepper hair. He wore no hat. His face was as thin as a sapling pine with a long-pointed nose. His hair was combed and neatly trimmed.

The coat he wore was black as night with a broad collar and light blue piping. Black trousers with white stockings matched the coat. Dainty shoes covered his feet, each with a brass cross buckle. His shirt was snow white. The outfit was finished with a red tie that hung loose down front.

As he approached Stevenson and Bennett, he displayed a wide smile. "Good evening, Mr. Bennett."

"Reverend," acknowledged Bennett. "Mr. Stevenson I would like you to meet the deputy Magistrate, Mr. Pierce."

Stevenson shook hands with the man. He had to admit, if he was to imagine a deputy magistrate, he would certainly look like this fellow.

"How do you do, sir?" said the thin man, nodding politely. The voice did not seem to fit the man. It was deep, clear, and decidedly British.

"I am well, sir. Thank you," answered Stevenson.

"Shall we be on our way, gentlemen?"

"Reverend," said Bennett, "you ride in the back of the wagon until the driver calls you. He will know when. At that time the canvas cover will be removed, you will then take your place beside the driver. Please do not forget to wear your magistrate hat."

"Why, yes, of course," answered the reverend in that deep, rolling voice. He climbed into the wagon.

Stevenson looked at Bennett. "A reverend?"

"Have no fear, Mr. Stevenson. The Reverend Pierce is the most persuasive man I have ever encountered. He could talk the devil out of an apple tree. Now in the wagon if you please, Mr. Stevenson."

"Should I ask what happened to the real magistrate, Bennett?"

"Trussed him up like a turkey and thrown into the hold of our ship."

THE LONGHUNTER

Stevenson's eyes went wide. He was about to say something.

"A jest, Mr. Stevenson," answered the sailor, holding up his hand. "It was only a jest."

Stevenson blew out air from his inflated cheeks in frustration.

"Is this the time for a jest, Mr. Bennett?"

"Yes," said Bennett with an innocent expression on his face. "Actually, the magistrate and his wife received an invitation to the military governor's ball tonight. Mrs. Magistrate was beside herself with joy. She had been seeking an invite for some time now."

"And what of the magistrate officers?"

"They were sent a gift from the magistrate himself, a lovely barrel of Jamaican rum including a note to enjoy themselves as the magistrate and his wife will surely do this evening."

"An invitation to the military governor's house?" asked Stevenson skeptically. "How was this managed?"

"Same printer that makes the warrants for arrest also prints party invitations," answered Bennett flatly.

Stevenson wagged his head in wonder. Even so, he felt as though a pinewood knot was lodged in the center of his belly, irritating as well as indigestible. Taking a seat on an empty crate, he looked around the small space, scanning each man's face. Everyone seemed quite calm.

Bennett stuck his head inside and handed the scrolls to Reverend Pierce. "Do not forget, Mr. Stevenson. You are to stay in the wagon no matter what occurs. If Mrs. MacEwan sees you and calls your name, we will be undone and most likely forced to a violent end. Understood?"

"Yes," answered Stevenson stiffly.

"Good luck to you all."

The first part of the trip was relatively straightforward. The wagon rolled up the street, clapping the cobbles with steel-rimmed horseshoes. Stevenson noticed for the first time that a pile of blankets and soft pillows were stacked in the rear of the wagon. *For the Mrs. and her children*, he thought. *Did Bennett think of everything?* The pine knot in his gut wasn't getting any better.

With the docks far behind now, the streets became eerily quiet. The wagon rolled to a stop. The reverend and all three crew members clambered out as if the maneuver was practiced. The reverend headed to the driver's seat while the crew removed the canvas cover. In seconds, they were again on their way.

Stevenson had the ridiculous notion that the reverend may have forgotten his hat. He asked one of the crew.

"Gave it to him myself," answered one man. "Not too worry, sir. The reverend baptized me hisself."

It wasn't clear to Stevenson how that helped, but he accepted the answer.

"Getting close now," said the same man as he peered out the back of the wagon.

"Lord, help us," muttered Stevenson.

"Amen," said the man sitting beside him.

The wagon came to a halt.

The three crew men climbed out, and the reverend could be heard descending from the driver's seat. Stevenson dared a peek out the back, and there before him was the infamous Weatherly house, painted German blue.

The house was well lit with several lanterns displayed in the large bay window. The sounds of a fiddle and pipe could be heard drifting through the night, accompanied by the laughter of men and women. The driver of the wagon came down and held the draft horse by its reins. The four conspirators approached the Weatherly house, looking every inch the officials they pretended to be. Each of the crew, apart from the reverend, carried a Brown Bess in a casual manner. The reverend approached the single guard near the front entrance of the home.

"Good evening, sir," said the reverend, addressing the soldier.

The soldier looked over the wagon that just arrived. "What's this then?" he asked politely.

"I am Deputy Magistrate Emerson. I am here to arrest"—he stopped and studied one of the papers he held—"Mrs. Elspeth MacEwan and children." He rolled the document closed.

"No, sir," answered the soldier. "We have orders from Captain Alden. These people are to be held here until further notice."

"Well then," answered the reverend confidently, "this is your further notice. You will have these people brought out immediately. It is late, and I wish to go home to my supper."

"I cannot release the prisoners without direct orders," snapped the soldier with finality.

"Here then," said the reverend, handing both documents to the man. "As you can see, they are orders from the military governor as well as an arrest warrant from the magistrate's office."

The soldier studied the papers briefly. "I'll have to get me sergeant, sir. I cannot read a word of these papers."

"Do so quickly. We do not have all night, sir."

The reverend took on a ruffled appearance, stiffly tapping his polished shoe at a rapid pace on the stone path. The soldier hurried off to collect his sergeant.

The sergeant came out of the house, buttoning his jacket and jamming a tricorn on his head. He approached the reverend.

"A sinner, I see," said the fake magistrate with disgust.

"I was a sleeping, if you must know," answered the sergeant irritably.

"These are for you," said the reverend, passing the papers to the man.

The sergeant studied the papers closely. "I thought this was all cleared with the magistrate's office. Why is this happening now?"

The reverend had rehearsed this part. He knew precisely what to say.

"A body was discovered washed ashore a mile south of Collier's Landing. It has been identified as Tom Evens. There was a large hole in his chest. As far as we are aware, Mr. Evens was killed here in this house. We have two complaining witnesses attesting to this. Once the body was discovered, we immediately began an investigation, thus a warrant for arrest. To avoid any unpleasant conflict with your army, we gained the permission of your military governor. Please have these people brought out immediately for transfer to the Walnut Street Jail."

As the reverend wound his tale, a look of heightened concern crossed the sergeant's face. As Bennett expected, the men involved in the disposal of Tom Evens's body would now see the seriousness of their actions.

Stevenson sat hidden in the dark of the wagon, listening intently. He marveled at the audacity of the reverend. The three crew members behaved as though this were just another day, another arrest for the magistrate. They peered inside the bay window of the house and chuckled at the men inside, cavorting with their paramours.

"One of my men will have to accompany you to the jail."

"That is just as well, Sergeant. A colonel from the Twenty-Third Dragoons is waiting in my office to question you and your captain Alden about how Mr. Evens's corpse wound up in the river."

The sergeant's face began to take on a look of panic. He began to sputter. "We have strict orders, Deputy Magistrate. We are not to leave our post under any circumstance."

"Hmmm," muttered the reverend. "Fine then. I will inform the colonel. Now will you kindly release these people to me?"

"Yes, sir," answered the sergeant meekly.

Hurrying back to the door of the Weatherly house, the sergeant entered. To Stevenson, his return seemed an eternity.

Finally, the door opened, and out came Mrs. Weatherly. She stood at the top of the steps, hands on hips, glaring at the fake magistrate. Behind her, a small knot of bundled people made their way down the front stairway and across the cobbled path. Peeking out a hole in the wagon, Stevenson recognized Elspeth MacEwan immediately. The children were mostly enclosed in blankets as it was a cool evening. Suddenly awakened, they shuffled along, confused and slightly dazed. Stevenson smiled to himself. *This is happening*, thought the hunter.

Elspeth, pleading with Mrs. Weatherly, cried out, "You must inform the captain, Mrs. Weatherly! Please tell me you will!"

"I will, Mrs. MacEwan. Be certain of that."

Mrs. Weatherly looked down on the reverend skeptically. "Since when does Philadelphia have a deputy magistrate?"

The reverend locked eyes on the old woman.

"I was elected to this office nearly two months ago, madam. And," he declared, "I am not only the deputy magistrate, I am also an ordained minister. You should be aware that I have made several attempts to shutter this house of yours. With this arrest, you will no longer house prisoners here. Your protection from magistrate law will not apply. You can be certain of my return on that matter."

"Wait," called Weatherly. "We have no arrangement with the British."

"That is not true, madam. Your captain Alden has held several prisoners here." The reverend turned sharply on the sergeant. "My information is that they were all women prisoners, Sergeant. Is this true?"

The sergeant held mute, his mouth ajar.

The reverend turned back to Mrs. Weatherly. "Oh yes, Mrs. Weatherly. The magistrate knows of these abductions, women taken from their homes by British irregulars, all held as rebel conspirators here in this very house by you and your captain Alden. You can claim no innocence in this matter, madam. The commander of the Twenty-Third Dragoons is currently seeking the whereabouts of your captain. This whole affair has the stench of skullduggery about it and will be found out. You may be certain of that."

As still as a statue, Elspeth caught every word of the reverend's little speech. She cocked her head to the side and glared up at the old woman. "Several other women, Mrs. Weatherly?" shouted Elspeth aloud.

The idea began twisting in her mind like a rope turned to a coil. She reeled at the words. What fate, she wondered, had been awaiting her at the hands of John Alden and this wicked woman perched at the top of the steps?

"Mrs. Weatherly!" screamed Elspeth. "You lied! You knew all along what he was doing, and you lied. You have been conspiring with Alden this whole time, haven't you? What did you intend for my children?"

Weatherly said nothing.

"You are a wicked woman, Mrs. Weatherly, and I will see you in hell for this," finished Elspeth.

Mrs. Weatherly ignored Elspeth, asking only, "Where are you taking them?"

"The Walnut Street Jail," answered the reverend in a clipped tone, "where they should have been taken at the first." The reverend then turned to his three crew members. "Assist these prisoners into the wagon, gentlemen. I wish to be home as swiftly as possible."

The children were passed into the wagon first. They made little sound beyond the occasional sniffling. As Elspeth climbed aboard, she spied a dark figure tucked in the corner. The man was dressed as a simple farmer. Elspeth stared at him, trying to adjust her sight to the darkness. She could not clearly see the man's face. Suddenly stricken with a new fright, she recoiled.

"Howdy-do, Mrs. MacEwan?" whispered Stevenson softly.

Elspeth recognized the voice. But she could put no face to it. She leaned in closer to the seated figure, trying desperately to make out anything in the darkness of the wagon's interior. As she did so, the three crewmen climbed in. Each man settled on an empty crate. The reverend hoisted himself up onto the driver's buckboard. The wagon began to roll.

"It is I, Mrs. MacEwan. Olaf Stevenson," said the farmer.

Stevenson slid closer to Elspeth. The old longhunter lit a night lantern, illuminating his face. At the sight of Stevenson, realization hit Elspeth like a falling tree. Stevenson smiled broadly.

"We are taking you home, Mrs. MacEwan," said Stevenson, "home where you belong."

Elspeth lost herself. She let out an anguished wail, audible all the way back to the Weatherly house. She began to shake and sob in sudden relief. The children heard their mother and became agitated. Aelwyd began crying and shaking visibly. David, on the other hand, knew this man, a friend. He also understood what was happening.

"We're escaping, Mother!" cried David happily.

A loud thump came from the top of the wagon, a warning from the reverend.

"Everyone, quiet," commanded Stevenson.

David placed an arm around Aelwyd, calming her. He whispered to the frightened girl, "Quiet now, Aelwyd. We are going home. We are going back home."

The girl stared at her brother in disbelief. David nodded and said simply, "Really."

The twins sat silently, snapping their heads from one person to the next. They gripped each other's hand tightly, attempting to adjust their sight to the near-total darkness. They had heard their brother, but to them, it meant little. This was just another adventure for the boys.

Brian said, "Are we really going home, Mama?"

Elspeth managed to control her emotions and placed a hand on Brian's shoulder. "Yes, Brian, we are. You and Duncan must be very quiet now. And you as well, Aelwyd. If we wish to get home safely, we must all be very, very quiet."

"I'll help, Mother," whispered David, smiling.

Elspeth took a deep breath and sat up. She turned toward Stevenson and wrapped her arms about the large hunter, hugging him with all the force of a brown bear. He was having difficulty breathing. She held on to Stevenson for a long time as tears of happiness ran over her face.

The wagon began picking up speed. The farther away from the Weatherly house, the faster they moved. Taking a sharp turn away from Walnut Street, they ran along for several blocks. Then pulling beside another wagon facing the opposite direction, they suddenly stopped. The crewmen piled out of the back as quick as a sack of freed rabbits.

Helmut held his draft horse by the bit, keeping the butcher's wagon steady. The side of the wagon read, "Becker & Rohs, Deutsche Butchers."

Ulli scrambled around the back to supervise the transfer. Between Stevenson and the three crewmen, it took only seconds to get everyone in the butcher's wagon. Ulli quickly piled up a series of boxes, concealing the MacEwan family and one large hunter. The crates were filled with salted beef.

The magistrate wagon took off without so much as a fare-thee-well. It quickly vanished down the dark street. The canvas cargo cover was back in place.

Ulli and Helmut made straight for the Philadelphia docks. Once they arrived at their destination, they came to a quiet halt. The dock was deserted this time of night. Mr. Stevenson swiftly grasped each of his friends by the hand and bid them farewell.

"Come back to us, Olaf," said Ulli.

"Ja," echoed Helmut stoically.

"I will, my friends. Thank you for this. It will not be forgotten."

It was well past midnight before the MacEwans were transferred to a slow-moving garbage scow, the only fully functioning barge on the river this time of night. The smell was awful, but it had little effect on the mood of the passengers. Sitting quietly, huddled up in a pile of blankets and pillows, Elspeth and the children were all smiles. Ulli had placed a sack of apples in the back of his wagon, and David, Brian, and Duncan were munching on them with delight. Mr. Stevenson sat on a barrel beside the steersman, smoking his long Dutch. They drifted past Collier's Landing sometime around two o'clock in the morning.

Two miles farther downriver, the scow came to a halt and was tied up to a line of oaks standing off the shoreline. Except for Stevenson and the barge pilot, everyone was sound asleep. The hunter hated to wake them, knowing it was a difficult night for all, but they had to keep moving, and Stevenson was determined to keep at it.

Once everyone was safely ashore, the scow untied her lines and drifted back out to the middle of the river. They walked a wide path toward an open wagon standing by a leafless maple. A stocky man wearing a long peacoat dressed as a sailor came around the wagon, holding a night lantern.

"Mr. Bennett," said Stevenson, surprised.

"Mr. Stevenson," replied Bennett, unsmiling.

"I have no way to thank you, Bennett. You can believe me when I say you are a maker of miracles. You have my sincerest gratitude and the thanks of Mrs. MacEwan and her children as well. I believe William will be the most grateful."

"I am happy that all went well, Mr. Stevenson. Perhaps someday we can do this again."

"I do not believe I would enjoy that," said the hunter, tipping his hat kindly.

"Fine then," said Bennett with feigned grievance. "Did you bring any rum . . . or just yourself." He laughed softly.

"I fear it is only us, sir," answered Stevenson with a positive nod. He reached out and shook Bennett's hand.

After helping the children into the waiting wagon, Elspeth approached the two men. She locked both hands around Stevenson's own and looked up at the square Swedish face.

"Thank you, Mr. Stevenson. Thank you for our lives."

"Oh, not me, Mrs. MacEwan. Your thanks is owed to this gentleman," said Stevenson, turning to Bennett. "May I introduce Mr. Richard Bennett. Bennett, this is the benefactor of your escape plan, Mrs. Elspeth MacEwan."

Bennett whipped the cap from his head and shyly offered his hand. Elspeth gently held it, smiling up into the face of the pug-nosed sailor. His short choppy brown hair fluttered in the evening breeze.

Elspeth said, "I do not know you, sir, but I can easily say I am forever grateful for everything you have done for us—everything. Thank you for my life and the lives of my children."

Bennett looked down modestly on his hobnailed boots, scuffing the earth as he did so.

"One question, if you please," asked Stevenson, interrupting.

"Yet another question, Mr. Stevenson," said Bennett tiredly.

"The reverend, he was telling the truth about Alden and the women held prisoner at that house?"

"Yes," answered the sailor grimly. "The only thing that saved Mrs. MacEwan here from an unknown fate were the children. Alden had to find a way to rid himself of the little ones but was unable to do so for some reason. That allowed us time to rescue the family."

"How did you learn of this, Mr. Bennett?" asked Elspeth. "About Alden and the house, I mean."

"I gained what information I could about Captain Alden from one girl at the house. Her name is Amelie. She told me that Alden had taken as many as six women to the Weatherly house, some even before the British occupied the city. When he was through with them, they begged the captain for release. And this he did. They were never heard from again. I believe Alden killed them all."

"My god," said Elspeth. "If that is true . . ." Elspeth trailed off, thinking of what might have been. "I could see such behavior from a savage Indian but from an English officer?" A cold shiver ran through

Elspeth at the thought. Unable to fully comprehend Alden's crimes, Elspeth shook visibly.

"I will go to my children now," she said quietly. "I thank you again, Mr. Bennett. I wish you well, sir."

Bennett acknowledged her thanks with a sharp nod. "Safe journey to you, Mrs. MacEwan." At that, Elspeth climbed into the wagon. Sitting beside David, she placed her arm about her son's small shoulders and fell to an exhausted sleep.

"I should have killed Alden when I had the chance," said Stevenson angrily. He stomped his foot in frustration.

"Alden is no longer your concern, Mr. Stevenson."

"Are the British really after him?"

"Not that I am aware," answered Bennett, placing the cap back on his head. "They may be, but it is unlikely. Don't burden yourself about Alden, Mr. Stevenson. I will deal with the man myself. Now if you follow this road less than a mile, you will find Major Clark and Captain Gunnarsson waiting. Once there, you will be safe."

Broken Tree

THEY WALKED IN the rain. Just south of Bemis Heights, the American forces were assembling for a march east. The Hessian and British captives from the Battle of Saratoga would now be marched to an American fort, there to be paroled or imprisoned. As Timothy strode through the camp, all eyes fell on him and the odd group that trailed behind.

Directly in Timothy's wake was Broken Tree. Despite the rain, wet leaves, and mud, the tall Indian moved effortlessly along using his staff to support his crippled leg. He stared straight ahead, Shawnee proud. Uncertain if he was going to his death, he displayed no curiosity or fear.

Wallace and Bowling trailed behind on each side of Broken Tree, their rifles at the ready. As they passed the exhausted men of the Virginia company, conversation ceased long enough to witness the little parade. The Shawnee chieftain was a sight to these men as he rocked side to side, keeping pace with Timothy. Several of the men hurled insults at the Indian as they passed by, some tossing clods of dirt or worse. The Indian ignored it.

Morgan propped up and, leaning back on his cot, read the latest correspondence from Major Clark. He learned something from the communiqué that angered him. The MacEwan family had been discovered imprisoned in a Philadelphia bordello.

"A bordello," muttered Morgan to himself. "Good god."

He understood now why the MacEwan boy had taken for the city. Morgan's hips ached fiercely this day, further spoiling his temper. The message from Clark did not help. As the rain continued, he considered what Timothy had relayed between William and the Shawnee Indian Broken Tree.

Broken Tree was known to Morgan. He had heard of the crippled chief many times before, Tenskwatawa's broken brother. The reputation of the tall Indian was somewhat of a mystery. He supposedly spoke

English better than most white men. This mattered little to Morgan now. His interest lay in the short conversation between Broken Tree and William MacEwan.

When Tim Murphy mentioned the name of Alden, it drew Morgan's attention instantly. He remembered the Englishman's name. The British plan that William had given Morgan had been passed onto General Washington. And George, rightly so, took it to be a British ploy. When word came down that Burgoyne had invaded south from Canada, it only solidified Washington's thinking on the matter. The American general ordered Morgan and his riflemen north to meet with General Gates's forces. Together, they would face Burgoyne's threat.

As Tim approached Morgan's tent, the ever-present corporal Hand stood at the entrance. Ezra eyed Broken Tree closely.

"Does he carry any weapons?" asked Ezra.

"No, Ezra, he was searched thoroughly. He has no weapons."

"What about that big stick?"

"He needs that to walk," answered Timothy impatiently.

"Give it here," said Ezra. "You can help him in."

He took the staff and leaned it carefully on the side of the tent.

Timothy offered his shoulder to Broken Tree. The Indian's grip was painful. He leaned heavily on the young rifleman, nearly collapsing Tim to the ground. Timothy thought a bear had climbed his back.

As they entered, Morgan sat up, swinging his legs over, placing his stocking feet on dirt. He did not stand. The center pole hub was tall, but the sloping cover forced Broken Tree to remain standing in place. He was simply too tall for the short-pegged sides of the tent.

Morgan indicated a blanket-covered crate beside his cot. "Will you sit with me and smoke Broken Tree?" said Morgan wearily.

"Why, thank you, Colonel. I would be delighted," answered the Indian in a clipped English accent.

Morgan's eyes opened wide with astonishment. "I was told you spoke English well. I see now it was no exaggeration."

"No more exaggeration than any other tale said of me." The Indian went right to it. "Why am I here with you now, Colonel? Am I to be executed?"

Morgan looked hard at the man but made no reply. The thought came to him that this Shawnee chief not only spoke like a white man but also thought like one. He could be the most dangerous Indian Morgan ever encountered. And that said something.

"What do you know of British plans?" asked the colonel. He raised a hand to Tim. "Timothy, would you be kind enough to pass that box over? The one on my table there."

Timothy brought the box over, handing it to Morgan. Morgan opened it and gingerly passed a clay pipe to Broken Tree. He pulled his own pipe from his coat pocket and then offered a sack of cut tobacco to the Indian. Broken Tree took a long draw on the Dutch pipe, blowing out a cloud of fine smoke with deep satisfaction. He smiled with pleasure.

"I am sorry, Colonel. The British rarely, if ever, share their plans with the Shawnee. Excepting the possible disposition and deployment of our warriors for battle, we know nothing."

Morgan anticipated this reply and considered it mostly true. Still, this wily Indian was impossible to trust. "How many white captives do the Shawnee have?"

Broken Tree was taken aback by this question. He had assumed the Americans' only interest would be the British—where they were, where they were going.

"White captives, Colonel?" repeated the Indian, mildly confused.

"Yes," said Morgan, raising his voice. "How many white captives are in your village?"

"Two, maybe three dozen. I am unsure of the exact number. Why do you ask?"

"I have a proposition for you, Broken Tree."

Morgan turned to Timothy. "How many Shawnee prisoners do we have in our possession, Mr. Murphy?"

"Seven, I believe, Colonel. The others ran when we opened our cannon, sir. They have vanished."

Morgan continued addressing Broken Tree. "I want to trade your white captives for you and the other Shawnee we hold. Are you amenable to this?"

"I am," answered the tall Indian, taking a puff on his pipe. "Fine tobacco, Colonel. I thank you."

"All right then, we will exchange you and your brothers for all the white captives you have in your possession. Now," said Morgan, straightening up, "I want to know what words passed between you and William MacEwan."

Broken Tree's eyes narrowed, pinching his thin face even further. "MacEwan, the longhunter?"

"Yes."

"He asked for the return of his family," replied Broken Tree simply. "I explained to him the Shawnee did not have them. They were taken to Philadelphia by the English."

"And he believed you?"

"Not until I mentioned Alden's name, a man he seemed familiar with." Broken Tree blew out another wave of smoke. "Once I explained that Alden was involved, he knew I was telling the truth."

"How is it you know this Alden?"

"We came on the captain escaping Black Feather's village."

"Captain, you say?" said Morgan.

"Yes. As I understand it, he is a captain in the Twenty-Third Light Dragoons."

Broken Tree then relayed how the Shawnee had stumbled upon Alden running from the Cherokee village.

"He told my brother Tenskwatawa where we might find American rifles. Naturally, my brother was interested in acquiring these rifles. On the trail north, we came on Alden's irregulars, a rather nasty group, I must say."

"A British officer was going to provide you with American rifles?"

"Yes. Alden explained they could be found at the MacEwan settlement."

"My rifles!" shouted Morgan, looking as though he might explode.

Broken Tree sat calmly, smoking the long thin pipe. "We found no rifles, Colonel."

"Only by the grace of God," said Morgan through his teeth. "So you killed the people at the MacEwan home, burned the place to the ground, and kidnapped MacEwan's mother along with her children?"

"As I said, Colonel, the Shawnee took no one. The captain and his people took Mrs. MacEwan. They were found in a hideaway from the cabins."

"Why did Alden take these people?"

"I have no idea, Colonel. The captain seemed interested only in the woman. He offered the children to Tenskwatawa, but my brother refused them. I would have taken them myself, but Tenskwatawa would not allow it."

Now it was Morgan's turn to be confused. "Why did Tenskwatawa refuse the children?"

"Fear, superstition, the longhunter." Broken Tree shrugged as if this was answer enough.

"Do you mean William MacEwan?"

"Yes, William MacEwan. The longhunter fought alongside Black Feather's Cherokee when we invaded the village. He killed several Shawnee. I saw this with my own eyes, a courageous young man. Then from an impossible distance, he shot Tenskwatawa, knocking him from his horse. If my brother had not been wearing his Spanish armor, he would most likely be dead now. It was enough to hold the Shawnee until Cherokee warriors came in relief, a remarkable shot really.

"In any case, my brother now has it in his mind that the longhunter will someday come to take his life. Tenskwatawa refused the children knowing this would give William cause to hunt my brother down and kill him. I tried to explain, but Tenskwatawa would not listen."

Every man in the tent looked at Broken Tree, amazed. They knew nothing of this from William.

"Wallace, Bowling," said Morgan, suddenly grabbing the attention of the two cousins, "get two good mounts and provisions. I want you to trail William immediately. *And* I want my horse back. If possible, get William to Major Clark's headquarters and have him wait there. Go now."

The two men bolted out of the tent.

Morgan turned back to Broken Tree. "I thank you for the information, Broken Tree. You may return to your confinement. We will arrange for one of your people to bring my offer of prisoner exchange to your brother. I would make haste if I were you, Broken Tree."

The Indian locked eyes with Morgan, but the colonel showed no expression. "And the reason for this haste, Colonel?"

"I leave here in two days. Those are my orders. If your Shawnee runner does not return in two days with the white captives, I will hang you and the remaining Shawnee captives."

Broken Tree looked mildly surprised. "You would hang prisoners of war, Colonel? I think that rather bad form, wouldn't you say?"

Morgan looked up at the now standing Indian. "No, I would not hang prisoners of war. However, I would hang murdering Shawnee, the men who killed Ian MacEwan, burned his home to the ground, and assisted in taking an innocent family against their will."

Broken Tree snapped his head up, took hold of Timothy's shoulder once again, and exited the tent in silence.

Alden

ALDEN STEPPED OFF the jolly boat onto the Philadelphia dock. This night, he would finally have Elspeth MacEwan in his arms.

He had donned his full dragoon uniform. The jacket, dark green with large brass buttons down the lapels, was tapered along his upper body with form. The britches were white along with the high-necked blouse. Two leather belts crossed his chest, each carrying a flintlock pistol. His boots were polished and high to the knee. The brass helmet he wore was topped with a spray of feathers dyed black with a dark band cloth wound round it.

He waited patiently for his horse. The raucous activity on the dock was in full play. Supplies of every type were lining up along the wharf; food stuff, animals, powder, cannon, shot, wine, and cotton were being discharged off the ships as men of every stripe scurried here and there. Alden ignored it all.

Two other officers of the Twenty-Third Regiment, one a captain, the other a colonel, wandered up alongside Alden as they, too, came onto the dock. Each man inspected his uniform, jerking the dark green jacket down tight to ensure its proper arrangement after the jostling jolly boat ride.

"Hallo, Captain Alden," said the colonel pleasantly.

Alden nodded politely. "Good afternoon, Colonel Tarleton."

Tarleton went on, "I have heard your special exploring assignment did not go quite as planned, Captain. General Howe was most disappointed you were unable to retrieve the American rifles. What are your plans now? I imagine you are anxious to return to the fight on the back of a horse."

"Yes, of course, Colonel, most anxious," answered Alden distractedly.

"Ah," said Tarleton, tilting his chin up, "our mounts have arrived. A pity we must stay in this dung heap of a city. When Cornwallis arrives, you will see some real fighting then."

"Yes," said Alden, "I imagine so. General Howe seemed reluctant to leave the confines of the city."

"You mean the confines of his bed." Tarleton scoffed with a laugh. "Good day to you, Captain."

Tarleton and his companion climbed their respective animals, each giving Alden a bonny salute. The colonel and the silent captain rode straight up North Avenue.

Alden had dealt with Banastre Tarleton previously. The man was vicious in a fight and incredibly brave. His reputation was that of a savage winner. Having spent weeks—nay, months in the American interior, Alden knew only too well that to truly defeat the American soldier, it would take men of Tarleton's brutality.

Tarleton was a rare animal in England. Unfortunately for the British, that could not be said of the Americans. They, too, were brave, vicious, and fierce. Most importantly, they were in this fight of their own will. Without their ruthless, unbending courage, the American soldier simply could not survive this wild country. But they did. *Yes*, thought Alden, *it will take more than Banastre Tarleton to win this war.*

Riding leisurely along the abandoned streets of Philadelphia, Alden approached his commandeered quarters. A sergeant from the Twenty-Third stood waiting outside. The man rushed down to Alden, handing him a slip of rough paper.

"An urgent message, sir," said the sergeant.

Alden read the note quickly. Without acknowledging the man, he remounted his horse and made straight for the Weatherly house.

Alden pounded up the short entrance steps, burst through the front door, and called out in a thunderous voice, "Mrs. Weatherly!"

The old woman came down the hallway from the kitchen in no hurry. She held out both her hands in supplication. "It was the magistrate, Captain. I could do nothing to prevent it. They had a legal warrant for their arrest."

Alden looked at the old woman, his face flushed with anger. "I told you no one was to remove them from this house. How could you let this happen?"

"I let it happen?" queried the old woman sharply.

"Ask your sergeant outside there," she continued angrily, pointing at the front door. "Your soldiers read the orders. There was nothing to be done. We were forced to release them."

"Where is she?" growled Alden.

"The Walnut Street Jail. They took the whole lot."

Alden stormed out of the house, stopping in front his sergeant.

"What happened?" asked Alden, clearly upset.

"It was the deputy magistrate, Captain. They come with a warrant and a note from the military governor."

"You had your orders, Sergeant. No one was to take those people from the house."

Dropping his voice low, the sergeant whispered, "He knew about them other ladies, Captain. He knew all about them. Said he was coming back to investigate, sir. Said there was a colonel from the Twenty-Third looking for you."

Alden's face suddenly went pale. He spun his head about as if searching for the mysterious colonel among the trees lining the street.

"Are you certain of this, Sergeant?" asked Alden, keeping his voice low as well.

"Aye, sir. The man seemed well informed about . . . everything. He challenged the Mrs. in the house too."

Alden's concern mounted. Who was this colonel from the Twenty-Third? Was he really searching for him? He had received no message except for the note from Weatherly. That was strange. He would have to see what this was about. He doubted his sentries would talk as they were as guilty as he. Each of Alden's four permanent duty guards at the Weatherly house had taken those women after Alden was through with them. They were all guilty. Every one of them would hang if they so much as uttered a word of this. Realizing he would have to go to the Walnut Street Jail if he wanted to discover the truth of things, he remounted his horse.

Before riding, he looked down on the sergeant. "What name is this deputy magistrate?"

"Said 'is name was Emerson, sir, Deputy Magistrate Emerson. He was a minister too, like a religious one."

Alden swept his horse with one fluid motion and took off. He made straight for Walnut Street.

Panting heavily in front of the jailer at the open desk inside the city jail, Alden looked down on the man, trying to catch his breath. The jailer was layered in clothing of multiple colors. It was cold inside the low-ceiling building and dark. Amazingly, it smelled even worse than the streets outside.

The jailer wore a ruddy face with an enormous round bulbous nose crisscrossed in dark blue spiderweb veins. His head was nearly bald, with thinning sprouts of hair poking out along each side. He scratched his bald pate.

"We have no one jailed of that description, Captain. In fact, there are no women prisoners here currently and certainly no children."

"May I look for myself?" asked Alden, not quite ready to believe this person at face value.

"Do as you wish, Captain. I cannot prevent you."

The man called to a person beyond a dark oak door with steel bars in the upper section. The door swung open. Alden marched down the long aisle, inspecting each cell as he passed. He moved quickly. Coming to the end of the cells, it was obvious to Alden that Elspeth MacEwan and her children were not being held in this jail. Expressing his frustration, Alden let out a strangled "Damn, bloody hell!" Outside once more, Alden climbed his horse and headed for the magistrate's office.

The day was ending, and what little light there was fast diminishing. Alden rode the streets at a quick trot, avoiding carriages, horses, and British soldiers. He was becoming increasingly impatient, his temper losing control.

"The magistrate is not here, sir. He has gone home."

Alden glared at the man. "May I speak with the deputy magistrate, please? A Mr. Emerson, I believe. I wish to know what happened to the woman and her children who were taken into your custody Thursday last!" He was shouting now, unable to control himself.

The official looked decidedly confused. "We have no deputy magistrate, sir. That office was abolished over a year ago. And as far as I am aware, we have taken no one in custody, Thursday last or otherwise. Our office has not issued a warrant for arrest in more than a fortnight at least. What is this about, Captain?"

Alden looked at the man, stunned. The realization that Elspeth and her children had somehow made their escape was unthinkable, but there it was. She was gone. *How?* wondered Alden. *They have no friends in the city, no family. No one could even know where Alden had taken them. So how did this happen?* His first thought came to Mrs. Weatherly. The old bitch was paid for this somehow, maybe the Americans. Alden knew she would do anything for money.

Back on his mount, Alden raced through the city, his horse bumping people, horses, and even wagons. The animal's shoes slid out from underfoot as it cut sharp corners in its rider's haste. By the time he reached the Weatherly house, Alden was as lathered as the animal he sat on.

"Follow me," commanded Alden, indicating his sergeant.

"Bring that fellow with you," he continued, pointing to the second sentry standing guard by the now open gate. All three men entered the Weatherly house.

Alden stormed into the kitchen. He gripped Mrs. Weatherly by the arm and began dragging her toward the long hallway. "Get those two sentries out the back of the house in here!" he shouted at the sergeant. As he continued to pull on the old woman's arm, she desperately clung to an open doorframe, resisting the captain's efforts with all her strength. The sergeant returned with the remaining guards, and Alden gave his orders.

"Get everyone out! Out of this house, get them all out now!" he screamed in near hysteria. Mrs. Weatherly looked at the English captain she knew to be a defiler, murderer, and God knew what. She wondered if the man had lost his reason.

"What are you doing, Captain?" she wailed. "Please stop this. You must stop."

"You knew!" cried Alden, spittle spraying from his lips. He pulled his helmet off by the jaw strap and swung it loosely by his side. "You knew it was not the magistrate. You knew all the time. How much did they pay you?"

"I did not know, I swear to you. I know nothing of the magistrate, nothing!"

Holding the old woman by her arm, Alden watched as the sergeant and his men began forcing the ladies of the Weatherly house out the front door.

"Please, Captain, do not do this!" cried Mrs. Weatherly. "We are innocent of any offense, I swear it."

The screams and cries of the women as they vacated the house rang throughout the closed neighborhood. What customers there were in residence fled through every conceivable exit available. They knew all too well what was happening. The Weatherly house was about to close—suddenly.

Alden, still pulling on Mrs. Weatherly's arm, was unable to dislodge her from the doorframe. The strength the old woman displayed was extraordinary. She simply refused to let go. Alden tugged once more, and when this failed to release the old woman's grip, he swung his brass helmet in a wide arc, smashing it squarely to the side of her head, knocking her senseless. She fell to her knees.

The women of the house were lining up beside the low picket fence around the property. What customers there had been disappeared into the night, running as fast as their feet would carry them. They put as much distance between them and the bordello as possible.

The sergeant came up the stoop and stood in the doorway. "Everyone is out, sir," he called to Alden. The captain reached down and, once more, gripped Mrs. Weatherly by the arm. He pulled her up, flinging her toward the sergeant.

"Take this outside." He snarled.

The sergeant, hauling Mrs. Weatherly by her armpits, backed out of the house, dragging the old woman's heels across the rough wood floor.

Alden marched back into the kitchen, grabbed a candle lantern, and plucked the lit candle from its base. He then held the flame under the blue cotton curtains that covered the kitchen windows. They ignited instantly. Then still in a rage, Alden walked down the hall to the open parlor. He fired the curtains there as well and then the embroidered tablecloths. He dropped the heavy candle onto the seat of an upholstered chair and watched as it burst into flame.

As Alden exited the house, the array of weeping women stood along the outer fence near the gate. Some were wrapped in blankets while others huddled together in the cool night air barely dressed. They all wailed in misery as they watched the flames begin to consume their home.

As they looked on, the fire took the second floor. Within minutes, the entire building erupted, throwing embers skyward. The front bay window shattered, sending glass fragments to the ground below. Alden stood by the fence gate, breathing heavily. He watched with pleasure as the house went up, the flames engulfing the dry wood as it cracked and split loudly. Then in the background of this cataclysm, a screaming wail came from within the house. Several of the half-naked girls shrieked in realized horror.

Mrs. Weatherly, on her knees, was just coming to a degree of sense when she tilted her head up. She, too, heard the muffled wails from inside the burning house.

Weatherly sat back on the cold grass and shouted, "Gwinn, Bell! They're still in the house. In the basement they sleep. What have you done? They've no way out." She turned on Alden. "You murdering bastard, you killed my slaves!"

Alden looked down on Weatherly without the least concern. "What do I care for your slaves, you old witch? I told you what would happen if you defied me. I told you I would put you out in the street and burn this place to the ground. I warned you."

"You'll pay for this, Alden, you bloody bastard. Those women cost me over £700."

The cries from the house basement came to a hysterical crescendo, and then suddenly, they heard nothing.

All the women were crying now, weeping silently or struck numb by the violent eviction and burning of the only home they knew. Alden faced the women as ash and cinder floated down on them. The odor of burning flesh now added to the smoky black air.

Amelie saw him first, a dark figure walking slowly round the corner of the blazing house. He appeared from behind the fire, stepping through the leaping flames and black smoke. He wore a long dark peacoat. Standing so close to the fire, smoke clung to him like a spectral cloud. A sailor's cap covered his head. It was pulled low. He appeared like a phantom. It was Bennett.

Framed before the fire with a long-barreled French navy pistol gripped in his hand, Bennett walked with deliberate strides toward his target. The women, hypnotized by the roaring inferno, noticed Bennett for the first time. The sailor raised the pistol as Alden began to turn his attention.

Bennett intended to shoot Alden at the center of his back, but the waves of heat from the fire obscured his vision, his sight awash with tears. Bennett pulled the trigger. The ball flew low, striking Alden at the back of his thigh, tearing a hole through muscle and tendon before passing on and dropping silently onto the cobbles of the street.

Bennett muttered a silent profanity. Turning round, he strolled calmly back through the flames and smoke, disappearing into the fire. Two musket balls whizzed after him as Alden's men fired at the startling ghost. Alden fell backward, rolling on his side, screaming and crying in much the same fashion as the women who surrounded him. As the Weatherly house collapsed in on itself with a mighty roar, rendering the structure to a pile of charred lumber, broken lanterns, porcelain, and brick, it began to rain hard in Philadelphia.

Mrs. Weatherly looked up at the pile of burning timber that was once her home and cried aloud, "My money! You've burned my money!"

Little Cornstalk

IT WAS A cool morning, but the sunlight on her shoulders felt warm and comfortable. Little Cornstalk sat back on her haunches, arranging a small circle of stones. Her belly made it difficult to lean forward, but she managed to reach out and arrange everything just so. In the center of the circle was a simple slate gray stone on which she scratched a symbol—three wavy lines with two straight lines shooting out on each side.

Reaching up, she untied a thin buckskin string and pulled it from her hair. The thin leather carried the delicate snow-white feather her father had given her during her fifteenth season. She laid it reverently beside the flat stone. Next, she took the beaded purse from her belt, a beloved gift from Adsila, her mother. From this, she gently withdrew a single bear claw and placed it beside the feather. Her brother Shadow Bear had given her this claw. She placed the claw beside the feather.

Finally, she laid the colorful corn purse alongside the other gifts, leaned back, and reviewed the tiny circle. She closed her eyes, tilted her head, and began singing a soft, undulating tune that seemed to come from the back of her throat.

Seamus Murphy stood off some distance, waiting in silence. He fidgeted as children do, shuffling his feet and staring off distractedly into the tree line or the clouds overhead. Little Cornstalk went quiet.

"Is this what your Cherokee people do, Little Cornstalk?" asked the boy innocently.

Little Cornstalk turned and looked at Seamus. "I ask the Mother Spirit to return William to me. I have a vision dream about William, so I will offer these." She indicated the small circle with the few items within. "She will help me."

"Was it a bad dream?" asked Seamus, suddenly interested. "I have nightmares sometimes. They frighten me."

He added hastily, "Not all the time."

"I have dreamed William was taken away to a far, far land in a great canoe. I cannot see this land, but I know it is too far for Stevenson. He will not find William."

"How do you know?"

"I know," answered the girl simply.

"Can I put something in the circle? Will it help if I do?"

Little Cornstalk smiled at the boy. "Yes, it will help. You must place something in the circle near the flat stone. It must be something you love, something important to you. That way, the Mother Spirit will see your heart, and she will help."

Seamus thought mightily about what best to put in the circle, and when it came to him, he took off for the tavern at a dead run.

He raced past Kathleen in the kitchen, practically bouncing off the walls; dived under his bed; and reached back for something tucked beneath in a small nook. Clamping the object firmly in his fist, he took off, passing his mother again.

Kathleen let out, "Seamus?" The boy disappeared in a flurry of pounding feet and the smell of fresh earth.

When he returned, Little Cornstalk was still sitting quietly, her eyes closed and her back straight as a tree.

"I have something," muttered Seamus. "Not much of a thing, but it means the world to me."

Little Cornstalk opened her eyes, and there in the center of Seamus's small hand was a brilliant red stone. Reflecting the sunlight just so, Little Cornstalk thought the small rock very beautiful. She had never seen a stone like it.

"I was going to give this to Ma, but she doesn't fancy rocks too much. She likes furs and money. When I go hunting, I'll bring Ma some furs."

Seamus stepped up beside Little Cornstalk, leaned over, and nestled the little red stone between the feather and the purse. He looked up and smiled at the Indian girl. He knew this was for William, but Seamus did it anyway. If it made Little Cornstalk happy, then it had to be a good thing.

"Thank you, Seamus Murphy. It is very beautiful. The Mother Spirit will see this." She smiled.

Kathleen decided to see what her errant son was up to and so stepped out of the tavern and followed the boy with her eyes. From where Kathleen stood, she was just able to see Seamus and Little Cornstalk kneeling on the ground. It looked as though they were planting something. She wagged her head and clucked to herself. More popcorn? Kathleen loved her Seamus dearly, but sometimes she wondered about that boy.

That evening at the Murphy dinner table, the subject of Little Cornstalk's prayer circle came up. Seamus was more than willing to tell all. As he described the purpose of the stone circle and the importance of the objects therein, it became clear to the Murphy clan that something had to be done.

The following morning, Little Cornstalk approached her prayer circle. She was astonished to discover an assortment of added objects. There was a crow feather, a length of ribbon, a broken knife blade, three coins, and a small sack of popped corn. The girl looked about as if searching for whoever may have left these items. She saw no one nearby. A few heads did turn her way as she scanned the Murphy compound, but those who did so only smiled knowingly as they continued with their daily chores. Little Cornstalk was very pleased.

The Delaware Crossing

IT HAD TAKEN William nine days to arrive north of the Delaware. He stood silent on the bank, watching the black water rush by. His expectation of crossing to the opposite shore was dismal. Only with the aid of a boat, raft, or canoe would it be possible.

Standing in the freezing rain as it poured down in cascading, wind-driven sheets, William was chilled to the bone. After days of hard travel, he unbound the bandage so carefully applied by Mr. Moses and tossed it aside. The wound was healing well now, itching ever so slightly. William's horse nickered as she, too, shivered in the cold rain, swishing her tail. Both horse and longhunter were beaten like a drum.

Good fortune had been with William on the trail south. Those few settlers living north and west of the main road passed along food and water for him and his mount. Some, believing William to be an American soldier, offered him a bed to rest and feed. He never lingered. His ride far too urgent.

He was forced to swing west round two British patrols as he came south, but they were noisy and all too easy to avoid. The British never laid eyes on him as he passed by them in a broken arc.

It was night now, and with it came the first cold weather of the season. William walked beside the riverbank, searching for any sign of a boat or raft that might carry him over the tumbling water. He saw nothing. As he moved along the water's edge, his moccasins sunk and slipped in the fine silt mud, leaving deep tracks that quickly washed away. The trees lining the high-water mark were nearly bare of foliage, the rain knocking loose the last of the fall leaves, affording little cover from the downpour. He moved cautiously, guiding his horse best he could. Up ahead, he thought he spied a flickering light through the darkness.

In the withering rain, an oblong shed with a wooden top came into view. Skins of different variety hung down on all four sides of the tent like hovel, enclosing it. The light flickering within was meager, wandering to and fro with the wind. Longhunter and horse stood some thirty feet off the structure.

"Hallo, the tent!" called William loudly.

No reply.

William tried again, this time with greater volume. "Hallo, I say! Is anyone there?"

Moving in closer, William tied the red mare's reins to a stout tree just off the riverbank. Stepping up to the strange little tent, he could see that it was only five feet in height thereabouts. He reached out and tapped the wooden top, eliciting a sharp cry from within. Standing with his rifle in hand, William tried one more time.

"Hallo, is anyone within?" He knocked again on the wood top.

A small head appeared in the gap of skins. "Who's there?"

"My name is William MacEwan. I seek a boat or raft to cross the river. Can you tell where I might find one?"

The figure inside muttered, "A moment, if you will."

The rustling sound of animal skins moving about caused William to peer across the little tent.

"I mean no harm to you. I merely seek a boat to cross the river," continued William, frustrated.

The man stuck his head outside again. He wore a broken tricorn bearing a series of small holes. "Be you English or Yankee?" he asked.

"I am no soldier, if that is your meaning."

The man scanned William from foot to head and then pulled himself inside, calling in a pleasant tone, "Come in then. I'll not be going outside in this."

As William ducked inside, the first thing to catch his attention in the dim firelight was the large horse pistol in the man's hand. He waved it gently at William's middle.

Although seated on a woodbox, it was clear the man was short legged. He had a mop of sodden hair that spilled out from neath his broken hat. What was visible hung in loose strands along his narrow face. He carried a full beard that grew to his chest. Both scalp and beard were shocked with gray. He was an old man.

His feet were bare, completely black, and apparently missing one or two toes. The britches he wore were dark felt, ragged and torn. He wore a buckskin coat too large for his thin frame. It kept the water out.

"You cannot be too careful these days," croaked the old man, still waving the horse pistol at William. "Don't be making any fuss now. I was a pistoleer in my day. And I will shoot you. Empty your purse now and place everything there," he said sharpish, pointing to another long box with his pistol. "You have the look of a rifleman. American?"

"I am no rifleman," answered William, eyeing the old man. He stood a couple of feet off from the dirty pistoleer, hunched over to avoid the low wood cover. He held his rifle by the barrel upright.

"That is a fine piece you have there," said the pistoleer, indicating William's rifle. "Bring it here."

The man smiled at William, exposing fractured brown and yellow teeth. William said nothing as he leaned in close to the man. Sweeping his rifle butt upward while pivoting the long gun in his left hand, William knocked the horse pistol from the old man's grip. He then swept the tricorn from the pistoleer's head and clutched a fistful of soaking hair. Jerking the little man from his seat, he forced him forward onto his knees. The old man squirmed desperately, trying to free himself from William's hold.

Casually placing his rifle against half-cured animal skins while still holding on to the head of hair, William pulled out his long knife. He pushed down on the man, straddling his small frame like a horse. Standing behind the old pistoleer, he pulled the tuft of hair taut, tilting the man's head up. He displayed the blade in the flickering light. The old man's eyes widened in terror. He let out a whimpering, mewl-like sound.

"Please don't take my life. I thought you would rob me. I swear to it," he blubbered in a squealing, cracked voice.

A flood of emotion suddenly overwhelmed William. Anger, frustration, and grief welled up inside the young longhunter in a wild rush. For the first time in William's life, he *wanted* to kill a man. All the pain, the anguish, and suffering twisting in his mind drove him nearly out of control. Tears welled up in his eyes, obscuring his vision. He looked down on the pathetic river pirate.

Leaning in close to the man's ear, William said in harsh, clipped words, "Where do I find a boat?"

The old man cocked his head, looking up. "There," he said urgently, pointing with his eyes. "Up there."

William looked up and discovered, to his amazement, a boat. It was the wooden tent top, overturned. The vessel itself was flat bottomed with low gunwales. It was eight feet long with two slat boards across the beam. It narrowed to a blunt prow with a broad stern.

Staring up at the structure, William barked, "Take it down!" He backed away from the pistoleer, releasing his grip on the man's oily hair.

"But the rain," complained the little man.

William reached down and pulled his tomahawk with his free hand. The man jerked away, stricken with fear. William then grasped the buckskin coat surrounding the man and dragged him outside. The heavy rain continued. Hacking at the line of skins strung along the outside gunwales of the boat, William worked quickly. The skins dropped one by one. Still hanging on to the man's buckskin, William shook him violently.

"Take it down!" he hollered through the pelting rain.

The little man did as he was told. The boat slid down across two wood slats, flipping upright and landing neatly at the old pirate's feet. It was a practiced maneuver.

"Oars, paddles, where are they?" said William impatiently.

"There," said the little man, pointing to a pile of loose hides just feet away.

"Show me."

The man gingerly moved toward the skins as William followed. He reached down to lift one hide, and William said coldly, raising the tomahawk, "If you come up with a weapon, I'll take the back of your head off. Understand?"

The old man rapidly bobbed his head. Pulling back the animal hide, he revealed two flat oars. He grabbed one.

"Take them both," said William.

The man plunged his hand back into the pile of skins, and William quickly came up on the fellow. As he watched, the old pistoleer pulled out two strange horseshoe-looking mechanisms. The man held them up for William see.

"Oar locks," said the man desperately. "We will need them for the oars."

William said nothing as he followed the old man back to the boat.

"Pull the boat to the water," said William tersely. Turning away from the river, William looked over at his tethered horse. She was tied to a sturdy limb with good grass underfoot. He knew she would obediently stay where she stood. She was a trained soldier's animal. She would wait.

Placing his long rifle in the boat, William shoved as the little man pulled, forcing the boat to the water's edge.

"We must head east first to take in the eddy," said the old man in his croaking voice. "From there, it is a short distance through hard water. Have no fear. I will cross you safely."

William and his unwilling pilot set off. As the man explained, they turned east into the current.

The water here was slow moving, becalmed with the aid of a jutting sandbar that reached out halfway into the river. As they passed through the eddy pool, they came into rough water that threatened to swamp the low-sided vessel. Anxious to end this trip, the little man rowed furiously. Water began spilling over the gunwales into the hull, and William looked on with concern. He pointed down. "Will we flood?" he asked loud enough to be heard through the rain.

The man looked down quickly, never ceasing a stroke. "We'll make it right enough. We're close now."

William could see the opposite bank looming in the darkness, a black wall of grass and mud. It was steep. As the small boat hit the bank, the stern was quickly swept sideways along with the river's current. The little pistoleer leaned out and grabbed hold of a tree root jutting up from the mud and quickly tied the boat to it. The boat stopped.

Lifting his rifle, William placed the long knife back in its sheath. He stepped out into knee-deep water. The boat rocked heavily. Scrambling up the embankment, his feet slipping to find a hold, William made slow progress. Holding fast to his rifle made it more difficult to gain purchase. Halfway up, he turned back. He could see the boat, with the old man sitting motionless in the pouring rain. The pistoleer's little ferry was still tied to the tree root. Turning back to continue his climb, William wondered why the man had not left. There was no reason he should remain, and the thought vexed him.

The pistoleer quietly fished around inside his buckskin cover, attempting to retrieve his horse pistol. He had slipped the weapon into his belt when he had taken the boat down. He only needed to pour dry powder in the pan. He leaned over using his tricorn as cover and threw a dash of powder down.

By this time, William had made the crest of the embankment. Once again, he turned back to look on the old man; and as he did so, the pistoleer drew up his pistol and fired. It was a slow, wet burn, but the weapon did ignite, sending the ball well wide of William. Getting his footing and standing at the top of the riverbank, William pulled his own pistol, aimed it directly at the figure crouched inside the boat, and pulled the trigger. The pistol would not fire as William knew it would not, but the little man frantically grabbed his oars and quickly set himself adrift, pulling away with the aid of current. He disappeared in the darkness.

William turned back to the open field before him. The tree line was many yards away. He wiped a hand over his face to clear his sight. As he looked down, he could see the entire field trampled in boot print. To the right, some fifty yards off, burned a middling fire struggling to stay lit in the rain. He moved left. William heard them before he saw them. They came from every direction except the river. Redcoats descended on William at a pace.

"Stop!" called one as he approached the longhunter.

"Halt!" cried another.

William looked about for an avenue of escape, but it was plain he was surrounded. The pistol the old man fired had gained the soldiers' attention. William realized it was the old man's intent. Holding his rifle horizontal with both hands, he stopped.

"My name is William MacEwan. I am here in search of my family!" he said aloud.

"Look here, Sergeant," said one man, pointing to William's long gun. "'E's a bloody widow-maker! They're the ones been killing our mates."

The sergeant advanced on William and ripped the rifle from his grip. "So," said the broad-shouldered sergeant, "slithering into the city for more killin', are ya?"

"No, sir," answered William carefully. As I said, my name is William MacEwan. I am no soldier. I came here only in search of my family."

"A likely tale that," said the sergeant doubtfully. "You men, take his weapons and anything else he carries." Putting his face inches from William's, he snarled. "You're done for, Yank." Then he struck William a blow to the side of his head.

Little Cornstalk

"WHAT DO YOU mean she's gone?" asked Kathleen. "I cannot find her anywhere, Ma. I have asked everyone," answered Seamus with a note of desperation.

"Did you look in on the blacksmith?"

"Oh yes, Mr. Cummings has no notion of her whereabouts."

"Well, she can't have gone far. She's five months pregnant. Go fetch your da."

Little Cornstalk was outside Murphy-Borough. She was searching for mushrooms. Mushrooms happened to be Connor Murphy's favored dish. The man could eat them every meal if allowed. Having been to this place in the trees once before with Seamus and a group of others, she noticed a fallen pine just east in a copse of tall shaded oaks. She knew her best luck would be there. It was damp in the low draw, with lichen covering the dead timber and damp earth covering the ground, a good place for mushroom.

She did not see or hear them. When they came at her, it was from three directions. The first knocked her hard to ground as the other two grabbed her arms, jerking her to her feet. She dropped the small basket she carried, struggling furiously with her assailants. Little Cornstalk was strong and long limbed, making it difficult for these men to control her.

As she reached down for her blade, one of her assailants came alongside, swinging a stout branch, striking Little Cornstalk on the side of her head. She staggered back, falling again, hard on her bottom. The men released their grip. She wagged her head to steady herself. She looked up.

Dragging Canoe stood before her the offending branch, swaying idly at his side.

"Dragging Canoe," said Little Cornstalk without understanding.

"Yes, Little Mother," answered Dragging Canoe with a wicked smile. "It is your Cherokee brother."

Continuing to survey the men around her, Little Cornstalk now recognized them as Cherokee brethren. She looked up into the faces of Walking Bird and Winter. They stood beside her, their faces impassive. A look of utter confusion adorning her face, the girl held mute. Dragging Canoe laughed aloud.

"Why do you do this, Dragging Canoe?" said Little Cornstalk.

"I am taking you," answered the brave.

All three Cherokee wore cold-weather deerskin shirts with muskrat and beaver moccasins. Their legs were covered with a variety of buckskin and fur. They smelled of smoke, skins, and sweat. Walking Bird and Winter wore fur caps.

"For what purpose have you done this? I have brought no harm to you."

"It is for muskets, rifles, powder, and ball, Little Mother," answered Dragging Canoe as if this was explanation enough.

"I do not understand."

"I have made a peace with Tenskwatawa, the Shawnee chief. We have a bargain—you for muskets and rifles."

"You would put Little Cornstalk under Tenskwatawa's knife? The daughter of Black Feather?" said Little Cornstalk, astonished at the idea.

Dragging Canoe laughed again. "I do not stand with Black Feather. I will not fight beside the white man anymore. English, American, this has no meaning to me. They are the same. White, Dragging Canoe will only kill white men now."

He continued as he paced to and fro before Little Cornstalk, "I have my own tribe now, Little Mother. And I do not fear your father. I am Dragging Canoe."

Little Cornstalk locked eyes with Dragging Canoe. An unpleasant smile crossed her face.

"You are right, brother," she answered quietly. "Black Feather will not kill you." She hesitated. "The longhunter will take your life."

Dragging Canoe revealed a brief strike of fear in his eyes, his dark face clouding with anger.

"I do not fear your longhunter. He is just another white man. I will kill him quick."

Little Cornstalk laughed as she swept her gaze over the three Cherokee. "You will all die for this."

Winter turned to Walking Bird. "I told you. She is a witch."

Headquarters of Maj. John Clark

DAG GUNNARSSON PULLED the door open. He stepped inside, stripping the tricorn from his head. He tucked it neatly beneath his left arm as he deftly avoided the head jamb.

"You sent for me, Major?"

"Yes, Captain. Would you be kind enough to invite Mrs. MacEwan in to speak with me? I have news for her."

"Yes, sir," answered the giant Swede.

Elspeth sat quietly, her back stiff against the hardwood chair. She clenched her hands repeatedly as they lay in her lap. She looked steadily on Major Clark.

Wearing a simple blue cotton dress with a light-colored leather belt cinched about the waist, she patiently waited for the major to speak. The dress, she learned, had been found among the belongings in the house, now being used as temporary headquarters. Elspeth offered to pay for the garment, but Clark graciously refused.

It had taken some days for the children to adjust to their new station. David seemed comfortable with the surroundings, but Aelwyd would still frighten at the slightest commotion. She also begun sucking her thumb again as a babe would do. This vexed Elspeth, but she said nothing of it to the girl.

The children were eating well now. The food provided by the major and his troop was both welcome and healthy. As it turned out, the twins were a favorite among the rough army men. They galloped around the camp, cavorting everywhere, sticking their little heads in and out of occupied tents, lean-tos, and even the main headquarter house with simple curiosity. They would often follow Captain Gunnarsson about the camp, convinced that the Swede was a *real* giant. Elspeth explained to the boys that Captain Gunnarsson was just another soldier, albeit a large one, but her explanation went to no effect. Whenever the twin boys saw the great Swede, they raced like mad to stand beside him and look up.

"Mrs. MacEwan," began Clark, "I have news from Colonel Morgan concerning your son William."

Elspeth leaned forward, gripping her small hands tightly. "What news?"

"Well," said Clark, clearing his throat with a cough, "your son is definitely in the company of the colonel. However, it appears William was wounded at Saratoga."

Elspeth pulled in a shock of air, throwing her hands to her mouth.

Clark quickly added, "The colonel writes it is but a minor injury, Mrs. MacEwan."

Clark continued in a rush, "Your son will be fine with a day or two of rest. He is in no danger and considered quite fit for travel."

"Thank god for that," said Elspeth, letting out a held breath. "When will my son return, Major?"

"The company may already be on the march, Mrs. MacEwan. The Eleventh Virginia, in fact, the entire regiment, has been ordered south. Unfortunately, due to this order, my men and I will not be able to take you and your children along with us. It simply is not possible. I trust that you understand?"

Elspeth slowly bobbed her head. "I understand, Major. How long is it we have?"

"The Eleventh leaves tomorrow next. If you wish to return to your home in the west, I would be willing to provide the loan of a small wagon and horse. I fear that is all I can spare at this time. Of course, we will give you what food and water we can spare for your journey as well. If you wish to stay here and wait for the Eleventh, you certainly may. But I am afraid I cannot spare any of my men to wait along with you."

Clark then leaned back as he studied Elspeth MacEwan.

She was a beautiful woman, he realized, petite with coal-black hair that shimmered in the morning light. Her recent ordeal had cast her alabaster skin to a shiny pale with sprinkles of fading color crossing high cheeks. Her lips were tuliplike and full. Deep brown eyes strained with exhaustion looked up at the major. They appeared at once tired and angelic to the army officer. He waited for a reply.

"How long before Colonel Morgan and William arrive?" repeated Elspeth.

"If the colonel is on his way as ordered, I would put their arrival here at a fortnight and a bit."

Elspeth gripped her lower lip in her teeth, concentrating. She and the children would have to wait here fifteen days, maybe more. She leaned forward and slapped both hands down on her legs with decision. She stood up.

"It appears I have some thinking to do on the matter, Major. I do appreciate all that you and your men have done for us. And I thank you most heartily, sir."

"There is something else, Mrs. MacEwan," said Clark seriously. He hemmed his thoughts for a moment before continuing.

"The house you and the children were held in, it has been set to fire, burned to the ground as I understand it."

Elspeth raised her brow. It was a moment before she replied. "That is for the best," she said matter-of-factly.

"I have also been informed that two slaves died in that fire and the . . . ladies of the house turned out to the street."

Elspeth's thought went immediately to Bell and Gwinn, the two kind slave women working the laundry at the Weatherly house. The ladies of the house, she knew, would find some accommodation and carry on as before, drinking, laughing, and losing their way. Mrs. Weatherly could go to the devil as far as Elspeth was concerned.

"I am sorry to hear this, Colonel. I worked alongside those Negro girls in the house laundry. They were innocents."

"One more thing," said Clark stiffly. "Our man in Philadelphia shot Captain Alden."

Elspeth's eyes flew open. "Is he dead?" she asked hopefully.

"We do not know if he survived his wound."

"That would not be my wish, Major," answered Elspeth emphatically.

Clark shrugged. "Captain Gunnarsson will assist you until we leave. He knows of the wagon and horse that I recommend you take regardless of your decision. Again, you have my apology. I realize this is most inconvenient for you, but it cannot be helped."

"No need for an apology, Major. You and your men have saved our very lives. We are more grateful than I can express."

"Save you gratitude, Mrs. MacEwan. It was Stevenson and Bennett who effected your rescue."

"Mr. Bennett," repeated Elspeth, wagging her head in amazement. "He is an odd fellow, is he not?"

"I would say so, yes."

"We owe him much. Please, if you would, Major, offer my best to the gentleman."

"If I see the . . . gentleman again, I most certainly will."

As far as Elspeth was concerned, Mr. Stevenson was heaven sent. The man had risked all for Elspeth and the children. She was more than appreciative. It was largely due to this that Elspeth found it nearly impossible to ask the stout longhunter for anything more. But did she have an option?

It could prove very difficult to remain here alone, waiting for William. If she traveled west back to her home, it would be a hazardous journey, even deadly. She had made the trek before, but could she do it alone with her children? It seemed unlikely.

Elspeth found Stevenson leaning over a fence rail that penned a large remuda. As she approached, she could see the stocky longhunter carrying on an animated conversation with a hatless young soldier.

"I must have that horse back," insisted Stevenson in ever-increasing volume.

"It is not possible, Mr. Stevenson. The mare cannot leave."

"I realize the army needs horses, young man. But surely, one pregnant mare would make little difference."

The corporal who had confiscated Stevenson's pregnant mare was about to answer when Elspeth stepped into the conversation.

"Ah, Mrs. MacEwan," said Stevenson, turning on the corporal. "I was about to have Connor Murphy's horse returned to me."

"No, you were not," replied the young soldier stubbornly.

"You cannot be serious!" bellowed Stevenson. "That mare is a loan from the owner. If I return without the horse, I will owe the value of the animal. I do not have forty pounds!"

"That is easily remedied, sir," answered the soldier calmly. "I will give you a voucher for the horse. We do this for all the animals we confiscate for the war effort. It is the least we can do."

"Oh, I agree," said Stevenson sarcastically, "the very least. How am I supposed to ride a slip of paper near three hundred miles? Do you have a notion on that?"

"I am afraid that is the best I can do, sir."

"May I interrupt?" asked Elspeth.

"Yes, of course, Mrs. MacEwan," answered Stevenson in a decidedly toned-down voice.

"Major Clark has graciously offered the loan of a small wagon and horse. Why not return Mr. Stevenson's mare," said Elspeth, turning to the soldier, "and simply use it as the colonel's offer?"

"I cannot, Miss," answered the soldier unhappily.

"Why not? Is the animal unfit?"

"No. When Mr. Stevenson brought the mare in, she was due to foal."

"Oh, I see," said Elspeth with a knowing smile. "Well, there you have it, Mr. Stevenson. I'm afraid another horse will have to do."

"Major Clark has offered you a wagon and horse?" asked Stevenson, surprised at the proposal.

"He has, Mr. Stevenson, and I intend to accept."

Stevenson looked up, brightening suddenly. "It takes a year for a horse to deliver a foal. I began my journey less than two months ago. If I could ride the mare here, then why not back? I could bring Murphy his pregnant mare, and he would have two animals in return."

"Too late," said the soldier, wagging his head sadly. "She delivered two days ago. The foal is just getting its legs."

Stevenson looked at the soldier bug eyed. "Then I want my mare back, and you can keep your paper and the foal," he said sharply.

Elspeth frowned at Stevenson. "Mr. Stevenson, you cannot separate a mother from her newborn. I am shocked you would consider the notion. I am sure another horse will do fine."

Stevenson, looking sheepish, answered, "As you wish, Mrs. MacEwan, as you wish." He scowled at the hatless private. "You will make a fine horse thief someday."

The soldier simply pulled out a voucher, holding it before Stevenson. The hunter swept it from his hand.

Stevenson and Elspeth returned to the camp, walking side by side. Elspeth seemed to be concentrating on the ground before her. She was silent.

"Is everything all right, Mrs. MacEwan?" asked the hunter, concerned.

"It seems the army here is leaving. Major Clark said they have been ordered south. He also tells me that William is returning to this place along with Colonel Morgan. They will be arriving in a fortnight and a bit. I have decided to wait here for William rather than head west with the children on our own. I feel it would be safer."

Now Stevenson's head was bent down in similar fashion to Elspeth. He was thinking. "If you have no objection, Mrs. MacEwan, I would very much like to remain here along with you and the children, at least until William arrives. Are you amenable to this?"

"I was hoping you would say that, Mr. Stevenson. I feel it is not fair of me to ask you for any more favor. You have done so much for us. Your proposal to stay is most welcome. I thank you." She looked up at the stout hunter and smiled.

"Actually," said Stevenson seriously, "we do have some things to discuss concerning William and his visit to the Cherokee village. I am unsure how you will find this news."

Elspeth gave the bulky Swede a questioning look as they strode along.

Philadelphia

WILLIAM WAS TRUSSED up like a roasting bird. He lay on his left side, facing the center of the room. It was a large space, perhaps forty feet across, forty long, with a high ceiling supported by two vertical posts. There were no windows. The floor was rough brick as were the walls. A solid oaken door stood at the far end of the room. It was locked.

They had bound William hand and foot with a solid length of rope. He could little more than roll side to side. He was beaten badly; his bones and muscles ached terribly. His father's moccasins were taken, leaving him barefoot. The hand weapons had also been taken along with his rifle. It was a cold place, this room. A patina of mold slick with age clung to the brick, holding in the chill. The man-made stone was slowly turning black. *Not unlike a brick-lined well*, thought William. A filthy chamber pot stood along one wall with a fetid bucket of water nearby. The only sounds that William could hear were footfalls on the floor above.

A rattle of keys against a lock came to him. The door was pushed open with a loud creak. William rolled over, staring anxiously at the oaken door. Three redcoats entered the room. One carried a high-backed wooden chair. The soldier brought the chair to the far vertical post, tying it securely to the dark brace. The other two men hauled William to his feet, plunking him down onto the chair. No one spoke. The man who had tied the chair proceeded to secure William to it with heavy rope.

"You have a visitor, widow-maker," said one.

"I am not—"

"Shut your gob, Yankee. I'll tell ya when to speak."

William had explained to anyone who might listen that he was not, in fact, an American soldier, that he had never fired on an Englishman in war or otherwise. His sole purpose for coming to Philadelphia was to search for his family. His pleas fell on deaf ears.

Still, William held out hope that someone would eventually listen and believe him. He wasn't certain of this, of course, but he seized the notion with both hands, repeating his innocence often and loudly. The door hung open before William, a tantalizing portal of escape, unreachable. Frustration and anger flooded his insides. A hard burning glare shone in his eyes.

Another soldier entered the room. This one wore a dark green jacket with a high stiff collar. His britches were white. The boots he wore were polished to a shine and knee high. He walked with a cane supporting a lame leg. A brass helmet with black feathers swung loose at his side off the uniform belt.

"Hello, William. A pleasure to see you again, my boy."

William recognized the voice but not the man. He stared into the eyes of the visitor wearing the green jacket. The officer simply smiled in return, waiting.

Slow realization came to William. "Mr. Alden," he said through thickened lips.

"Captain Alden, if you please. I am a commissioned captain in the Twenty-Third Dragoons. Didn't you know?"

Alden looked down on William, and several bruises and a black swollen left eye could be seen. The young longhunter's face had been badly battered. His lips ballooned and were discolored. Alden turned on the soldier nearest him. "I gave strict instruction. No harm was to come to this man. What have you done? It is critically important he arrive at his destination undamaged. That was to be understood!" shouted Alden, slurring his words.

"It weren't none of my men, Captain. When the patrol brung him in, he put up a fight is all."

Alden leaned heavily over his cane. The pain racking his wound demanded liberal doses of laudanum, and at the moment, he was well laced.

"I do not want this man injured," continued Alden more calmly. "He has a delicate task ahead, you see. He must be in excellent health to do so."

"Yes, sir," answered the redcoat stiffly.

"Leave us now. Wait outside. When I am through, you may have him."

The three soldiers silently passed through the door, making a loud squealing sound as it closed.

"Where is my mother, Alden?" said William menacingly. He struggled in the chair as he spoke, pulling desperately on the ropes securing him.

"You know," said Alden seemingly unconcerned, "that is the very question I have. Do you know where your mother has gone?"

William looked at Alden, uncomprehending. "I was told you had taken my mother as well as my sister and brothers. Where are they, damn you?"

Alden laughed. "I really do not know, William," he said, waving his arm and throwing himself off-balance. "They have disappeared, escaped my bonds. It was only your mother I wanted, you see. I cared nothing for the children, although the little girl did have an attraction. Still, they could all go to the devil if I had my wish."

Alden's eyes were swimming in laudanum. He swayed slightly side to side. The pain in his leg was powerful, but the dark liquid washed most of it away. His intoxication loosened his tongue, blending his speech.

"It was all part of my plan, you see, William. I was to travel west with your father's rifles! From there, I would move on to the Cherokee village, sign an alliance with the savages, then abandon the tribe to Shawnee attack as arranged. The blasted Shawnee came in too quickly.

"Still, the British plans I created had deliberately fallen into the hands of the Americans as intended. Stevenson was kind enough to accomplish that task for me," added Alden matter-of-factly.

"After leaving the Cherokee village, I was to move west to link up with the Shawnee. Unfortunately, like so many campaigns, it went awry. Tenskwatawa and his braves simply could not resist attacking their hated enemy, the Cherokee. I suppose the opportunity to kill was too great for them. In any case, I stumbled on the Shawnee after the battle. They nearly killed me, you know," he stated casually. "If not for that bloody lame Indian and a promise of your father's rifles, I most likely would be lying scalped in some wooded field. It was the lure of your father's rifles. That did the trick. Tenskwatawa was more than willing to attack your homestead to obtain those rifles."

Alden began to slowly shuffle back and forth as if speaking to a group. Limping in front of William, he rocked to and fro in mild motion. William looked on the man as if he had lost all reason.

"*You* brought the Shawnee to my home," said William angrily. "You killed my father!"

"Actually, a man named Evens killed your father," grumbled Alden. "Shot him with a large bore musket, put a hole through him the size of an apple. Funny thing that. Your brother David shot Evens dead, killed him in the Weatherly house. The Weatherly house. So you see how these things can go, William. Evens shoots your father. Your brother David shoots Evens. Serendipity, I say.

"Seeing your mother for the first time was so . . . unexpected, as if the world spins around and somehow spills over, tangling everything up. Amazing, really."

"And my sister Mary?"

"Ah, Mary, golden red hair like yours," said Alden, staring blankly, remembering the scene. "All I did was smile at the girl." It was as if this explained all.

"We came into the cabin after your father was killed, two Shawnee braves and me. Mary stood in the back near the books lining the cabin wall. Difficult to see with all the powder smoke in the air, you know. I never said a word to her. I simply smiled. She put the pistol to her head and pulled the trigger. Scared those Shawnee senseless. They ran out of the cabin."

William tried to stand. He pushed upward furiously against the ropes binding him. Struggling with monumental effort, he raised the chair off the floor.

"I will kill you, Alden."

"I know you wish to, William, but I fear your destination will end that hope." He laughed with a wet phlegmlike sound.

Alden turned toward the door, pulling it open with effort. The three soldiers quickly entered.

"Take him to the boat. He is expected in New York tomorrow."

Turning his back, Alden passed through the door. As he climbed the steps, William could hear the stump and click of the Englishman's cane as he unsteadily made his way.

Two Virginia Cousins

WALLACE GRANT AND Bowling Miller were close behind William. Or so they thought. William, it seemed, was traveling day and night. What little respite he took amounted to no more than an hour or two.

"By god, Wallace, William is moving quick. He's nearly a day ahead of us."

Wallace wagged his head in despair. "Cousin Daniel will have our ears for this, Bowling. We have to get that mare back, or we may as well quit. If we don't find William mounted, we'll have to pay for that animal."

"A moment of kindness to our friend, and look where it finds us," said Bowling sadly. "I think it best we make up ground, Wallace, instead of complaining on it."

When the rain came, William's tracks began to fade. Bowling followed the young longhunter's sign as well as he could, but as the heavy downpour increased, both prints of animal and man rapidly disappeared.

The two cousins squatted neath a dense set of red oak, walnut, and maple. There was no foliage overhead to relieve the downpour. Forced to wait for the battering storm to pass, both men hunkered down alongside their horses. Each worried on the ever-increasing gap between William MacEwan and themselves.

When the rain gave up, Bowling followed the direction of William's previous track, hoping the young longhunter held to a straight line. The trail led the two cousins to the edge of the Delaware just north of Philadelphia. British patrols were few on this side of the river and a considerable distance off. As the two young riflemen came up to the river's edge, a colorful dusk filled the sky. Night was coming on.

"Can you see well enough?" asked Wallace.

"Enough. Looks like William walked the horse here by the river." Bowling squatted down close to the tracks. "Ho now. This is not right," declared Bowling, turning to his cousin. "These are William's moccasins, but William's feet are not in them. Someone else is leading the colonel's horse. Small foot, bandy legged, definitely not William."

"How is that possible?" asked Wallace. "It makes no sense."

"Look here, cousin. These prints are from William's moccasins, but the feet inside them takes a short stride, small step, not like William's track at all. This fellow is bowlegged as well. See how he rolls his feet tilted out? That's not William. There's no doubt it's the colonel's horse though."

"Maybe William is riding the horse and this other fellow leading," said Wallace, scratching his jaw.

"No one's on the horse, Wallace. That's plain enough."

Bowling looked about, studying the tree line along the river's edge. He turned his attention back to the tracks. Looking over at his cousin, he said, "I'll follow along the waterline. You go some distance in the trees off the river. Stay with me as I move along. Keep out of sight though. It's not likely William gave his moccasins away. This might turn bad, so keep your wits about you."

Bowling followed the riverbank. The tracks wandered in and out from the water's edge, meandering along on a senseless path. It wasn't long before the riflemen came on a small tentlike structure displaying various animal hides hung along its sides. The top of the structure was covered with dark wood. A small smokeless fire stood just outside.

Off the water's edge back in the tree line, Bowling could see the colonel's mare tied to a low branch. Taking a quick glance at the animal, he turned back and approached the hide-covered tent. A sharp query came out of the dark.

"What do you want?" demanded the bandy-legged pistoleer in his dented voice. He held his large horse pistol, aiming it in Bowling's general direction.

Bowling threw his hands out wide. "No need for that, sir!" he called quickly. "I mean you no harm. My name is Bowling Miller. I have a place west of here. I come by the river often. Do not shoot."

"Are ya English or Yankee?"

"Born to the colonies, sir, but I hold allegiance to none. I keep as far from that scrap as I can. I came this way looking for horses. The Americans took every animal I had, even the ones that don't ride."

A gleam came into the old man's eye. He swept his gaze over Bowling and took a step back. "You look to be a rifleman. I see you carry one," he said, pointing to the long rifle in Bowling's arms.

"The only men without a rifle out west are dead. You must carry one. If not, the savage Shawnee, Delaware, and Mohawk would have eaten my liver long ago."

The old man shivered at this. "It happens I have a horse. And it is for sale."

Bowling flashed a broad grin on the old man. "I have interest in that, sir."

"If you meet my price and have the money, the horse is yours." The river pirate nodded.

Bowling turned toward Morgan's horse. "Is it that red mare?"

"It is."

"How much?" asked Bowling.

"Fifty pounds and worth every shilling. She's a well-trained animal, curried and combed, fed only good oats, and she rides smooth as a boat on the river."

"She does sound good. However, I would not buy a horse without knowing its provenance. She could be stolen."

"She is not!" answered the pistoleer indignantly. "She was taken in fair trade. I brung the owner cross the river in my boat. He paid in kind with this horse. Said he had no need for her. He was fair desperate to cross the river."

"You have a boat?" asked Bowling, curious.

"I do. She's right here," answered the pistoleer, rapping the barrel of his horse pistol hard against the flat hull. He brought the barrel down a second time with a heavy thunk to emphasize his point. The result was an enormous explosion of metal, black powder, and ball. It rattled the surrounding tree branches, echoing through the air and startling the mare as she jerked her reins in an attempt to flee. A fine spray of hot metal shot through the air. The barrel of the horse pistol splayed out like a daisy. The pistoleer stood dumbfounded before Bowling; his mouth hung open.

Bowling instinctively swung his rifle barrel down on the old man. A hot shard from the exploded pistol drilled its way through Bowling's heavy buckskin coat, nipping his right arm. It burned. Another piece just missed his head. The old pistoleer looked on his damaged weapon in disbelief. He began a keening wail. Noticing the large hole blown through the hull of his flat-bottomed boat, he wailed again in earnest.

Bowling waved his rifle frantically above his head, calling out loudly, "Do not shoot him, Wallace! The old fool double-loaded his pistol!"

The pistoleer whirled about, finding himself staring down the barrel of a second rifle held in Wallace's hand. He backed away from Wallace, nearly bumping into Bowling's rifle doing so.

"No!" screeched the distraught old pirate. "You've blown my pistol to pieces. Look at my boat! I will see you in hell for this, rifleman."

"That is a bold statement coming from you, sir. We know well and good you have stolen this animal. Tell us what happened to the man riding it. Where is he?" demanded Bowling harshly. "Choose your words carefully, old man. If you tell me false, I will kill you where you stand."

"'Tis true!" wailed the pistoleer. "I carried your man across the river. He was dressed as you with hair colored red. He carried a long rifle, knives, and a hatchet. He left this horse here with me and has not returned. It has been two days since. To my shame, I did try to sell her." He ducked his head in mock humiliation. "I am a poor old man with little food and small shelter. The winter months are cold here."

"Is that why you wear his moccasins?" asked Wallace sharply.

The old man raised his eyebrows with a look of surprise. He stared down at his moccasin-covered feet. "He . . . gave them to me?"

Bowling spun his rifle around and smacked the old man square in the forehead with the weapon's butt. The pistoleer went down in a crumpled heap.

"Throw him over the colonel's horse, Wallace. We'll carry him back to Major Clark. He'll discover the truth from this old thief."

New York Harbor, 1778

THE OPEN SLOOP sailed over the water at a brisk pace. She made four knots or better with the aid of a stiff northeast wind. William slept fitfully through the night, snapping awake on every jostle and bump of the vessel. There were many. Sitting on his bottom with the other prisoners, William did what he could to shelter himself from the biting October wind. He bunched himself up alongside the gunwale, shivering as wave upon wave of freezing sea spray flew over the deck, dousing every man aboard.

As he sat rolling side to side with each pitch of the boat, a single thought burned like fire in William's chest. It was a black hatred overwhelming every notion and refusing to leave go.

The treachery of John Alden was beyond William's calculation. Bitter thoughts of Elspeth, Little Cornstalk, his brothers, and his sister burrowed into his heart in painful bursts. The things Alden said were etched into his mind like words on a stone.

I just smiled at the girl, said the intoxicated Englishman, articulating his words with a lopsided grin on his face, spittle on his lips. *She put the pistol to her head and fired.* William shook with fury as he imagined his sister's last moments.

Evens killed your father, and your brother David killed Evens!

The words turned through William's mind but made no sense. What happened to his mother? How had David come to kill this man Evens? William had no idea.

The fast-moving sloop entered New York Harbor. The steersman, well experienced at his work, pushed his rudder hard over, swinging the boom cross deck to pop out the jib, catching the last of the ocean breeze as the boat moved into the harbor. The mainsail came down as the boat deftly drew toward a series of open moorings alongside the wharf.

They passed three anchored British ships of the line. These were enormous vessels, the likes of which William had never seen. Two bore three masts as tall as trees while the largest carried four. They were all anchored, gently swaying in the harbor swell. William could see many men scrambling up the rigging like squirrels, scurrying over the ropes, calling out to one another. Their shouts echoed clearly over the water. Across the bay near Wallabout, three broken hulks lay anchored. They carried no mast and appeared to ride low in the water, almost grounded. They were British navy prison ships.

Two wide estuaries merged at the southern tip of Manhattan Island, the East River flowing alongside the Atlantic and the Hudson on the west. The four-man crew of the little sloop hustled over the rigging. One man stood at the ready with a swaying anchor in his grip.

Two crew members held lines to be cast. Each man was ready to lash the forty-foot boat to the dock pilings jutting from the water. The four redcoats guarding the prisoners held fast to the gunwale ropes, their gaze only for the solid relief of the wharf. Coming alongside the mooring, the anchor flew out and the lines quickly cast and tied off. Bumping up along the stone and wood pilings, the sloop was swiftly secured. A wooden gangway slid off the wharf, communicating boat to dock.

The ropes binding William had been replaced in Philadelphia with riveted shackles and heavy chain. Each prisoner on the sloop was ordered to stand and climb the quivering gangway. It was a difficult process as the steel links that bound each man made progress awkward and slow.

A gaggle of redcoats blended with civilians, and dockworkers milled about over the long wharf. Crates and bales of goods leaving and arriving seemed to be everywhere. Wheelbarrows rattled over cobblestones that covered the dock end to end. A wooden shelter stood at the far end of the wharf, with a line of beaten men standing shackled one to the next.

Sir Jeremy Skelton stood patiently as the sloop tied up. Two naval officers in British blue along with three redcoat marines stood behind the administrator, shifting their weight foot to foot in the chilly air. It was middle day. The sky was clear with few clouds overhead. The wind blew cold on this October day. The sloop prisoners were lined up and marched toward the shelter near the dock entry.

As he stood in line, William could feel the cold stone of the wharf numbing his bare feet. It was almost a relief. The surface of the wharf was covered in a scatter of gravel and small broken stone that dug into the bottom of William's bare feet. It was a painful shuffle. As he waited with the others, William looked about.

The city of New York lay just beyond a large battery of cannon mounted on high stone walls. Four or five tall spires stood out above the smaller buildings. Each carried the cross of Christ. The buildings themselves were colorful, closely packed together, and well built with wood slat, brick, and stone. A pall of woodsmoke mixing with the smell of salt air, timber pitch, and fish hung over the wharf like a shroud. Crying seagulls swooped through the air, mingling with the sounds of stevedores, soldiers, and sailors.

As William advanced along the line, he noticed a well-dressed woman passing small packages to the prisoners before him. The bundles were small white-cloth-wrapped parcels tied with a colorful ribbon. The woman spoke briefly with each recipient.

The lady stepped up to William. "You have no cap, sir." She stared down at William's battered feet. "And no shoes," she declared.

William swung his head round, hesitating, unsure whether to answer. "No, miss. I lost my hat. My moccasins were taken."

She clicked her tongue in disappointment.

Elizabeth Burgin was of medium height. Her narrow waist and buxom form filled a dark blue dress trimmed in delicate white lace. A complementing shawl covered her shoulders, pinned at the neck with an ivory broach. Beside her stood a young black boy bearing a basket filled with small white bundles. Her hair was shimmering black, pulled back in a tight queue, and held in place with a fine mesh. A spray of small white flowers decorated one side of her hair.

She was a handsome woman with high dark brows, blue eyes, and a kind smile. Sympathy marked her face as she surveyed the line of broken men held in chains. Her smile tempered through the misery of what she witnessed.

Recognizing the blond-red-haired prisoner standing before Elizabeth Burgin, Sir Skelton pointed toward William and spoke to the naval officer by his side. The officer approached William and Mrs. Burgin.

Elizabeth reached in the basket and handed William a small package.

Stepping up, the lieutenant bowed his head, touching his cap in deference to Elizabeth. "This one is not for the Jersey, Mrs. Burgin. He has no need of your gift."

Elizabeth turned her sharp blue eyes on the officer. "This man has no cap or shoes, Lieutenant Perkins. What harm could my parcel be?"

The lieutenant stood silent under the harsh glare of this formidable woman.

She turned back to William, ignoring the lieutenant. "You may keep the package, young man," she said softly. "It is only a bit of biscuit with dried meat and a small portion of camphor. You may well need them before your ordeal is over."

The lieutenant grasped William by his arm. "Is your name MacEwan?" he asked sharply.

William did not reply. The officer shook William violently, rattling his chains. He repeated the query.

"That will be enough, Lieutenant!" cried Elizabeth, appalled.

The lieutenant stopped.

"Answer the lieutenant, young man," said Mrs. Burgin calmly. "It will do less harm and make little difference to your circumstance."

William stared at the lieutenant again, unsure. Then he shook his head in resignation. "Yes, my name is MacEwan."

The officer pulled on William's arm. "You are to come with me."

Elizabeth Burgin asked, "Where, Lieutenant Perkins? Surely you are not going to hang this young man?"

"We are taking him aboard the *Victory*, Mrs. Burgin, and that, I am afraid, is all I may say on the matter."

With that, the lieutenant pulled William away from the line of prisoners, leading him toward the shelter and Sir Jeffery Skelton.

Skelton looked William up and down. He asked, "You are William MacEwan?"

"Yes, sir," answered William, nodding.

Skelton turned to a marine at his side. "Where is this rifle of his?"

"They are bringing it up from the sloop now, sir."

"Excellent. Lieutenant Perkins, please take possession of this man's weapon. Bring your prisoner aboard the *Victory* and notify Captain Ford."

"I beg your pardon, sir," interrupted William, half-believing this stately Englishman might hear his plea. "I am not an American soldier. I swear this to you. I came to Philadelphia only to find my family. This is a terrible mistake, sir. I am no widow-maker, nor have I ever been. You must believe me, sir!"

"That is a bold statement," replied Skelton, clucking his words. "I have it on good authority you are indeed an American rifleman. In fact, it is well known that you are one of Col. Daniel Morgan's best marksman and that you have murdered several of His Majesty's finest officers. You are nothing but a murdering mongrel. Men such as you run like cowards from the field when the king's forces descend upon you. You, sir, are the most despicable of all, without an ounce of honor." Skelton stared at William hard, pursing his thin lips like a fish.

"I am telling you the truth, sir. I swear to it."

"Yes, Captain Alden said you would plead such lies," announced Skelton, shaking his head. "I will not hear it! I will not."

William's face went pale at the sound of Alden's name. He clapped his mouth closed and stared at Skelton with intense malevolence. His deep green eyes closed in on the man before him.

The look on William's face caused Skelton to step back a pace. He had never experienced such raw hatred directed at his person. The look in those American eyes was frightening.

"Take him, Lieutenant," said Skelton in a shaky voice. Then he turned his back on William.

As he did so, he came face-to-face with Mrs. Elizabeth Burgin.

"Where are you taking this man, Lord Skelton?" demanded Elizabeth as she watched the marines and naval officers drag William toward a jolly boat.

"If it is any concern to you, Mrs. Burgin," answered Skelton in a mealy tone, "that murdering scoundrel is being shipped to London. He will demonstrate this so-called American long rifle before the king's Privy Council. I understand the king himself wishes to be present, an honor afforded few men, let alone someone of his ilk.

"After that, he will be hung inside a caged gibbet from the Newgate Prison arch until the flesh rots from his bones, a gift to the people of England."

Elizabeth Burgin stared at this self-important dandy in utter disbelief. "You could do such a thing to a man so young?"

"It is no less than he deserves. As you know, Mrs. Burgin, English law has little tolerance for criminals, treason to the Crown being the ultimate crime. We have done far worse to common thieves. And they were much younger than this MacEwan fellow."

"This law you speak of, Lord Skelton, will bring only shame and disaster to you and your country."

"Oh, do spare me, Mrs. Burgin," drawled Skelton in mock concern. "We know your political views. We have an eye on you, Mrs. Burgin. Oh yes, we are watching."

The king's representative to America's colonies turned on his heel and stepped away at a regal pace, smiling and nodding to all he passed.

The Ohio

DRAGGING CANOE PEERED out through naked trees, barely concealing himself. His eyes were drawn to the open field and bald hill that lay before him.

It was a sunny day, dry and cold with few clouds overhead. A light breeze wandered through the thin line of white oak, pine, and maple. Tenskwatawa would meet Dragging Canoe at this place. Here, the Shawnee chief and Cherokee renegade would make their agreed exchange—rifles and muskets for the daughter of Black Feather.

Tenskwatawa, the younger brother of Tecumseh and elder brother to Broken Tree, was in his thirty-seventh season in 1778. He was known to all as the Shawnee prophet, holding enormous sway over the Shawnee through spiritualism and belief in the way of the Indian. He found he could affect his world profoundly with his words and did so often.

Tribal leaders from all over the Ohio journeyed to Tenskwatawa's lodge to consult the great Shawnee chief. Known for his intelligence, courage, and superstition, he decorated himself liberally with Spanish silver, a broad beaded medicine belt, tiny silver arrows, and triangle earrings. These adornments were meant to keep the touch of death away. Largely because of this, he believed himself safe from that shadow that takes all men.

He was no longer certain of this.

The longhunter had come to his hated enemy, the Cherokee. Tenskwatawa was convinced that the rifleman could end his life. He had seen it in a dream. The longhunter with the golden-red hair had struck Tenskwatawa's Spanish armor and with it a fear that rang loudly in the Shawnee chief's heart.

Winter came up beside Dragging Canoe.

Both men wore paint, anticipating a fight with the coming Shawnee. Dragging Canoe carried a series of horizontal and vertical tattooed markings down his chest. A white and red blanket hung from his shoulder. He held an old musket by the barrel, the stock resting firmly on the ground.

"Have you heard this woman, Dragging Canoe? She speaks words all day and night, words of the white tongue, Cherokee words about spirit dreams and terrible death! Walking Bird listens to her. He has become frightened with her words. She talks and talks the full day! When she looks at you with those silver eyes, it is a wolf looking at you. We must cut the tongue from her mouth and the eyes from her head. This is the fate of an evil witch."

"You make too much of the girl, Winter," said Dragging Canoe. "That is Little Mother you see sitting there. You have known her your whole life. She is no more wolf than I am. She makes no magic," declared Dragging Canoe, emphasizing his words as he continued to stare out at the open field.

"She is only a woman who talks too much. She is not even full Cherokee. You and Walking Bird are weak minded. You frighten like children."

Speaking urgently, Winter leaned in close to his friend. "She has told us the longhunter impaled a bear to a tree with only his knife. Walking Bird has heard this! You must take her tongue, Dragging Canoe. I will burn it in a fire. Black smoke will come. You will see."

Dragging Canoe turned away from his vigil. With a deep scowl, he looked Winter in the face.

"The longhunter *did* trap a bear to a pine with his knife. I heard this story spoken by Shadow Bear. I heard it with my own ears."

Winter's eyes grew large in shocked surprise. "That is not good," he said, wagging his head side to side. "Not good."

"Let Tenskwatawa burn her tongue," said Dragging Canoe. "What do I care? I only want the guns."

Little Cornstalk sat in an open, sunny spot. The dry, cold autumn grass bristled beneath her. Her legs were splayed out for comfort. The pony she rode was deep backed with a sharp spine and thin blanket. It did her bottom no good.

Walking Bird draped a colorful Shawnee blanket over her shoulders, which helped ward off the morning cold. She took note of its artistry.

The Shawnee woman who had made this blanket was skilled in her work. It had tight weaving. The threads were locked well. It had good colors. She wondered briefly if Walking Bird had killed the woman who made this blanket. She hoped not.

As she squinted up at the cold sun, she thought of William; her mother, Adsila; the Murphy clan; and her friend Stevenson. Little Cornstalk knew William was too far away from her and would not be able to save her from Tenskwatawa, Stevenson as well. She was also aware she carried no value to Tenskwatawa except as bait with which to capture and kill William.

For the first time since learning of her unborn child, she wished it was not so. She prayed Tenskwatawa would wait to kill Little Cornstalk, wait long enough for her child to be born. If he did this, she knew the Shawnee would readily adopt the child. At least then it would live. This prayer gave Little Cornstalk some small peace. Yes, she would plead for her child's life. She would beg the mother of all things, the sun, the trees, and the sky itself for her child's life, William's child. For herself, she cared nothing. Her days in this dream life were given and taken as it was for every man and woman. She had known love, pain, family, friends, laughter, grief, and happiness. She was satisfied with her life.

Dragging Canoe threw up an arm as he stared out across the field. "Hold. They are coming."

A tall figure ambled down the hillside. He sat on a small Appaloosa pony, his feet dangling low, nearly touching the earth. This Shawnee sat erect, his head held high, his gaze straight on the hammock. He carried a long staff in his left hand that he intermittently poked into the ground every few feet as he advanced. It was Broken Tree.

Broken Tree had been contemplating his brush with death when he spied the little group of Cherokee. Daniel Morgan, true to his word, released Broken Tree and the others when Tenskwatawa gave up the white Shawnee captives he held. Broken Tree knew if he had not sent along the token of the longhunter's hair, more than likely, he would be hanging from a Saratoga elm. He knew his elder brother enough to know that.

Dragging Canoe stepped out from the hammock, holding a hand up high. He called a peaceful greeting. Broken Tree did not respond. Behind the riding Shawnee, several braves followed. They walked a single pony carrying a bundle wrapped in blankets. The group stopped several yards ahead of Dragging Canoe.

With Winter by his side, Dragging Canoe felt a hard stone riding in his belly. He knew who Broken Tree was, the younger brother of Tenskwatawa and Tecumseh, the white-speaking Shawnee with the broken body. *Where*, he wondered, *is Tenskwatawa?*

Dragging Canoe looked about nervously. He had no trust in this Shawnee who spoke the white tongue.

"Greetings, Dragging Canoe," said Broken Tree in formal Cherokee.

This surprised Dragging Canoe. There were many Indians who spoke the language of different tribes but not like this Indian.

"You have the woman?" continued Broken Tree.

"I have kept my word. She is here," answered Dragging Canoe. "You have the guns Tenskwatawa promised?"

Broken Tree swung his staff around, pointing to the pony with the tied bundle. "They are here."

Dragging Canoe began to walk over to the pony.

"I will see the woman first," said Broken Tree, halting the Cherokee renegade.

Walking Bird stood quietly beside Little Cornstalk. He could hear words spoken but did not know what was said. He looked down on the girl. He was unhappy. Bringing Black Feather's daughter to this did not sit well with Walking Bird. Once, he considered taking Little Cornstalk as his wife, but this feeling faded over time. He came to realize she was too hard, too smart to make a good Cherokee wife. She had the eyes of a wolf. Still, a tiny corner of his heart refused to release the old feeling.

He pulled Little Cornstalk's knife from his belt and carefully passed it to the girl. Little Cornstalk saw this, and without turning her head or speaking, she slipped the knife under the Shawnee blanket into the sheath tied under her skirt. She turned to look up into Walking Bird's eyes. He gave a simple nod.

Winter came to them and instructed Little Cornstalk to rise. Stepping out of the trees, Little Cornstalk shaded her eyes from the sun. She looked at the collection of men but said nothing.

Broken Tree awkwardly slid off his pony. He approached Little Cornstalk with an ambling gate. The first thing he noticed was the color of her eyes, a piercing silver-gray, much like that of an animal. Standing before the girl, he reached into a pouch hanging from his side. He took out a small thing. Opening his hand, he presented the bundle of William's hair to the girl.

"William," whispered Little Cornstalk, recognizing it instantly as she reached for the bundle.

"This is William. Did you take his hair?" asked Little Cornstalk sharply as she reached beneath her dress for the knife.

"No," answered Broken Tree, shaking his head. "I asked him for a token, and he gave this to me. It saved my life."

Little Cornstalk passed the bound hair back to the tall Shawnee.

"Do you know where the longhunter is?" asked Broken Tree, not expecting the girl to reply.

Little Cornstalk looked into Broken Tree's eyes. She saw sadness there, hard and lonely.

She answered, "William was taken away on a great canoe. I do not know where. I have seen this in a dream. He is far from me now, but he will return. I know this."

A great canoe? wondered Broken Tree. If he was taken by the British and put aboard one of their ships, then William MacEwan may never return.

"Are you certain he is coming back?" asked Broken Tree kindly.

"Yes," said Little Cornstalk seriously. "I have seen this in my dream too."

Broken Tree looked down on the girl, the Shawnee blanket shifting over her shoulders. He realized for the first time she was pregnant. A question appeared in his eyes, and a small smile lit his face. He said in English, "Is this the child of the longhunter?"

"Yes," answered Little Cornstalk, stroking her belly.

"I think my brother Tenskwatawa can help you. He will tell you where your longhunter is."

"How can he know?"

Broken Tree held out the bundle of hair. "He speaks with the English. I think they have taken the longhunter."

Little Cornstalk looked down on the bundle. She searched Broken Tree's face carefully with her silver-gray eyes. She did not reply.

Headquarters of Major Clark

MAJ. JOHN CLARK slammed the door behind him as he stepped inside the commandeered home. He slapped the rain off his field cloak with the use of his tricorn, scattering water in every direction. He carefully pulled his cloak, hanging it and the hat on a stout wood post attached to the wall.

It had been raining now for days, and his order to move the Eleventh Virginia south in this deluge was worrying. The roads from here to the Carolinas would be muddy rivers near impassable for his cannon. It would make for slow progress.

Close by, Wallace and Bowling stood at attention, each man holding his rifle by the barrel while their right arm captured their hats neatly. A small ragged figure sat bunched up on a low hardwood chair on the opposite side of the long room.

Clark scanned the men quickly as he dropped wearily into his seat. "At ease, gentlemen. My orderly tells me you have news concerning Mr. MacEwan. What is it?"

Bowling stepped forward and proceeded to relay how he and Wallace had come on the old river pirate. Their orders from Colonel Morgan were clear: retrieve the colonel's horse and bring Mr. MacEwan back if possible. Bowling was careful not to implicate himself and Wallace too deeply in the matter of the horse.

"How did Mr. MacEwan gain access to the colonel's horse?" asked Clark sharply. "Did he steal the animal?"

"Oh, no, sir. It was loaned by fault," answered Bowling, bobbing his head innocently.

"We didn't know it was the colonel's horse, sir," piped up Wallace.

Bowling gave his cousin a hard look and then continued, "We came upon this river rat in possession of the colonel's horse and William MacEwan's moccasins, sir. We have questioned him about it, but he has little to say on the matter."

Clark took a sniff of the air and scrunched up his face in distaste. "Good god, what is that offensive odor?"

"I believe it is that man's feet," answered Bowling, pointing to the old pistoleer across the room. "We took the moccasins off him."

Clark stood up to get a better view of the little man seated across the room.

The man's battered hat sat beside him on the floor. A white bandage was loosely wrapped about his head, hooding his eyes slightly. Filthy black and gray hair hung down alongside his face. He had an equally filthy beard. The clothes he wore were little more than rags, torn and dirty. As Clark looked down, he saw two black stumps vaguely resembling feet. Three toes were missing on the left foot and only one clinging to life on the right.

"Good god! Get something to cover his feet," said Clark desperately. "And whatever information you two have to impart, do it quickly and get this . . . person out of my headquarters."

Wallace pulled a thin blanket from the roll strapped over his shoulder and threw it over the gnarled limbs. He went back to stand by his cousin.

"What precisely is it you want from me, Mr. Miller?" asked Clark.

"This fellow will not tell us how he came by the colonel's horse or the moccasins," said Bowling. "He claims William gave them to him. Now William may have left the horse in this man's care, but he would never give up his moccasins. I am certain this fellow has stolen them and most likely killed William MacEwan to get them."

Clark directed a piercing look at the ragged man. "What is your name, sir?"

"My name is Ezekiel Bitterman, Major," declared the little pirate proudly. "I am innocent of these accusations. I have killed no one."

"I am a major, sir, and you will refer to me as such. How then did you come in possession of the horse and moccasins?" asked Clark sharply. "Tell me true, and I will see you fed and on your way."

"They was given to me, Major, as I told these men. I am no thief. I live a hard life off the river, and I take what's given is all."

"He's lying, sir," said Bowling heatedly. "This rascal pulled a horse pistol on me. Would have shot me too if the mechanism had not exploded.

"Major, William would no more give up those moccasins than he would his rifle. And I don't believe William would hand over a loaned horse to this character. This old pirate tried to sell the animal to me."

"Ease yourself, Mr. Miller. Hot words will not aid us here."

Clark turned back to the old pistoleer. "I would ask that you tell us the truth, sir. How is it you came to possess the horse and footwear?"

"As I said, sir, I am no thief, and that's the God's truth."

"Did you hold a pistol on Mr. Miller as he claims?"

"I did, sir, but I thought they was river trash. I been robbed before, you know. Had many a thing stolen from me in the past and from men just as these. That one"—he pointed at Bowling—"knocked me in the head with his rifle and for naught."

"Why, you dirty little—" said Wallace, taking a step.

"That will be enough, Mr. Grant!" barked Clark, halting Wallace.

Clark continued to stare at the old man and then slowly wagged his head. He addressed Wallace and Bowling. "I am afraid there is little more I can do considering what I have heard, gentlemen. You have the return of Colonel Morgan's horse at any rate. The whereabouts of Mr. MacEwan will have to remain undiscovered for the time being."

Bowling said slow and clear, "Let me shoot off one of those bloody feet of his, sir. I doubt it would be missed. He'll tell the truth then."

The old man let go a shuttering squeak, pulling himself deeper into the chair.

Major Clark pondered a moment when the door flew open, and his corporal entered. "Captain Gunnarsson to see you, sir," began the corporal.

Gunnarsson barreled into the room, shouldering the corporal aside before he completed his sentence. Following in Gunnarsson's wake was Olaf Stevenson and Richard Bennett. All three men shed a cascade of water as they pulled their caps and shook themselves. Gunnarsson eyed the old man seated across the room and then turned to Wallace and Bowling.

"Is this the man?" asked Gunnarsson, pointing to the old pirate.

Swinging his gaze from one person to the next, the pistoleer began to quake. The sheer size of Gunnarsson was intimidating enough, but it wasn't the captain who shook the old man; it was the hardened sailor, Richard Bennett.

Bennett strode over the wood floor, dripping water. He stopped directly in front of Ezekiel Bitterman.

"Hello, Ezekiel," he said with a wicked smile. "I've been looking for you."

Clark said, "You know this man, Bennett?"

"Yes, sir, I do. We have been trying to catch this old thief for months. He has turned in some of our best people to the British when they tried to cross the river to gain entrance into Philadelphia. The English pay him well as I understand."

"How say you, Mr. Bitterman?" said Clark angrily. "It appears you *have* been lying to us."

"Just as I said, sir," said Bowling, nearly shouting the words.

"You're not looking well, Ezekiel," continued Bennett, looking down on the old pirate.

Unable to shrink further into his chair, Ezekiel Bitterman began nervously rolling his hands one over the next as if making a pemmican knob. His eyes were cast to the floor, no longer looking up. He made little squeaky grunts, taking rapid breaths. His narrow frame was shuttering visibly.

Clark repeated the question firmly. "How did you come by the colonel's horse and Mr. MacEwan's moccasins, Mr. Bitterman?"

Bitterman held silent.

"Answer the major, Ezekiel, or it will go badly for you," said Bennett, menacing in his tone.

"Don't kill me, Mr. Bennett!" squealed Bitterman. "The English forced me. They did. They were to shoot me as a spy if I did not help them. Please don't kill me, please."

"I'll make a bargain with you, Ezekiel," answered Bennett, looking over at Clark and nodding. "I will not harm you if you answer the major's questions truthfully."

Rolling his hands quickly now and not looking up, Bitterman cleared his throat.

"Was raining it was when he come by, looking for a boat."

"I take it you mean Mr. MacEwan," said Clark.

"The fella with the horse it was, dressed like a savage with no hat. He had long reddish gold hair and a wound the side of his head. Walking the horse along the river he was. Said he come to find a boat. Said he weren't no soldier, but how was I to believe that, I ask you?

"When he come, I was tucked inside me little tent cause of the rain, so I invite him in. I thought maybe he was a scoundrel, so I pulled my horse pistol on him. 'Tis true, it is. He had that look about him," continued Bitterman, swinging his head up, looking for a sympathetic expression. He found none.

He continued, "Quick as a wink, he knocks the pistol from my hand and puts a knife to me throat. He tells me he needs my boat, and I was to take him cross the river. I told him it was bad weather, but he made me do it at the point of his blade.

"Anyways, I rowed him over to the other side. And when he walked up the bank, I fired my pistol at him, but I missed clean. It's what any man would have done. That's when the redcoats come and took hold of him."

"What did they pay you, Ezekiel?" asked Bennett softly.

"I only just asked for his moccasins," answered the old pirate, hanging his head.

"So William is a prisoner of the English?" said Stevenson bitterly. "Where would they take him?"

"Where did they take him, Ezekiel?" repeated Bennett.

"I swear, I don't know," stuttered the old man. "The red bellies knocked him cold and dragged him away is all I know."

"And the horse?"

"Well, I kept the horse as you can see. No use to that savage fella, was it?"

The silence in the room hung like a pall of smoke. All eyes were on the ragged old river pirate.

"You promised no harm to me, Mr. Bennett," said Bitterman quickly as he continued to roll his hands. "All in this room heard it clear."

"That is true, Ezekiel," answered Bennett, nodding in agreement. "And I will keep my word."

Major Clark stood up, looking Bennett in the eye. "Captain Gunnarsson, take this man out and see he is given food."

Ezekiel Bitterman looked up with a broken-toothed smile. "God bless you, Major. I can see you as a man of faith, a good Christian soul."

Clark continued solemnly, "Then hang him from the big oak south of here. You will place the sign of ***Traitor*** upon his hanging corpse."

"Yes, sir," answered Gunnarsson, grabbing a shocked Bitterman by the scruff of his oversize buckskin.

The old man let loose a scream that shook the timber of the house. He struggled violently as Gunnarsson lifted him bodily off the chair with one hand. He began blubbering and squealing incoherently, pleading for his wretched life as he wriggled and squirmed.

HMS Victory

ADM. RICHARD HOWE was comfortably seated in a red tufted leather chair. Eagerly leaning forward, he looked aft through the bank of wide glass windows covering the stern of the HMS *Victory*. It afforded an amazing view of the ship's wake and following sea. Once again, he marveled at the workmanship of the hand-carved frames surrounding the glass in ornate design.

He loved this ship. Howe considered her the finest sailing vessel in the world. He was continually amazed with her beauty, artistry, and seaworthiness. Like a lovely woman, she captured his heart whenever he stepped aboard.

At the of age of fifty-two, first Earl Richard Howe, KG, was admiral of the British fleet. Howe was fit for his age. Standing just under six feet, he wore no wig. His hair, long since rendered a ghostly white, required no such display. He had a sharp, prominent nose with windblown ruddy cheeks and thin colorless lips. His uniform of the day was dark navy blue trimmed in green and gold piping.

Turning in his chair, he looked down at the lone object lying across the dark oaken desk before him. It was an American long rifle, William MacEwan's long rifle.

Delicately sliding a finger over the polished surface, Howe examined the silver patch box mounted inside the hardwood stock. The cover of the patch box was held fast with a tiny swing latch that he now released. Peering inside, he discovered a small bundle of square cloth patches used to pack powder and ball into the lethal weapon. The rifle, he noted, had been well cared for.

The stone flint wedged in the hammer was in good condition as was the mechanism of the hammer itself—trigger set, pan cover, and pan. The silver-filled trigger guard was thin and artistically curled yet stiff. The rifle itself was truly long in comparison to a British Brown Bess. The barrel reached thirty-six inches while the rifle itself was close to sixty. The tip of the barrel held a silver ring almost two inches long with a sight and clip for the ramrod. This rifle fired a forty-caliber ball. The ram was made of split hickory straight as a string with a flat silver tip.

Leaning back in his chair, the admiral considered his brother's oft-repeated claim. Gen. William Howe, commander in chief of British forces in the colonies, fully believed the American long rifle to be the most effective weapon in the colonial arsenal. And no one—not the king, Lord North, or for that matter any member of the Privy Council—believed him.

The admiral considered the prisoner they were now ferrying to London, England. This American rifleman was to demonstrate the accuracy and lethality of the long rifle before the king and council, proving beyond a shadow of reason the truth of the matter. He wondered now, *Could this young man, a boy really, be the murderous widow-maker he is so labeled?*

Howe had taken a glimpse of the American before he was stowed away and, for the life of him, could not reconcile the three descriptions—assassin, murderer, and widow-maker. All were attributed to this fellow yet so young. Howe's brother hated and feared these American riflemen, and he began to wonder how true it all was.

***

William found himself locked in a storeroom closet with a hefty steel tumbler on the door latch. On one bulkhead were rows of shelves. They held a stack of empty ship ledgers ready for entry. The opposite bulkhead carried a thin wood shelf just able to hold a washbasin. There was no chair or bench to sit, only a thin blanket bunched on the floor next to a brass chamber pot.

A line of books sat on the bottom shelf. Titles of the leather- and wood-bound tomes ranged from *The Plays of William Shakespeare* to *The Old English Baron*.

The storeroom itself was narrow, measuring about seven feet in length and no more than six feet plus overhead, wide enough to allow shoulder room but no more. A small wooden plank with a center plug was clapped over the porthole mounted in the far bulkhead. It was secured with a wedge. William managed to remove the wedge, taking in his first view of the open sea.

The shackles and wrist restraints that William bore as he boarded the *Victory* were removed by the ship's carpenter as soon as he came aboard. The grizzled carpenter was careful not to injure William as he drove the rivets out with the aid of a steel rod and heavy mallet. William thanked the man, receiving a smile in return.

The sailor in charge of William, Boatswain Gibbon, was a gruff fellow and foulmouthed. He pointed to the chamber pot sitting on the deck. "Do you know what this is?" he asked sourly.

"Yes," replied William, "a chamber pot."

"Be sure to use it, and that means when you empty your belly too. I'll not be cleaning up any mess from you. Is that understood?"

William nodded without really understanding.

"You'll be fed midday same as everyone. You'll get water, no ale or rum. That's for sailors only. At six bells, I'll come collect you so's you can use the head. Don't be touching any of the purser's ledgers." He indicated the heavy bound ledgers on the shelf. "The captain will flog you for that. Keep yourself quiet. Don't be banging on the bulkhead or makin' a fuss. You're right close to the admiral's quarters, and he likes his quiet, he does. Understood?"

William looked at the man quizzically. "Yes, except for the part about bells and the head, I mean. What are they precisely?"

The boatswain wagged his head at the sorry ignorance of the American lubber. "Forget the bells. You'll know when I comes to collect you. The head is the privy on the ship. There be eight, and they lay forward close on the bow. You do know what a privy is, don't you?"

"Yes, of course, sir," replied William innocently.

"Thankee for that," said the boatswain sarcastically. "I've heard you American bastards shit in the street." Then he left, locking the door behind him.

When William first took sight of the *Victory*, he thought she was a floating castle of sorts. Painted dark brown with alternating bands of light tan, each deck of the ship was clearly outlined. An array of port covers lined both sides of the ship, all decks. Stepping aboard through a heavily decorated portal, William viewed the interior of the beautiful ship.

She was adorned in blue, green, red, and gold colors. The structural beams overhead and underfoot were painted a clean white. The deck itself was made up of spotless wood slat planks tightly sealed one to the next and scrubbed raw. Intricate carvings lined every portal. William had never seen the like of it.

Grateful to be unbound from his chains, William began to think a little more clearly now. His head wound, it seemed, had healed well and the swelling of his left eye considerably reduced.

At noon, Boatswain Gibbon entered. He dropped a pair of ditchers' boots stuffed with wool stockings on the deck. "For your bloody feet," said the surly sailor.

Gibbon handed a plate of food to William along with a flask of water. William finished the meal before the boatswain had a chance to exit. Politely passing the empty plate back, he downed the water provided in three quick gulps. He had been hungry and thirsty.

***

A hard knock came on the admiral's hatchway. "You may come in," called Howe.

Captain Ford entered. He pulled his hat and stood at attention before the seated admiral.

"At your ease, Captain."

Ford looked down on the rifle. "Is this the prisoner's infamous weapon, sir?"

"Yes, apparently," answered Howe. "It's well made as you see. Hard to believe a long musket like this could wreak such havoc on a battlefield. My brother swears it so. He tells me this weapon can strike a target over 250 yards away. Do you think it true, Captain?"

Ford continued to study the rifle as he slowly shook his head. "I find that difficult to believe, sir. Still, I am in no position to question General Howe's assessment. I am sure the general is far better equipped to judge than I am."

"Yes, he would be. And what do you make of our prisoner, Captain?"

"I've only seen him once, sir, when he came aboard. He seems quite young to me, unusual for a hardened soldier. His hair is an odd color certainly. Quite tall too. Dressed like a savage with all that leather and beaded fringe hanging off him. I know little else."

Admiral Howe stroked his chin absently. "I would certainly like to see that."

"See what, sir?"

"A man strike a target 250 yards away," he said, laughing. "I would hate to contradict my brother, but it does seem impossible. A shame we cannot prove it one way or the other."

Captain Ford cleared his throat. "There could be a way, sir, with your permission."

"Oh?" said Howe, looking up at Ford.

***

William bundled himself in a corner, pulling his knees up close. He threw the thin blanket over his shoulders. It was cold in this little room, and the damp salt air seemed to seep into his bones. His thoughts fell back to Little Cornstalk, Elspeth, and the children. He suddenly missed his mother very much. He wondered how he would make his way back to her and Little Cornstalk. It seemed an impossible task given his situation. If they were really taking William to England, how then could he ever escape and return home? He did not know.

Tenskwatawa

LITTLE CORNSTALK KNELT calmly on her Shawnee blanket. Her legs were neatly folded beneath her. She sat, head bowed, before the Shawnee chief, Tenskwatawa. His brother Broken Tree stood nearby, silent.

Council members from the surrounding Shawnee tribes were in attendance, sitting on either side of Tenskwatawa. A line of young and old warriors perched stoically as they looked down on the girl.

Little Cornstalk was surprised to see some of the older council chiefs wearing wampum belts. The beautiful beaded belts of white and purple shells were wound round the chieftain's waist a full fathom long. Once common to Indian trade, they were now more decorative than functional.

It was cold and sunny this morning, with many fires burning throughout the Shawnee village. Woodsmoke lay over the lodges like a blanket. The still air drifted softly about from the shuffling Shawnee gathered round. They wanted a view of this Cherokee girl, the daughter of Black Feather. Many had come to see if it was true what was said. She was known to hold great medicine, a true seer, a witch.

Little Cornstalk scanned the line of warriors with her silver-gray eyes. She appeared calm, but beneath her buckskin shirt, her heartbeat was as fast as a snared rabbit. She waited for Tenskwatawa to speak.

Tenskwatawa held up a hand. The crowded Shawnee fell quiet.

"You are the longhunter's woman?" asked the great chief as he peered down on Little Cornstalk.

"I am," answered Little Cornstalk clearly.

"You carry the longhunter's child?"

"I do."

"The Shawnee are enemies of the Cherokee. This we all know. When we came to your village, the longhunter fought beside the Cherokee.

Because of the longhunter, we were defeated by your father's people. This will not happen again.

"I did not see the longhunter in my dreams, and so he was able to shoot Tenskwatawa from far away. *Look now!*" shouted the chief, pounding his breastplate with a closed fist. "He could not kill me because of my Spanish plate. I can see the longhunter now. And I will see him when he comes for you."

Little Cornstalk rose on her knees and addressed Tenskwatawa.

"You can see the longhunter through his token, yes?"

Tenskwatawa opened his eyes, surprised at the girl's knowledge. He turned carefully toward his brother Broken Tree, standing silent.

Little Cornstalk continued, "The longhunter did not want to shoot Tenskwatawa, so he struck your Spanish plate to save your life."

All heads turned toward Tenskwatawa. What this Cherokee girl was saying made no sense.

Tenskwatawa stood up. "If the longhunter did not wish to shoot me, then why did he?"

"I told him to shoot you," answered Little Cornstalk simply. "He refused. So I told him again to shoot you. That is when he struck your Spanish armor. He did this to keep his own mind and to grant what I had asked of him. There are not many men who could do such a thing. He is a great man, Tenskwatawa, the father of my child."

Tenskwatawa sat dumbfounded at this revelation. For this Cherokee girl to say such things, it was not right.

Then Little Cornstalk climbed to her feet and walked slowly toward Tenskwatawa. She held out her hand. Lying in her palm was a bundle of hair identical to that of William's, only black as a crow wing. She passed the offering to the chief of the Shawnee.

Turning now to look on the whole council, Little Cornstalk said, "The longhunter gave his token to Tenskwatawa so he could always see him no matter how far away he was. I give my token to Tenskwatawa for the same reason. Now you will see me in your dreams and know where I am always."

Silence fell over the Shawnee chiefs. Tenskwatawa stared down at the small stack of bound hair and smiled. Then he laughed aloud. He looked up at Little Cornstalk, wagging his head in amusement.

Broken Tree was stricken to his core by Little Cornstalk's performance. She had taken Tenskwatawa's own words and used them like a blade against the chief. He wondered when the girl had cut her hair or how she did it. He took in the scene before him and knew beyond doubt that this beautiful Cherokee girl was far more dangerous than he ever imagined.

New York

THE BRITISH EVACUATED Philadelphia. Boats, ships, rafts, and canoes plied their way north in a mass exodus. Every type of conveyance was employed including horse, carriage, wheelbarrows, and wagons. Loyalists crowded the Philadelphia wharf with whatever belongings they could carry. The fortunate were already on their way to England. Those with money and connection were given ready transport to London. Fear gripped the city of Philadelphia. Fleeing was the only option left to those loyal to the Crown. Take flight or suffer the wrath of returning American rebels. Captain Johnathon Alden was among them.

When he stepped onto the pier in New York, Alden took an unsteady breath. A biting cold gripped Manhattan, bringing with it the threat of snow and stiff winds blowing down from the Canadian north.

Wearing a heavy winter cloak over his uniform, Alden made his way past the gun battery mounted just beyond the wharf. His leg was paining badly, which was worrisome. He was nearly out of laudanum. As soon as opportunity allowed, he would have to find an apothecary.

Pushing his way through the pack of bodies crowding the New York docks, he waved his cane violently as he called for a carriage. Though his wound was healing, he still relied on his cane for occasional support. As he made his way to the office of his cousin Sir Jeremy Skelton, Alden wondered if his plea for help would be answered.

Several sentries stood around the building, pushing people along to keep the entranceway clear. Waves of displaced humans flowed past, clogging the streets with belongings balanced in their arms. It looked to Alden as if New York itself was under siege.

"Johnathon!" cried Skelton as Alden arrived at the office of the king's representative.

A major general lolled quietly beside Skelton's fine oaken desk, stretched out in a tufted leather chair. Alongside the overweight general stood his adjutant. As Alden entered, he quickly saluted the general, nodding politely to the second officer.

"I imagine you have come to inquire about your rifleman, cousin," said Skelton cheerily. "Rest assured he is safely on his way to London aboard the *Victory*. And I have passed along your instructions to Captain Ford as requested. Admiral Howe is also aboard the *Victory*, heading home for a much-needed rest. The ship is due to arrive in England sometime early December. You must be pleased with yourself. Another coup heh, cousin?"

"I am, cousin. It was a difficult task finding the right man, but I believe I have done so. William MacEwan is an expert with the long rifle, one of Daniel Morgan's deadliest widow-makers. He will be able to demonstrate how lethal these riflemen can be on the battlefield."

"They are nothing but cowards as far as I can see," harrumphed the general as his adjutant nodded in agreement. "We should hang them all."

"Have no fear on that account, General," said Skelton with a smile.

Alden began walking across the room with the snap of his cane on the hardwood floor clearly audible.

"Cousin!" cried Skelton, concerned. "You are injured? How so?"

"It's nothing really," answered Alden, bowing his head modestly. "I took a ball in Philadelphia. Bloody rebel spy shot me as I was attempting to move my prisoners. The Americans burned the house down where I was holding them, killing two innocent slave women in the process. My captives made their escape."

"Bloody hell!" shouted the general. "These Americans have no sense of decency."

"To be honest, Jeremy," continued Alden, "that is the reason I have come to see you." Reaching into his bloused jacket, Alden pulled the original orders General Howe had given him. "I need men to go after these escaped prisoners. General Howe tasked me with the mission to stop the flow of weapons to the western colonies, and I intend to complete that mission. Currently, I am on injured absence from the Twenty-Third. But I'll be damned I will sit here convalescing while these rebels get away. Can you assist me?"

"What are you proposing, cousin?"

"If I can recapture these people and extract the information I need, I'll be able to halt the transport of these weapons. It's vitally important to the war effort."

"By god. Say no more, Captain," said the oversize general." I will find a contingent of men for your mission. How many do you think you'll need?"

"I think a company will serve, Colonel. No more than fifty men, I should think, certainly no more than that."

"A company you shall have, Captain." The general turned on his adjutant. "Lieutenant, would you see what units are available to the captain? Provide information you gain to Sir Skelton here when you have it."

"Thank you, General," said Alden with a wide smile.

"Splendid," added Skelton airily, clapping his hands. "In the meantime, you will rest and repair yourself at my residence, Johnathon. And Mrs. Baldwin is having a party tonight too."

West of Philadelphia

ELSPETH SAT ON a discarded shipping crate just outside the small tent Stevenson constructed for her and the children. A wood fire burned weakly beside her feet, billowing smoke. She stared into the feeble flame, lost in thought.

Her worry over William was painful and inexplicable. Bennett had provided the information of William's capture by the British. How he came by this evidence Elspeth had no idea. The man seemed to know all when it came to the city and the British.

Why, she asked herself, *would the English imprison my son?* He was no soldier. Was he simply caught up in this terrible conflict? She knew this could be possible. Her concern for William grew palpable with each passing day. The English might even hang William given reason. She shut this notion down, pushing it away from her mind.

Without William, I just don't know, thought Elspeth. A cold shiver went through her like a wind.

Mr. Stevenson was repairing one of the wagon wheels or at least attempting to. A steady string of mild profanity hovered over the wagon as Stevenson grumbled and swore at the offending lug. He was no wheelwright, that was certain. His frustration and volume rose accordingly.

Elspeth smiled as she listened. She was grateful to the grizzled hunter, more grateful than she could express. Among all this mayhem, Stevenson had somehow found winter clothes for her children, food, and blankets. He even discovered an old canvas sail they used as a makeshift tent. Meant to tolerate incessant rain and oncoming cold of winter, the sail was more than adequate.

"Mr. Stevenson," called Elspeth, "it is late, sir. You cannot work in the dark. You should wait till morning to complete your repair."

Stevenson gratefully stood up, dropping the steel pry he held in his grip. He brushed his hands together, slapping off loose dirt and animal grease. "Perhaps you're right, Mrs. MacEwan. It is dusky, and my eyes are not what they used to be."

"Come sit by the fire. I will reheat this terrible coffee you found."

Elspeth picked up a small wood-handled pot with liquid swirling around inside. "What do they call it?" she said, looking down at the black mixture. "Chicory?"

"Yes. Not a very tasty concoction, I'll admit, but it does serve. I apologize about the wagon, Mrs. MacEwan. It appears I have little skill for such things."

Stevenson plunked himself down on a wide cut log and stretched his legs. Elspeth placed the small pot on the dying embers and cleaned two cups with a small cloth. She turned to Stevenson.

"Any news from Mr. Bennett?" asked Elspeth, trying not to sound overanxious.

"Not yet," answered Stevenson reluctantly. "Perhaps tomorrow. It is dangerous work as you know, Mrs. MacEwan. It takes time."

"You have a troubled look about you, Mr. Stevenson. What is it?"

"Oh well," answered Stevenson as he leaned back. "I do have something to tell, Mrs. MacEwan. I had hoped William would be here to explain, but given the current situation, I see no way past it."

"What is it, Mr. Stevenson?" said Elspeth as she gingerly handled the pot.

Stevenson's eyes wandered upward into the leafless branches overhead. He shook his shoulders as if chilled. "Perhaps we should wait to hear from Bennett."

Elspeth was suddenly struck with a singular fear. She had not considered the idea that Stevenson would have to leave her and the children. The notion unsettled Elspeth terribly. She knew only too well there was nothing she could do if Stevenson wished to depart. He was, after all, a freeman with no obligation to Elspeth or her children.

"Mr. Stevenson," said Elspeth, her voice thick with emotion, "I am so terribly sorry. I was not thinking, sir. I should have realized that you have family and friends to return to in the west. You have selflessly stood by our side all this while. And I thank you for that. In fact, I cannot thank you enough. You literally saved our lives."

"No, no, Mrs. MacEwan," said Stevenson, staring down on his booted feet, "it's not that. It's just . . ." He hesitated.

"It's a girl," he finished, looking up.

"A girl? You have a girl?" asked Elspeth with a smile.

"No, not me," blustered Stevenson. "When William came to Black Feather's village, returning Shadow Bear to his family, he met a girl."

Elspeth snapped her head up. "William met a . . . girl? What girl?"

"She is Black Feather's daughter, Shadow Bear's sister. Her name is Little Cornstalk."

"Well," said Elspeth cautiously, "I suppose it only natural that two young people might be interested in each other. Other than his sisters, William has had little exposure to girls. What did you say her name was? Little Cornstalk? It seems a pretty name. Is she pretty?"

"Oh yes, very," said Stevenson, nodding.

Elspeth scratched one side of her head idly as she collected her thoughts. "I imagine she is short, much like me. I mean, her name, Little Cornstalk, it would seem so. You know how literal the Indian can be."

"Oh, no. You misunderstand, Mrs. MacEwan. An Indian cornstalk is tough, strong. Able to hold a heavy load of corn, they are hard to cut down and even harder to pull from the earth. Little Cornstalk is an apt description for this girl. As to her height, I would say she is as tall as William."

Elspeth squinted, trying to envision this mysterious girl. She looked over at Stevenson, who was now studying his boots intently.

"Was there something you wanted to add, Mr. Stevenson?"

"It is not what I wish, Mrs. MacEwan. But I feel I must."

Stevenson's look was that of a condemned man about to be hanged.

Elspeth caught the look in the hunter's eyes. Her hand flew out, pointing a finger at Stevenson.

"What is it, Mr. Stevenson?" said Elspeth sharply. "You look thoroughly vexed."

"The girl is going to have William's child," said Stevenson in a rush.

"That is the truth of it. There, I have said it," he finished with a rush of expelled air. He looked Elspeth squarely in the face, delivering a single firm nod.

Elspeth sat silent; her mouth hung open in shock. She stared at Stevenson as frozen as a stone. Of all the things Stevenson might have said, this was the farthest from Elspeth's thoughts. The absolute quiet between the two friends lingered in the air several minutes before Elspeth finally spoke.

"Where is this girl?" she asked carefully. "With her people?"

"No. She came along with me in search of William. I left her with the Murphys when I came east."

"Tell me about her," said Elspeth, calming down somewhat.

Stevenson did.

He described a beautiful half-Cherokee girl with silver-gray eyes and crow-black hair, a young woman with remarkable intelligence. "She was stubborn to a fault," said Stevenson with a laugh. "Brave and capable in every way. Much loved by her family and tribe and most everyone else who meets her. She is hardworking, tough, and most of all a happy spirit." She loved William in a way that Stevenson found difficult to describe, although he tried.

"And William loves this girl?"

"He was reluctant to leave her when I asked him to return home with those documents. I would say yes. He loves her very much."

"She's staying with the Murphy clan, you say?"

"Yes."

"Well, at least she is safe there. Connor and Kate are good people. They'll take care of her."

Murphy Settlement

CONNOR SAT QUIETLY waiting. He sipped his ale casually as he stared up at the moon illuminating the night. It was silent in the small community, every soul not on watch, fast asleep, with one exception.

Connor could hear Seamus rattling about in the tavern. The boy was making so much noise that it was almost comical. It brought a smile to Connor's lips. He took another sip.

Stepping out backward through the door of the tavern, Seamus trod lightly. Even so, he stumbled in his step, banging the musket against the wood post supporting the porch. He twisted his head around in panic.

He was wearing Connor's winter hunting buckskin, which was considerably larger than his frame. Heavy woolen trousers covered his legs, and on his feet was a pair of his sister's winter moccasins. An oversize coonskin cap was perched on his little head, and in the stumble and rush, it fell over his eyes, blinding him momentarily. He pulled the cap back and waited in the silence that followed. Satisfied that he had not woken anyone in the tavern house, he turned.

"And where is it you think you're going?" asked Connor from the shadowed moonlight.

Seamus whirled about, losing his balance. He fell on his bottom with a thump, dropping the musket with additional clatter. The coonskin cap once again fell over his eyes. He shook his head in despair as he rearranged it.

"Da," squeaked Seamus, "what are you doing up this time a night?"

"Waiting for you, me boyo. If I had any sense, I would tie you to the porch post and tuck myself back in bed. Instead, I'm out here on a cold night, waiting for me idiot son to arrive. Now where is it you think you're going?"

"I'm going save her, Da! You can't stop me. No one else will. She needs me, Da."

"I presume you're talking about Little Cornstalk?"

"Aye. I'm go'n' to save her, Da."

"Well, I must say, you do look well fit for the task. What have you got there?"

"I took your hunter buckskin, Da. Had to do it," said the boy seriously, shaking his head.

"I see that. Those trousers look good for the weather, and I see you have your sister's winter moccasins. Very smart. Do you have powder and ball for that musket?"

"I do," said Seamus, pulling out a horn and pouch and displaying them proudly.

"Now what about your sharps?"

"Sharps?" asked Seamus, mildly confused.

"Yes, your knife and hatchet. A man cannot travel this part of the country without them. You do have them?"

"Oh, I was planning to get them, just now."

"That's good."

"And you have a flint, char cloth, and strike in hand, me boyo?"

"Why would I need a flint, Da?"

"To start a fire, of course. You don't want the poor girl to freeze, do you? It's biting cold out there. And surely, you have a flintlock buried in that buckskin somewhere. Where is it?"

Looking sheepish, Seamus peered down at his hands. He made no reply.

"Ah, now don't you worry, son. Follow me, and we'll gather the necessaries."

Connor stood up, heading for the tavern doorway. Seamus followed in his wake, dragging the heavy musket behind, thumping along the wooden porch.

Rummaging behind the bar, Connor pulled out an Indian knife nearly the length of Seamus. The blade glistened in the dim light of the candle Connor had fired up. He reached back and came up with a large flintlock pistol, placing it on the bar next to the blade. Looking down on his son over the opposite edge of the bar, Connor said, "Sit yourself down, son."

Seamus scrambled up on a stool. He looked at the knife and flintlock, flinching at the sight.

"Now where did I put that flint?" said Connor as he feigned searching.

"I could start a fire Indian-style, Da."

"That's right. That's right," said Connor excitedly. "You'll need a bowstring and a good hard stick with a cut base. You know how to make one, don't you?"

Seamus hesitated as he decided on how to answer this question. "No," he said honestly.

"Ah, now that's a shame. We'll find that flint, don't you worry."

Seamus said nothing as he continued examining the knife and pistol on the bar.

"I almost forgot," said Connor. "You'll need a canteen for drinking water." He pulled a large canteen off a hook behind the bar and laid it next to the knife and gun. The necessaries were starting to pile up.

"Here we are," said Connor, laying a large flat flint on the bar that must have weighed two pounds at least. He quickly added the char cloth and steel strike. "There you have it, Seamus. I think you're all set now. Oh wait, I near forgot. A man going out to save an Indian princess will surely want a drop before he goes. You know, your old da always takes a drop before I go Indian fighting. Sturdies the spine, it does."

Reaching behind him, Connor pulled out two open top flagons. Popping the cork on the ale barrel sitting on the bar, he poured out the foamy liquid. He pushed one flagon toward his son.

Seamus's eyes popped open as large as the tavern window. His face glowed with anticipation. Having a drop with his da in the tavern? He could barely contain himself.

"You want to drink with *me*, Da?"

"Why, of course, son. You can't very well go off without taking a drop now, can you?"

"No," said Seamus, wagging his head and smiling ear to ear. He grabbed the flagon. Filled to the top, Seamus struggled to hold the heavy pewter cup up, spilling some ale on the bar. He grabbed the flagon with both hands to steady it.

"Now that's what I like to see in me son. A two-fisted drinker, he is."

Seamus took a sip and rapidly wiggled his head, shuttering from the impact. A small white foam mustache appeared on his lip. He smiled again.

"Go on then, drink up," said Connor.

Several minutes later, Seamus began to wobble on his stool. After every sip, he looked up at his da and delivered a smile. Seamus had never realized how much he loved his father.

They began a comfortable conversation. They spoke of Little Cornstalk. "I love her, Da," mumbled Seamus.

They laughed about the time Seamus accidently shot Connor. "I didn't mean to, Da. I swear, it were an accident."

Seamus began dropping his head every few minutes as if it were too heavy to hold up. "You look a wee bit tired there, Seamus. Rest your head a bit while I get some jerky for your journey."

Seamus happily did as instructed and promptly fell asleep.

Kathleen stood leaning on the kitchen doorframe leading from the tavern. She hung there with her arms crossed as she observed her wayward son and husband.

"Is he finished?" asked Kathleen.

"Aye, I think so," answered Connor tiredly as he yawned and stretched. "Can I go to bed now, Kate?"

"Go on with you then. I'll bundle up his nibs and put him to bed. As I said, Connor, desperate love leads to desperate measures."

"Hmm," mumbled Murphy as he trundled off to bed.

Kathleen pulled the shaggy coonskin off Seamus and gently stroked his light brown hair. "Desperate love," she repeated softly.

The Victory

SHE WAS 227 feet long stern to bow with a 49-foot walking beam. The *Victory*'s keel was laid down in 1758, built in Chatham, England. As a first rate, the *Victory* was a sturdy fighting ship. Sixteen days out of New York with every sheet waffling in a light wind, she was making just under four knots.

It was required that every crew member aboard the *Victory* work, and so they did. At sea, she was a hive of commotion.

On this day, her decks were scrubbed as a matter of course. Kneeling sailors grunted with effort as they pushed and dragged their holystone over the hardwood deck. A chanteyman breaking into song would drive the sailors on with his audible cadence of a good, bawdy chantey.

"What do you do with a drunken sailor? What do you do with a drunken sailor? What do you do with a drunken sailor early in the mornin'? Throw 'em in the scuppers with a hosepipe on him. Throw 'em in the scuppers with a hosepipe on him. Throw 'em in the scuppers with a hosepipe on him early in the mornin'."

The rigging, spars, and ratlines crawled with barefoot blue-jacketed sailors.

She was a happy ship, the *Victory*. Music aboard her filled every evening. Mandolins, penny whistles, fiddles, and drums drifted through the bulkheads, soothing the rowdy sailors as they made their way across the cold Atlantic.

Boatswain Gibbon was a whistler. He arrived every day as he said he would be taking William his midday meal and guiding him to the head at six bells. He would look in on William throughout the day, ensuring his charge was in good spirit and the chamber pot properly relieved. He spoke little to William, pinching his eyes in distaste at the young widow-maker while whistling a tuneless melody.

Over the last couple of days, William had been greeted with a cold bucket of seawater. The sailor who managed this feat waited both evenings for William to emerge from below deck. As William made his way to the head, the unknown sailor would stumble as if losing his balance. Then in the throes of righting himself, he would accidently toss the cold-water bucket over William. The surrounding sailors guffawed and slapped their thighs in delight. After two such soakings, William was more than angry.

Sitting with his back against the hull just under the little porthole, William pulled his knees up for comfort. He was wet and cold. The narrow purser's closet had little airflow for drying out, so he was forced to spend all night and the following day close to freezing. Draping his single thin blanket over his head and shoulders, he did his best to keep warm.

It was close to six bells, and William knew this most likely meant another cold-water bath. He was not going to allow it this time. As the whistling boatswain Gibbon approached the purser's closet, William stood up. When the little door creaked open, he scowled at the boatswain and said, "Not today, Boatswain Gibbon." This caused the sailor to pinch his eyes.

"What's the trouble then?" asked the boatswain. "Are you sick?"

"No, sir, I am not," answered William shortly.

"Well, come on then."

Up on the main deck, William swiveled his head about. He looked up into the rigging and then fore and aft. The ship had a gentle roll to her as they made their way. William, feeling the deck beneath his feet, scrubbed them hard for good footing. Sailors separated as the two men passed by, leaving a narrow, open pathway. Then two by two, they trailed in the wake of the older boatswain and the young American. They all knew what was coming, and the smiles they displayed glowed with anticipation.

William caught sight of the bucket sailor. He was a stout fellow not much older than William himself. He was a short man with long arms and solid legs. He was barefoot as he gripped the bucket rope, slanting his gaze sideways to get the pace of William. It was a practiced maneuver that William was now familiar with. Leaning over and crossing his feet to assume his feigned stumble, the sailor swung the bucket out, ready for delivery.

As he crossed William's path in his little dance, William spun to his left and stuck out his right foot, catching the sailor's ankle. The bucket went wild, missing William and sloshing the deck. The sailor tripped, sprawling out on his belly across the deck, taking much of the cold water to himself.

Jumping to his feet in a flash, the stout sailor came at William like a mad bull. William stood his ground and, when the sailor was within range, kicked out his right booted foot, striking the man squarely in the crotch. The sailor went down on his knees, gripping his groin. He rolled over on his side as he moaned in agony. William stepped over to the man.

"I'll kill you for this," croaked the bunched-up sailor as he choked on his nausea.

"You are welcome to try, sir," answered William calmly. Then he turned and continued his way to the ship's head.

Boatswain Gibbon looked down on the moaning sailor. A smile crossed his face. "You don't look well, Halfpenny. You should see the surgeon." Following William, the boatswain began whistling a bouncy tune.

The crew of the *Victory* fell over with laughter. Two of his mates lifted Halfpenny to his feet and helped him below.

"Kicks like a Frenchman, he does," said one sailor as the party broke up.

***

"Is he injured?" snapped the admiral.

Boatswain Gibbon stood before Admiral Howe's desk, rolling his cap in a tight circle between his hands. He was worried about catching the cat. He hoped he would not.

"Oh, no, Your Lordship. 'Twas the other way about."

"You'll refer to His Lordship as Admiral or sir while aboard the *Victory*. Is that understood, Boatswain?" said Captain Ford, standing beside the admiral.

"Aye, sor," answered Gibbon, bobbing his head. "My apology, sor."

"How did this happen?" asked Ford.

"It were the men, sor. They been tossing insults at the boy mostly, but then Halfpenny got the idea to give him a cold soak."

"Seaman Halfpenny?"

"Aye, sor. He loves a good scrape, you know. Anyway, done the first time, the boy even apologized to Halfpenny. That really tossed the crew a laugh. So Halfpenny decides to do it again yesterday. The boy realized right off he was being put on. That got him mad."

"I take it this was the third time?" asked Admiral Howe.

"Aye, sor, indeed, it were. The boy put Halfpenny down with a solid blow to his privates. He was wearing good boots when he done him too."

The cabin went quiet for a minute as Howe digested this bit of information. "Would you say he's a fighter then?"

"I would, sor."

"What else do you know of the man, Boatswain?"

Boatswain Gibbon reached up with one hand and scratched the top of his nearly bald head in thoughtful concentration. "Oh, I don't know, sor. He's quiet much of the time. Has lots of questions, he does, about the ship. He's right polite though. I'll give 'em that."

"What questions?" asked Captain Ford.

"'What's that?' he asks. 'It's a capstan,' says I." The boatswain flung his arm out for emphasis. "'And what is that called?' he asks. 'They be spars,' says I. Questions like that, sor."

"How does he spend his time?" asked Howe quietly.

"Reads, he does. Most all day too, sor."

"Reads! Reads what?" asked Ford, surprised.

"Books, sor. The purser has a stack of 'em in that closet of his."

"Which books?" queried the admiral with interest.

"I wouldn't know, sor, as I don't read m'self. Can sign my name good and do numbers, but I can't read a lick."

"And the man has said nothing else about himself?" asked Captain Ford. "Where he's from? What company he fought with?"

"Well, he did have lots to say when first he come aboard, sor. I told him to shut his gob about that nonsense, some crooked yarn about not being an American soldier and the like. A pack a lies is what it were, sor. I wouldn't have it."

"What precisely did he say, Boatswain?"

Gibbon pinched his eyes as he tried to recall the words.

"Said he weren't no American soldier and never was." The boatswain delivered these words as if he were driving a nail. "Said he went to Philadelphia to find his mother. *Of all things to say to an honest man!*" The boatswain shook his head.

"Then he says he was took up by a British patrol in Philadelphia and taken for a soldier, but when he tried to explain, they didn't believe him. And who would? I ask you."

There was silence.

"Is that all, Boatswain?" asked the admiral.

"Oh no, sor. He said the patrol took him to a black-hearted captain named . . . Alden, sor."

"Hold there," said the admiral, holding up a hand. "Did you say Alden? Captain Johnathon Alden?"

"Aye, sor, Alden it were. Don't know the captain's given name, just the Captain Alden part."

"Continue," said Howe, nodding.

"Well, sor, the boy claims this Captain Alden murdered his father and sister in some Indian raid or other, then abducted his family. Took the lot to Philadelphia, he did. Said this captain confessed the whole matter right to his face. Then some red bellies knocked him around a bit and sent him off to the *Victory*."

Boatswain Gibbon looked from one officer to the other expectantly. "I ask you now, who would believe a fairy tale like that, sor?"

Admiral Howe looked over at Captain Ford. "I wish to speak with the prisoner, Captain. Please have him brought to me, in ten minutes, no less."

"Boatswain," cracked the captain.

Gibbon pulled himself erect. "Sor?"

"You heard the admiral, man. Go collect the American and bring him back here in ten minutes."

"Aye, sor."

Captain Ford stood idle, his hands clenched firmly behind his back. His head was tilting downward in thought. "You know this Captain Alden, Admiral?"

"I do. I have met the man twice. I found him to be . . . an unpleasant fellow. My brother William assigned him to an exploratory mission. He was attached to the Twenty-Third Dragoons at the time. It was considered a dirty and dangerous assignment."

"Surely, you're not taking this American's word over a captain in the British army. It's impossible to even consider."

"You may be right, Captain Ford, but I cannot help recalling a story my brother relayed to me about this Captain Alden. He said the captain had kidnapped a family of western colonists involved in gun running. It was a woman and four children. He was holding them prisoner in a local bordello in Philadelphia. My brother, the general, was most uncomfortable about the affair. This fellow Alden assured him that it was temporary and only meant to extract information concerning the gun running. Now I wonder."

"A bordello, sir? Why not take these people to the local jail?"

"Exactly my thought, Captain Ford. The first time I met Alden, I found the man to be ingratiating, sly, and basically distasteful. If the American is telling the truth here, we may have a tiger by the tail. If it became known that the army has captured an innocent, the embarrassment to the government could be untenable."

"Captain," continued Howe, "would you be kind enough to retrieve the orders you received for the prisoner? Any other documents as well if you have them."

Admiral Howe then stood up and made his way to a tall thin cabinet holding an American long rifle.

When William entered the admiral's quarters, his eyes immediately locked onto his rifle.

"That's my rifle," he blurted.

The admiral sat calmy, reading the orders that Captain Ford had given him. He made no acknowledgment of William's presence. A straight-backed chair sat before the admiral's desk, and Captain Ford directed William to it. "Have a seat, Mr. MacEwan."

Taking his gaze from the rifle, William looked about the beautiful cabin. Every surface of the ornate woodwork was spotless and highly polished. There were several brass lanterns hanging here and about, swaying with the rhythm of the ship in a hypnotizing gesture. The bank of windows at the stern looked west, displaying a setting sun just above the ocean horizon. William was struck by the beauty of the view, finding it difficult to turn away.

"The chair, if you please, Mr. MacEwan," repeated Ford.

Boatswain Gibbon nudged William's elbow. "Sit, boy," he said firmly.

William sat, shrugging slightly.

All eyes went to the admiral as he continued his reading. He turned another page with a soft, scraping sound. William continued his examination of the room.

A small alcove stood on the port side of the space, and in it was a sturdily built bed rack with a comfortable mattress, coverlet, and pillow. Just outside the alcove was a small table with two chairs similar to the one William occupied. The admiral placed the papers on the desktop and looked up at William.

"Do you know why you are aboard the *Victory*, Mr. MacEwan?" asked the admiral.

"Yes, sir, I have been told."

"Captain Ford's orders are to convey you to London for the purpose of demonstrating your skill with this rifle." The admiral nodded at the rifle. "You are to perform this task before the Privy Council, General Command, and Lord North. Even the king may be present."

William shrugged again, noncommittal.

"I also have here," continued the admiral, sliding a sheet out from the others, "the action report on your capture. It states here that you were captured outside the city of Philadelphia in a skirmish with a British patrol, that you have been identified as an American soldier attached to the Eleventh Virginia Rifle Company, that you are, in fact, a rifleman, also referred to as a widow-maker. Do I have this correct?"

A smile began to cross William's face slowly. He bent and shook his head. The world, it seemed, was far off-balance. Excepting his name, none of what the admiral said was true. And although William recounted the truth several times while imprisoned, not one person bothered to ask if any of it was true. He held silent.

"Well, Mr. MacEwan? Is this true or not?"

William looked up sharply. "It is a lie, sir."

"How is it a lie?"

"I am not an American soldier, nor have I ever been. I came to Philadelphia to find my family. I was captured by a patrol when I made my way into the city. I tried to explain my reason for being there, but your soldiers refused to listen."

"These orders were signed by His Lordship Jeremy Skelton, a key administrator to the Crown," said Howe. "And the action report of your capture was signed by the officer who effected it, Capt. Johnathon Alden."

At the sound of his tormentor's name, William shot up from his seat, clenching his fists and scowling at the admiral. Boatswain Gibbon quickly stepped in front of William as the admiral snapped, "Calm yourself, Mr. MacEwan. Please, sir, sit down."

The anger that William displayed was palpable. His entire frame was vibrating with fury. He wagged his head and sat back down.

"You say you are not an American soldier, Mr. MacEwan, and yet you carry this rifle. Why?"

"I am a longhunter, sir, from the western region of the colonies, just east of the Cumberland Gap. That is why I carry this rifle," answered William simply as if that explained all.

"A longhunter? I am unfamiliar with the term. What, pray tell, is a longhunter?" asked the admiral, curious.

William looked up at the admiral. He saw no animosity or ridicule in this man's eyes, just a gentle patience. He seemed in earnest, but how was William to know?

"A longhunter, sir, is a man who goes out into the wilderness on a long hunt. He could be two or three months away, hunting furs, pelts, and meat as needed. It requires certain skills, of course. You must track what you kill, dress out your game, and skin the hide. You must navigate trails no white man has ever set afoot too. The most important skill, of course, would be shooting and, when the occasion arises, fighting Indians as well."

"I see," said the admiral. "Perhaps you can tell us the truth of the matter then. I would be willing to listen."

William looked at the man in surprise. He considered the admiral's request. He also considered the notion that this man was merely setting some sort of trap for him. He was unsure of its making or why.

"Why?" asked William.

"Why what?" replied the admiral.

"Why are you willing to listen when everyone else is unwilling?"

Admiral Howe thought about his answer. He had no wish to reveal his thinking on the matter just now but felt he owed some measure of honesty to this young man. He made his decision.

"I have met Captain Alden, Mr. MacEwan," said the admiral matter-of-factly.

William was about to eject himself from the chair once again, but the admiral cut him off in a commanding tone. "Please, Mr. MacEwan, if you insist on bounding out of your chair at every mention of the captain, I'll have to ask the boatswain to restrain you. Now tell us what you know, sir. How is it you know this Captain Alden?"

William took a deep, shuttering breath to calm himself. Then he spoke.

"I first met Mr. Alden at our homestead," began William.

As the details poured out, William became more and more animated from the telling as if a weight was being lifted from his shoulders. Someone was willing to listen, and that in itself helped William clear some of the anger from his mind.

He began by explaining how he had accidently shot Shadow Bear. This led to his journey to the Cherokee village in the company of Alden, Stevenson, and Shadow Bear. He told of the deadly fight with the bears; of how he fell in love with an Indian maid, Little Cornstalk; and of his affection for the Cherokee people. The more he spoke, the easier the words came.

He described the battle with the Shawnee and the loss of his Cherokee brother, Shadow Bear. He whispered these words. Looking up with a small smile, he told the admiral of Alden's cowardice in the fight with the Shawnee and how Alden had swum away, leaving all behind.

Realizing the compromise of the matter, William opted to leave out the details concerning his delivery of Alden's plans to Colonel Morgan.

As he continued, he told of his return home, finding only destruction. His family was gone. His father and sister were buried by the hands of a neighbor.

Then he told of the race to catch the villains and rescue his mother. On the trail of the Shawnee, he came on the American Army at Saratoga. During the battle, he was wounded without firing a shot. Afterward, he discovered the whereabouts of his family from a captured Shawnee chieftain named Broken Tree. He returned to Philadelphia as quickly as he could fly. After being taken up by the patrol, William was brought to Alden, where the captain confessed his crimes, exposing his devilish plans.

Alden's desire to violate his mother and dispose of his brothers and sister all came out. But William's family had somehow made their escape from the city and disappeared, infuriating the captain. The injured Alden had William placed in chains and sent to New York. To what purpose, William did not know at the time.

When William stopped speaking, only the hum of bare feet racing over the ship's deck could be heard overhead. A distant penny whistle played through the bulkheads as the ever-constant sea slapped wave after wave against the *Victory*'s hull.

William looked at Admiral Howe, his face an open question.

"Thank you for telling me this, Mr. MacEwan," said Howe finally. A look of deep concern shadowed the admiral.

"And in the telling, sir," asked William, "have I done myself a good turn? Am I a free man now that you know the truth of it?"

Howe held himself silent for several seconds and then said, "Without proof, Mr. MacEwan, there is little I can do for you right now. That being stated, I intend to investigate your claim with every instrument available to me. As I said earlier, I have met your captain Alden. Both I and my brother William have a low opinion of the man, and if there is a kernel of truth to what you say, I will find it out. My brother has hanged men under his command for less than what you describe here. That is the best I can offer you at this time."

"Well, sir," answered William, "that is more than I had yesterday."

"I do have one favor to ask of you," said the admiral. "Would you be willing to demonstrate your long rifle to Captain Ford and myself? I would like to know if you can really hit a target 250 yards away."

William drew his eyes down to the rifle on the admiral's desk. He longed to hold it. The rifle brought into focus a vivid image of his home, his family, and Little Cornstalk. And like those he loved, the rifle was no less a companion to William's life. He could imagine nothing else.

"I have never fired a shot aboard a rolling ship, sir, but I will do my best."

The admiral turned to Captain Ford. "See to it that Mr. MacEwan has more deck time, Captain. Boatswain?"

"Aye, sor."

"Find some warm clothing for Mr. MacEwan. He will be demonstrating his rifle and should be properly dressed for it. And he is to be given a ration of rum once a day."

"Aye," answered the boatswain without understanding.

***

The order to lower the sails and turn into the light wind came early the next morning. The seas were low with one- to two-foot swells. Word of William's shooting exhibition came to every sailor's ear. Luffing in a cool wind with little else to do, the notion of an American widow-maker giving a demonstration of shooting was a rare delight to the crew. Every man allowed was up on the main deck or decorating the rigging in an attempt to get a good view of it. Officers crowded the quarterdeck. Several Dutch eyepieces were on display as well.

At the bow of the ship, a small raft was set to sea. It had a square structure on top, standing no more than four feet tall. Above this, a Union Jack flew, fluttering sweetly on a short, stout pole. A long rope was attached to the raft and slowly paid out. As the raft floated away from the ship, an estimate of distance was determined.

William stood calmly on the quarterdeck. He watched the little raft drifting away. The two problems, as William saw it, was the rise and fall of the raft and the roll and dip of the *Victory*'s deck. This would be a difficult shot requiring perfect timing.

William loaded the rifle rapidly. A pair of marines were assigned to keep a close watch on the prisoner. When the raft reached a distance of about 200 yards, the captain gave William permission to shoot when ready.

A northern gannet circled the raft, deciding to alight on top of the stout pole holding the Union Jack. With that, a chorus of sailors began taunting William. "Shoot the bird! Shoot the bird, Yank, why don't ya?" The call rippled through the ship, accompanied with waves of laughter.

Captain Ford turned to Admiral Howe, wagging his head. "This seems an impossible shot, sir. Never mind the distance. The man has never fired his rifle under such conditions. Even our marines, who are well trained to do so, would have difficulty making that shot at 30 yards close quarters, sir."

"Never mind, Captain. Let us see what happens."

William stood straight as a tree, his feet planted apart with good purchase to the deck. His sight followed the little raft as he rolled gently along with the rhythm of the deck.

"There is no need to try and hit the bird, Mr. MacEwan," said Captain Ford, frustrated with his men's caterwauling. "Please—"

In that moment, William—ignoring the captain—brought his rifle up in a single swift motion, aimed, and fired. The bird exploded in a cloud of feathers, sailing briefly into the air and then crashing back into the sea.

"Good god," said Ford, flabbergasted.

William reloaded and fired three more times, striking the upright column in the center of the target raft with less than two inches spaced between each shot. The distance from the ship to the little raft on the last shot was close to 300 yards.

Admiral Howe smiled. He was delighted for his brother William, who had correctly assessed the effectiveness of the American long rifle.

He turned to William. "Thank you, Mr. MacEwan. I am suitably impressed."

For the first time in her history, the HMS *Victory* sailed in muted silence. Only the slapping waves, singing ropes, and flutter of loose sails could be heard.

The Letter

WALKING AT A pace, Stevenson circled the wagon one last time. After repairing the faulty wheel lug with David's help, Stevenson decided to check the remaining lugs. He was glad he did. He even replaced a sideboard that was rotting out.

It was midday and cold, with a brace of heavy gray clouds overhead blocking out the warmer sunlight. Stevenson wore a heavy brown wool coat with red facing. His racoon pelt cap was pulled down tight, covering his ears just. He examined the wagon closely. David, standing in the bed, assisted Stevenson with the examination.

The shock of learning William's situation had faded some for Elspeth. Still, her anxiety over her eldest son's fate had her barking at the children, leaving her generally out of sorts and miserable.

When Bennett explained that William had been taken to London on the orders of Alden, Elspeth cried, declaring, "If only my pistol had been dry. My one opportunity to kill that man taken on the whim of wet powder!"

Bennett had agreed, nodding vigorously. He, too, regretted his poor shot that night at the Weatherly house as it burned to the ground. The memory plagued him.

David was about to hop out of the wagon when he spied a rider in the distance. The man was heading directly for their little camp at a dead run. Dressed in black, the mysterious rider pounded up the sloping hill, slowing with the effort.

"A rider coming, Mr. Stevenson," said David, pointing in the direction of the oncoming stranger. "It looks like a preacher."

Stevenson turned, peering at the rider. The man wore a black pulpit robe cape that flew in the wind. A broad-brimmed black round topped hat sat clapped to the rider's head, held in place with the aid of his free left hand. *The dress of a pastor*, thought Stevenson as he scratched his head. "Better climb down from there, David, and fetch my rifle if you would."

As Stevenson stood behind the wagon, their unknown visitor began to come into focus. The man's head was dipped low, the hat brim covering most of his face. Then Stevenson relaxed. He recognized the dark red stud underneath the man. David stepped up and handed the long rifle to Stevenson.

"I don't believe we'll need that, David, but I thank you."

"Who is it then, Mr. Stevenson?"

"If I am not mistaken, it is that scoundrel Bennett. Come dressed like a preacher of all things. I swear to God, if that man was not doing good and brave things, I believe he would be destined for the gates of hell."

David looked curious. As Bennett approached, the strange preacher called out Stevenson's name. "Olaf, don't shoot me! It is I, Bennett. I am in disguise," he finished with a laugh.

Upon hearing Bennet's voice, Elspeth rushed from the small tent. Close behind her followed Aelwyd, Brian, and Duncan. As the children tumbled out, falling over one another, they gathered round their mother expectantly. A steamy cloud of exhaled breath emerged from all three, emphasizing the cold, damp air.

"Back in the tent, you three!" shouted Elspeth. "And don't come out until you have a proper coat and shoes on. Go on then." They piled back into the tent.

Bennett climbed down from the stud, tying the reins to one of the wagon wheels. Pulling the pastor's hat from his head, he delivered a broad smile as he rushed over to Elspeth.

"Mr. Bennett," said Elspeth, wonder in her tone, "I did not know you were a man of faith."

"Today I am, Mrs. MacEwan," said the sailor. "A useful disguise for our purpose.

"Who is this then?" continued Bennett, waving his hat at David.

"This is my son David," answered Elspeth proudly.

"David!" cried Bennett, throwing his arms in the air, still clinging to the hat. He offered his hand to the boy, giving it a hearty thrust. "You are a hero of mine. Did you know that?"

"No," said David, mildly confused.

"Well, you are," said Bennett. "You are the man who killed that vile bastard Tom Evens."

David's eyes went wide; his face, turning pale, fell like a stone. He drew his head downward, staring at the earth. His knees began to tremble. Bennett looked up at Elspeth, uncomprehending. She shook her head fiercely, giving Bennett a look of warning. Bennett caught the gesture, realizing his mistake.

"David," said Bennett cheerily, "would you be good enough to feed and water my mount? We have had a hard long ride today, and he is lathered some."

David pulled his head up. He studied Bennett closely. "You were the drunken sailor who fell into our room at the house. I remember you."

"Aye," said Bennett carefully. "That is me, although I was not as drunk as I appeared. You have a good eye, young man. Most would not recognize me in this costume."

David continued to look at Bennett in silence. Then he said, "Thank you for helping us, sir."

"You are most welcome, David."

"David, please take care of Mr. Bennett's horse," said Elspeth impatiently.

David pulled the reins free from the wagon wheel and walked the animal over to a large bucket trough filled with water. He began removing the heavy saddle.

Elspeth could contain herself no longer. "What news of my letter, Mr. Bennett? Were you able to post it safely?" she asked in a rush.

"Aye," said Bennett with satisfaction. "Sealed and posted it as you requested. Four days ago, I hand-delivered it to the captain of the *Pelican*, a packet making for London, an urgent letter posted at the request of Pastor Hemlington of the Baltimore Protestant Congregation."

Elspeth leaped at the man. Wrapping her arms about his neck, she planted a delicate kiss on his cheek. As Stevenson stood watching the scene, a sudden pang struck his chest. His affection for Elspeth, it seemed, had become somewhat ungoverned. This perplexed the hunter as he had never before entertained such notions. Yet this overwhelming feeling had somehow crept up on him.

"You used a *church seal* on my letter?" asked Elspeth, laughing in surprise.

"Indeed, I did," answered Bennett, feigning insult. "I have the seal in my saddlebag just now."

"Well, this is wonderful news indeed. Come now and sit by the fire. I am just making some food for the children and Mr. Stevenson."

Elspeth wore a long cloak of gray wool over her simple blue dress. Her black hair was drawn back and tied neatly. Stevenson noticed a twinkle in her look and a lightness to her step, something that had been missing over the last several days. This brought another jolt of envy to the man. Curious about this letter himself, Stevenson had yet to inquire on the matter. It was something between Bennett and Elspeth, he knew, but he was ignorant of its meaning. His hesitation to pry was fast losing way.

"May I ask what this letter is about, Mrs. MacEwan?"

"Of course, Mr. Stevenson," answered Elspeth. "As you know, Mr. Bennett discovered that William had been taken prisoner in Philadelphia and from there was being taken to London. Because of this, I decided to write a letter to my brother-in-law. In the letter, I explained William's circumstance. I also revealed that scoundrel Alden and his involvement with the death of Ian." She added this with emphasis.

"Do you believe your brother-in-law can help William?"

"That is my hope, Mr. Stevenson," answered Elspeth excitedly. "You see, my husband's brother is a powerful laird in Scotland. The clan MacEwan has held title there for hundreds of years. It is my hope that Hamish MacEwan, of the clan Ewan of Otter, will have some influence on the government. I do not know if he will help us, but I pray he will. There is little more I can do now except wait. Even if Hamish manages to succeed, it will be some time before we know anything." Elspeth looked up at Stevenson. "Now that I know the letter is safely on its way,

Mr. Stevenson, I think it time we went home. We will wait for news of William there."

"Home," said David, thrilled. "When do we leave, Mother?"

"As soon as Mr. Stevenson allows, David," answered Elspeth, continuing to gaze at the hunter.

"We leave tomorrow then, David," said Stevenson decisively, "that is, if you and your band of little frights can get the wagon properly loaded in time."

As if on cue, Aelwyd, Brian, and Duncan once again flew out of the tent, tending to buttons and shoelaces as they did.

"Let's eat," said Elspeth happily.

Bennett looked a little grumpy to Stevenson, and he couldn't have cared less.

Manhattan Island

"YOU LOOK POSITIVELY rustic, Johnathon." Skelton laughed as he scanned his cousin head to foot.

Alden stood before his cousin Jeremy, holding a long rifle in his arms. He wore fringed leather buckskin britches, a jacket with colorful beads, and a wide black leather belt. Included was a pair of knee-length moccasins and a solid wool coat with drawstrings. Beneath this, he wore a dark waistcoat. The shirt was blue cotton and full sleeved. Wrapped about his neck was a white linen scarf. Atop his head sat a battered tricorn, completing the outfit.

A French pistol was tucked into the belt along with a large hunting knife strapped down to his right leg. He no longer needed the cane for support, discarding it happily. His leg wound, still painful on occasion, was swiftly relieved with a healthy dose of laudanum.

"Now how are you to command a company of regulars dressed like a local?" asked Skelton. "You have no rank or insignia?"

"I travel with the scouts, cousin. The regulars follow at a discrete distance for support. There are five of us in the scouting party, all professionals in this work. You can be certain. It's important to approach the enemy with stealth, you know. Besides, we have a capable lieutenant in command of the company. He knows his business."

"I see," said Skelton, bobbing his head. "I suppose you know where these gun smugglers are. Somewhere out in the wild, I imagine. Do be careful, cousin. With the exception of New York, Generals Clinton and Cornwallis have moved to Halifax and South Carolina respectively. Philadelphia is now deserted. Where you travel can be quite dangerous. Even the Hessians have left the region."

"Have no fear, cousin. I know what I'm about. I expect to capture the lot quickly, if they survive."

"How utterly chilling," mewed Skelton, rubbing his hands together.

"Would you like me to bring you an Indian scalp?" asked Alden, raising an eyebrow. "I imagine we'll be collecting a few."

"Ouuh," cooed Skelton. "Wouldn't that be delicious, Johnathon? I can carry it home then and frighten the refined ladies of London. They'll faint and shutter at the sight. What fun!"

"I'll see to it then."

The Shawnee Village

LITTLE CORNSTALK SAT tethered to a tree. A long leather rope, twisted tightly around her ankle, held her to a ten-foot circle. It was cold this morning, but the Shawnee blanket that Walking Bird had given her was warm enough. She was offered food of a sort, corn mush mostly with bits of unknown dried and smoked meat.

This village smelled strange to Little Cornstalk. It did not smell like her Cherokee village. The lodges here were large and well built with timber, heavy tree bark, and pine brush, much the same as a white man's lodge. An array of weapons, shields, lances, and bows were stacked outside each structure, ready to be taken up at a moment's notice.

Across the valley, huge fields of corn were grown. The stalks were naked of any crop this time of year. Sacks of harvested corn were plentiful, though, and the Shawnee shared all with the members of the tribe.

Whiskey was readily available as well, and several Shawnee partook. Small knots of braves could be seen at any given time of day or night wandering along, laughing, stumbling, singing, and passing a whiskey bottle among themselves. This was very strange to the girl.

Little Cornstalk needed to speak with Tenskwatawa, but the great chief continued to refuse her. On several days, Broken Tree would come and visit. He was curious about Little Cornstalk, always asking questions. She knew he was dangerous and his interest in the Cherokee girl a fleeting curiosity, but still, it was odd, she thought.

Her anger was rapidly fading to despair. She found herself constantly reaching down along her skirt to feel for the certainty of the knife as if it might suddenly disappear, leaving her defenseless. She needed to think, but it was becoming increasingly difficult. Adsila taught her long ago that, as a Cherokee woman, her only real protection in life lay within her mind. A woman had to think to survive.

***

"This woman tied like a dog outside my lodge," said Tenskwatawa wearily, shaking his head, "she comes to my dreams now. I think I should kill this woman. Anyone can see she has the eyes of a wolf. Yes, I should kill her and take the child. If I keep the child alive, the longhunter will not come for me. He will know that Tenskwatawa will have his child under my knife. If I keep his Cherokee woman, though, the longhunter will come for me. Yes, I think he will. When the child is born and nursing life, I will kill the longhunter's woman so he will know my heart."

Broken Tree sat beside his brother in the smoky lodge, idly tapping his staff on the moccasin-packed earth.

"Let the Cherokee woman go. Then perhaps the longhunter will not come," said Broken Tree. "She has vision dreams the same as you. It could be a bad omen killing this woman and taking the child. You have her token of hair. You will always see her."

"She carries the name of the Shawnee chief, Cornstalk," said Tenskwatawa, frustrated. "I do not know how this can happen. And I do not know if this is an omen or not. It makes me angry to think these things. If she is the woman of the longhunter and if I set her free, he might seek revenge. No, I will wait for the child and then burn the Cherokee witch in our fire."

Broken Tree wagged his head. "You forget, brother. I have met the longhunter. He is young but a man of purpose, certain, quick, deadly. Do you really wish to have such an enemy on your path? If you kill his woman and take his child, he will not stop until you are dead, or he is. I have seen this in his eyes."

"I will think on this," said Tenskwatawa. "If I see an omen, I will consider your words. If not, I will kill the Cherokee witch and take the longhunter's child. Then he will not kill me."

She is no witch, thought Broken Tree, considering his options. *But she is clever.* He owed a debt to the longhunter. If not for him, Broken Tree would have been shot by that old American rifleman or hanged by Morgan and his men. He would have to think about how best to repay this debt.

***

The screams, cries, and shouts came before the crowd of Shawnee were seen. They were surrounding captives and moving them slowly toward Tenskwatawa's lodge. Little Cornstalk prayed it would not be Connor Murphy. She knew the rough Irishman would search for her despite his feelings. Could it be Murphy? She was uncertain.

At the commotion, Tenskwatawa stepped out of his lodge, followed closely by his brother Broken Tree. Tenskwatawa looked over at Little Cornstalk. She was instantly struck at the coldness in his eyes. She understood only too well what this could mean. This was a look of death. Was it for the coming captives taunted by the Shawnee crowd or for Little Cornstalk? She did not know. Understanding, Little Cornstalk realized she had little choice now but to escape and quickly. It was a question of how.

The mass of Shawnee moved closer to the chief's lodge, allowing Little Cornstalk to see who the captive was. She was shocked to find Dragging Canoe and Winter being pushed and dragged forward through the mass of vengeful Shawnee. Both men had their upper arms bound tightly behind their backs, pulling their chest out like a strutting bird, rendering their hands all but useless. Blood ran freely from several wounds inflicted on both Cherokee braves. Their heads had been dashed with Shawnee clubs, the blood obscuring their vision. Dragging Canoe shook his head violently, clearing his eyes. The crowd pushed Dragging Canoe and Winter to the front, all the while cursing, batting, and sticking as they threw insults at the two captives. Tenskwatawa raised his left arm. The mob settled, but the cries and insults continued.

"You have betrayed me, Dragging Canoe," said Tenskwatawa loud enough so all could hear. "Is this how the Cherokee bargain? The longhunter's woman for my guns. That was our bargain. And for this, I allowed you and your men to go free to kill many whites as you promised. Now you do this to Tenskwatawa's brother, stealing six horses from Blackfish and killing two Shawnee braves. Because of your broken mind, I now have my guns back along with your lives."

"Where is Walking Bird?" cried Little Cornstalk above the din. "Is he dead?"

Dragging Canoe shook his head. "No, he ran away many days ago. He believed your words."

"I am glad," answered Little Cornstalk, bowing her head.

Tenskwatawa shot a hard look at Little Cornstalk and then turned to Broken Tree. "Does the woman plead for their lives?" he asked his brother.

"No," answered Broken Tree. "She asks, where is the other Cherokee, Walking Bird?"

"Walking Bird?"

"Three Cherokee braves brought the girl to me," said Broken Tree. "You have captured two."

"Where is this Walking Bird? Did we kill him?"

"No," answered Broken Tree with a small smile. "She warned him, so he ran away."

Clouds of foot dust began to rise in the air, engulfing the scene. Many feet were scrambling for a better view of the enemy and their journey to the afterlife.

Tenskwatawa glared at Little Cornstalk. "Take them!" he shouted, waving his hand.

Winter began singing his death song. Dragging Canoe remained silent. They were taken to a large post buried into the ground. They were quickly tied to it back-to-back. Then a pile of brush, kindling, and wood was added, pushed into a tight circle about the Cherokee's feet.

Their hands were then cut off and tossed in among the brush, wood, and kindling. These would be consumed by the fire along with their owners. The Cherokee would enter the next life without their hands, which were needed to fight and make their way. The scalps of the two condemned Cherokee were then torn from their skulls and pinned on lances, waving high above the smoky air.

Winter cried out as a Shawnee brave stepped up, driving a blade deep into his side, meant for pain, not to kill. The tangled knot of Shawnee writhed like a serpent coiling, crawling, constantly in motion circling, flowing, and growling.

The fire was set, and as the two Cherokee burned, the shouts and screams of the gathered Shawnee came to a wild crescendo. The odor of burning wood, flesh, and bone filled the air.

Later, as the crowd grew weary of the spectacle, the Shawnee began to disperse. Little Cornstalk sat alone in the cold darkness. Her colorful Shawnee blanket was wrapped carefully over her shoulders. A full moon peeked out from the clouds, drifting overhead, temporarily illuminating the village at regular intervals. Little Cornstalk waited patiently as the lodge fire died away. The old Shawnee woman sat hunched over close to the fire, occasionally delivering a barking cough in the quiet as she picked lice from her thick hair. She was to keep watch over the young Cherokee witch.

"Bring wood," said the old woman with another cough. "It is cold."

Little Cornstalk understood the demand and dutifully stepped over to the woodpile, selecting a sturdy limb of elm about two-inch wide. She came up silently behind the old Shawnee. Swinging the limb in a short arc, she hit the back of the old woman's head with an audible thunk. The old woman crumpled over, sliding off her blanket as she fell toward the dying fire. Little Cornstalk reached out, grabbing hold of her hair. She pulled the Shawnee away from the hot embers.

Little Cornstalk did not like this Shawnee woman, but she also did not wish for her to burn. Gently laying the woman aside, she quickly cut the leather rope tied to her ankle.

Little Cornstalk heard the snapping twig and froze. She whirled about on her heels, knife in hand, set to strike. She stopped at the sight of Broken Tree standing idly with a pistol in his hand. The barrel was pointing at the escaping Cherokee girl.

"Where is it you are going, Little Cornstalk?" asked Broken Tree in a soft English whisper.

Little Cornstalk did not reply. Holding her place, she studied the lame Shawnee carefully.

"If you travel far, you will need a pony," added Broken Tree, again in whispered words.

Little Cornstalk tilted her head, narrowing her silver eyes on the man. Her suspicion of the tall Shawnee was well deserved. Why did he not shoot or cry out?

"I have no pony," said Little Cornstalk cautiously.

"I know where you can get one," answered Broken Tree as he flipped the pistol about and offered the butt to Little Cornstalk as she crouched beside the old woman.

She took the offered pistol and quickly tucked it in her belt. "You will call out. Your people will kill me then."

"I will not call out."

"Why do you do this?" asked Little Cornstalk, bewildered.

"I have met your longhunter, William MacEwan."

"William," whispered Little Cornstalk.

"When the longhunter gave his token to me, I was captured by the Americans. The longhunter saved my life. I am repaying my debt to him. Since I cannot separate you from your child without killing you both, the longhunter will owe *me* a life. Take the old woman's blanket and cover her with yours. Tie the rope to her ankle."

Little Cornstalk quickly did as Broken Tree suggested.

"Follow me."

They moved swiftly down a worn path, coming to a small open field with a rail fence corral. Several ponies could be seen wandering along the fence line.

"Take the black. He is fast and familiar with the path. This trail," continued Broken Tree, pointing to a narrow path, "will take you west. When you cross the river, head south. The way is difficult, but it is safe. In three days and a bit, you will come close to the Murphy Fort. I know you have friends there. You will be safe."

Little Cornstalk grasped the pony's shaggy mane and threw herself up on the animal's bare back. She turned to Broken Tree. "Little Cornstalk will not forget this, Broken Tree of the Shawnee. I will tell my William."

"Do not forget this as well," said the tall Shawnee, leaning forward. "The longhunter owes *me* a life."

"I will remember," answered Little Cornstalk. Then she pulled the pony's mane and took off at a gallop, the intermittent moonlight guiding the way.

Woolwich to London

WILLIAM HAD BEEN allowed to walk the deck three or four times a day, sometimes at night as well. He was feeling much better in his mind largely due to this. William had never been confined in such a way, like a caged animal. His life was home to open spaces, endless trails, forests, lakes, mountains, and rivers. A longhunter could track the frontier of America for a year and never step on the same path.

As William passed, strolling along the deck, the crew of the *Victory* made way for the strange longhunter. The men were uncertain what to make of this American rifleman. What they did know about William was frightening. This young American sharpshooter could kill a man at an incredible distance. And there was nothing the target could do to prevent it.

William was not allowed to step on the quarterdeck as was the custom of the British navy. This courtesy was afforded to officers, midshipmen, and those invited only. The night gave William a rare open view of a star-filled sky at sea. When he learned the vessel navigated the ocean by the stars and sun, he was utterly amazed. Longhunters often followed stars this way but without the use of sextant or timepiece.

One evening Boatswain Gibbon came to the purser's closet, crashing open the door, and in a rush of words said, "Come with me, MacEwan. There is something you should see."

Up on deck just off the starboard bow, a pod of blue whales broke water. The behemoths were wallowing in the sea, rolling, and blowing streams of water into the cold night air. The blues were less than a hundred yards off, but when they thrust that great tail up out of the water, the sheer size of the beasts thrilled William with delight. His heart raced with excitement at the awesome sight.

It was very cold now. A freezing wind filled the sails of the *Victory*, stinging William's ears and cheeks. He was moving along the starboard railing toward the bow. As he passed the mainmast with its collection of storage cabins mounted at its base, he spied a bare foot jutting out from the shadows.

William watched closely as the owner of the foot suddenly sprang forward, a thin shiny blade in hand. William spun to his right, taking the knife thrust to his leg. The knife drove hard into William's thigh, eliciting a sharp cry from the longhunter. Swinging back to his right, William threw out his elbow, catching Halfpenny a blow to the side of his head and sending the man in a rolling tumble across the open deck. The blade skittered over hardwood, disappearing under the rail.

Halfpenny sprang up onto his bare feet and once again charged William. Without any thought to their previous encounter, Halfpenny came straight at William as before. For his part, William simply waited for Halfpenny to arrive before he snapped his boot out, once again catching the errant sailor squarely in the crotch. This time, William put every ounce of energy into the boot, lifting Halfpenny several inches off the deck. The man came down on all fours, groaning in agony. Tossing up a full belly of food and rum, he rolled onto his side and then his back, drawing up his knees in a poor attempt to alleviate the sudden crushing agony.

Boatswain Gibbon quickly came up to William. "Are you all right, MacEwan?" asked the boatswain nervously, concerned more for himself than William.

William looked up sharply at the boatswain. Anger crossed his face. "I think so, Boatswain!" he barked. Then he clapped a hand hard over the wound, stemming the blood flow.

"Let's get you below to the surgeon. Captain's not going to like this," finished the unhappy boatswain's mate, shaking his head.

Admiral Howe stood back from the surgeon's table where William lay. He looked down on the longhunter, clucking and wagging his head. "Is it serious, Doctor?"

"It is deep, but it looks to be a clean wound, Admiral," claimed the physician as he stood up, wiping his hands free of blood. "I believe it was a fish knife used, sir, thin and sharp. He's a strong lad though. Should be fine in a day or so, I would say. Some pain, of course, but this will pass soon enough."

"And this other man, Seaman Halfpenny?"

"Well," said the doctor, smiling at Halfpenny as he moaned and rolled side to side on the other table, "Seaman Halfpenny will not be climbing any ratlines for a while. He'll walk lopsided for a week at least. Should be fine after that."

"Thank you, Doctor," said Howe. He then turned his attention to the boatswain. "Boatswain Gibbon."

"Sor!" shouted the boatswain nervously.

"Please escort Mr. MacEwan back to his cabin. Provide a ration of rum as you see fit."

The admiral then turned to William. "I can make no excuse for this, Mr. McEwan. I only ask that you understand. There are men aboard the *Victory* that wish you ill. That is a matter of circumstance. The war, you understand."

"Yes, sir," answered William, wincing as he rose from the table.

"We will be dropping anchor at Woolwich tomorrow. From there, a barge will take you to London proper."

Howe cleared his throat to continue. "I realize you have no good reason to perform your shooting demonstration, Mr. MacEwan, but I hope that you will cooperate in the matter. Refusing to do so is your right, of course. As a prisoner of war, you cannot be compelled. Still, a demonstration of your weapon would be critical to opening certain blind eyes. The British government must understand the danger of your rifle."

"As I have said, Admiral, I am not a soldier. On the other hand, I see no reason why I should aid the British in your war. My family and I have been abused, sir. We have not been treated fairly! Would you do otherwise?"

"You misunderstand, Mr. MacEwan," said Howe regretfully. "My brother and I have always thought this war ill advised. It is my belief, and my brother William's as well, that war with the Americans can only come to a bad end. If you can show the council the danger they face in this fight, it is my hope they will reconsider this foolish action and make a peace, one that is satisfactory to both parties."

William considered Howe's words. He nodded slightly. "Do you really believe it could help end the war?"

"If it shortens this war by one day, I would say yes, it is well worth the effort."

"All right, Admiral. I will do my best, but once I am in the hands of your council, I make no promises. For you, however, I will try."

"Fair enough."

***

Woolwich Wharf was enormous. As the jolly boat pulled alongside the dock, William could see a long valley of houses, barns, and storerooms that ran clear out of sight. The activity on the dock was similar to New York but on a grander scale. In the ice-cold air, smoke rose from a forest of chimneys billowing out black clouds over the township of Woolwich.

The Thames was very wide here with a good harbor. In it lay anchored several ships, both fighting and merchant. Once again, William witnessed commerce on a scale of immense proportion. This was a busy seaport.

The admiral and Captain Ford accompanied William along with two marines. William bid farewell to Boatswain Gibbon, thanking him for his rough attentions. He would always remember the fantastic sight of breaching blue whales. On the east end of the dock, an array of red- and blue-coated soldiers stood waiting. The officer in charge stepped forward with a sharp salute.

"Admiral Howe, Captain Ford. Lieutenant Bellamy at your service, sirs. I am to take possession of your prisoner. We will board the London barge and, from there, transfer the prisoner into the Royal Barracks Jail. I understand I am to retrieve his weapon as well. Is this agreeable, sir?"

"Yes, Lieutenant." Captain Ford crooked a finger at the marine carrying William's long rifle. "Hand over the rifle and accessories to this lieutenant, Marine."

The lieutenant then passed the weapon, powder horn, and shot pouch to one of the men in his party. Barking a harsh order, the group turned about and escorted William to the barge.

As they made their way upriver, William could see ice floes in the Thames, something new to him. The river often froze over in the winter, allowing the citizens of London to set up stalls like a holiday bazaar on the thick, frozen ice. These makeshift fairs were popular among London's populace and were frequented daily when the ice allowed.

Approaching the city of London was another first for William. The city was beyond description. Dark with a thick layer of fog and smoke, the buildings rose high in the air, some as tall as a great pine. The building themselves were a mix of brick and wooden structures ranging as far as the eye could see. Once again, innumerable chimneys belched out clouds of smoke, adding to the fetid fog, placing a haze over the entire city.

When the barge docked, William bade farewell to Admiral Howe and Captain Ford. He thanked the admiral for his help and concern.

William was taken by closed wagon into the city. As he peered out of the barred window, he viewed the bustling streets of London. The smell was unusual as it included woodsmoke, cooked meat, fresh and dried fish, horse sweat, and the odor of thousands of people. Manure littered the streets as well, but there seemed to be a cadre of ragged children sweeping the waste away and then begging for pennies for their effort.

Men, women, and children hawked goods of every sort from trays strung about their necks, calling out what fare they had for sale. There were roasted potatoes, mussels, clams, dried fish, pies, and chestnuts. Eel pie and mash, whatever that was, seemed the most popular. The wagon passed three or four fiddlers. Their half-gloved fingers glided over the neck of their instruments as they fiddled with enthusiasm, begging for coins.

The wagon then traveled through a quieter portion of the city. It was not nearly as busy or raucous as the streets they had just passed through. Moving into a fine cobblestone courtyard, the wagon came to a halt. This was the London military garrison. William climbed down from the wagon, looking around.

It was a fine building made up of yellow brick and stone. There were several archways ringing the courtyard, tall and wide, with beautiful keystones crowning each arch. Some held writing carved into them. The words appeared to be Latin. William was unable to read their meaning.

Surrounded by the clutch of soldiers, William was marched through a large archway into the building's interior. Stopping in front a single enclosure with heavy bars, he was guided inside and told to sit on the bunk and wait. The steel-barred door slammed shut behind William and, with a rattle of keys, locked.

Western Boundary of New York Colony

LIEUTENANT TIBBITT WATCHED as Alden and his men rode out of the camp. He had never received orders of this nature before and was uncomfortable with them. He called for his sergeant.

"How are you with navigating these trails, Sergeant?"

"I can follow them as well as any man, Lieutenant. Why do you ask, sir?"

"I am curious about Captain Alden and his intentions here. He has asked that we remain at a distance from his scouting party. We are to follow some three or four miles back. That seems a bit excessive for a support mission. If we are to align our efforts with Captain Alden in an emergency, I can hardly do so from three miles away."

"What do you suggest, Lieutenant?"

"Take two men with you. Strip off your uniform jackets and attire yourselves with dark cloaks. Follow the captain, but keep out of sight. Captain Alden may not appreciate our initiative. If all seems right, no harm done. If you find otherwise, I wish to know immediately."

Alden sat his horse, gnawing idly on a fingernail. He waited patiently to advance on the small plantation. Sitting beside him were two of his scouting recruits, hard men these. Alden knew them well. They had operated together on previous occasions. It was not easy for Alden to discover such men—men who could kill with little thought or conscience to the act, men who enjoyed taking human scalps; Indian or white made no matter. Human hair could still bring a good price on the English market. These men would steal anything if worth the effort. They had murdered male defenders, raped women, and enslaved the innocent. With their bloodlust sated, they burned all to the ground in their wake. Children were taken only to be sold or killed along the trail simply because they were unable to keep pace with their captors. These were Alden's people.

Ranging west even before the British army occupied Philadelphia, Alden and these very same men raided homesteads along the frontier, killing and taking what silver they found along with young girls and women.

Alden and his irregulars had scouted this particular property the previous day while holding themselves out of sight. It appeared to be a ripe plum for the taking.

The homestead plantation was large and comfortably arranged. Well-built cabins and storage barns ringed a field of cornstalks cut close to the winter ground. A vegetable garden lay alongside the main cabin, but it, too, was bare. The harvest was taken more than a month ago. It was cold and dark now. The sun had not yet risen. Alden waited. He was anxious to gain this first conquest. It had been some time since the MacEwan place. When he thought of Elspeth and her escape, his mind went to heated frustration. There were three men present in this homestead as well as four women. The first concern for the raiders was the dogs.

As the sun rose, Alden and his two companions made their way steadily toward the main cabin. A single male was seen leaving the structure. The man stretched his arms out, focusing his attention on the task at hand. Making his way to the livestock where some milking cows grazed, he carried a wooden stool and bucket, swinging them jauntily as he marched along.

Sitting his horse some distance from the man, Alden called out, "Hallo, the house!"

The farmer whirled about, dropping the stool and bucket. Throwing his hand up to block the morning sun, the farmer replied in a mild Swiss accent, "Who is there?"

"I am Capt. John Alden, sir. We are British army scouts searching for deserters."

"We are Quaker here, Captain. You will find no such men at this place. We do not make war or condone it in any manner. We are a peaceful people."

As the farmer walked over to Alden, a second man exited the cabin along with two large dogs. The new arrival held a long musket. He was barefoot and dressed in a nightshirt only. His dark hair was tousled as he looked about half asleep. Sweeping a free hand up to rub his eyes, he called out, "Karl?"

"It's all right Erick, we have English visitors."

"You say you are peaceable," declared Alden as he eyed the snarling dogs. "And yet this man carries a musket to our approach."

"There are Delaware west and north of here," said the farmer. "They have attacked us in the past. We must defend ourselves when necessary."

As one dog crept closer to the three riders, Alden drew his saber and gave a signal to his cohorts.

The milking farmer was shot first. Struck midchest, he dropped where he stood. The scout to Alden's left fired on the man in the nightshirt, striking him in the face. He fell back straight as a tree. His corpse blocked the doorframe.

One of the dogs jumped at Alden, attempting to seize hold of his leg; the British captain swung his saber down, splitting the animal's skull, killing it instantly. The second dog was dispatched with a French flintlock.

Screams from inside the cabin followed as the occupants desperately tried to dislodge the man in the nightshirt, lying in the doorway. For all their effort, the door stood open.

The three other scouts approached the cabin on foot from the south. They circled round the back of the structure, looking for any runaway victims. There were none.

A rifle shot came out the open door as Alden gave the order to rush the cabin. The first scout through was hit with a small-bore pistol. Injured, the man rolled to his left, allowing the second scout just behind to enter. This man carried two flintlocks, one in each hand. As he entered, both pistols fired. The screams took on an urgency that was near deafening. Backing out of the open door, he stepped over the dead man and waved the others inside. Alden rushed in.

Four trembling women stood clustered in the center of the space, staring wide eyed. The body of a third farmer lay at their feet as they wailed in despair. Their lives were over. Their men were killed, and they were at the mercy of vicious killers who had no soul.

Three hundred yards away, tucked behind heavy brush, Lieutenant Tibbitt's sergeant pulled the glass away from his eye. Lying flat on his belly, the sergeant let out a blast of held breath. "Mother of God!"

The private lying beside the sergeant asked in an excited whisper, "What is it you see, Sergeant?"

"The devil at play!" growled the sergeant. "That bastard Alden and his men just murdered everyone down there in that cabin."

"Why would they do that, Sergeant?" asked the private, bewildered.

"Lord knows. This is evil work."

The screams of the women now carried through the morning air, echoing over the low hills and empty field. The private began to rise.

"Get down, you fool. They have a guard outside the cabin. He may see you."

"Shouldn't we go down there, Sergeant? Shouldn't we stop this?"

"Have you gone mad?" whispered the sergeant in harsh tones. "Five murdering killers down there and you still with a shine on your face! You slide back down this hill and get to your horse. Go straight to the lieutenant. Don't let them see you, boy. If they do, we're all dead."

London-Greenwich

WILLIAM SAT BUNDLED up under three layers of blankets. It was freezing cold. Even the saltwater soaking from Seaman Halfpenny seemed warm in comparison. He would have to get up and walk soon just to pump some blood. The food here was poor in comparison to the *Victory*'s mess, some type of vegetable stew in a weak broth that William had never tasted before. Dry, coarse bread the consistency of wood came with each bowl of the noxious soup, filling William's belly just enough to avoid hunger.

Three or four times a day, a Sergeant Dunn would come by to inspect William. After a week of near-freezing weather, the sergeant finally brought William a small brazier. Charcoal wood was provided along with a flint and fire strike. The brazier provided little relief from the cold and damp air.

The city garrison, known as the Royal Artillery Barracks, was near the center of London located in the borough of Greenwich. And a busy place it was. Four battalions were garrisoned here at the barracks with room to house three more.

Any number of marching feet could be heard daily passing outside William's cell, all stomping in tight unison and high precision. Some of these soldiers were shipping out to the colonies, others to the West Indies, Africa, India, or Australia. Those deployed were swiftly replaced with new recruits.

With little to do, nothing to read, and no conversation to speak of, William's detention was becoming tedious and horribly frustrating. His desire to return to his frontier home and the people he loved was beginning to overwhelm.

The cell was twenty by ten feet, allowing William to walk a tight circle only. He did this daily to clear his mind and pump blood to his limbs. Constantly marching round and round, it became a full-time necessity. As he walked the tiny loop, William could feel his anxiety growing with each turn of his foot.

Number 10 Downing Street

FREDERICK NORTH, SECOND Earl of Guilford, was the prime minister of England. He walked an even pace into his spacious chamber clothed in the cloak of his office, a black velvet garment with intricately laced gold piping that ran the lapel and covered both sleeves. His waistcoat and breeches were rust-colored velvet. White frilled cuffs poked out of the sleeves. A dark green ceremonial sash from right shoulder to left hip lay over the waistcoat. He wore white stockings and dark brown shoes. His wig was curled short and smoothly powdered a bone white.

His chubby pale cheeks and bulging blue eyes roamed the room as was his habit. The prime minister was about to begin his day.

As he moved toward the great desk, Lord North shuffled through a bundle of correspondence clutched in his hands. These were letters and messages determined to be most important. As he flipped through the dispatches, a single missive caught his attention. He stopped.

"Ho now. This is a letter from our admiral of the fleet, Lord Howe, officially sealed."

North turned his gaze on Lord Germain, secretary of state for the colonies.

"George," he said, addressing the secretary, "why have I received this? Is there some issue I should know about concerning the admiral?"

"Not that I am aware of, Prime Minister."

"Well, he has clearly addressed this to me. Let us see what our admiral has to say."

Three clerks sat in strategic locations about North's office, each with a specific task. Alongside Secretary Germain stood Field Marshal Jeffery Amherst, commander in chief of North America. Both men waited patiently as North read the unexpected letter.

"Hmm," hummed North. "Most curious, most curious indeed. George, this letter says we have in our possession an American rifleman. He is being held at the Royal Barracks. Is that correct?"

Secretary Germain deliberately stepped in front of Amherst, blocking his view of the prime minister. The secretary was not overfond of sharing his time or opinions with Lord North.

"Why, yes, Prime Minister, that is correct. The American was captured and shipped here by my nephew Lord Skelton. He is to demonstrate the efficacy of this so-called long rifle.

"There is some level of disagreement concerning the weapon," continued Germain, turning to Amherst. "Would you agree, Field Marshal?"

North looked at Amherst as he wheeled around the secretary. "There is some question as to the actual facts, Your Lordship," said Amherst. "We've received several action reports, specifically from General Howe, telling us that his officers and cannoneers are being killed in the field from great distances with the use of this American rifle. We are attempting to determine the validity of these reports. They do appear to be in earnest."

"Good heavens, Amherst." Germain scoffed. "You know as well as anyone in the army. These reports must surely be in error. It is not possible for a man to shoot another at a range over two hundred yards. The idea is simply ridiculous. Impossible!"

"Ordinarily, I would agree, Secretary Germain," replied Amherst. "However, General Howe's reports have since been seconded by other officers in the field, sir. Both Generals Clinton and Burgoyne have made similar reports backing Howe's assessment."

"Nonsense!" declared Germain smugly. "The American prisoner will demonstrate this rifle, and then, gentlemen, the truth of the matter will be revealed."

The prime minister glared at the two men most responsible for leading the war effort in America. He scowled. Holding up Howe's letter, the argument came to a halt.

"You may factor in another issue, gentlemen. It appears our admiral of the fleet has cast doubt on the true character of your prisoner,

Secretary Germain. He has officially requested that we conduct an inquiry into the matter. The admiral believes this man could be a simple farmer-hunter, a civilian caught up by our forces while trying to locate his family."

Germain cleared his throat with a rattle. "I have it on good authority, Prime Minister, that the prisoner is, in fact, an American rifleman, a so-called widow-maker. I cannot guess at Admiral Howe's motivation here. He may simply be trying to buttress his brother's tale of amazing assassins in the wilds of America."

"How would that serve the admiral, George?"

"If the admiral claims the prisoner to be an impostor, then when he demonstrates his rifle and fails, as he surely will, the admiral can make the case that this man was not an American rifleman. Simple."

Lord North pursed his lips unpleasantly. "What is the nature of your good authority, George?"

"Why, my nephew Lord Skelton."

"Do you mean to say Lord Jeremy Skelton captured this man? I find that difficult to believe."

"No, no, Prime Minister. It was Jeremy's cousin Captain Alden who effected the prisoner's capture, a decorated officer in the Twenty-Third Dragoons. I have the action report in my possession."

Lord North rolled his bulging eyes, looking at no one in particular. "I see. Admiral Howe mentions the captain in his letter. A cousin, you say?"

"Distant to me, sir. He is connected to the Skelton family through marriage. I believe his mother wed one of Lord Skelton's younger brothers."

North stared at the letter, considering his options. *The familial connection with Germain will certainly explain Admiral Howe's addressing this letter to me*, thought the prime minister.

"Sir," said Germain, interrupting the prime minister's thoughts, "these Americans all claim to be simple farmers, teachers, merchants, et cetera whenever captured. It is a poor ruse our military hears every day from the scoundrels. It is all they can think to say when they are captured."

"Thank you, George," snapped North irritably. "You do realize, of course, that I have been acquainted with the Howe brothers for more than forty years. I am fully aware of their opinion concerning the war. I am also aware of their character. I can comfortably say that both Richard and William Howe are two of the most honest, sensible, and courageous English gentlemen I have had the good fortune to know. They are completely devoted to the empire and to His Majesty, the King.

"If Admiral Howe wishes an inquiry into this matter, then by god, George, an inquiry he shall have. Has anyone even questioned this prisoner? George?"

"Me! Why, no, of course not. You hardly expect a man in my position to personally question a captured soldier, surely."

North studied Germain's face, delivering a withering look.

Continuing on, the secretary quickly added, "I would leave such a task to one of my officers naturally."

"I'll question the man," said Amherst. "The matter is important enough, surely. I would like to settle this to my own satisfaction, sir. If there is any validity to General Howe's concerns, I want to know. I'll provide a report of my findings in the morning, Prime Minister."

"Splendid solution, Jeffery," said the prime minister, smiling. "Thank you. I look forward to your discovery."

Smirking at Secretary Germain, Amherst turned on his heels and departed.

Cell Number Six, Royal Barracks, Greenwich

"YOUR NAME IS William MacEwan? Do I have that right?"

"Yes, sir," answered William as he studied the well-dressed officer standing outside his cell.

Amherst looked down on the documents he held and then up at William and then down again. He was distracted by a notion he had not considered previously.

"I would like to ask you a few questions, if I may. You are a prisoner of war and therefore not obligated to answer, but it may help your position here. Are you willing?"

"If it will take me home again, I would answer the devil himself."

"Let us hope that will not be necessary," answered Amherst with an unpleasant smile. "Now what military company are you attached to?"

"None."

Amherst looked up again. "How do you explain your being *here* then?"

"If you care to listen, sir, I will tell you."

And so William did. As his odyssey unfolded, Field Marshal Amherst listened intently. His eyes grew widely concerned; his head dipped ever lower as if a weight was being pressed on his skull. William finished with an intensity that clearly displayed a painful anguish. Amherst found himself believing this young man's story. The tale he had listened to could not possibly be imagined.

"Well, Mr. MacEwan, I find myself at a loss. If you are telling the truth, I do not know how to answer just now."

William responded by advancing to the cell bars. He gripped the cold steel with white knuckles. "It is not a lie, sir! It is the truth before man and God. I would swear it now and forever before any man."

Amherst stood mute in front of the longhunter. He considered William's words and realized there may have been a mistake made. But he was struggling with how to deal with it.

"I have two final questions, Mr. MacEwan. First and most importantly, is it *really* possible to hit a mark at two-hundred-plus yards with this rifle of yours?"

"Yes," answered William simply.

Amherst raised an eyebrow. He had a look of doubt, tilting his head slightly.

"Ask your admiral Howe if you do not believe me," said William. "He can tell you the truth of it."

"All right, I will ask the admiral. My last question concerns your family."

William pinched his eyes, giving Amherst a hard glare.

"Do you have relatives here in Great Britain? In Scotland perhaps?"

"My father was born in Scotland. As far as I am aware, he does have family there."

"And your father's name?"

As he attempted to understand the purpose for these questions, William studied the field marshal carefully. The reason for the question eluded him. He considered Admiral Howe's advice and so answered, "My father's name was Ian MacEwan."

Lenape

THE AIR WAS crystalline cold. A brilliant sun stood high above, with few clouds drifting overhead. There was a soft breeze blowing down the hillside that shuffled the dry, fallen leaves. There was no trail here, just open space between the pine, elm, beech, and white and red oak.

Little Cornstalk walked the pony carefully over the carpet of leaves, ensuring each step to keep the small horse from stepping into a covered hole or some other unseen broken ground. It was a slow pace but necessary.

Snow had come to the mountaintops, not yet reaching this far below the tree line. She knew it would arrive soon. Occasional patches of casual ice was another hazard to be avoided. Little Cornstalk had not eaten for days. The ice patches provided small water, but it was enough. Still, she was terribly hungry. She considered slicing the pony's throat and cutting off meat but thought better of this. The pony might be needed for a quick escape. She looked about for anything she could forage from the brush and windblown leaves. There was nothing. The unwelcome scent came to her suddenly. She stopped. Stroking the pony's face to calm his breathing, Little Cornstalk listened intently as she peered into the surrounding trees.

Animal hides—there was no scent like it. Little Cornstalk knew well that if there were animal skins, there, too, were men. Moving cautiously forward along the base of a high hill, she picked up the scent again. It followed the light breeze, rolling down the hill. If there were men on the other side of the hill and she downwind, she might be able to sneak past them without notice. The pony nickered.

The Delaware brave sprang out from a gathered pile of leaves like a panther. He was no more than thirty feet from Little Cornstalk. Three more Delaware came up out of the ground behind her in similar fashion, blocking her path of escape in that direction.

The first Delaware tilted his head as he approached Little Cornstalk. She was a strange sight to see. A lone Cherokee woman walking a black pony in this place. Ten feet off, Little Cornstalk pulled the pistol Broken Tree had given her, pointing it at the oncoming Indian. The Delaware slipped a red-oak-handled tomahawk from his waist and spun it deftly. Little Cornstalk pulled the trigger.

Staggering back from the girl, the Delaware lost his footing on the dry leaves. The pistol misfired. With a screaming howl, the Lenape charged Little Cornstalk. The girl threw her pistol at the attacking brave as he swung the tomahawk high in a tight arc. She ducked her head sideways, and the blade edge caught Little Cornstalk just over her right eye, slicing a thin gash.

Backpedaling desperately, Little Cornstalk lost her balance. As she fell, she wrapped her arms about her swollen belly, landing hard on her bottom. The Delaware was on her in an instant. He raised the tomahawk for the kill.

A fraction of a second before she heard the shot, a small hole appeared in the Delaware's forehead. The report echoed through the trees. The Lenape-Delaware crumpled over the top of Little Cornstalk's legs, pinning her to the ground.

The three Delaware standing back away from the pony whirled in unison toward the direction of the rifle shot. A volley suddenly came out of the dense tree line as Little Cornstalk watched all three Lenape-Delaware went down. Two lay dead. The third began crawling toward a pine for cover. Two other Delaware braves who had been scrambling down the hill, unseen, reversed course, making their way over the crest of the hill and out of sight.

Little Cornstalk pushed the dead Lenape off her legs and stood up. Blood ran freely down the side of her face. She was shaken and dizzy. She grasped the pony's mane to steady herself. Peeking over the animal's neck, she watched as six men, all white hunters, slowly emerged from the trees. Each carried a long rifle.

Little Cornstalk slipped her knife from her dress and held it firmly at her side. As the men advanced, it became more difficult for Little Cornstalk to see. Blood flooded her right eye, and the other teared heavily. Hiding herself behind the horse as best as she could, she waited. She knew these men could be worse than the Delaware. She began to shiver.

The hunters were covered in fur hides head to foot. They marched side by side, slowly spreading outward. They were bearded with cold-weather caps, heavy coats, and winter moccasins. The man in the center of the group came straight toward Little Cornstalk.

When the hunter was no more than twenty yards away, he pulled his cap, revealing his face.

Little Cornstalk let out a rush of air in a cold cloud. She bent her head down on the pony's neck, shaking in relief. She looked up.

"Little Cornstalk is happy to see you, Connor Murphy!" she called out.

The stocky Irishman stopped short and wagged his head in disbelief. "Jesus, Mary, and Joseph! Little Cornstalk!" shouted Murphy. "You're alive."

Murphy and one other large-framed hunter rushed up to the girl as she collapsed on the ground. The other hunters circled the scene, making certain there were no other Indians lying about under the leaves. The crawling Lenape-Delaware was swiftly dispatched with a single shot to the back.

"You're hurt, girl!" cried Murphy.

"Come now. Sit here while I get you fixed up. This is work for my Kathleen," said the Irishman as he carefully wrapped a linen band about her wounded head. "But I'll do me best."

As Murphy wound the linen neckerchief around Little Cornstalk's head, he could feel the girl almost vibrating from cold and shock. He felt an overwhelming urge to protect this young Cherokee girl. She was as much family to the ruddy Irishman as his own.

"You are a good shot, Connor Murphy," said Little Cornstalk in a shaky voice. "Thank you for saving my life."

"Don't thank me, girl. It was Cummings. The smithy made that shot, and a fine shot it were too."

The large-framed hunter pulled his cap and smiled down on Little Cornstalk. "I knew it was you," said Cummings with certainty. "Connor here didn't believe me, but I knew it was you."

"Mr. Cummings!" cried Little Cornstalk, reaching up to the big blacksmith. "Your magic has saved Little Cornstalk. I am very happy to you."

Cummings barked a hearty laugh as he reached down and took Little Cornstalk by the hand.

"All right now, girl," said Murphy, helping Cummings get Little Cornstalk to her feet, "I think it's time we took you home. I know a lady and her son who are yearning to see you again."

"Home," repeated Little Cornstalk. "Yes, I want to go home, Connor Murphy. I am very hungry."

The MacEwan Homestead

"WOULD YOU TAKE me to their graves, Olaf?" It was the first time Elspeth addressed Stevenson by his given name. It came as a small shock to the hunter when he heard it. Making no reply, he simply nodded.

As they made their way up the steep grade, Elspeth could only look down. Crossing the same path she and the children used when running to the hide brought a flood of hard memories. To distract herself, Elspeth said, "You'll forgive my addressing you informally, Mr. Stevenson, but we have been through much. It would seem natural after all. You don't mind, do you?" she asked softly.

"No, Mrs. MacEwan, I do not mind at all."

"And you shall call me Elspeth in return. I think it time."

David trailed well behind Stevenson and Elspeth. When they were taken by Alden those many months ago, he and the other children never saw the destruction that was now their home. The burned skeletal remains of the animal stock, black charred cornfield, and fallen timber that once made up their happy life were a wrenching experience for the boy. He was sad and angry at the sight.

Aelwyd, only steps behind her brother, clenched her hands in a tight ball. It was clear she did not want to look or remember that terrible day. The home she loved and felt so secure in was gone along with her father and sister, Mary.

The twins, Brian and Duncan, chattered away as they wandered behind Aelwyd. About halfway up the hill, they became quiet. Seeing the others with bowed heads and solemn expression, they instinctively joined the mood without understanding why. Duncan took Brian by the hand. His brother did not resist.

They crested the hill and came up on a plateau that stretched out to a small open field covered in dead grass. Along the elevated ridge of the hill, five graves overlooked the MacEwan homestead. The five crosses were still there, slightly battered from wind and weather. The little parade clustered up around the pile of heavy stone neatly arranged over each grave.

Stevenson indicated with an open hand. "This would be your husband, Elspeth. As Murphy explained, he thought you were here," continued Stevenson, pointing to the second grave. "This third one, I believe, is your daughter Mary. I am sorry, Elspeth. Murphy did the best he could, but it was impossible to know who anyone was except for your husband."

"This is father's grave?" asked David, touching the loose stones.

"Yes," whispered Elspeth, bobbing her head.

"Father is here?" asked Brian. "Under these rocks?"

"Yes," answered David.

"Dig him up, Mama!" demanded the boy as he glared at Elspeth.

Elspeth burst into tears, burying her face in both hands.

"Don't be foolish, Brian," said David harshly.

Stevenson placed his hand gently on David's shoulder. "The boy doesn't understand, David."

Aelwyd began to cry. "I want to see Father!" she wailed.

With the rain of tears now coming from two directions, the twins took up a chorus of their own. David resisted the urge, but the moment was too overwhelming, drawing the boy in. He, too, began to weep.

Stevenson stood completely flummoxed. With his hand on David's quivering shoulder, the rugged hunter found *himself* tearing up. He let out a rough cough to settle his emotions. Tears were something Stevenson had little understanding of. Still, in that moment, he came to realize that Elspeth and her children were suffering terrible pain, loss, and grief, something he had all but forgotten in his life. So Stevenson let the MacEwan family cry. And cry they did. It was a necessary thing and had been for a good long while.

That evening, Elspeth and Stevenson busied the children with chores, collecting kindling for a fire, setting up the small tent, and laying out blankets to keep the cold ground at bay. The sun was falling, and soon it would be very cold. After their meal, they all bundled up close to the blaze. Everyone was quiet except the twins, who continued to rattle on about missing chickens and Stick, the dog.

"We will start rebuilding in the morning," said Elspeth to no one in particular.

Stevenson looked up from the fire. "It's near mid-December, Elspeth. This is no season to start cutting trees. It would take weeks of hunting just to get enough food for such an effort. I think it best we wait till spring before we begin rebuilding here. Until then, we can seek shelter with the Murphys. It is a safe place with lodging and food. Just until the spring, you understand. I really think it best."

"No," said Elspeth emphatically. "This place is the only thing we have left. Ian and I put everything into this piece of land. I'll not leave our home again."

"But, Elspeth—"

"No, Olaf, we stay."

"I think Mr. Stevenson is right, Mother," said David in a clear voice.

Elspeth snapped her head up, looking at her son. She turned to Aelwyd. "Aelwyd, take your brothers into bed for the night. They look to be half asleep as it is."

Aelwyd slowly got up and began herding her two reluctant brothers into the black interior of the canvas tent.

Slowly nodding, Elspeth said, "You are my son, David, and I love you very much, but this is a decision I must make myself. Mr. Stevenson has been a good friend to us. And I appreciate that. But now we are home and on our own. My decision is we stay."

David stood up, dropping a stick he had been swirling in the dirt. "You are nothing but wrong, Mother," said the boy stiffly. "Mr. Stevenson saved our *lives*. We wouldn't even be here if not for him. We have lost enough, Mother. Can't you see that? Last winter was as harsh as they come, and you know this. There is no reason to think this winter will be any less so. We have no shelter, no food, and no tools! We do not even own that horse or wagon. If you wish to make decisions, Mother, they must concern all of us. I say we follow Mr. Stevenson's advice."

"And what happens if we return to find someone here stealing our land?" said Elspeth angrily.

"Then I will remove them, Mother!" snapped the boy as he kicked a spray of dirt into the fire. Turning on his heels, David walked sullenly toward the empty wagon.

Elspeth sat staring after her son, her mouth open. She turned to Stevenson. "Now what do you make of that, sir?"

Stevenson looked at Elspeth with a knowing smile. "That boy killed a man saving your life, Elspeth. I think you should listen to him."

Stevenson and David slept in the wagon that night. In the morning, they could hear Elspeth starting a fire and bustling about. She was humming as she wandered round the little campsite. The twins emerged from the tent, sleepy and yawning. They immediately began demanding food. Aelwyd chose to remain in the bundle of warm blankets left behind by her mother and brothers.

David sat up, looked at his mother, and shook his head. He knew he would do as his mother wished. She seemed determined on the matter. Resigned to Elspeth's decision, he would do as he was told. Still, he was not happy with it.

The last of the salt bacon began frying in a pan over the open flame. With the smell drifting in his direction, Stevenson lifted himself and stretched his injured leg. Stiff with morning pain, he slid off the rear of the wagon and stood. After pounding himself with both arms to warm up, he made his way over to the frying bacon. Elspeth looked the hunter over and smiled lightly. David came over and sat quietly on the cold ground. He picked up a stick and began swirling a spiral pattern in the dirt.

"You two, gentlemen, look like you just lost your best friend," quipped Elspeth. She offered bacon to David and then Stevenson, holding the hot pan with the hem of her dress. "Come on then, eat up. We have to load our wagon if we are to travel as far as the Murphys'. And I would like to get there before Christmas."

David's face lit up like a brass lantern. His rosy cheeks clicked up on his face in an enormous smile. He eagerly began stuffing hot meat and fat into his mouth.

Chambers of Lord Jeremy Skelton, New York

"YOU MUST BE mad!" cried Skelton. Standing in front of the oaken desk of His Lordship stood Colonel Sims. His hands were clasped tightly behind his back. The colonel leaned forward slightly to emphasize his words.

"I take no pleasure in telling you this, Your Lordship." Actually, Sims took enormous pleasure in delivering this particular message. "I am as shocked and disappointed as you, sir. The fact of the matter is Captain Alden has completely lost his reason. He is roaming the western edges of the colonies with a band of marauders, attacking and killing innocent civilians and worse. Something must be done, sir."

Skelton began sputtering and slapping his hands on the desktop. "But this is impossible, Johnathon killing innocent women! Impossible, I say."

"We have witnesses, Your Lordship."

"Witnesses? What witnesses? Some filthy Americans who speak nothing but lies? How can you take the word of such people?"

"These witnesses are British regular soldiers, sir, one a master sergeant, the other a company lieutenant, the men who accompanied your cousin on his mission west, sir.

"Aside from that, General Clinton has received orders to investigate Captain Alden on another matter entirely. It concerns prisoners he had taken while stationed in Philadelphia. Three British regulars acting as guards under your cousin's orders have been taken into custody over the affair. These men were part of Alden's operations in the area. They were assigned to guard prisoners being held in a civilian house."

Skelton recalled his cousin's tale of escaping prisoners in Philadelphia when he was wounded. "Yes," said Skelton defensively, "Johnathon was wounded, shot by an American spy when he was moving his prisoners to a safer location. The Americans burned the place down, killing two women."

"Sir, every prisoner that Captain Alden took to that house were women and in one case children. According to the testimony of the guards we have taken into custody, that house was a brothel. And the Americans did not burn it down. Your cousin fired the house, killing two women slaves who worked therein. At the very least, Your Lordship, General Clinton has demanded Captain Alden's presence so he may answer these charges. Have you any idea where your cousin may be, sir?"

"Why, no," answered Skelton, now thoroughly confused. Shaking his head, Skelton looked down on his desk. "You'll forgive me, Colonel Sims, but I just find this all so impossible to believe."

"Impossible or not, Lord Skelton, we must find the captain. Only he can answer these charges. We must act swiftly before any more damage is done to the captain's reputation."

"Yes . . . yes, of course."

The MacEwan Homestead

WHEN ALDEN RODE up to the charred rubble that once was the MacEwan home, he scowled. "They should be here! Bloody hell, where are they?"

There were now some twenty-one raiders with Alden. Eight of them were a mix of Shawnee and Iroquois. These Indians held loyalty to no one. Their only purpose for tying themselves to Alden was the opportunity to kill and rape. Plundering the white settlements for gain was only an afterthought. The remaining troop was made up of renegade white men who felt much the same as the Indians. Three of them were deserters from the British army, one a Hessian, mercenaries all.

The group ranged over the property, searching for tracks or anything of use they could find. When they discovered the small campsite Elspeth and the children used, they called Alden over.

"Someone was here, maybe three, four days ago. Horse and wagon tracks heading north."

"What lies that way?" asked Alden.

"One or two homesteads and the Murphy Fort."

"Don't forget Blackfish," said one man sarcastically.

"That's where they went," said Alden, kicking a blackened piece of cabin wood. "The Murphy Fort, safest place for her to take the children. How far is this fort? Can we catch them?"

"It's a few days' ride. If they move slow, we might."

One man sidled up to Alden. "Why chase this woman, Captain? She steal something from you, or did she give you the pox?"

Alden pulled his flintlock and smacked the man on the side of his head with the heavy barrel, knocking him down. "It's my bloody business, not yours. If you wish to continue riding with us, you'll follow and do as you're told."

Alden looked at the other men, turning in a circle to address them all. "You all have money in your pocket, whiskey, and food. It is due to me that you have these things. Me, you understand?"

As he spoke, the original five raiders who came west with Alden began gathering round their captain. Each swung his rifle in a casual manner as their captain spoke.

These men knew well what they had gained under Alden. They also knew that if captured, they would be hanged for what they had done. Protecting Alden was more a survival instinct than anything. Besides, they had more money now than they ever imagined. They had raped, killed, and plundered every homestead they came on, some victims no more than infants. Those they did not kill outright were sold into slavery to the Choctaw, Creek, and Chickasaw. It was making them all rich.

They had better clothing, better food, and good whiskey. They rode stolen horses now, shoed and saddled. Their lot in life had improved enormously since following the English captain, and they had no intention of abandoning that.

"Get mounted," called Alden. "I want to catch these people before they make this Murphy Fort."

Number 10 Downing Street, London

THE PRIME MINISTER, Lord Frederick North, continued reading the report that Field Marshal Amherst provided. If not damning, it was certainly suspect. Amherst had carefully recorded William's statement as well as Admiral Howe's. He read them again. If Howe was to be believed, and North had no reason to think otherwise, this was an unseemly affair that had the potential of embarrassing the Crown and injuring England—a captured American soldier who was, in fact, not a soldier at all but rather a common American civilian. He could hear the howls from the back benches now. For those in Parliament who opposed the war in America, this would be grist for the mill. Ford frowned.

The report was complete in detail. Attached were the original letters to the Privy Council from Generals Howe and Clinton. There were also notes from General Burgoyne. Gen. Simon Fraser's field notes were included. Fraser himself had been killed at the Battle of Saratoga purportedly with a long rifle. Each man contributed to the report, describing in detail the impact of the American rifle in the field.

When North read Amherst's speculation that the young American might be related to the MacEwan clan in Scotland, he muttered a profanity under his breath. North was familiar with the MacEwans. They were powerful, wily Scotsmen. Given the rare right to possess a coat of arms, the clan oscillated between committed English ally and implacable enemy. The family was enormous, with a history spanning five hundred years.

Members of the Clan MacEwan sat in Parliament as well as the House of Lords. They voted as a block and could be counted on to aid or resist as they saw fit. North was becoming rattled over this affair. Things were beginning to spiral out of his control, and Lord Frederick North did not like that at all. He looked up.

Standing at the far end of the room were Field Marshal Amherst and Secretary Germain. They were whispering heatedly, clearly in disagreement. Looking unusually perturbed, Lord Germain stood red faced, fluttering his arms and hands as if he might take to the air like an enormous bird.

"George," said the prime minister sharply.

Germain turned on his name. "Yes, Prime Minister?"

"I have a question, George. Why, in heaven's name, did you ignore these reports from your general officers in the field concerning this long rifle?"

"They were not ignored, Prime Minister," said Germain huffily. "I had our general staff look into it. It came to nothing. The weapon was deemed less than useless in the field."

"Hmmm," hummed Ford as he stared down on the papers before him. "It appears your assessment conflicts with these reports."

"As it should, Prime Minister. The rifle is overlong, making it clumsy to carry on the march. They are slow to load compared with the Brown Bess, and they cannot carry a bayonet. Therefore, they have no strategic value whatsoever."

"That strikes me false, George. A weapon that can kill from a distance of two hundred yards would definitely have strategic value."

"That is just my point, Prime Minister. There is no musket, rifle, or any other weapon on earth that can fire that distance accurately."

"But you haven't proved that, George."

"I will with this rifleman," said Germain, his face flaring red again.

"If he can strike a mark at that distance, I'll eat the feather in my cap," finished Germain.

Cell Number Six, Royal Barracks, Greenwich

WILLIAM HEARD THEM.
"Is it a man or a bundle of rags?" asked one voice in a clipped Scottish accent.

"I dinna believe it's a pile of rags, brother. See the hat," replied the other man.

William was slow to raise his head in response. Several soldiers and cadets tramped past his cell daily, providing heckled comments and profane insults. He had come to ignore them. Still sleepy from another miserable night, William finally peeked out from under his hat. Focusing his attention on the two visitors, he considered the idea that he still might be dreaming.

Standing in front of his cell stood two gentlemen wearing the most colorful array of clothing William had ever seen.

The man on the right wore a bright red coat that hung to his knees. Beneath the coat was a green vest and a fine white linen shirt. Ruffled sleeves peeked out from the coat cuffs. A neatly wrapped scarf collared his neck.

A kilt of tartan pattern circled his waist that also came to his knees. The front of the kilt displayed a fox head pelt hung by a thin silver chain. Across the man's chest was a buckled leather strap that carried a pistol and a large knife. Dark stockings and heavy shoes covered his lower legs and feet. Atop his head sat a large black bonnet trimmed in tartan with a jaunty green feather attached to one side. Tufts of brilliant red hair poked out from under the bonnet.

His face was flushed red with large green eyes and a flat nose. An enormous red mustache covered his mouth, hanging down near his chin.

The gentleman on William's left wore a forest green velvet coat, long sleeved and buttoned high to the throat. He, too, had a buckled leather strap with both pistol and dirk. No bonnet adorned this man's head. He wore an identical patterned kilt minus the fox head. His hair was soft brown. His face was clean shaven. He smiled with even white teeth.

"Are you William MacEwan?" asked the man in the red coat.

William shook his head to clear his senses. He stood up slowly. "And who are you to be asking, sir?" answered William, scrunching his eyes together.

"Can you not answer a simple question, lad?" said the big red man testily.

"Yes, I can," answered William. "However, it is customary to know who is asking and why."

"We'll get to that, lad. Have no fear. Now are you William MacEwan?"

Wearily, William answered, "Yes, I am. Now may I know your name, sir?"

"One more question first. What's your father's name?"

"Ian," said William sharply, losing patience. "Ian MacEwan."

The man in green shot out his arm, striking the man in red on the shoulder. "I told ya it was him, brother. You owe me a guinea."

Ignoring the man beside him, the big red man pulled a sheet of paper from his vest pocket and held it out to William. "Do you know your mother's hand, lad?"

William reached through the bars and took the offered sheet. He began to read.

"God in heaven," proclaimed William, "this is my mother's writing. How did you come by this, sir?"

"Your mother sent it to me from America. I am your father's brother, Hamish, your uncle, lad. And this is your uncle Robert."

William was barely listening as he read Elspeth's words. He snapped his head up. "She's alive and safe! The children are as well," said William, suddenly dizzy. He sat down on the bunk.

"It's true then? What your mother claims in the letter? You're no American soldier?"

William continued reading without answering. Hamish turned impatiently on his brother.

"Is the lad deaf?" he asked.

"Let him read, Hamish. I'm sure it's been long since any word from his family has come his way."

Hamish harrumphed.

The two colorful Scots waited patiently for their nephew to finish. William rose, holding the letter out. "Isn't Mother amazing?" he cried.

"Sending this letter just for me. Remarkable," muttered the young longhunter as he reread the letter. "She intends to return home. The children are safe, and that bastard Alden is far from her reach."

William looked up, smiling. "Thank you for this, sir. It is the best of news. Uncle, I mean," finished William hurriedly.

"Now answer my question, lad. Is your mother's claim true? You're no American soldier?"

"My mother does not lie, sir. Nor has she ever."

"That's all I want to know," said Hamish crisply. He turned on his heels and marched straight down the long hall.

"Where are you going, Hamish?" called his brother Robert.

"To see our prime minister. You stay with the lad, Robert. See no harm befalls him. I'll be back," replied the big Scot over his shoulder.

Number 10 Downing Street

"GEORGE, IF THIS American is indeed a rifleman as you say, then you will have proved your point one way or the other with a shooting demonstration. Am I correct?"

"Yes, Prime Minister, you are."

"However," continued Ford, "if he is not an American rifleman as he claims, then you will prove nothing. Have you considered this, George?"

"Why should I? My nephew Lord Skelton has verified the prisoner's identity. He is an American rifleman. Would you take the word of an American liar over the king's representative? My nephew Jeremy would never blunder in such a way. I stake my reputation on it."

"Careful in your declarations, George. If Field Marshal Amherst's report finds otherwise, this could put us in a damnable position. I have to deal with Parliament concerning the war, George, and it's becoming more and more difficult with each passing day. You had better hope you are correct because if the Whigs find otherwise, there will be hell to pay."

A clerk rushed up to the prime minister and whispered in his ear. Ford slammed a meaty palm down on his desk. He looked up at the men before him.

"Lord Hamish MacEwan is waiting outside my office just now. If this turns out as I suspect it may, you better have ready answers for His Lordship, George." Ford turned to his clerk. "Show His Lordship in."

First Lord Hamish MacEwan stomped into the room, marching straight for the prime minister.

"Good day to you, Hamish," said Ford in a friendly manner. He did not stand.

"And to you as well, Frederick," answered Hamish, rolling his Rs.

"I think you know Field Marshal Amherst and Secretary Germain," continued Ford, nodding at the men.

MacEwan nodded politely at Amherst but made no acknowledgment of Germain. He found the man distasteful.

"What brings you to London, Hamish?" asked the prime minister politely. "It must be important to travel this season of the year."

"I think you know well and good what brings me to London, Frederick. You have my nephew locked up in your barracks jail and for no good reason. The lad isn't even a soldier, yet you hold him as such. Do we imprison the innocent now, or has something else influenced your judgment?"

Ford raised his brows. This was indeed a surprise. Amherst considered the idea that the prisoner named MacEwan could be related in some distant fashion to the MacEwan clan, but nephew to the clan's laird? If the prisoner was truly Hamish MacEwan's nephew, then what?

"Your nephew," repeated Ford, raising his eyebrows, bulging his eyes further.

"Aye," answered Hamish firmly.

The prime minister was beginning to tire of this. With each passing day, his life became more and more complex. King George III was mad as a hatter. This everyone knew. In his rare moments of lucidity, the king spoke only of the war in America.

How could they do this to me, Ford? the king railed. *After all we have done for them. Their largest trading partner. I have protected her shores, fought the French and savages for them. We've brought goods and commerce to them all. I only ask they pay their tithe like any good citizen of the Crown. It's for their benefit and the empire, by god. And for this, they turn on their king. They must be taught better, Prime Minister. You need to punish them. Punish them all.*

Prime Minister Ford looked across his desk and saw only disaster. He wanted to throw everyone out of his office, clear his mind, and simply rest his head. Instead, he said, "Can I offer you a chair, Hamish?"

"I'd rather stand, if you don't mind, Frederick. I intend to return to my nephew's side so I may be with him when he is released," snapped the Scotsman.

"As you wish, Hamish. Now to be clear, you say we have captured your nephew, a noncombatant. We have documented reports that say otherwise. He was captured on a field of battle outside the city of Philadelphia."

"Lies," answered Hamish simply. "I have a letter from the lad's mother, my sister-in-law. She was quite clear in the fact that her son has never been a soldier and is not one now."

Germain audibly mumbled under his breath. Hamish turned slowly to the man. "Have you something to add, Secretary Germain?"

"Any mother would do likewise to free her son."

"Are ya calling my sister-in-law a liar then, Germain?"

Secretary Germain caught the look in Hamish MacEwan's eyes and froze. Turning a shade whiter, he visibly wagged his head. "Certainly not, Lord MacEwan. I only suggest—"

"I know what you are suggesting, Germain. If you persist, sir, I'll be calling your second and happy to do so."

Germain went white as a linen sheet and then red with anger.

"Calm yourselves, gentlemen," interrupted the prime minister. "There is no need for such talk here."

"Why did ya bring the lad to London in the first place, Frederick? Even if he was a soldier, why bring him all this way to England? To what purpose?"

Amherst cleared his throat. "If you'll allow me, Lord MacEwan, I'll explain."

The Royal Barracks

"HOW OLD ARE you now, William?" asked Robert.

"I am eighteen, sir, November last."

"Aye, that's a fine age to be upright. I almost remember it myself," said Robert nostalgically. "Now then, laddie, what can I give you for your birthday?"

"Give me, Uncle?" William chuckled with a smile.

"You're locked away like a hunting dog here, William, your birthday missed and no one to celebrate with. Surely, you have a desire for something. What is it?"

William thought the offer over and knew instantly what he wanted. "A potato, Uncle, one of those enormous roasted potatoes they sell on the street. Can I have one of those?"

Robert stared at his nephew with renewed curiosity. "A potato, you say?"

"Aye," answered William, nodding in the affirmative.

William watched as Robert turned on his heel, laughing as he ran down the long hallway. The tall Scotsman disappeared along with his echoed laugh.

William thought about the request he made for a moment. He suddenly realized his uncle must think him mad. Of all things to ask for, a potato? William shook his head, disappointed with the idiotic appeal. He knew very well what he wanted. He wanted to go home, back to his family.

Number 10 Downing Street

"DO YOU MEAN to tell me you brought the boy all this way only to shoot a rifle?"

"That is the very thing, Lord MacEwan," answered Amherst earnestly. "If he is as skilled as Admiral Howe claims, it could prove very important to our troops in America. We must know if this long rifle can really perform as described. It will settle matters here with the secretary and the general staff as well. It is most important, Your Lordship."

"God in heaven, man, anyone can shoot a rifle. You have to kidnap my nephew to do that? I want him released immediately, Frederick," demanded Hamish, raising his voice for emphasis.

"I am sure you understand, Hamish," said Ford. "This puts me in a difficult position. I have conflicting information here and so must sort it out properly. If you'll just give me a few months, I will get to truth of it. In the meantime, I will see to it your nephew is made as comfortable as possible. Can we agree?"

Hamish MacEwan surveyed the men standing about and scowled. He leaned over Ford's desk and wagged a finger at the prime minister. "Two months, Frederick, no more. I'll not wait a minute longer. Gentlemen," he said, making his way out.

"Well now, that's just fine," said Ford quietly. "Do either of you two have any suggestion on how we might deal with this?"

"If I may, Prime Minister," said Amherst. "I do have an idea that might work to everyone's satisfaction. It would require cooperation from His Lordship MacEwan, but I think it could solve our problem nicely."

Murphy-Borough

ELSPETH WAS IMPRESSED with Murphy-Borough. Ringed by a twenty-foot wall of sturdy triple pine, the entire space was well protected. Inside, an array of cabins lined the inner walls with tidy paths traversing the whole community. A large open field lay within. More than a hundred souls were in residence now, working and wandering the narrow paths that communicated the entire borough. A patrol of sentries walked the parapet atop the walls, constantly peering out at the tree line. For the first time in many a day, Elspeth felt safe. Olaf and David had been right to insist they come to this place, at least until spring.

Stepping into the Murphy Tavern, Kathleen welcomed the MacEwan children warmly, bustling the lot into the kitchen, offering food and drink. She turned to Elspeth. "I imagine you'll be wanting to meet William's young lady, Little Cornstalk."

"Yes," answered Elspeth meekly.

Leaving the children to warm themselves in the heated kitchen, Kathleen guided Elspeth into the tavern proper. Sitting a table at the far side of the long room was Little Cornstalk. Her back was turned toward Elspeth and Kathleen. A young boy sat across from Little Cornstalk, quietly conversing. Their heads were bent close together. As the two older women approached, Seamus looked up.

"Hello, Ma," said Seamus cheerily. "Little Cornstalk was telling me of her adventure with the Shawnee. It's terribly exciting."

"That's grand, Seamus, grand. Now do me a turn. Go to the kitchen and welcome our new visitors. I would have a word with Little Cornstalk."

Little Cornstalk stood up, turning as she did so. She examined Elspeth closely. Her silver-gray eyes suddenly flew open. She clearly saw William in this strange woman's face and became very excited. "You are William's family," she announced proudly.

Looking on the girl, Elspeth was stunned by her beauty. Her face, framed in long black hair, held an equally stunning smile. She had high cheekbones under those silver-gray eyes. She was tall and well proportioned. Her swollen belly stood out like a basket as she wrapped one arm beneath. Little Cornstalk noticed Elspeth eyeing her tummy. She began stroking it gently.

"Little Cornstalk," said Kathleen, "this is William's mother."

The beautiful eyes shot open again. She let out a small squeaky sound. For once, the girl was speechless. She stepped close to Elspeth slowly, reaching her hand out. Tears slid down her perfect face in silence. "William's mother," repeated Little Cornstalk, awed. "I am good to meet William's mother."

Elspeth, smiling shyly, took the offered hand. It was an experience Elspeth found endearing. The Cherokee girl and Welshwoman held each other's gaze for a full minute. Little Cornstalk, looking down on her belly, once again began stroking it gently. "This . . . is William's son."

Elspeth turned to Kathleen, who was fighting tears herself. "So certain it's a boy?" she asked her friend with a laugh.

"Aye," Kathleen answered. "She insists and will have it no other way. Mind you, I feel the same as you. But with Little Cornstalk, it is a closed matter. It's a boy."

"Yes," agreed Little Cornstalk, smiling. "William's son is a boy." She said this as if this settled the matter.

The two older women laughed in unison.

***

After caring for the horse and wagon, Olaf Stevenson strode purposely for the Murphy Tavern, all the while arguing with the man trailing in his wake, Connor Murphy.

"You lost my bloody horse!" cried the Irishman, throwing his hands in the air.

"You gave me a pregnant pony, Connor. It was only good fortune that I made it all the way to Philadelphia on that beast. There was nothing I could do. The army took your animal, and that is the way of it. The horse I came with is all I can offer you, that and this paper. They call it a script or some such thing." Stevenson tried passing the worthless script to Murphy, waving it in his face.

"Wait," said the wily Irishman, "I gave you a pregnant horse, and you return without her or the foal?"

"Yes, Connor, as you can plainly see."

"Then you owe me two horses. You only came back with the one."

"Have you lost all your reason, Connor? Did I not just explain what happened to your *pregnant* horse?" shouted the Swede angrily.

Ignoring the irate Irishman, Stevenson stepped briskly into the tavern. Spying Elspeth and Little Cornstalk together, the big man came over to them. "I see you have met Little Cornstalk, Elspeth."

"Stevenson!" cried Little Cornstalk. She jumped up and down and threw her arms out. "You are back. I am happy to see you, Stevenson."

"And I you, girl." The two friends embraced.

"May I ask for a drop of rum, dear Kathleen?" said Stevenson wearily. "I have a thirst."

"Make sure you get his money first," said Connor sarcastically.

Ignoring Connor, Stevenson turned back to the ladies. "You look fine, Little Cornstalk. Are you well?" he asked, turning to Kathleen for confirmation.

Kathleen nodded a yes as she quietly poured a healthy portion in a pewter goblet. Stevenson took a mouthful.

"Where is William, Stevenson? You did not find him?" asked Little Cornstalk.

"William is being held by the English. I am sorry, Little Cornstalk. I did try to find him. Do not despair though. William will be back."

"I know. William was taken in a great canoe to a place I cannot see. But he will return to me," said the girl confidently.

"Yes, he will, Little Cornstalk. William's mother has been helping too," replied the older hunter, nodding at Elspeth. "Tell me now, what have you been doing since last I saw you?"

"I am learning to blacksmith with Mr. Cummings. He is a good man. He saved Little Cornstalk from a Lenape tomahawk."

Stevenson turned to Connor Murphy with a hard look. "That is a good thing," he said crisply. "I will thank Mr. Cummings for this."

Little Cornstalk continued, "I was taken by Dragging Canoe to the Shawnee while you were away, Stevenson," announced the girl matter-of-factly. "I have spoken words with the mighty Tenskwatawa."

Stevenson shot out a spray of rum over the bar boards. "What!" He turned on Connor Murphy again. "Did I not ask you to keep the girl safe, Connor? What mischief is this then?"

"Drink your rum, you surly Swede," replied Murphy with a downcast look. "When you settle yourself, I'll explain."

Kathleen waved Elspeth and Little Cornstalk toward the kitchen. Elspeth explained to Little Cornstalk how William was taken by the British and sent to London, England, a land far away. She told the girl of her letter and the hopes she held for it.

"I have worry for William. I will pray for the Mother Spirit to keep him safe so he may return and see his mother and Little Cornstalk. Your words on the paper will save William. He will come home now."

"Would you like to meet William's brothers and sister?" asked Elspeth.

"Oh, that is good," answered the girl, wrapping her arms about her belly and smiling.

The following morning, two riders approached the high walls of Murphy-Borough, holding a white flag. At a hundred twenty yards, a shot rang out, striking the earth ten feet in front of the men, halting their progress. Connor Murphy was the first up the parapet, peering out at the two mounted men.

Murphy asked, "Who are they?"

"Never seen 'em before, Connor. They're horse mounted and well armed. Don't like the look of them. That's certain."

"Mmm," hummed Murphy. "Give me the glass."

The sentry handed Murphy a Dutch glass that he clapped to his eye, scanning the two riders. He did not recognize either man, but he did recognize the horses. He collapsed the eyepiece with a snap. Looking down on a gathering of the curious, Connor called to one man. "Take a pony. Ride out to those two and ask what they're about. Take care," he added. He turned to another sentry. "Give me your rifle."

As the lone borough resident rode out, Stevenson climbed up the rough ladder to the sentry walk. Standing beside Connor Murphy, he asked, "Who are they?"

"Don't know yet. Mitchell out there will take their measure. I do know this. I sold those two horses they ride to a farmer who lives well east of here. They may have purchased the animals, but I think not. There's been a number of raids on settler homesteads east and south of here. I was told a mix of Indians and white men are involved. They've been raiding homesteads up and down the foothills, stealing and killing their way. It's a rotten bunch they are. This could be two of them."

Stevenson studied the two riders intently. "The one on the right has three scalps tied to his saddle."

"How the devil did I miss that?" said Murphy, grabbing the glass again. "By god, you're right, Olaf. That settles it. Those two are not entering here."

When the rider sent out returned, he called up to Murphy.

"Well?" asked the Irishman.

"They look bad to me, Connor. Carrying scalps they were and well armed too."

"What do they want?"

"They say they look for a woman and her children named MacEwan. Told me they were friends of the woman's son William. They've been following and want to make sure Mrs. MacEwan and her brood were safe. I don't believe a word of it."

Connor looked over at Stevenson, confusion in his eyes.

Equally confused, Stevenson spoke. "The English would never send out Tories to chase down Elspeth and her children. And those wicked two are no friend to William MacEwan."

Stevenson scratched his head. Who would ask for Elspeth? Certainly not the British. She and the children had escaped Alden with their lives. Could it be the captain?

"Tell me of these Tory raiders, Connor. What do you know of them? Who leads them?"

"My friend Samuel Blue of the Catawba heard of a renegade English officer in their mix. Said the man leading was a captain, name of—"

"Alden," finished Stevenson with menace.

"Why, yes," said Murphy, "the very name. Do you know the man?"

"I do," answered Stevenson simply. "Hand me that rifle."

Murphy did so, asking, "What do you intend, Olaf?"

Without answering his friend, Stevenson rested the rifle barrel on the stockade, aiming the weapon on the rider bearing the scalps. He fired. The man twisted in his saddle, falling from the horse. The second rider spun his animal about and took off at a high gallop. The man drove straight south at breakneck speed. Connor Murphy sighted a second rifle and fired at the fleeing villain. His shot was high and wide, missing the intended target by several feet.

"Fine shot, Connor. I think you hit a squirrel," said Stevenson with a sarcastic grin.

"What the devil do you know, you damned Swede? My eyes don't hold to much these days. Comes with age, you know. What are you grinning at?"

"I'm grinning at you. That second horse I owe you stands just out there. Now I owe you nothing."

Connor Murphy brightened up considerably. "Right you are, Olaf. Right you are."

One Mile South

ALDEN WAITED ANXIOUSLY for the two men he sent to Murphy-Borough. He was almost certain that Elspeth had taken refuge in the fort, but he needed to be sure. He had to know if Elspeth was there. The weather was turning colder now, making it difficult for the raiders. Three of the white men and two Indians had already left the group. Alden was angry, but there was little he could do about it.

A single rider came barreling down the road at a full gallop. It was one of the two Alden sent out. The man pulled his horse up short, sliding in the loose dirt. He jumped off the animal and strode purposely toward Alden. He pulled a flintlock from his belt.

"Where is Gladwell?" asked Alden as the man approached.

"Dead," said the rider, pointing the flintlock at Alden.

"They shot Bone out of his saddle as we waited for your precious information. He never had a bloody chance!" shouted the rider. "I told you this was a bad idea, Alden. Now we've lost a good man. I could kill you right here, you bloody bastard."

"Stay your hand, sir," said Alden, backing away from the rider. "How could I know they would fire on you? You carried a white flag, did you not?" Alden cared nothing for the dead man. His only interest was Elspeth.

The dead rider, Bone Gladwell, could be replaced easily enough. The woods were teeming with such men since the war started, murdering thieves in a lawless land. If the Indians weren't killing whites, then the whites were killing Indians. Add the war to it, and chaos prevailed. The fight against the rebellion cut loose these monsters like a spreading disease. Each one was given a weapon and told to kill their fellow man. And kill they did.

Resting his hand lightly on his own pistol, Alden asked, "Was the woman there?"

"We never found out, damn you. They sent someone to talk. We asked about this woman you want so badly, like you told us. Over the last few weeks, they've had many families enter Murphy-Borough. The old bastard we spoke with could not recall the name MacEwan. Said he would find out and return with an answer. They answered, all right. They shot Bone Gladwell dead and damn near killed me too."

"Then she is there," said Alden thoughtfully.

"Look here, Alden," said the rider, waving his pistol. "I know nothing of this woman you seek or why you want her. I only know this. Because of you, my friend is dead. This wild fantasy you hold for some woman has unhinged your mind. From here on, I decide where we go and what we do. Is that understood?"

"Fine, fine," said Alden, looking down. "The woman is important to me but not to the loss of any man here."

"All right then," said the rider, tucking his pistol back into his belt, "we need a place to stay for a bit. Without winter shelter, all these men will leave. Then you have nothing—no money, no woman."

"Is there something nearby that would serve as good shelter?"

"Thirtysome miles east. A Quaker lot built a settlement village. It was wiped out months ago by a Cherokee renegade, Dragging Canoe. Most of the cabins still stand. It would be a good place to hold up. We have supplies enough. Attacking Murphy-Borough with this small number now will only fail. In the spring, we can gather more men. The people within the fort will come out then as well. You'll just have to wait for your slut," finished the rider.

The man turned his back on Alden, heading for his horse.

"Just one thing, Pittman," called Alden.

"What?" hollered Pittman as he spun about.

Alden fired his pistol, striking Pittman directly midchest. He fell back dead as stiff as a pine. Stepping over the corpse, Alden declared, "She's no slut, Pittman."

A scramble of white men and Indians who stood some distance off rushed to the scene. Each held a weapon. Three of Alden's original killers were included in the group.

"You shot Pittman?" asked one man, glaring at Alden. "Why?"

"The damn fool gave our position and numbers to those people in the Murphy Fort. He tried to threaten them with attack. They answered his threat, shooting Bone Gladwell off his horse. Then the coward ran straight back here, begging me for help. He knew they would follow. So I killed him. Pittman has placed us all in jeopardy. Now we have to move and fast. It won't be long before that fort sends out a party to hunt us down."

"Where shall we go?" asked another.

"We have to get to good shelter. Winter is upon us. We need to find a place that's safe. There is an abandoned Quaker settlement thirty miles or so south of here. We'll go there. They won't track us that far."

Alden's man looked down on Pittman's body. "What about him?"

Alden looked at the faces arrayed in a semicircle before him. Painted savages and fur-covered white men stood frozen in place as they peered down on Pittman's corpse, sniffing the air like a pack of dogs.

"You may have what you like, gentlemen," announced Alden. "Everything of Mr. Pittman's is now yours. Do as you please."

The raiders charged the body, taking everything possible. They fought one another over the two pistols he carried and his knife. His cloths and moccasins were swiftly pulled off. The horse he rode was stripped of its saddle, rifle, and bags. In less than a minute, Pittman lay naked facedown in the dirt. He was brutally scalped, with one ear missing. One of the savages had taken his right pinky finger. There were three or four knife wounds to his back. Alden could only wonder why. After all, the man was thoroughly dead.

Walking toward his horse, Alden realized these men were, in fact, little more than a pack of animals. And he was becoming more like them with each passing day.

Manhattan

COLONEL SIMS ENTERED the office at a smart step. Removing his tricorn, he addressed Lord Skelton. The man was as white as a wig.

"Are you quite all right, Your Lordship?" asked Sims, not really caring.

"I am being recalled, Colonel Sims, back to London," answered the bewildered representative as he waved a sealed letter through the air. "It seems the young rifleman we sent to London is not, in fact, an American soldier. And he is related to a powerful Scottish family, Clan MacEwan."

Sims could hardly contain his glee at this news. Still, he held his face as motionless as a stone. It would not do to display pleasure at the moment. Skelton was a peer after all. Insulting the man would only invite damage to Sims's career. Sims would hold his tongue.

"Have you any news of my cousin, Colonel?" asked Skelton desperately.

"Captain Alden has not returned, sir. As far as we are aware, he is still out west somewhere on the frontier."

"We must find him. I have orders to return him to London as well. Surely you can find him?" finished Skelton hopefully.

"Unless Captain Alden turns himself in, sir, there is little hope of finding him. It is a large country as you are aware. Our priorities at the moment are to move the army south to the Carolinas. I am sorry, Lord Skelton, but there is nothing more we can do but wait. The military has opened a court-martial inquiry into the captain's activity. Your cousin, sir, is at considerable risk."

Skelton bowed his head. All the good work he had done was for naught. His wild cousin had brought the British Empire down on his head. Skelton's reputation, the very honor of his family, was now in jeopardy. His uncle Lord Germain was quite clear in his desire to have Skelton and his renegade cousin brought back to England immediately.

"Will that be all, Your Lordship?" asked Sims quietly.

"What? Oh, yes, of course, Colonel," answered Skelton distractedly. "You are dismissed."

Colonel Sims turned sharply and, with a happy smile, left the room.

Number 10 Downing Street

"YOU'RE BEING UNREASONABLE, Hamish," said the frustrated prime minister.

"Am I?" said Hamish MacEwan angrily. "I think not. It's now seven weeks gone, and you still have no agreement with the French. Is this idea of yours going to work or not, Frederick?"

"Please, Hamish, I have invited you here for a reason." Prime Minister Ford looked up at the tall Scotsman, craning his neck. "I must insist you take a seat, Hamish. You're hurting my neck, looking up at you this way."

Hamish MacEwan called for a chair, which was swiftly delivered.

"As to the time, you know as well as I that negotiations with the French can be difficult. We're not exactly on good terms."

"Well, you have asked me to come, and I am here. What news is it you have? Has there been any progress at all?"

"First, you must understand. The man we want returned to England was the most effective spy we have ever had in France. He provided information on the French fleet, Louis court, as well as diplomatic contacts with other nations, specifically the Spanish. Your nephew carries no value to the French. He is considered a prisoner of war, nothing more. For the French to release our man, we must provide an exchange equal in value, and your nephew simply does not qualify.

"With that understanding, I have devised a plan using your American nephew. I've taken the liberty to write Benjamin Franklin. He is the colonies' representative to France. I have advised Mr. Franklin that we currently hold six American naval officers as well as your nephew. With that in mind, Mr. Franklin has taken responsibility to persuade France's chief minister, Count Vergennes, to make the exchange on behalf of the American cause. The chief minister is besotted with Franklin. God knows why. I found the man to be insufferable. Now we have but two problems."

"And what is that?" asked an exasperated Hamish.

"First, the French have demanded that fifty thousand pounds be included in the exchange. I am attempting to gain those funds now. The second is your nephew himself. He has not agreed to this shooting exhibition. Once I have the funds in hand and your nephew agrees to demonstrate his rifle, we can make the exchange. Your young nephew can go home, and France will have returned to us a most important person, Col. Marcus Burke. So the question remains, Hamish. Will your nephew agree or not?"

"I'll speak with the lad."

Cell Number Six, Royal Barracks, Greenwich

UNLIKE THE BUSY Hamish, Robert MacEwan had come to visit William every day of the week. The tall Scotsman was growing very fond of his young nephew.

With Robert's prompting, William reluctantly relayed the account of his travels, searching for his kidnapped family, being wounded at the Battle of Saratoga, and his eventual capture at the hands of the wicked captain Alden.

It was a tale of adventure, hazard, misery, and joy, causing Robert to pepper William with questions about his wayward brother, Ian MacEwan. William complied.

He told of the hunting trips at his father's side, tracking game and gathering pelts for trade, how they planted early corn to the freshly plowed field that lay beside the MacEwan cabin, how William learned to shoot the long rifle. He described the home his mother and father provided east of the Cumberland; the books his mother collected; his brothers, David, Brian, and Duncan; the girls, Mary and Aelwyd; how the MacEwans lived; and how Ian and William's sister Mary died.

"You look poorly, nephew. What is it that pains you, William?" asked Robert.

"It is nothing, Uncle," answered William quietly. "My only wish is to return home."

"Yes, of course. Nevertheless, you seem inconsolable these few days last. It must be something. Pray tell, what troubles you?"

William looked up, pain ringing his eyes. "It is my own guilt, Uncle. My father and sister were murdered, taken in my absence. If I had been where I belonged, home, I might have prevented it. At this moment, I would gladly trade my life for theirs."

"You would make a bargain with God then?" asked Robert, astonished.

"If it were possible, yes."

"I can tell you, William," answered Robert, wagging his head, "you cannot. Men have tried that very thing since the birth of our existence. Think of it. What would you have to offer in trade?"

"My life, of course," answered William, surprised at the question.

Robert laughed. "Every soul offers that. Think of it. You have nothing to offer. Your life is his to take and his alone. Even you do not have the right to spurn such a gift. The trade you seek has already been made the moment you were born. Rejoice in the gift you have been given, William. When God is ready, he will trade with you then and only then."

William hung his head at the words. They struck him in a way he did not yet understand. Perhaps someday he would. "I miss Little Cornstalk," said William suddenly.

"What?"

"A girl. Her name is Little Cornstalk."

"What an odd name for a young lady. How did she come by it?"

"Her mother and father, I would imagine. She is Cherokee, you see, the daughter of a chieftain, Black Feather. I was good friends with her brother, Shadow Bear. He died fighting the Shawnee. I miss him terribly too, but most of all, I miss her."

"Are you in love with this girl, William?"

"I think so," answered William, bowing his head. "I fear I may never see her again. When I think on it, my heart thumps in my chest like a water drum. I am miserable over the thought."

"Well, that certainly sounds like love. Have no fear, William. Hamish and I will get you home. You will see your love again and your mother as well. The prime minister has called Hamish to his office. He would not do so without cause. We should learn very soon when you will be released."

"I pray to God you're right, Uncle. If I must stay here much longer, I will lose what little reason I possess."

The door at the end of the long hall banged open with crash, and the heavy footfalls of Hamish MacEwan came down there way.

"Hamish," called Robert. "Have you news for William?"

"I do," answered the big Scotsman. "Lord North has made all the arrangements. William and six American naval officers will be part of the exchange. Some funds are involved as well. There is only one remaining question."

"And what is that, brother?"

"Yes, what?" added William eagerly.

"Your agreeing to a rifle exhibition, William. You must demonstrate this rifle of yours to the general officers and the Privy Council. It is the last remaining request. What say you, William? Will you?"

"No," said William, shaking his head. "I will not aid the English in any fashion. The bastards have killed my father, beaten me, jailed me, stolen my family, and forced me here. Why should I do anything they ask?"

"So you can go home." Hamish snarled. "Don't be a fool about this, William. Do you really believe a simple demonstration of your rifle will change anything?"

"No, I imagine it will not."

"All right then. Consider what I have told you. Make your decision. Yay or nay? Robert and I will stand with you whatever you decide."

Hamish then turned to his brother. "Walk with me, Robert."

The two men strolled down the long hall. Hamish spoke softly. "I am going to visit Admiral Howe."

"Whatever for, Hamish?"

"The admiral persuaded William to fire that damn rifle of his while aboard the *Victory*. Perhaps he can tell me how to do so on land."

***

Sitting across from each other, William was listening to Robert recite Scottish poetry. The words were soothing and, to William, a healing potion to his mind and heart. If nothing else, knowing his two uncles had been a boon to the longhunter. He would never forget these two kindly Scotsmen and all they had done for him.

Once again, Hamish came down the long hall, this time with a sprightly step. Robert stopped reading and stood up to greet his brother.

"How was your visit, Hamish?"

"Illuminating," answered the big Scotsman.

William rose from his bunk.

"William," said Hamish, "I have been to see Admiral Howe. He remembers you well."

"The admiral was very kind to me, Uncle. I would thank the man if ever I see him again."

"He wanted me to remind you of something, William, something you should not forget."

"And what is that, Uncle?"

"When you fired your rifle aboard the *Victory*, you accomplished two things." Then Hamish fell silent, waiting.

"For heaven's sake, brother, what did the man say?" said Robert, about to burst.

"He said William amazed the entire complement of the *Victory* with his shooting skill, every man aboard. And . . . he frightened them.

"I know you have no wish to aid the British, William. And your loyalty to your home is laudable, but consider this. Frightening a pack of overstuffed English generals and officers would strike me as a good incentive to shoot that rifle of yours. Don't you think so, William?"

William looked up at his two uncles, both men smiling ear to ear. "That does seem a good reason, Uncle. Yes, very good indeed."

The Cherokee Way

CHRISTMAS CAME AND went in Murphy-Borough. Christmas here was celebrated in solemn fashion. A sermon provided by an elected pastor was given with passages from the good book, read out for all to hear. Candles were lit and prayers made. It was a comfort to the residents of the community and well received.

The New Year held little to no fanfare. To many, it was merely the marking of another year gone by. In remembrance, the names of those lost to the previous year were read aloud from the front porch of the Murphy Tavern. Connor Murphy called six names in all—three men, two women, and a newborn. A harsh winter brought snow to the hills now, the promise of spring a distant wish on everyone's mind.

"Fetch more hot water, Seamus, and bring along some of the clean towels and cloths I have in the kitchen. Make certain they are clean, mind you."

"Yes, Ma," answered Seamus as he turned and ran for the kitchen.

Elspeth sat beside Little Cornstalk, clutching her hand. The girl made no sound as she experienced wave after wave of gripping spasm. How she could hold her cries from such terrible pain, Elspeth had no idea. The only response from Little Cornstalk was to grip Elspeth's small hand so tightly that she thought it might break.

"You may cry out if you wish, Little Cornstalk. There is no shame in this," said Elspeth, catching her own breath.

"It is the way of the Cherokee, Mother Elspeth," said Little Cornstalk through clenched teeth.

And so it went.

It seemed the entire population of Murphy-Borough was holding its breath. People milled about outside the Murphy Tavern. The blacksmith, Mr. Cummings, sat dolefully, perched on the wooden steps leading in. His knees pulled up under his chin. Wagging his head occasionally as if a fly was pestering him, he mumbled incoherently to no one.

Stevenson and Murphy were enjoying each other's company up on the parapet, swinging their legs back and forth as they passed a bottle between.

When the baby finally made its way into the world, the little room exploded with excitement. Elspeth and Kathleen laughed with relief. The baby popped out with a thick sprout of red hair upon his head. Scrunching up his tiny face, the infant let out a wail that traveled to every ear within hearing. A cheer went up, and the loitering crowd began to clap hands, breaking into spontaneous dance. A fiddle player alongside a piper played a lively tune, encouraging the happy folk.

Kathleen quickly tied the umbilical cord in two places. The baby lay on Little Cornstalk's tummy, already bundled in a warm blanket. Cradling her newborn with one arm, Little Cornstalk reached down and grabbed hold of the cord. She brought it to her mouth. Clamping her teeth over the slippery cable, she sheared it in two. With blood dripping down her chin, she smiled at Kathleen and Elspeth.

"It's the Cherokee way," said Kathleen, shrugging with a shiver, her hand holding useless shears.

"Apparently so," answered Elspeth, shocked as she watched Little Cornstalk spit out the bit.

That evening, the residents of Murphy-Borough celebrated. Connor Murphy brought out three barrels of ale and one of rum. To the stunned populace of Murphy-Borough, he charged nothing for any of it. Seamus Murphy made mountains of popcorn for everyone, handing out warm handfuls to anyone who wanted.

Stevenson became very drunk. Elspeth had never seen him in his cups before, and she found it amusing. The older hunter sat beside her son David atop a table, singing Swedish folk songs, swaying to and fro. He smiled continually.

As the spontaneous gathering began to dwindle, Elspeth made her way back to Little Cornstalk. The girl was murmuring softly to her child as she fed him. Elspeth marveled at her newborn grandson. Knowing this was William's child, a sudden comfort came to Elspeth. She wished her beloved Ian could see this moment and was saddened to know he never would. Still, she realized this was life. And everything it brings.

Looking on her grandson, she knew then that Ian MacEwan would never be gone. He was right here in this very room, right now.

Sitting on the bed next to Little Cornstalk, Elspeth cupped her hands in her lap. "Now," she said quietly, "what name are you giving my grandson?"

Little Cornstalk gazed up into Elspeth's eyes. "That is for William, Mother Elspeth. He must name our baby."

"Oh," answered Elspeth with a troubled look.

Although she was completely exhausted, Little Cornstalk did not miss the disappointment on Elspeth's face. Just about then, Kathleen Murphy stepped into the room, closing the door quietly behind.

"And what are you two ladies chatting on about?" asked Kathleen.

Elspeth said, "Little Cornstalk tells me that William is the one who must name the child. I imagine that is the Cherokee way."

Little Cornstalk nodded in affirmation. "This is true," she said. "It is the way of the Cherokee." She tilted her head. "How do the whites name their babies?"

"Well now," said Kathleen, "to that, we name them the day they are born. We would choose a name and then write it down in a family Bible so it is never forgotten."

"How do you choose this name?" asked the girl.

"It's usually a family name, like the name of a father or grandfather, a brother, or maybe a good friend, someone important to you. Connor was given his da's name, and he is very proud of that. You understand?"

"Yes," answered Little Cornstalk thoughtfully. "It is a good thing to do this, I think. William's son is white with the red hair of his father." She giggled as she said this. "We will name our baby for William's father, Ian. William will be happy for this."

Elspeth was ecstatic. She had hoped for something like this. Still, she immediately realized that Little Cornstalk had given up a cherished tradition to please her—or perhaps William too.

"We often give a third name to our children," said Elspeth quickly. "I have a good one."

"What is a good one?" asked Little Cornstalk.

"Shadow Bear," announced Elspeth, remembering the young Cherokee boy she cared for and who had become fast friends with her son, the brother of Little Cornstalk.

"Oh," squeaked Little Cornstalk, "this is a good name. William will be happier."

"That's settled then," said Kathleen.

Addressing the child, she announced, "Welcome to the world, Ian Shadow Bear MacEwan."

"Are you happy with this name, Little Cornstalk?" asked Elspeth expectantly.

"Yes," answered the girl. "This is a good name. We will write it in a book so it will never be forgotten."

Royal Barracks, Greenwich

THEY WALKED WILLIAM down the long hall and out into the courtyard, where a waiting carriage stood. Four redcoats accompanied the longhunter as they drove through the streets of London. Once again, William peered out the window, watching the busy citizens pass by, hawking food and wares. The journey to the target range was short. Pulling up outside a low brick building, William could see some of the attendees milling about.

Several officers in full uniform stood conversing with one another. All manner of ribbons and medals hung from their chests. William spied his uncle Robert standing alone. Hamish was nowhere to be seen. Atop the roof of the low building were a series of chairs, some of which were occupied. A heavyset gentleman in a white wig sat center front, bundled up in dark fur blankets. Two clerks sat on either side of the prime minister.

William recognized Field Marshal Amherst standing to one side. The man beside him he did not know. Dressed in their finery, the nonmilitary guests began to congregate and seat themselves. After some instruction, William was guided to the front rail of the range. Special effort had been made to increase the distance of the targets. One side of the range was cleared of debris and ice, making a clear path to each target more than 250 yards away.

A soldier came up to William and handed him his rifle. William examined the piece closely, pulling the hammer mechanism and staring down the long barrel. He opened the patch box in the stock and rubbed the delicate cloth between his fingers. A second soldier handed William his powder horn and shot bag. He carefully fingered the lead shot for smoothness. They were good.

Robert MacEwan strolled up behind William. "Is everything to your liking, nephew?"

William turned and smiled at his uncle. "Yes, Uncle. My rifle appears to have suffered no damage. A speck of rust in the pan, but I rubbed that out. I am ready when they are."

Amherst came up to the firing rail and nodded to William. "You have all you need, Mr. MacEwan?"

"I do, sir."

"Then proceed at your leisure."

Virtually every man there held a glass. The target was a long way off and impossible to see with the naked eye. From the distance of 250 yards, even an eyeglass would barely suffice. To simplify things, a series of flags were used. Green was a direct hit to the target center. Yellow meant the center target had been missed within twelve inches. A red flag suggested a complete miss outside the twelve-inch boundary.

The target itself was designed in concentric circles, black against white. A four-inch diameter patch at its center seemed tiny this far away. William began to load his rifle.

"Notice the time it takes to load this weapon, gentlemen!" called out Secretary Germain, who had been standing beside Amherst. "It is a glaring flaw in the weapon's design. Also, as you can plainly see, the long barrel is incapable of holding a bayonet, useless in a charge."

Listening to the man speak did nothing to hurry William. He knew well that to rush loading a rifle invited disaster. His father would never approve. As he continued, William could hear the generals tittering and clucking in disapproval at the time it took to load.

Standing at the ready, William turned to Amherst. "You may fire, Mr. MacEwan," said the Field Marshal.

Feet slightly spread, William eyed the target. In one sweeping motion, he pulled the rifle up, aimed, and fired. Silence followed as the spectators drew their eyepieces up. One or two with good sight let out a small cry. Then the green flag came up.

There was a grumble from the spectators, especially the general staff. Several eyes fell on Secretary Germain.

"Again, if you would, Mr. MacEwan," said Amherst.

This time, William loaded quickly, less than a minute. The target being replaced by the attendants was ready. William performed exactly the same. Sweeping the rifle up, he aimed and fired. Once again, there were cries from behind William, this time louder. The green flag went up again.

Amherst turned and looked up at the prime minister. He waved the field marshal to continue. The prime minister leaned over to one of his clerks and spoke. The man pulled a watch from his waistcoat. At Amherst's request, William fired ten shots, loading his rifle as quickly as possible. When he fired the last ball and the final green flag made an appearance, it was clear to those who witnessed the demonstration that the American was a remarkable shot.

"Well, George," called the prime minister, "it looks as though your assessment of the long rifle is incorrect."

"Partially, I would agree, Prime Minister." Germain sniffed. "However, it is still slow to load and incapable of holding a bayonet!"

Prime Minister Ford leaned over once more, speaking softly with his clerk. He nodded. "George, according to my clerk, it took Mr. MacEwan just under a minute to reload his rifle. To march a line of men 250 yards over open field takes three minutes. That would mean your enemy can fire three times before your troops are even within range of their own weapons."

"Isn't it more like two times, Prime Minister?" asked Germain sarcastically.

"You're quite right, George. It is closer to two times, unless, of course, they have more than one line of fire. I believe they would, George. Wouldn't you agree?"

Germain clapped his mouth shut, turned on his heel, and walked away.

"My compliments to you, Mr. MacEwan," called Ford. "Have a safe journey home, sir."

Robert was pounding William on the back. "Well done, William. Well done."

"Where is Uncle Hamish?" asked William.

"I'll tell you a little secret, William. Just between us, you understand? Your uncle is a fierce man in battle, none braver. But if he is forced to sit idly and watch as others perform, he simply cannot bear it," finished Robert, laughing.

Quaker Settlement

ALDEN ROLLED OVER onto his side and emptied his belly. Yellowish brown fluid came up, burning his throat as he spit furiously over and over. His head was pounding. He had taken to drinking large amounts of whiskey along with the last of his laudanum. He was trying to make his supply last. He knew he would have to do something about that. He was now thoroughly addicted to the vile brew.

An argument could be heard outside the cabin, shouted words in anger, an audible scuffle between men who could barely spell their names. Alden was tiring of these daily conflicts, and they seemed to be getting worse as the days passed.

The Quaker settlement turned out to be a good choice for Alden and his crew of mercenaries. There were three good cabins in all, quite large. A temporary corral was repaired to hold the horses. There was good water from a deep well. The only wanderers passing through were Indian, and they were from various tribes—Mohawk, Delaware, and a few drifting Shawnee. A single Huron had come into the camp, dragging three women intended for the slave market south. Not all these misfits stayed with Alden and his men. Many simply moved on.

Alden stood up and relieved himself on the cabin wall. The argument outside grew intense as the belligerents bellowed curses at the top of their voice. They hurled words at one another as if they were weapons. A single pistol shot rang out and with it the ominous silence that followed.

This cabin had no door. The opening was covered in a makeshift blanket cobbled together with pelts and leather strips. Robichaud swept it aside. Still half-dressed and draped in a large woolen blanket, Alden turned to the violent Frenchman.

"What happened?"

"That goddamned Huron, Smoke," answered Robichaud, "he wants the girl back."

"What?" said Alden, incredulous. "I paid that bastard twenty pounds. Does he think it for nothing? He has no claim on me."

When the Huron, Smoke, came into the camp, he had three captive women with him. Two were black slaves recently escaped. The third was a fourteen-year-old white girl with pale blond hair. The instant Alden spied the girl, he wanted her. She was desperately thin, filthy but comely. The dress she wore was in near tatters, exposing her bony frame. *Good food will fix that soon enough*, thought Alden. Knowing the Huron intended to sell these women, Alden naturally made an offer for the white girl. The Huron agreed. Money was exchanged, and Alden took possession of his latest conquest.

The girl was sweet. Willing to do whatever Alden wished, she delighted the captain. Her only plea was that he not harm her. Alden assured her he would not.

At first, he found the girl to be simpleminded but a pleasure, nevertheless. After two weeks, Alden began losing patience with her. It wasn't long before he grew thoroughly disgusted with the waif. He began berating her and even striking her, demonstrating the promise he made as hollow. Having had enough, Alden took the girl out for a walk one morning into the trees. Pointing out broken limbs and wood branches, Alden ordered her to pick up the dry pieces for the evening fire. As she turned her back on the captain, he slipped his flintlock out and shot her in the back of the head. Stuffing the body under fallen tree trunks, he kicked wood leaves, dry brush, and dirt over the corpse, leaving her.

Stepping outside the cabin with Robichaud, Alden was instantly confronted by the irate Huron. Smoke stood holding a musket in one hand and a rope tethered to his two slave women in the other. He was ready to depart.

"Where is the girl?" asked the Huron in broken English.

"You cannot have her back," said Alden. "I paid good money for her."

"Not enough," said Smoke angrily. "Slave markets pay much more for white girl. You pay nothing."

"Well, you cannot have her. She is gone."

"Gone," repeated the Huron. "Where gone?"

"Far away," said Alden. "You will not find her."

Smoke knew that Robichaud had already discharged his pistol and so was unloaded. He looked down at the barrel of his musket aimed toward the ground. Judging his chances, he drew his eyes up on Alden with undisguised hatred, another white man stealing.

As he pulled his musket up, Alden thrust aside his blanket. Holding his drawn flintlock on the Huron, he hesitated only a second. When the ball struck Smoke, he let out a small cry. Firing his musket uselessly into the dirt, he fell back. Still alive and struggling to rise, Robichaud descended on the hapless Huron, cutting his throat with a single swipe of the blade.

"Take the slaves," said Alden casually. "They are worth good money."

France

WILLIAM BID FAREWELL to his uncles in Woolwich. It was an awkward parting. Hamish wanted William to visit Scotland and meet the rest of the Clan MacEwan. William refused. Hamish took it badly.

William was grateful to both his uncles for all they had done, and he told them so. He knew his time in the Royal Barracks would have been far worse without them. Still, he was determined to return to America as quickly as possible. Hamish, God bless him, had insisted all of William's property be returned in full. This included his long rifle. The British were reluctant, of course, but Hamish made a grand fuss over it, pointing out the absurdity of capturing a single rifle from a lone American hunter. "It would only make England look petty," declared the Scottish laird.

Crossing the English Channel was a rough affair. The wind and weather pushed the small British ship in corkscrew fashion, causing several crew members to become seasick. William soaked it all, enjoying every minute of the passing. Unlike many aboard, he held his footing and food.

The actual prisoner exchange took place close to the French coastline due to the heavy seas. William's concern here was that he not fall from the transfer boat rocking precariously in the water. Drowning, after all he had been through, would be awkward, to say the least.

After landing, the exchanged prisoners made their way to two large carriages. Painted a polished black enamel with fleur-de-lis designs, the coaches immediately sprang forward, making for Paris. A French guide assigned to each coach kept the men informed along the journey. It was a two-day trip to the City of Light with stops only for food and rest, allowing the riders and horses some respite.

William's companions in the coach were open and mostly delirious over their pardon exchange. They asked many questions of William, noting his rifle and dress. Whenever they stopped, the French offered wine, brandy, and ale to the men. Having nothing to drink over the past year, the naval officers quickly became inebriated. William had no interest in imbibing, although he did find the food wonderful. Their final stop at a roadside tavern served a farmer's stew made with mutton and root vegetables. William thought it the best thing he had ever eaten.

As they rolled into the city, it was just coming dark. Looking out the coach window, William could see that Paris was heavily populated with the desperate souls of the destitute. Many hands were held out, begging for coin or bread. The clothes they wore were little more than rags. Several were shoeless in the freezing weather. The coach drivers forced these unfortunates off the road with whips, driving them away, shouting obscenities. It was a disappointing introduction to the city of Paris.

The coaches drew up to a single red brick home on a narrow lane just inside the city proper. The modest structure was half-covered in a spiderweb of leafless vine. In the summer, William knew the vine would blanket the walls in deep green leaves.

Each man emerged from their respective coach, stretching and stomping their feet. Pointing to the door of the home, the French guide bade them all enter. A naval lieutenant marched up the steps and banged on the door. The door flew open by the hand of a thin young man dressed in finery. He was of medium height with dark brown curls covering his head, pulled back in a combed tail. His outfit was crushed velvet blue with ruffled sleeves and a high collar. He backed away from the entrance, bowing and waving his hand for the group to enter.

"How do you do, gentlemen!" cried the young man.

"We have been waiting anxiously for your arrival. My name is Temple Franklin. I am very happy to see you all," he said with a laugh. "We had no idea when you would actually arrive, so you must forgive our lack of preparation. If you would be good enough to follow me to the study."

The line of tired men including William trailed behind at a pace. They came into a large room whose walls were covered in books. Sitting in an ornate chair was a large man of wide girth. This man had a balding pate with long loose graying hair that fell untied to his shoulders. A pair of tiny spectacles, perched on the end of his nose, sparkled with the reflection of a table lantern. He wore baggy trousers of gray felt, a dark red coat with fur collar, matching red waistcoat, and a rumpled white linen shirt. His face was large and long with a fine nose. His complexion was pale with ruddy patches on the cheeks. He stood up.

"Gentlemen, gentlemen, I am delighted to see you. I am Dr. Benjamin Franklin, currently representing the Continental Congress here in France. Come in and be welcome. Temple, would you be good enough to bring some extra seating for our guests?"

William entered the room last, carrying his long rifle in cradle fashion. As he pulled the hat from his head, he immediately caught Franklin's attention. Still dressed in buckskin and fringed trousers, William naturally stood out from the others. As the representative to France approached the young longhunter, he thrust out his hand. "You would be William MacEwan?" asked the older man, smiling.

"Yes, sir," answered William as his gaze fell over the hundreds of books lining the walls.

"I have a letter for you to read. It is from your friend, I think, Col. Daniel Morgan?"

"Why, yes, sir. I know the colonel well. Has he written to me?"

"The letter is addressed to me, of course, but it does concern you. Please follow me while I have Temple fetch it."

Franklin directed William to a small office, and the two men entered. William sat quietly, reading the two-page letter. In it, the colonel had explained William's situation, urging the good doctor Franklin to expedite the longhunter's release. William considered the notion that his mother had a hand in all this somehow. The thought was both comforting and extraordinary. Standing from his chair, William returned the letter to Franklin.

"I thank you for that, Dr. Franklin. I had no idea anyone knew where I was, other than my uncles, of course."

"Oh yes. Your capture and journey to England is well known. Colonel Morgan's letter provided further detail. The search for your family, being wounded at the Battle of Saratoga, and your eventual capture in Philadelphia—all are known. It stands as quite an adventure, I must say. As to the information of your being sent to England, you may thank Mrs. Elizabeth Burgin for that."

"Elizabeth . . ."

"Burgin," finished Franklin. "You met her on the wharf in New York City. She passed you one of her kind packages. She was very concerned about your welfare."

"Yes, of course," said William, recalling with a smile. "The woman on the wharf."

"Just so." Franklin nodded. "I'll be honest with you, William. It was Morgan's letter that brought me to your aid. The fact that the British captured an American innocent and claiming you as a combatant was too delicious for me to ignore, an incredible blunder on their part. It was an excellent opportunity to embarrass the Crown, you see." He laughed.

"How is it you come to this information, sir?" asked William.

"Oh, well, the British have their spies, and we have ours," answered Franklin vaguely. "In war, every scrap of information has value."

"I see," said William, pondering the words.

"And now when you return to America, what will you do, William?"

"I will reunite with my family and Little Cornstalk. I will secure their safety."

"Little Cornstalk?" repeated Franklin, confused.

"Yes, sir. She is a girl I fell in love with and left behind. She is Cherokee," said William by way of explanation.

"I see," said Franklin, understanding.

"And then?" asked Franklin, suddenly serious.

William's face took a hard turn. "I will hunt down the Englishman John Alden and kill him."

Franklin raised his brows, clearly surprised at this. His expectation had been that William would join up with Morgan's riflemen and enter the fight for America's freedom. He studied the longhunter closely.

"Perhaps you should know this then," said Franklin slowly. "Capt. John Alden has deserted his command. He is now a wanted man by the British for crimes of murder and theft."

"Have they captured him?" asked William in a rush.

"Not that I am aware of," answered Franklin, shaking his head.

William turned as if concentrating on something. He remained silent.

After a time, Franklin rose from his chair and, placing a hand on William's shoulder, said, "Let us rejoin the other gentlemen, William. I am certain you wish to learn how soon you can be on your way."

Having turned out a table of food and drink, Temple Franklin bid all to sit and partake.

"Your transport, gentlemen, will be an American ship," announced Franklin. "She arrives on the morning tide three days from now at the port of Nantes. The ship is called the *Ranger*, captained under John Paul Jones. The captain has strict instructions to carry you directly to the colonies. Just now the British have deserted Philadelphia, moving men north and south. New York is out of the question as English soldiers still roam the city. Even so, the situation is a fluid one and may change at a moment's notice, so be prepared for any eventuality."

"Is Captain Jones taking any officers, sir?" asked one of the naval men.

"For that, you will have to consult the captain. I would very much like to introduce you all to the fine city of Paris, but alas, it is not to be. The *Ranger* will linger no more than a few days before heading back to America.

"Now, gentlemen, we will feed you and bundle you straight back into your coaches. It is a three-day trip to Nantes. You begin this very eve. I must tell you all that your country is most grateful for your sacrifice and courage. I am sorry it took this long to realize your parole. Now, gentlemen, let us eat."

Murphy-Borough

"WAKE UP, MOTHER Elspeth! Wake up!" Elspeth found herself being shaken violently by the shoulders. She opened her eyes to find Little Cornstalk hovering over her. She sat up, rubbing her face awake.

"Is it the baby?" asked Elspeth, concerned.

"No," said Little Cornstalk, shaking her head. "Ian Shadow Bear sleeps now. He is good."

Ian Shadow Bear, thought Elspeth. *That will take some getting used to.* "What is it then?"

"It is William," whispered the girl.

"William?" said Elspeth, suddenly alert. "What of William?"

"He is coming," said Little Cornstalk with a brilliant smile.

"He is coming," she repeated excitedly.

"But how do you . . ." began Elspeth as Little Cornstalk grabbed her hand, hauling her up from the bed.

"We must go to the prayer circle and bring a thing from our heart," said Little Cornstalk. "I have cut a patch from Ian Shadow Bear's blanket. This is good."

"You wish me to bring something as well?" asked Elspeth, mildly confused.

"Oh yes, it is too very important. We must hurry before the Mother Spirit shines her face on my circle. This will help bring William home to us."

Elspeth looked on the girl with affection. She was so simple, so direct and earnest that it was infectious, childlike but not. Being raised a Christian, Elspeth considered Indian mysticism nothing more than nonsense. Still, the girl's obvious devotion was not to be ignored.

"What shall I bring?" asked Elspeth, unsure.

"You must bring something from your heart," answered Little Cornstalk as though this was obvious.

"I cannot think of anything," replied Elspeth, frustrated.

"Something close to you," insisted Little Cornstalk. "Hurry. We must go."

Elspeth looked around and could think of nothing suitable. Then she considered the knife. It was the bone-handled knife she had taken from the Weatherly house. Although she came close, she never actually used the blade. Still, it was important to her. She felt her safety and those of her children had depended on it at one time. It was tucked in with her meager belongings; she quickly retrieved the small blade.

"You will put this in the circle?" asked Little Cornstalk, staring at the knife. "Did your mother make this knife for you?"

"No," said Elspeth, shocked at the thought. "I took it from a woman in Philadelphia."

"Did you kill this woman for the knife?"

"Good heavens, no!"

"This is not good," said the girl, wagging her head. "You have no other thing?"

"We lost everything when the Shawnee came—my books, all our silver, clothing, everything. It was all taken or destroyed. My wedding band was stolen on the road to Philadelphia along with the cross my father gave to me. I have nothing else."

"Head har," said Little Cornstalk bluntly.

"Har?" Before Elspeth realized what was happening, Little Cornstalk snatched a lank of her hair and sheared off a small bundle with her knife. Elspeth looked at the Cherokee girl, dumbfounded.

"Hair," she said, suddenly understanding.

"Yes, har," repeated Little Cornstalk simply. "I will tie it." She dashed out through the door.

The two women ran straight for the small circle. Slipping on the half-frozen ground, running as fast as her feet allowed, Elspeth stayed close behind the girl. Almost there, she realized she was barefoot, wearing only a thin nightdress. She began to laugh at herself.

Upon reaching the circle, Little Cornstalk dropped to her knees. Elspeth did the same. Swiftly tying the bundle of loose hair, the girl passed it to Elspeth and pointed at the flat rock near the center of the circle. Elspeth placed the hair gently beside the stone. She turned to Little Cornstalk and smiled.

Little Cornstalk placed the blanket clipping next to the bundle of hair and began chanting in a soft whisper. Within moments, the sun peeked over the eastern hills, lighting up the circle and all its contents. Little Cornstalk bowed her head in one final gesture and then rose to her feet.

"Is it done?" asked Elspeth, looking up expectantly.

"Yes," answered the girl. "Now William will come soon."

"Thank heavens," said Elspeth, rising to her frozen feet.

"Come along then. Let us go inside and breakfast. *I am very cold!*" she shouted with a laugh.

***

Connor Murphy stood idly on the tavern porch, having just finished a hearty meal. Chewing noisily on a tough strip of bacon, he sniffed the late winter air eagerly. The promise of spring was near. The bandy-legged Irishman could smell it.

Murphy-Borough had a new alarm bell. It was a heavy strip of forged steel that swayed freely near the main gate. Striking the piece with a solid bar, it produced a resonating ring that sailed throughout the community. Made with the hands of Little Cornstalk, it was manufactured under the close supervision of Cummings, the smithy. To date, it was Little Cornstalk's proudest work. In fact, Murphy himself had to stop the girl from banging on the damn thing.

This late morning, the Murphy-Borough alarm bell rang with a jarring echo as it traveled through the air. Connor spat out the last of the chewed-up bacon and rapidly climbed the parapet. Snatching the eyepiece from the watchman, Murphy focused in on a lone Indian sitting motionless some hundred fifty yards off the main gate.

He was clearly Shawnee and finely dressed. Sitting on a low-backed black and white Appaloosa, the Indian held a long staff in his left hand, topped with a small white sheet. He made no attempt to advance.

"Saints, preserve us," said the stocky Irishman. "I don't believe me eyes."

"Who is it then, Connor?" asked the watchman.

Ignoring the question, Murphy called down to a man standing close by the gate. "Go fetch Stevenson and be quick about it!"

"By god, Connor, who is it out there?" repeated the watchman.

"If I'm not mistaken, and I don't think I am, that would be Broken Tree out there, the Shawnee chieftain and brother to Tenskwatawa and Tecumseh. Lord knows what this is about, but I'm thinking it's no good."

Stevenson, half-dressed, began climbing the parapet ladder. He was grumbling fiercely as his head popped up beside Murphy's boots.

"What is this about, Connor?"

"I want you to take a look at this Indian sitting out there."

"Whatever for?"

"Come on then. Get up here and take a peep at this Indian, damn it."

Stevenson held the glass up and peered out at the lone figure standing idly in the open field.

"I'll be damned," said Stevenson. "That's Broken Tree, the Shawnee brother. What the devil is he doing here? Have you seen any others?"

"No, and I have men outside watching the trails that lead in. I have no idea how he got past them without notice."

"What are you going to do?" asked Stevenson.

"I'm going to open the gate and let him in," said Connor matter-of-factly.

"Are you mad, Connor? That Indian is deadly."

"So I am told."

"Why let him in then?"

"Curiosity." The Irishman shrugged as he descended the parapet ladder.

***

Broken Tree slid from the pony's back down onto his feet in his usual manner. Standing at the center of the community, holding the staff erect, he looked about the surroundings with interest. An array of curious silent faces stared at the tall Indian.

On the tavern porch stood Little Cornstalk, Kathleen, and Elspeth along with a gaggle of nattering children. Kathleen chased the little ones back inside. Little Cornstalk stepped off the tavern porch and approached the crippled Indian. She stopped, facing the Shawnee.

"Good day to you, Little Cornstalk," said Broken Tree in his clipped British accent. "It is most gratifying to see you safe and in good health. I see you are no longer with child. I trust the baby is also safe and in good health?"

Little Cornstalk answered with a question of her own. "Why do you come to this place, Broken Tree? You have repaid your debt to the longhunter. I am here, a life for a life. What reason brings you?"

"It is for the sake of your child that I come, Little Cornstalk. You must hear my words. Then I will leave you."

Elspeth studied the lame Indian closely. She was afraid of this man but also indebted. Broken Tree watched over her and the children as they traveled to Philadelphia. It was a kindness under difficult circumstance she could not forget. She never discovered the reason. Elspeth came off the porch. She stopped beside Little Cornstalk. The tall Shawnee smiled.

"How lovely to see you again, Mrs. MacEwan," said Broken Tree with an elegant half bow. "It appears our paths have once again crossed. I trust you and your children are all in good stead?"

"Yes, we are, Broken Tree," answered Elspeth quietly. "I thank you for asking. Won't you come inside and warm yourself? I am sure you have traveled far and a good bit cold for it."

Connor Murphy raised a brow at the invitation. Stevenson looked equally perplexed. Both men, unwilling to act as the gracious host, held their tongue in deference to Elspeth.

Inside the tavern, Elspeth asked David to bring the fire up. The boy smiled at Broken Tree, remembering his kindness on the trail to Philadelphia. Seamus lent a hand, and soon a healthy blaze filled the tavern space, warming it nicely. Everyone sat at the long rough table. All eyes were on the crippled Broken Tree. The lame Indian sat quietly, tapping his staff on the rough wood floor.

"Why are ya here?" snapped Connor.

"As I told Little Cornstalk, I have come for the sake of the longhunter's child."

"What does this mean?" asked Little Cornstalk, not understanding.

"The reason I helped you escape our village, Little Cornstalk, was to save you and the longhunter's child. You know this. I wished to repay the debt I owed the longhunter—my life.

"Tenskwatawa knew if he held the child under his knife, the longhunter would never dare to attack him. He was going to wait until you gave birth to the child. Then he was going to take your life and hold the child prisoner. He believed the longhunter would never seek revenge knowing this."

"Wait," said Elspeth. "Who is this longhunter you speak of?"

"Why, it is your son, Mrs. MacEwan, William," answered the Indian, surprised at the question.

"William?" said Elspeth. "My William?"

"Yes," answered Broken Tree, "your William. We know he was taken prisoner and brought to England, Mrs. MacEwan. Let me assure you the Shawnee had nothing to do with your son's capture. This was accomplished by the British alone. When I explained this to my brother Tenskwatawa, he realized your son would be helpless to interfere in any attack on Murphy-Borough. I tried to reason with him but to no avail. I came here partly due to this. I feel somewhat responsible."

"William is coming," said Little Cornstalk forcefully. "He travels here now. Tenskwatawa will not take Ian Shadow Bear. William will kill him, and I will help."

Stevenson snapped his head from one face to the next. He was beginning to understand this conversation, and his temper rose accordingly.

"Tenskwatawa is attacking. He comes here to steal the baby?"

"Yes," said Broken Tree. "He is coming with many men. This fear he holds because of the longhunter has gripped his soul, broken his mind. I have tried to dissuade him of these thoughts, but it is hopeless. He is coming, and he will fight."

"Let him come," said Connor Murphy, slamming a hand down for emphasis. "Blackfish and his whole tribe have tried to take down Murphy-Borough more than once, and they have failed at every turn."

"He will come, I assure you, Mr. Murphy," said Broken Tree sadly. "He intends to bring a large host, not just Shawnee but also Iroquois, Mohawk, Delaware, Abenaki, and Huron. The English captain Alden—"

"Alden!" cried Elspeth, halting Broken Tree.

"What has Alden to do with this?" asked Stevenson angrily.

"He has allied himself with Tenskwatawa," said Broken Tree. "He will come and fight alongside my brother. He has several good fighters with him. And they carry a small British cannon."

"A cannon, you say?" asked Connor. "What size cannon?"

"I believe it to be a three-pound Galloper. It was stolen from a British armory near Montreal with help from the Abenaki. As you may be aware, my native brothers very much fear the cannon. They will not fire it, but Alden certainly will. It could wreak havoc here, Mr. Murphy."

"Why do you tell us this, Broken Tree?" asked Elspeth.

"As I said, Mrs. MacEwan, I wish to repay a debt. But honestly, I am not entirely sure," answered the tall Shawnee. "Your son saved my life in Saratoga—twice. For this, I returned Little Cornstalk and her child. I grow weary of these wars, Mrs. MacEwan. The killing of men, women, and children—the misery of it can be . . . overwhelming. For the Shawnee, it is an endless struggle. Does this answer, Mrs. MacEwan?"

"Perhaps. It does appear your healthy foot stands in the world of white men, Broken Tree," said Elspeth knowingly. "I fear your mother and father would be heartbroken over this."

"As you say, Mrs. MacEwan." The Indian nodded. "On the other hand, Father Faraley would consider me blessed."

Philadelphia

WILLIAM STEPPED ONTO the Philadelphia wharf in one long stride. The air was cool and dry just now. The sun was pleasantly warm on the longhunter's face. He stopped a moment, spreading his arms out wide, taking in a lungful of air. He tapped the butt of his long rifle lightly on the worn wooden dock with satisfaction. A smile crept across his face. He was home again.

The return journey aboard the *Ranger* was a swift one indeed. Fair winds and good weather brought the *Ranger* to America in record time. Even her captain, John Paul Jones, was impressed with the speed with which she made the crossing.

Captain Jones happily enlisted two of the freed officers, taking them into the ship's complement. The others continued their journey, making their way north as far as Boston and beyond. Each former prisoner was delighted to be back in America.

As he looked about, William could see that the docks of Philadelphia were busy indeed. Men, carts, wheelbarrows, mules, and boats all seemed to be jostling over the entire port. American soldiers with ready muskets resting in their arms roamed the wharf in casual fashion. No one paid William the slightest attention. Looking west, he began making his way straight for the Schuylkill Bridge. At the end of the wooden dock stood three roughneck sailors. One carried a rolled blanket of red and blue print. He wore an odd-looking hat with a white feather. The man to William's right held a rifle in hand with a musket and tumpline slung over his back. The third sailor looked William over as if he were a good boat for sale.

Of average height, this man stood out from the other two. He wore a heavy dark blue woolen peacoat. A small sailor cap sat on an unruly mass of hair. Striped trousers and hobnailed boots covered his legs and feet. He carried nothing in his hands as he made directly for William.

"You would be William MacEwan?" asked the pug-faced sailor.

William pinched his eyes on the man. "And who might you be, sir?" asked William closely.

"My name is Bennett, Richard Bennett. I am a friend to your mother and Olaf Stevenson. You are William, am I correct?"

"You are, sir," answered William as he studied the sailor head to foot. "I recognize your name, Mr. Bennett, from my mother's letter. It appears I owe you thanks, sir."

Without answering, Bennett reached into his peacoat and withdrew a sheet of paper. "I've another letter for you, this one also written by your mother with the aid of Stevenson. It's why we're here," finished Bennett as he passed the letter to William.

William hurriedly read the message. The news was good. William's mother and surviving children were all safely grounded in Murphy-Borough. Little Cornstalk was there as well. Stevenson made no mention of a baby. This was requested by Elspeth. She did not want her son to receive such news in a distant letter. At the mention of Bennett's name in the letter, William looked up at the fellow.

Bennett turned to the man on his right, holding the blanket, and nodded. The sailor bent to a knee and carefully unfurled the red and blue blanket. Inside lay a pair of moccasins, William's moccasins. The sailor then pulled the peculiar hat from his head, laying it on the blanket as well.

Without words, Bennett swept his arm toward the second sailor and pointed to the blanket. This man slipped the musket and tumpline from his back and gently laid the rifle and musket down alongside the beaded moccasins. A powder horn, shot, and ball pouch were quickly added.

"Stevenson was most insistent that you have these," said Bennett, waving his hand over the blanket. With that, he swung his coat open and revealed two French pistols tucked in a wide brown belt. He placed both on the blanket beside the other weapons.

"Apparently, you need these items to survive your trip west. It must be a wonderful place, this home of yours," finished Bennett sarcastically, scrunching his face up in distaste.

William chuckled. "I assure you, sir, it is most wonderful. But tell me, how on God's green earth did you retrieve my moccasins?" Sitting gingerly on the edge of the old dock, William dragged off his scuffed boots and pulled on the beloved moccasins.

"They were taken off the feet of a dead river pirate," said Bennett matter-of-factly, "if you can call them feet. He was an old man with a wicked, unrepentant soul."

"I almost killed that man," recalled William, looking down at the moccasins now mounted on his feet.

"His name was Ezekiel Bitterman. We hung him from an elm as a thief and traitor to the cause. A well-deserved end, I would add."

"God's soul," said William, shaking his head in wonder. Both men stood silent for a moment, considering the lost soul of Ezekiel Bitterman.

"Mr. Stevenson mentions a horse here?" continued William, indicating the letter. "Do you have a horse as well?"

"I'm afraid the matter of the horse is somewhat more complicated. You see, it's far easier to acquire weapons these days than a horse. The Continental army seems to be confiscating every four-legged animal within five hundred miles. On that, however, I may have a notion. If you would be good enough to join me."

The other two sailors broke off, waving a farewell to Bennett. William gathered up the weapons, tucking the pistols in his belt and tumpline that now crossed his chest. He slung his own rifle over his back.

"Don't forget your hat," said Bennett as he draped the blanket over his shoulder, twisted his head in the direction of the street, and began walking. Moving silently beside Bennett, William gave the hat a closer look. He liked it. It was black felt with a round dome and wide brim. One side of the brim was sewn up against the dome in jaunty fashion. A white feather poked through a series of holes in the folded brim and trailed a good four inches off the back of the hat.

"Your mother wanted you to have that hat. It's a preacher's hat. God knows why. It's a foolish thing if you ask me, but then I find most hats are."

William plunked the hat on his head without comment, tossing his old one aside. It was swiftly snatched up by a passing hatless citizen.

With that done, he examined the new rifle and musket carefully. He began loading them.

After a bit, Bennett came to an abrupt stop, forcing William to look up from his task. Overhead, attached to a solid brick-faced structure, was a long flat wooden sign with colorful dancing cows, sheep, pigs, and chickens painted across it.

"What place is this?" asked William, looking left and right.

"German butcher," answered Bennett as he banged on the shuttered door.

"Go away! We are closed!" called a heavily accented voice. "Come tomorrow, please, if you would."

"Open the door, Ulli!" shouted Bennett in reply. "It is Bennett. I must speak with you."

Ulli Becker slowly opened the door, peeking out the gap. "What do you want, Bennett?"

"I have someone here who wants to buy one of your horses."

"We do not sell horses, Bennett, only meat. You know this. We need our horses for the wagon."

"Ulli, you have two horses and one wagon. Clearly, you require only one horse."

Ulli peered around Bennett, taking in a view of William. He bobbed his head in the young longhunter's direction.

"Who is this with the feather in his cap?" asked the short German suspiciously.

"This is William MacEwan, the eldest son of the woman we rescued. You remember her?"

"*Mein Got, ya!* Of course, I remember. We helped save her and the children!" cried the German. "Come in, come in."

William and Bennett stepped into the open shop space.

"Helmut!" roared the short German, nearly blowing William's new hat from his crown. "Come quick! We have guests."

"I am coming, *ja*," came the surly reply.

Thunderous steps pounded down the short stairwell, rattling the glass windows and shivering the door. Helmut hit the floor with a thud. He looked at Bennett and smiled broadly.

"Richard, my friend, it is good to see you," said the tall German, slapping Bennett solidly on the back.

"*Und* who is this?" asked Helmut, looking William up and down.

Ulli piped up, "This is William MacEwan, Helmut. This is the lady's son, the one we rescued from the Weatherly house."

"Da woman with the children?"

"Ja," said Ulli.

"*Mein Got!* We saved your mother and da children!" cried Helmut, throwing his long arms in the air as if surrendering. "We did good, didn't we, Bennett?"

"Yes, we did," answered Bennett, smiling.

William looked at the unfamiliar faces surrounding him and blinked several times. He began shaking hands and thanking the men profusely. Helmut's grip nearly broke William's wrist. It was a struggle to release his hand.

"I am in your debt, gentlemen. Truly, I am," said William. "Just now, however, I am need of a horse. Mr. Bennett says you may have one."

Ulli wagged his head no while Helmut bobbed his up and down with an assenting smile. Both men spoke simultaneously.

Ulli said, "*Nein*, we have no horse to sell."

Helmut said, "*Ja*, we have two horses, a good one and an old one."

William turned to Bennett for resolution.

"Ulli, surely, you can part with one of your horses," said Bennett in a reasonable tone. "The lad needs a horse to get back to his family. You understand?"

"Ja," said Helmut. "You take the red one. It is a very good horse. The other is a draft horse with long teeth."

"Nein, nein," repeated Ulli. "If you must have a horse, take the gray. He is a little old, but he is good."

Helmut then said something in German that William did not understand. Ulli replied. Within seconds, both men were in heated argument, shouting at each other in German.

William looked to Bennett once again, only to have the bandy-legged sailor shrug while tipping his head.

William interrupted the German butchers with a shout. "Gentlemen!" cried William. "I do not care which animal you sell. Just sell one, if you please. Now! I am very sorry, but I must be on my way."

There was some further grumbling in German.

Finally, Ulli reluctantly said, "You may take the red horse then. What can you pay?"

William's uncle Hamish had tried to give William fifty pounds, but the longhunter refused as this was far too much money. He settled for five pounds, which he now produced.

"Five pounds," said Ulli, raising his eyebrows in disbelief. "The saddle is worth more than that."

"Oh," said William, looking down on the floor. He was disappointed. "Well then, I thank you for your help with my family, gentlemen. I will not trouble you any longer. I must be on my way."

"Hold a moment if you would, Mr. MacEwan," said Bennett, turning on the two butchers. "I will stand for the cost of the animal. Mr. MacEwan can repay me when he is able. How much is the horse, Ulli?"

"Forty pounds, and the saddle is eight," answered the German, folding his arms over his chest with finality and raising his birdlike chin. "You have forty-eight pounds, Bennett?"

"Not just now, but I will. You know you can trust me for the amount."

"Ha!" said Ulli. "You who spends your monies in bawdy houses with painted women and rum. Where would you get forty-eight pounds?"

"That would be my business, Ulli," answered Bennett, clearly insulted.

"Gentlemen," said William in frustration, "the horse, if you please!"

"Ja," said Helmut. "She is out here."

The group bundled their way out the back of the butcher shop across an open corral and into a small barn. Two horses were stabled comfortably within. Helmut led the red horse outside while Bennett grabbed the saddle hanging on the wall. Ulli remained silent throughout, mumbling guttural German the whole time.

The saddle was quickly added to the animal along with bridle and bit. Looping the reins up, William caught the stirrup and swung himself into the saddle. He nodded gratefully to the men.

"Do you have everything, William?" asked Bennett.

"All except a hunting knife and hatchet. I can do without them for now."

"Wait!" cried Helmut as he rushed out the barn. Returning, he held a long butcher knife in a wooden sheath in one hand and a gleaming long-handled cleaver in the other.

"These will do?" he asked politely.

"Yes, sir," answered William, taking both. "They will do nicely."

Tenskwatawa

TENSKWATAWA AND BROKEN Tree sat opposite Alden in the great lodge. A smokeless gathering of glowing embers sat between the men. Alden had hauled the cannon to the Shawnee village, impressing the warriors and squaws standing around it. They declared it good thunder medicine before lightning. The problem, as Alden saw it, was shot. There were few three-pound cannonballs available, only twenty to fire and no more.

"We may need more cannon shot," said Alden, wagging his head. "Twenty is a paltry number. We could lose three or four just getting our range and direction, maybe more. That leaves seventeen at best. If the fort has heavy timber, it may not be enough."

"What do you suggest then, Captain?" asked Broken Tree in perfect English.

"I have nothing to suggest," said Alden irritably, "unless you know where we can find more shot."

"I still think this is an ill-advised adventure, Captain. I have told my brother so. Even with the warriors that Tenskwatawa will be assembling, it looks to be a very risky enterprise. Many Shawnee will die, and for what?"

"You will rid yourselves of the Murphy Fort. It lies within Shawnee lands, does it not? You will be helping your British allies as well. Over one hundred white lives will be taken and many scalps for your brothers' lodge poles. The plunder alone will fortify the Shawnee for a year or more. Food, barrels of rum, weapons, good horses."

"But for you, it is the white woman MacEwan you seek, is it not?"

Alden flushed angrily at this. He shook his head. "My desire is to help your brother Tenskwatawa, nothing more. As allies to the British, I would think this a mutual goal between us."

Tenskwatawa broke his silence. Speaking forcefully to Broken Tree, he spoke at length. Alden sat quietly listening. The great chief spoke at length, a cadence of words without the least understanding to the renegade English captain. Divining nothing from the conversation, Alden could only sit patiently as he waited for this insufferable savage to complete his monologue.

Finally, Tenskwatawa stopped speaking. Broken Tree turned to Alden. "My brother does not trust you, Captain. You have lied to us in the past, and he believes you will do so again."

"What lies?" sputtered Alden. "I have told no lies."

"You lied about the long rifles," said Broken Tree calmly. "You also did not tell Tenskwatawa that the homestead we attacked was the home and family of the longhunter. Because of this, the longhunter haunts his dreams. He is an enemy to Tenskwatawa now."

"The longhunter! He is far away in my homeland of England," said Alden emphatically, throwing his arm out in the general direction east.

"I," shouted Alden, pounding his chest, "sent him there myself! I am certain he hangs from a gibbet, dead by this time. He cannot harm your brother. As to the rifles, they were well hidden. Even your own people did not find them. How is this a lie?"

"Oh, I believe you, Captain. It is my brother who carries this doubt. As far as the longhunter is concerned, I have it on good authority he is indeed on his way here now," said Broken Tree softly.

Alden laughed. "Impossible," he said simply. "William MacEwan is hanging dead or imprisoned."

"We have your word on that, Captain?"

"Of course. How is it the great Tenskwatawa could fear a mere boy anyway?" asked Alden doubtfully. "The notion is ridiculous."

"Ridiculous or not, Captain, the Shawnee believe, as does my brother, that the longhunter is, in fact, an implacable and deadly enemy, a man of special power, if you will. You see, he spared my brother's life when we attacked the Cherokee village. And he saved my life at Saratoga. For a man to do such things only to have the Shawnee kill his father and destroy his family makes for a compelling tale among our people. In many ways, it makes us the weaker, less honorable of the two. It is a mystery white men do not understand.

"The Shawnee will speak of these things as we sit by our lodge fires, and with each telling, a fear grows in the belly. Every debt owed must be paid in kind. This is only natural law. From an Englishman's point of view, it would be considered a case of . . . dishonor, if you will." Broken Tree stared down on Alden. In his heart, he knew this Englishman to be a coward without the least understanding of true honor.

Ghost stories. Alden snorted to himself. He wagged his head in disgust. *These ignorant savages, so simpleminded. How can you deal with such nonsense? No right-thinking person will believe any of it.*

"You may assure your brother, Broken Tree," said Alden forcefully. "The longhunter is gone. He can no longer bring harm to your brother or his people. You have my word on that."

Murphy-Borough

"JUST KEEP DIGGING, Seamus," ordered Murphy, addressing his youngest son. "I see David here making good progress. You should as well."

"He's two years older, Da, and a good bit taller as you can plainly see."

"Tell you what?" Connor smiled. "You boys dig your way to that oak stump there, and I'll bring out something to eat and a couple of cups of ale. How does that sound?"

"Oh," said Seamus, "that would be grand, Da."

"Yes," echoed David. "Thank you, Mr. Murphy."

"Fine then. No more excuses, Seamus. Dig!"

Seamus Murphy and David MacEwan had become good friends over the last two months. On this day, they were given trench-digging duty. Several boys and men from the community were out digging long semicircular trenches encompassing the community walls. Others were busy felling nearby trees at a rapid pace, clearing the ground for good range of fire. It was hard and dirty work, lasting sunup to sundown.

More than four feet across and nearly three feet deep, the trenches were designed to slow down attempts to reach the timbered walls surrounding Murphy-Borough. Dry branches, leaves, and brush lined the bottom of these trenches. Poison sumac and long tendrils of poison ivy were then added. This foliage had to be handled carefully with hand-covered cloth so the men and boys packing the trenches did not infect themselves with the noxious sap. Some did anyway.

Once a sufficient quantity of kindling was laid down, the trench was set. As the enemy advanced, these pits would be fired with a flaming arrow. The burning kindling and poisoned leaves would bellow out smoke, obscuring the field. More importantly, when the smoke was inhaled by the enemy, raking lungs and eyes, it would seriously afflict the person breathing it in. Throats would close, and lungs would burn like fire. The eyes and face of the victims would begin swelling within an hour of exposure. The affected person would be unable to fight. Some would even succumb and die a terrible death, choaking on their own swollen tissue.

The smell of freshly cut wood filled the air. Sharpened pine rails were distributed, buried deep behind each trench, pointing outward, making further enemy progress more difficult. Joined together with long spikes, these flattened rails and pointed barricades were difficult, if not impossible, to get around. It was a mix of holes, trenches, and barricades alternating in progressive arcs. It left only one straight path to the gates of Murphy-Borough.

Inside the community was a hive of activity. Women and young girls were busy making bandages and rifle and musket patches, cooking ready food, and filling canteens. Water buckets were filled and stationed throughout, equipped to douse the many fires that would surely come.

Mr. Cummings and Little Cornstalk were hard at work forging twenty-penny spikes for shoring up the timber of the palisade walls and parapet. Additional sharpened pine rails were nailed to the top of the walls with long spikes. Scattered pieces of steel and iron were collected for the navy swivel guns. Molten lead shot and rifle balls were poured from a large melting pot at a frenzied pace, intended for the muskets and rifles used in the coming fight.

There were no idle hands in Murphy-Borough. Everyone understood the necessity for this effort, knowing their very lives depended on it.

Elspeth and Kathleen sat in the bustling tavern, cutting cloth patches intended to stem the flow of blood when it came. Ian Shadow Bear awoke in his cradle, releasing a lusty wail that filled the large room already consumed with chatter. Kathleen sent one of her girls to fetch Little Cornstalk. Baby Ian was hungry.

The three women sat congenially at the large table as Little Cornstalk nursed her son.

"I cannot help but wonder about this, Broken Tree. He is most unusual for an Indian. Do you think he told us the truth? Do you think the Shawnee will really come?" asked Kathleen worriedly.

"Yes," said Little Cornstalk, bobbing her head. "You cannot see Broken Tree's heart like other men. This is true. His words are twisted like the path he walks. But in this, he tells the truth. They will come. I can feel it. Tenskwatawa will bring many warriors to attack us. He will try to take Ian Shadow Bear, but he will fail."

"I have heard some talk," said Elspeth with an unsettled frown. "There are some men here who would hand over Ian to protect their own, his life for theirs."

"I do not fear of this, Mother Elspeth," answered the girl simply. "You, Connor Murphy, Stevenson, and Mr. Cummings would not let this happen. You are good people, even though you are white and without understanding. Good people are always good."

"Don't you worry, Little Cornstalk," said Kathleen fiercely. "If ever a man in Murphy-Borough tried something like it, he would answer to me."

Elspeth laughed aloud. Little Cornstalk added, "And Seamus Murphy."

At this, Kathleen let out a barking laugh lasting several seconds. "Aye," she stuttered through chuckles, "me lovely Seamus would as well."

West

WILLIAM FOLLOWED AN Indian trail leading north and west, almost a straight line to Kentucky land. Without haste, he moved steadily. Before parting ways with the stocky sailor Bennett and his bickering German friends, he was given a sack of food and a military pass written by Col. Daniel Morgan himself. The pass might be needed if William encountered any American forces.

As he approached the steeper hills of the Appalachia, it was a comfort to see the trees filling out with bright green leaves. The landscape opened before him with natural beauty. It was a sight that William had missed desperately. New grass sprouted everywhere, adding a sweet fragrance to the leafing trees. Spring was here, and William would breathe it in as it drifted through the air.

Stopping for a needed rest, William climbed down off the stiff leather saddle. Tying the pony to an oak, he pumped his legs out. He was by estimate some forty miles south and just east of Murphy-Borough. The German mare he rode turned out to be a good mount. Ulli Becker informed him of the animal's name. *Neeli*, he declared. *She vas named after a girl I once knew many years ago.*

Neeli rode well without tiring. Just now she was munching new spring grass and getting a well-deserved rest. William needed to stand and stretch himself out as well.

It was late afternoon, with good sunlight filtering through the trees surrounding the low draw. A fresh breeze began to climb over the hills from the southwest, and with it came an uncomfortable sensation. William had not experienced this feeling for many months. Still, the longhunter's skills had not deserted him. Someone was out there at a distance.

He could not see them yet, and there was no telling sound to be heard. Nevertheless, someone was definitely out there. They were well screened among the hills and dense trees. William decided to find out who it was. Leaving the pony tied, he pulled the butcher knife from its wooden sheath. Reaching up, he drove the blade deep into the oak above his head. William turned and disappeared into the forest. He left no track.

Walking Bird trailed the pony tracks carefully. He easily followed the marks of the single horse rider. This horse was shod, most likely the pony of a white man. More than a dozen warriors shadowed Walking Bird. It was a war party, painted and heavily armed. They searched for a band of English raiders, white men who had attacked the eastern village of the White Owl people. Everyone in that village had been killed.

These men traveled with renegade Indians of different tribes. They were led by an English captain. White Owl and Walking Bird had come to take their revenge. Most of the braves held back as Walking Bird continued to study the trail. Coming to a blind hill, the party stopped.

Keeping low and staying well hidden among the trees, Walking Bird crawled over the hilltop. From his perch, he could see a red pony down in a low, open draw. The animal was tied to an oak and carried an English saddle. Looking about into the draw and through the trees, he saw no rider. The braves began spreading outward in a line as they approached the red horse. Every few feet, they stopped to listen. Only the rustle of windblown branches could be heard.

Seeing nothing, the band came up on the tethered animal. As Walking Bird approached the oak, he looked up, and there saw William's blade embedded in the trunk at arm's length. He reached up, took hold of the blade handle, and began to pull.

The shot came out of the trees with a thundering echo. The ball struck the oak less than an inch from Walking Bird's grip. Walking Bird let out a sharp cry as he jumped back away from the tree. The entire band of warriors then crouched down, swinging round their muskets in the direction of the shooter.

"Why do my Cherokee brothers track the longhunter?" shouted William through the heavy line of white oak, elm, and red maple.

Walking Bird heard these words. Then he smiled. Standing proud, he let loose a passionate ringing war cry. "Longhunter!" he cried out. "It is I, Walking Bird, your Cherokee friend. Do not kill me, brother!"

Silence followed. The tall figure of William MacEwan emerged from the forest. He held his rifle low as he stepped toward the band of Cherokee warriors. A musket and a rifle were draped over his back with two pistols tucked into the leather tumpline strapped across his chest. A wicked hatchet the Indians had never seen before poked out from his belt. He wore a round domed black hat with a long white feather.

Stopping thirty yards before the band of Cherokee warriors, William dropped his rifle butt to the ground. Holding the barrel lightly with two hands in a gesture of peace, he spoke.

"Greetings to my brother Walking Bird. The longhunter is happy to see my Cherokee friend."

"Aye, yi, yi, yi!" cried Walking Bird joyously, throwing his arms up in welcome.

Murphy-Borough

THE FIRST SHAWNEE came before sunup. These were Blackfish people. There were many. Their passage down the northern trail was deliberately noisy, raising the first alarm for the residents of Murphy-Borough. Their presence sent a cold shiver through the community despite its expectation. Keeping well back of the tree line to avoid the long rifles protecting Murphy-Borough, the Shawnee and their allied warriors began surrounding the fort.

Alden's crew of mercenaries joined them along with an ever-increasing number of Shawnee, Ottawa, Iroquois, Mohawk, Chippewa, and Delaware. Alden's wagons were filled with shot, powder, and three-pound balls. The powder and shot was quickly distributed among the attacking Indians. Rifle and musket fire sporadically erupted from both sides. The fight was beginning.

Connor Murphy called for calm among the people of Murphy-Borough. "No need to waste your shot now!" he called. "Our time will come soon enough."

It was a clear day, sunny and bright, good fortune for Murphy's fire trenches. The Irishman worried that rain might come, diminishing the effect he hoped for. Murphy and Stevenson constantly made rounds, checking that everything was as it should be. Multiple muskets and rifles leaned up along the upper walls of the outer barricade, ready to fire. Casks of powder and shot were set out at intervals for reloading. The two navy guns were packed, ready to fire.

Connor chose a group of young men and boys along with some women for reloading. Their task was to replenish every musket and rifle with powder and ball as speedily as possible. The best shooters he spread out along the walls some thirty yards apart. These men were seasoned Indian fighters and good shots.

Little Cornstalk had objected vocally that Mr. Cummings be included in the group. After all, it was Cummings who had saved her from a Delaware tomahawk and at a good distance too. Murphy knew better. The fact that Cummings's shot had struck that Delaware square between the eyes was more than a miracle. Murphy knew full well that if Owen Cummings was to aim his rifle at the ground beneath his feet, he would most likely miss.

Connor had not the heart to tell the girl this, fearing it would diminish her opinion of the large blacksmith. Cummings's amazing shot was indeed just that, amazing. He was issued a musket and told to shoot close range.

David and Seamus were among those chosen to reload muskets and rifles. Instructed to keep low and close to the timber walls to avoid arching arrows, both boys would have to scramble along on hands and knees, loading and returning the weapons as quickly as they could.

Satisfied they could do no more, Connor Murphy and Olaf Stevenson took position along the wall, Stevenson with a long rifle and Murphy at one of the two navy guns.

The three-pound Galloper struck the palisade timber with a withering shutter. The shot was low, but it sent the message intended. Wild cries exploded from the tree line as the Shawnee and their allies prepared their first assault.

Tenskwatawa sat on his gray and white, overlooking the fort from a distant hill. Beside him was his brother Broken Tree. The battle plan was simple. Alternating waves of Shawnee, Ottawa, Delaware, or Chippewa would attack different sections of the fort and then retreat. The remaining Mohawk, Iroquois, and Delaware were held in relief, positioned to attack later in the day. Sending fifty or more braves at a time at different sections of the wall would keep the defenders off-balance, allowing Alden's cannon to do its work. The attacking Indians would kill as many defenders as possible, delivering fire arrows in their wake.

It took four cannon shots before Alden properly targeted the gate hinges. Knowing the basic construction of Murphy-Borough, Alden knew that if one set of the enormous hinges that swung the main gates was destroyed, only the brace between those gates would remain intact.

One or two cannon shots would then be able to knock the main gate open, allowing the attackers entry into Murphy-Borough.

Murphy could see what Alden was up to and began bracing the gates from inside, scolding himself for not anticipating the maneuver. Things began to get hot.

After the third wave of fighters, more fire arrows came. Most of them were easily doused with buckets of water sent cascading down the outer walls. Those arrows that reached inside the fort were taken care of by young men able to scramble up on the cabin roofs. Little Cornstalk seemed to be everywhere. She pulled flaming arrows from dry timber, helped the wounded into the tavern, and refilled water buckets.

As the fight continued, a wave of attackers made it to the first of the poisoned trenches. Murphy and Stevenson shot their own arrows, igniting the brush and ivy therein. Several braves ran straight through the billowing smoke and around the sharpened pickets for close shooting. Some were swiftly dispatched with long rifles from the fort. They soon retreated.

Alden was careful not to waste any of his three-pounders. His fire was steady with long intervals between shots. Murphy and Stevenson wondered at this until Murphy realized the only answer was the supply of cannon balls. If the enemy had a limited supply of shot, they would naturally conserve them. Knowing this, Murphy immediately went back to bracing the gates.

Inside Murphy-Borough, it was mayhem. Folks ran about, putting out fires and dodging falling arrows. After each successive wave of attack, it was clear to Stevenson and Murphy that the enemy was making headway. Almost all the poisoned trenches were ablaze now, sending black smoke through the air over the open field of fire.

More of Murphy-Borough's wounded were carried into the tavern. Little Cornstalk helped the best she could. It was a bloody mess. As the number of wounded increased, the day passed slowly. Keeping the younger children in the interior of the tavern was Kathleen's main concern. Checking on them periodically, she made certain they were safe. Aelwyd was keeping a close eye on the baby, Ian. The youngest of the Murphy clan were also in her care.

Owen Cummings was helped inside with a musket ball in his middle. He fussed mightily that he was fine, although incapable of standing properly. Little Cornstalk stood close by the big man with a worried look on her face.

"Let me have a look, Mr. Cummings," said Elspeth amid the chaos.

"I'm fine, Mrs. MacEwan," said the smithy. He turned to Little Cornstalk.

"I really am fine," he repeated with a grimace. "It's a minor wound as you can see." The girl smiled at him.

"Go now, Little Cornstalk," he insisted. "The others need you. Please, Mrs. MacEwan, take care of the others. Mine is but a small injury, I assure you. I have a good bit of padding on me as you can plainly see."

"Nevertheless," replied Elspeth sharply, "I will see the wound, if you please, Mr. Cummings."

She pulled up the blacksmith's blouse. The smell of human waste came to her, and she knew instantly the big man was in trouble. She packed the bleeding hole with cuts of cloth and applied a linen bandage.

Handing Cummings a flagon of rum, she ordered brusquely, "Drink this. It is for the pain."

By this time, fourteen Murphy-Borough residents lay dead. Three men inside the tavern died of their wounds while eleven others lay sprawled out on the compound grounds. It was turning into a massacre.

Many attacking Indians lay dead outside the walls as well. It was becoming a bloody day for the Shawnee too. Tenskwatawa thought the losses acceptable but began to worry as the numbers grew. His plan was working but at a cost the Shawnee chief had not realized. Broken Tree lamented the loss of life loudly and warned his brother that it would only get worse as the fight wore on.

Along with the sunlight, this terrible day began fading. It was clear now to both sides that Murphy-Borough could withstand little more. Despite the bracing, Murphy knew that five or six more cannon balls would demolish the gate hinges, leaving the community open to full-on assault. Just how many more cannon balls the enemy had, Murphy could only guess.

Seamus and David were peppered in black powder stains. Both boys had done a fine job reloading despite their obvious fear. Their faces and hands were now blackened with their effort. As the firing from both sides subsided in the waning light, David smiled at Seamus for the first time.

"Looks like they're giving up, Seamus," announced David hopefully.

"Aye," replied the boy with an answering grin. "My da said they would. I hope they took a bellyful of that sumac smoke. Did that once when we were clearing land hereabout. Near killed me."

Seamus scrambled forward, reaching out to grab an unloaded rifle. It was beyond his grasp. As he stood up to take hold of the weapon, a Chippewa arrow sailed over the wall. It took Seamus in the back just below the right shoulder blade, passing through his small body and jutting out his breast. The boy looked down at the unwelcome projectile in amazement. Then he tumbled from the parapet, hitting the ground with an audible thump.

"Seamus!" cried David. Jumping off the platform, David rushed to his friend's side.

Still alive, Seamus looked up into David's eyes. "They shot me, David," said the boy in a horse whisper.

Witnessing the scene, Little Cornstalk ran over to Seamus. Blood poured from the wound, turning Seamus a bluish white. His body went limp as Little Cornstalk lifted him into her arms. She made for the tavern.

"Kathleen!" screamed Little Cornstalk. "Kathleen!"

Hearing his wife's name, Connor Murphy turned on the scene and watched as his youngest son, Seamus Murphy, was carried into the tavern, an arrow protruding from his back.

The poisoned trenches began its work. Many Ottawa and Shawnee braves who jumped the trenches began exhibiting the symptoms of exposure to sumac and poison ivy smoke. At first, the Indians thought it some type of curse possessing their comrades. Welts and seeping pustules suddenly appeared on their faces, arms, and legs. For those who breathed in heavy quantities of the smoke, it was much worse. They began to choke, wheezing for air as their throats slowly closed, swelling shut. Their eyes bulging out obscured vision as they desperately gasped for air. The unaffected warriors watched in horror and fear.

The ever-superstitious Tenskwatawa saw this and called a halt to further attacks, prompting Alden to rush to the chief's side.

"Why have you stopped?" shouted Alden. "I can open the gates, damn you!"

Broken Tree answered, "The braves who inhaled this poison smoke have frightened the others. We are losing warriors, Captain. The Iroquois run away in fear. Tenskwatawa has no wish to waste more Shawnee lives. We will stop for now. Night is coming on, Captain. You will not be able to see your target, regardless. It would only waste your shot. We will finish the fight in the morning."

Kathleen Murphy sat beside the body of her son Seamus, inconsolable. Weeping as she gently wiped the powder stains from her son's face, she made soft, whining sounds. "Ahh, me lovely Seamus," she whispered, "what have they done to you?"

Kathleen shook in misery, wagging her head with incomprehension. Tears washed over her face in a constant flow. She began wailing, a keening vocalization that gripped every soul within the sound of it. Little Cornstalk sat beside Kathleen, holding the boy's hand gently, murmuring a quiet chant and bobbing her head down and back. As Elspeth tended the other wounded, she cried silent tears, knowing Kathleen's pain all too well. To endure this was more than a woman should bear.

Seamus Murphy died quietly as he lay on the big tavern table. His small body seemed to shrink visibly as his life spilled out across the rough wood table and onto the floor. A deathly silence filled the room as the tears of every witness continued unabated.

Connor Murphy burst into the tavern, passing David roughly as he stood by the open doorway. He held a smoking rifle in his grip. The burly Irishman looked down on his youngest son with a pitiful expression. It was indescribable. Kathleen looked up at her husband. She said nothing. The misery in her eyes told all. A touch of maniacal fury came on Connor as he continued to stare at the dead body in disbelief. He turned swiftly, leaving the tavern without a word.

The LongHunter

THE SUN SLOWLY broke over the eastern hills, illuminating a battered Murphy-Borough. It was cloudy overhead this morn, diminishing the early light. Added to this, a heavy fog encased the lower ground. Looking down from his stand at watch, Stevenson studied the chest-deep fog obscuring the open ground, trenches, and defense obstacles. He could see no movement along the enemy lines. The field itself appeared deceptively peaceful. An unusual quiet enveloped the land, aided by the heavy fog. Because of the thunderous echo of cannon, musket, and rifle fire the previous day, even the trill of morning birds was absent.

Tenskwatawa was unhappy. Several lively discussions were taking place between the tribal leaders. This was not unusual among the differing tribes. Opinions were put forth about how to proceed. Many of the chiefs complained bitterly at the loss of so many braves. Broken Tree spoke forcefully, urging his brother to abandon the fight as too costly. The three leaders of the Chippewa, Ottawa, and Delaware including Blackfish agreed.

Tenskwatawa argued just as forcibly that the lives lost must be avenged. Several of the younger Shawnee warriors were of the same mind and said so. They were willing to fight on. Their desire to destroy Murphy-Borough had only hardened with the death of their comrades. Anger and fierce cries of revenge whipped these braves to a killing frenzy. They would take more white lives and the scalps to prove it.

Alden, who refused to accept anything less than the total surrender of the fort, argued loudly to continue. He would not stop now. In strident words, he explained that the three-pound Galloper would finish the Murphy Fort once and for all, assuring the Shawnee prophet, Tenskwatawa, that his cannon alone could do the job.

"Your braves do not need to expose themselves to the white rifles. Once the main gate is blown down, it is only a matter of charging the breach and gaining entrance to the fort. Shawnee losses would be minimal," argued the renegade captain.

Asking he be allowed to commence the bombardment, Tenskwatawa agreed. Lining up the Galloper, Alden and Robichaud carefully packed the small cannon, delivering the first shot of the day. Again, war cries, whoops, and screams erupted from the gathering invaders.

Hidden in the trees to the southwest of Murphy-Borough, a band of sixtysome Cherokee and one white man carefully crept their way behind the line of Shawnee, Delaware, and Ottawa, holding positions south of Murphy-Borough. The Cherokee braves made little sound as they moved toward their enemy. Hidden within the heavy ground fog and brush, William and his companions slipped up silently on the unsuspecting Indians.

Walking Bird cut the first throat of a kneeling Chippewa warrior. Sliding the body quietly onto the grass, he moved along to his next victim. The wave of Cherokee death spread out behind the enemy line, picking off brave after brave in its bloody work.

Drawing his German cleaver, William ambushed an Ottawa. The Ottawa let out a fierce cry as William split his skull. The longhunter and his Cherokee cohorts were now discovered. A general brawl ensued, Indian fighting Indian, hand fighting hand.

After delivering the killing blow, William pulled the hat from his head and charged up the sloping ground through the thick white fog. He made straight for Tenskwatawa and the English cannon.

As the disturbance four hundred yards south took his attention, Tenskwatawa wheeled his horse in the direction of the commotion. He studied the swirling fog closely. It began to display a line of figures rushing in his direction. Shrieks and cries echoed up from the white smoky fog. William came out of it, leading a large body of Cherokee warriors, his golden-red hair clearly visible.

Initially, Tenskwatawa did not recognize the white man for who he was, the longhunter. But as William came within range of the Shawnee prophet, Tenskwatawa froze. Fear gripped his belly. As with any man's fate, death in the form of the longhunter had come for Tenskwatawa.

Pulling his pony's reins in an attempt to retreat, Tenskwatawa turned. William, sliding to a stop, pulled his rifle up, took aim, and fired. The ball struck the Shawnee chief's left temple, spinning his head and throwing him from the pony. The great Shawnee prophet fell to the ground, covered in a misty layer of white fog.

Robichaud, standing beside the three-pound cannon, prepared to send the next shot. He held a ready taper in his grip. Recalling Timothy Murphy's words, *We shoot the cannoneers*, William once again stopped, took aim with his second rifle, and fired. Robichaud was struck center chest, forcing him to stagger back several steps, falling dead.

Alden, stunned at the sight of the longhunter William MacEwan charging toward him with a loaded musket, turned and ran for his life.

Recognizing their feared enemy, the Cherokee, charging from the south, the Ottawa people fled the field, running away as fast as their feet would carry them.

Broken Tree, understanding the situation clearly, spurred his pony, disappearing over the hills into the misty fog. The bulk of his Shawnee brothers with the exception of a few took to the trees. The remaining attackers rapidly disbanded, breaking into small groups; they faded into the forest as quickly as possible.

Farewell

WILLIAM STOOD BESIDE Little Cornstalk, his arm draped around the girl's waist, holding her close. She held Ian Shadow Bear to her breast as the longhunter and the Cherokee girl leaned into each other. Elspeth, David, Aelwyd, and the twins stood silent before the line of sixteen graves.

The whole of Murphy-Borough came out to pay their respects to those who now lay in Mother Earth. Kathleen and Connor Murphy stood side by side before the small grave of their beloved son, Seamus. The two brokenhearted parents gripped each other's hands tightly. Kathleen cried silently as she listened to the comforting words of Olaf Stevenson.

Little Cornstalk looked upon two of the graves with great sadness, the lovable Seamus Murphy and the mighty blacksmith, Owen Cummings, who succumbed to his injury after two days of painful struggle.

Standing to one side was Black Feather, Little Cornstalk's father. He had come with a large contingent of Cherokee, ready to aid in the fight, but by the time he arrived, it was all over. Many of his warriors chased the Shawnee and their allies far to the north before finally giving up the chase. Bringing his speech to a close, Stevenson bid farewell to the souls that lie before him, asking only that God receive these good people to his bosom. Amen.

The rebuilding of Murphy-Borough had already begun. Many hands were hard at work before long. The main gate hinges were swiftly repaired as life began to return to normal in the community. Although it was reasoned that the Shawnee and their allies would not be returning anytime soon, Connor nevertheless posted several watches along the battered parapet. To ease his misery, the feisty Irishman kept as busy as possible. Then the warning bell was struck, and everyone in Murphy-Borough felt a cold rush of fear.

"Who is it, Mitchell?" called Connor as he approached the ladder to the walkway.

"It's that broken Indian again. Carries a white flag. He has people with him."

Connor peered out, and as described, there sat Broken Tree with a small group surrounded by an agitated ring of Cherokee warriors. He held up a white flag tied to his staff. Resisting the urge to shoot the Shawnee chief outright, Connor called down to a man tending the gate. "Go on out and ask him what he wants."

Connor, joined by William and Stevenson, watched the man approach Broken Tree. Words were spoken. Then the man sent out was given the reins to a pony that carried a white man clearly in distress. The man's arms were tied behind his back, jutting his chest out like a bird. His face was covered with a red scarf. It was Alden.

Recognizing the English captain, William raised his rifle, ready to fire. Stevenson placed a staying hand on the weapon.

"You would murder an unarmed man so readily, William?" asked the Swedish hunter.

"Yes," answered William angrily. Then he wagged his head. "No. I do not know."

"No is the answer to that," replied Stevenson flatly. "Alden will pay for his crimes. We will see to that. Do not sell your soul for a man such as this, William. It will only destroy you. It is justice we seek, not vengeance."

"And how do we answer that?" asked William.

"I have an idea," said the wily hunter.

Alden

IT WAS DECIDED that Alden should be given to Black Feather and his people. After all, it was the English captain who had cost the life of Shadow Bear, Black Feather's son. Understanding his fate now lay in the hands of the Cherokee chief, Alden blubbered like a child, begging to spare his life.

After consulting with William, Elspeth, and the community of Murphy-Borough, it was determined that Alden be taken back to the Cherokee lands to pay for his shameful behavior. William would ride along to witness the captain's fate. They traveled two full days.

Entering a wide clearing deep in the trees, the party came to a halt. Alden was roughly hauled from his mount. Before him was a large open pit some twenty feet long, just as wide and deep. Shaking with abject fear, Alden begged William to intercede.

"Please, William," wept the terrified Englishman, "do not let them cut me up and burn me. Shoot me if you will. I beg you. As a mercy, shoot me. It was only for the love of your mother. That is why I stole her away. As you see, no harm came to her, I swear to it. I only loved her as any man would. You cannot condemn me for this."

Four braves dragged the struggling Alden closer to the edge of the pit. Slamming his heels into the dirt to prevent forward progress, the Cherokee were forced to lift him bodily off the ground. He became incoherent, stuttering threats he would kill them all as he was a British officer. Then just as fervently, he begged forgiveness. Only Black Feather and William understood his jabbering words.

The braves then ripped the shirt from Alden's back. Cutting the bonds that held his arms, they forced a long knife in his grip. The bewildered Englishman turned toward William as if to ask a question. Then four eager hands flung the distraught Englishman into the pit.

Landing on his hands and knees atop a stack of black furs, he still held the knife. Alden was now both bewildered and thoroughly frightened. The furs began to move.

A low growl echoed from the pit as an enormous black bear rose on its hind legs, turning to face the terrified Englishman. Alden slid back, landing on his bottom as he desperately scrambled away from the bear. The Englishman's scream rang through the air, bringing a series of answering war cries from the surrounding Cherokee braves.

William was stoic as he listened to the horrifying sounds emanating from the bear pit. The roaring animal mixed with the screams of Alden careened off the surrounding trees. Then the shrieks of the slaughtered Englishman ceased, followed by the brutal tearing of human flesh and crunching bone.

Turning to William, Black Feather spoke. "What will you do now, longhunter?"

"I will bring my family home. We will rebuild."

"Will you fight the English now?"

"Yes," answered the longhunter. "I believe I will."

CPSIA information can be obtained
at www.ICGtesting.com
Printed in the USA
LVHW111650150622
721316LV00011B/306/J